———————————— ★ ————————————

Down the driveway I went, and back home, there was someone waiting for me at the doorsteps to my house, sitting there, legs stretched out, looking quite comfortable.

When I got to my house, I stopped, as if the snow about my feet had suddenly turned into ice, keeping me still.

For before me was Spenser Harris, fake Secret Service agent.

I stood, waiting to see if he would say anything, but that didn't seem possible.

For he was dead.

I gingerly walked around, checking to make sure he was as dead as he looked. He was on the snow-covered ground next to the doorsteps, leaning up against the stone foundation. His legs were out in front of him, his hands were folded primly in his lap. His eyes were closed. Thank God for small favors. I looked to the side of his head and saw a mass of blood and torn flesh and splintered bone just behind his right ear.

I didn't like him, and didn't like what he had done to me, but still...I didn't like seeing him dead on my doorstep.

———————————— ★ ————————————

*Previously published Worldwide Mystery title by*
*BRENDAN DuBOIS*

BURIED DREAMS

# BRENDAN DuBOIS

# PRIMARY STORM

**W✷RLDWIDE**®

TORONTO • NEW YORK • LONDON
AMSTERDAM • PARIS • SYDNEY • HAMBURG
STOCKHOLM • ATHENS • TOKYO • MILAN
MADRID • WARSAW • BUDAPEST • AUCKLAND

*To Jeannette Pinette*
*Paul Pinette*
*And the memory of Roland Pinette.*
Qui habitent dans les montagnes et dans mon coeur.

**PRIMARY STORM**

A Worldwide Mystery/February 2008

First published by St. Martin's Press LLC.

ISBN-13: 978-0-373-26628-9
ISBN-10:     0-373-26628-6

# Acknowledgments

The author wishes to express his thanks and appreciation to his wife, Mona Pinette, for her sure touch as an editor; to his St. Martin's Press editor, Ruth Cavin, and her assistant, Toni Plummer; and to his agent, Liza Dawson. Special thanks as well go to the dedicated staff at both the Stratham-Newfields Veterinary Hospital of Newfields, New Hampshire, and the Harvest Hills Animal Shelter of Fryeburg, Maine. And thanks, too, to those members of the news media and political campaigns who bring a special sort of madness to my home state every four years.

# ONE

TWO DAYS BEFORE I was arrested for attempted murder, I was driving down the snow-covered collection of ruts that mark my driveway when I spotted the man standing outside my home on Tyler Beach, New Hampshire. To get to my driveway, one has to pass through the parking lot of the Lafayette House, a huge Victorian-style hotel set on the opposite side of Atlantic Avenue, and past the odd collection of SUVs and luxury vehicles that belong to guests at the hotel. The past month or so had seen a rash of break-ins among the guests' parked vehicles, but I didn't see any broken glass as I drove through the lot, so maybe the forces of light were winning over the forces of darkness, or at least, the forces of vandalism.

What I did eventually see was my unanticipated visitor. The man standing at the doorway did not seem to be a hotel guest; there was no apparent luggage in sight. He was in his early thirties, slim, wearing a dark gray heavy coat that reached midthigh, dark pants, and some sort of sensible winter shoe. He looked at me and I looked at him as I pulled into the unattached shed that served as a garage, right next to my home.

I gathered up my mail—retrieved a while ago from my PO box at the Tyler post office—and got out of my Ford Explorer, knowing I would probably have to go back to town later in the day to take care of a forgotten errand at my local bank. Outside, the cold salt air felt refreshing, but I didn't like the look of the guy as I approached him. He had sharp hunter's eyes, and his black hair was cut close and trim, and looked perfect, like it had been trimmed by someone who charged three figures for a haircut. Up close, I could see that he was wearing a blue striped shirt and a red necktie underneath the long coat. There was a light snow falling from the gray sky.

"Lewis Cole?" he asked.

"That's right," I said. "What can I do for you?"

He said, "I'd like to ask you a few questions, if you don't mind."

Being the middle of January, it was cold, and I wondered how long my visitor had been waiting for me outside. "Sorry, I do mind."

"Excuse me?"

"I said, I'm sorry, I do mind. I don't know you, and I don't know why I should answer your questions."

He nodded. "A good point. My apologies."

He reached into his coat pocket, took out a thin leather wallet, and flipped it open. As I looked at his photo and the cardboard identification slip and the nice shiny badge, the man decided to be redundant and announce himself.

"Mr. Cole, the name is Spenser Harris. And I'm an agent with the Secret Service, from the Boston office."

I looked up to his sharp face. "All right," I said. "I guess I don't mind after all. Let's get inside."

"Thanks."

I unlocked the door, kicked the snow off my boots, and went inside. Before me was a closet and closed door that led to a small cellar, flanked by a stairway that aimed up to the second floor. To the left was the small living room and sliding glass doors for the rear deck. Next to the sliding glass doors was a tiny kitchen that had a nice view of the Atlantic Ocean. Most every room in my house was described as being small, which happens when one's house is more than a hundred years old and once was a lifeboat station that rescued mariners on their way in and out of Porter Harbor, just up the coast.

I tossed the mail on the couch and followed it up by my coat, and looked over at my guest, standing there, slim and polite. I said, "Curious to know why the Secret Service is visiting here today."

"Strictly routine," he said, offering me a smile that said the visit was anything but. He started unbuttoning his clean coat and said, "Mind if I sit down?"

"Go right ahead."

Any other guest I would have offered tea or coffee or some other liquid refreshment, but I didn't like the look of Agent Harris, and I didn't like the way he had barged in on my day, standing out there like that. He could have easily called me to make an appointment, away from my house, like at a coffee shop or something. Instead, he had stood outside in the cold January weather, knowing I'd be back soon. Which meant some sort of surveillance, which meant some sort of effort on the Secret Service's part, which meant this visit wasn't routine, no matter his cheery nature.

From his coat he took out a small notebook, flipped it open with an experienced toss of the wrist, and said, "Mr. Cole, in just over a week, the New Hampshire primary will take place."

"As a resident of New Hampshire, I don't think I need the reminder."

"I'm sure," he said. "And part of our duties within the Secret Service is to do a threat assessment of the area whenever prominent candidates come by to make an appearance. For example, tomorrow Senator Jackson Hale will be stopping by the Tyler Conference Center."

"So I've heard."

"And my job is to interview those people who appear on our list of…well, people we're interested in."

This was becoming fascinating. I eyed him and said, "Are you telling me that the Secret Service considers me a threat?"

"Not at all," he said, protesting just a bit too much. "It's just that we have a list of people who have come to our attention over the years. Most of the time, it's just cranks. Guys who tend to hate anything and everything. Guys who've been overheard at bars making threats against prominent candidates. There are also a couple of high school students on the list as well, who've written e-mails threatening to kill the president. Unfortunately for them, they're going to get visited every few years if they come within a certain distance of the president or a presidential candidate."

"And how did I come to appear on your little list?"

"Something about your background, Mr. Cole."

"I'm sure," I said. "But I've been a resident of New Hampshire for a number of years. Why now?"

He shrugged. "I gather that we've been tasked to be more wide-ranging and thorough in our reviews. Now, from the records I've reviewed, I see that you used to be with the Department of Defense. Correct?"

"Yes."

"You were a research analyst with a little-known intelligence interpretation group within the department."

"Also correct."

"Now," he said, shifting his weight on my couch, "this is where it gets a bit interesting. According to the records we've been able to review, you left this group under…under questionable circumstances. And being with the Department of the Treasury, we were also able to ascertain that you receive a monthly compensation payment from a certain disbursement fund within the Department of Defense. It appears that for a number of years, even with your position as a columnist for *Shoreline* magazine, that you have received a healthy payment from the government."

I looked at Agent Harris and wondered if I should boost the thermostat up a notch, for there was a wicked wind coming off the Atlantic, finding its way through some odd nooks and crannies by the sliding glass doors.

I kept on looking at him.

"Well?" he asked.

"Yes?"

"I'm sorry, I didn't hear your reply."

"Oh," I said. "I'm equally sorry. I didn't hear a question."

There was a tiny bit of a struggle on that composed face, and I wasn't sure if I had angered him or humored him, but he pressed on and said, "I guess I'm just asking you to confirm what I've just said."

Well, there you go. Aloud I said, "I'm sorry, when I left the employ of the Department of Defense, I signed a standard non-disclosure form. I have nothing to say."

"Can you tell me why you left the Department of Defense, Mr. Cole?"

"No, I cannot."

"Can you tell me if your departure had anything to do with your mental state or capacity?"

I was going to say something rude and sarcastic about that question, but thought better of it. Open that door, just a tiny bit, and Agent Harris could slip in and raise merry hell for the rest of the day, poking and probing. I was going to have none of that. So I said, "I'm sorry, I can't say anything more than what I just said."

"Can you tell me if your experiences in the Department of Defense have left you angry? Bitter? Holding a grudge?"

"Yes, yes, no," I said. "Clear enough for you?"

"Not really."

"But it'll have to do. I'm sorry."

A flip of the page. "Do you have any opinions about Senator Hale?"

I shrugged. "Last I checked, he's one of four candidates for his party's nomination. Having won the Iowa caucuses, he might be unbeatable if he were to win in New Hampshire."

"Excuse me, Mr. Cole, but that's not an opinion. That's a news report."

"Maybe so, but my opinions I keep to myself."

A tiny bit of a smile. "Good for you then."

"Are we almost done?"

"Almost."

"I believe that you are…let's say romantically involved with a member of Senator Hale's campaign staff. Correct?"

"Partially correct," I said. "She's a volunteer. She's not a member of his paid staff. That I know of."

"But you and a…Miss Annie Wynn have been together now for a few months. True?"

"Also true, and none of your damn business."

"Have you attended any of Senator Hale's political functions in the past?"

"Nope."

"Do you plan to attend the rally tomorrow?"

"Depends," I said.

"And what might that depend on?"

I looked him squarely in the eye. "It depends on whether my attendance there will improve my chances of later wining, dining, and bedding his fair campaign aide."

That brought a smile. He closed the notebook. "Very good, Mr. Cole."

I WALKED HIM OUTSIDE and by then, he had transformed himself from Chilly Secret Service Agent to Tired Guy with Lots of Work to Do. He said, "Sorry about being so inquisitive and such, but in these times, it's better to look at things more closely than have something slip by. There's a list and each name on that list has to be checked off by an agent who's juggling lots of cases. For every ninety-nine interviews like yours, we'll get one where a guy is sitting in his living room with a dozen dogs in the house, piles of pizza boxes on the floor, pictures of the candidate plastered on the walls, and an AK-47 across his lap."

"Seen any AK-47s lately?"

"It certainly isn't for lack of trying," he said. Outside he re-buttoned his coat, shivered. It was now dark. It got dark early in New Hampshire in January, a law of nature, but it didn't mean it was a law I particularly liked. The falling snow had stopped but no doubt it would return the next day, next week, and next month.

Agent Harris said, "In these particular times, you really have to make the extra effort to nail everything down. One missed appointment, one follow-up you don't make…well, if that guy shows up with a bow and arrow at a campaign appearance, and it could have been prevented by you, it's a hell of a thing."

"I can imagine."

"Sure. The news coverage alone would send you to a field office in Nome…but on days like this, Nome seems a hell of a lot warmer."

"Been here before?"

"Sure. Primary season, four years ago. When all the candidates, news media, and assorted hangers-on and campaign staff bustle around your fair state, the Secret Service follows."

"Sounds like the guy whose job at the circus is to follow the elephants with a broom and big shovel."

That got a laugh from him as he turned to me and said, "Thanks again for your cooperation."

"Not a problem. Are we done?"

Even in the poor light coming from my house, I could make out the smile on his otherwise serious face. "Sure we're done. Just don't write any threatening letters with crayon and grocery bag paper, and we won't ever see you again."

"It's a deal."

One brief handshake later, he trudged up the hill to the parking lot, and I watched him until he was out of sight. I shivered from the cold, walked into the house, stamped off snow from my boots, and went inside, shaking my head at what had just happened. Poorly run job, if this was what passed as Secret Service agents nowadays.

For I had a connection to the fair senator, a rather intimate connection, and I was surprised that the Secret Service agent hadn't called me on it.

But surprises and the thought of surprises could wait. It was time for dinner, and a special guest. My planned trip to the bank would have to wait. I turned on the outside lights for my guest, and went to work.

I WENT TO THE STOVE and began with the basic bachelor oooking technique, i.e., boiling water, and started two pots, one large, the other small. When they had boiled long enough and hard enough, I went into the refrigerator and took out a small paper bag, nestled within a plastic bag, secured earlier this day on a shopping expedition. I opened the bag and carefully reached in twice, pulling out two pound-and-a-half lobsters. Saying, "Sorry about that, guys," I tossed them into the water and put the cover on the larger pot. There was a faint clatter and then silence.

With the other, smaller pot boiling merrily along, I threw in some fettuccine noodles and set the timer. About ten minutes to go, which gave me time to microwave an Alfredo sauce I had made that morning, and to wash and tear some chunks of romaine lettuce. When the simple salads were complete, the lobsters were done and I pulled them out of the pot with a set of metal tongs.

There was a sound at the door. I turned, one steaming red lobster held in my hand, water dripping on my kitchen floor.

A redheaded woman came into the kitchen, wearing black slacks, small winter boots, and a heavy red cloth jacket, which she was shrugging out of as she came up to me. She dropped a leather purse and a soft black leather overnight bag on the floor. A quick kiss and Annie Wynn said, "Honey, I'm home."

"That you are," I said. "Thanks for coming back on time."

"You're welcome."

"Hungry?" I asked.

"Starved."

"Good. Earn your keep, why don't you, and set the table."

That earned me a swat on the rump, and she grabbed some silverware and dishware as I cracked open the lobster, washed the meat in the sink, and cut it up in small pieces. The fettuccine was done, which meant a trip to the strainer, and in a minute or two, we were at the bar side of the kitchen countertop, sharing the dinner, and a bottle of Australian pinot noir as well.

"How's things with you?" I asked.

"Great."

"Really?"

She shrugged. "Most of the people at Hale headquarters are eating two-day-old pizza. I, on the other hand, told my coworkers that I had a man waiting for me, a man waiting to cook me dinner. Be thankful I got out of Manchester in time."

"Thankful I am. How goes the campaign?"

"It goes," she said. "It goes. I've been doing a lot of phone work, trying to winnow out a list of campaign contributors here in the state that have yet to pull out their checkbooks or bank account for the good of the party."

"Are you good at taking money away from citizens?"

She smiled. "Quite good. Which will no doubt serve me well when I get my law degree, also known as a license to make money."

"Just what the world needs. A good-looking redhead lawyer who likes money."

"And likes magazine writers as well."

I smiled back. "Lucky me."

"Damn straight," she said, and we ate for a while longer, and she said, "So, what's new with you?"

"Well," I said. "When I came back from the post office today, like you, there was a man waiting for me at the house. But he wasn't here to make dinner."

"Really? A campaign volunteer?"

"Not really," I said. "A Secret Service agent. From their Boston office. Seems he's in the area, doing prep work for tomorrow's rally for Senator Hale."

"What kind of prep work?"

If I do say so, the fettuccine and lobster dish was delicious, and I hurried in another bite before replying. "The Secret Service maintains a list of what they call 'persons of interest' that they interview before a campaign appearance by a presidential candidate. Guys who write threatening letters to the UN. Guys who're known to be stalkers. Guys with interesting criminal records."

"You've got any of those things in your background?"

"Nope."

She pursed her fine lips. "Then you must be interesting indeed. Did he take you down to headquarters? Pull out the rubber hoses? The folded over phone books?"

"None of the above, Counselor. We had a nice little chat in the living room, he determined that I'm not watching for black helicopters to come kidnap me, and then he left. End of visit."

Another forkful of dinner went into her mouth. "So why the interest in you?"

"Because of my years at the Department of Defense, I imagine."

She shook her head. "No, I don't think so. I think it's because of what happened to you at the DoD, and the circumstances of your departure. That's why."

I didn't reply. She was skating into an area I really didn't want to visit, and I think she sensed it, for she smiled and said, "I guess they were looking for a disgruntled nut and came up empty."

I returned the smile. "I may be a nut, but I'm not disgruntled. If anything, I'm very gruntled."

That made her laugh and she tossed her napkin at me, and in a matter of minutes, dinner was complete.

In the living room I started a fire in the fireplace, and Annie took the couch and watched one of the early evening cable network shows, as I did cleanup in the kitchen. Before I started I gave her a kiss and she said, "Lacey, one of the communications people back in Manchester, she said if she had a man waiting to make her dinner and clean up afterward, she'd jump him on the kitchen table when he was done."

"Sounds like marvelous campaign advice."

She touched my cheek and said, "Kitchen tables can be so uncomfortable."

I nodded in agreement. "Sure. Crumbs. Butter dishes. Odd pieces of silverware."

"But your bed is nice and wide and warm."

"Sure is."

"Hurry up in the kitchen then, sport."

I walked back. "Free advice from a lawyer-to-be. Better not let the Massachusetts Bar Association hear about that."

I thought she'd say something sharp in reply, but by then, she was curled up on the couch, remote control in her red-painted fingernails. I kept an occasional eye on her as I scrubbed out the pots and washed the dishes and silverware and glassware. There were no leftovers—thankfully, for usually leftovers in my refrigerator transmute themselves into science experiments within a week or so—but there was entertainment as I worked. Annie takes her work and her politics quite seriously, and from the kitchen I heard her shout back at the television, "Moron!

"Idiot!

"No, you're behind in the polls because your candidate can only debate the issues when a script is written for him!"

I kept on cleaning and then wiped down the kitchen countertop, and when things were dried and put away and the lobster shells were put into the trash, I went out into the living room.

The television was still on, another cable news show was broadcasting a couple of campaign operatives screaming at each other, the fire had died down, and Annie Wynn, my Annie Wynn, was lightly snoring on the couch, the remote still in her fingers.

I gingerly pried the remote from her hand, set the television timer to shut down in fifteen minutes so the sudden quiet wouldn't wake her, and I gently picked her up. She started murmuring and through a quiet yet forceful touch, I got her off the couch and upstairs in my bed in just a manner of minutes, holding on to her tight as we maneuvered up the stairway. There were two highlights of bringing her into my bedroom: undressing her and seeing what manner of undergarments she had chosen that day, and the sweet wine-tasted kiss I got from her as I slid her under the sheets, and the way she murmured, "Thank you so much for taking care of me."

I pulled the sheet and blankets up. Taking care of someone. It had been a very long time since I had taken care of anyone, and though I was seriously out of practice, I found that to my surprise, I was liking it.

I checked the clock. It was not even 9:00 p.m. I wasn't tired but I didn't want to go downstairs and watch television by myself, so I got undressed and slipped inside the cool bedding, and switched on a reading lamp. By now I was learning about Annie and her habits and foibles, and one thing I knew was that once she had fallen asleep, it would take something on the order of a tidal wave to wake her up.

So I read for a long while, a biography of Winston Churchill, and I enjoyed the sensation of being warm and safe and having a woman slumbering in bed with me. I read until the book seemed to gain weight in my hands and fall on my chest, and soon enough, the reading lamp was out and I was asleep.

THE TOUCH WOKE ME UP, and I was startled for just a moment, wondering where I was, wondering where my weapons were. Then I felt the touch again, the light scraping of fingernails against my back. I kept still and silent, just liking the touch of her hand upon me, and then her lips were at my ear, whispering, "Are you awake?"

"I am now."

The scratches were wider on my back. She kissed and licked and nibbled at my ear, and then her hand moved about, so it was now scratching at my chest. She snuggled up against me, her warm skin upon my back and rear and legs, and she said, her voice still quiet, "I meant to tell you something earlier, but I forgot."

"You did, did you. What is it?"

Another kiss, a flick of her tongue against my ear. "You're a secretive man, Lewis, but I have secrets of my own."

"Keep on talking."

She giggled. "I'm part of a confidential organization, providing technical support to the Secret Service. And I've been tasked to subject you to a severe interrogation."

I rolled over and she was in my arms, and I kissed her and she kissed me back, and I looked up at her in the faint moonlight, and said, "I surrender."

She moved about, so that she was gently straddling me, and the bed suddenly got warmer. She bent down, her red hair tickling my nose. "Have you now, or have you ever been, a member of the Communist party?"

"No."

She started moving on top of me. I held her tight, with my hands against her side, her flesh smooth and warm. "Have you now, or have you ever been, a member of a group advocating the violent overthrow of the government of the United States?"

"No...ma'am."

I kissed her and she lightly moaned, and said, "Have you now, or have you ever been, a male with extensive lovemaking fantasies?"

"Guilty as charged," I managed to say.

"Good," she said, holding on to me with her strong hands. "Interrogation over."

"Best news I've heard all night."

"Oh, stop talking already," she said.

"You started it."

And she didn't say anything for a while after that, and neither did I.

# TWO

SOMETIME IN THE MORNING the shower was running, and I suppose a male who subscribed to *Playboy* magazine and worked out and was in top shape and form would have leapt out of bed to jump in the shower and wash Annie's back and see what else happened. However, since I'm one of those few who do buy *Playboy* occasionally for the articles and its fine fiction, I confess that I looked at the time and rolled over and went back to sleep. She's a dear but she can thrive and flourish on four or five hours of sleep, which I still didn't understand. I suppose I could give it a try, but I doubted I would live that long.

So when I eventually woke up, got dressed, and went downstairs, she was finishing an English muffin and a glass of orange juice, and she had gotten changed into the contents of her overnight bag, which was now slung over her shoulder. For some reason my stomach felt queasy and the sight of the food and drink made me just a bit nauseous. Probably the afteraffects of not enough sack time and a too-rich dinner.

Annie said, "I would have made you breakfast, except you were still snoring and sleeping."

"Only half true, Counselor. I was sleeping. I wasn't snoring."

"Says you. Give me a kiss good-bye."

"Sure," I said. "But not here. Up at the parking lot."

"Oh, you romantic, you."

I took the overnight bag from her shoulder and grabbed a coat from the downstairs closet. We both went outside into the early January morning. It was overcast. It seemed like every day this past week had been overcast.

Annie said, "Brrr. Damn cold. Sick of it, I really do get sick of it."

"Part of the grand plan," I said.

"What's that?"

"To make us appreciate summer more," I said.

"Bah," she said. "Sounds like crap our Puritan ancestors made up to justify the lousy weather, and for settling their poor butts in this part of the world. Come along, sport, let's go."

She slipped her arm into mine as we maneuvered our way up my frozen driveway. To our left were a mess of boulders and rocks that marked this part of the eighteen-mile New Hampshire coastline, and to our right was a sharp rise of land and more rocks, hiding Route 1-A—also known as Atlantic Avenue—from my house, and vice versa. Before us was the Lafayette House's parking lot and Annie's BMW—leased from a Boston law firm that she did work for as a paralegal—and I said, "Still can't believe the firm lets you drive that Beemer, seeing how you took a leave of absence and all."

She squeezed her arm against mine. "They see it as an investment, Lewis. All those potentially juicy contacts I can make during the campaign might pay off down the road. You know what the three biggest pastimes in Boston are, don't you?"

"Sports, politics, and revenge."

A quick laugh. "You've learned well."

At her BMW she turned and I gave her a quick kiss, and she said, "See you at the rally today?"

"I don't see why not. What time is it again?"

"Two p.m. At the Tyler Conference Center."

I had my hands on her hips. "Will I see you?"

"Probably from a distance, Lewis. But I'd like to know you were there."

"Then I will be."

She touched my cheek. "Two o'clock. Don't be late."

"I won't. Maybe I'll see my Secret Service agent friend."

"Maybe you will. Maybe he'll show you his gun and everything."

"Sounds like something you'd like."

That got a big smile and she got into her BMW, started it right up, and then left the parking lot, and I got a toot-toot from the horn as she turned onto Atlantic Avenue, and that's how this day started, a day before I was to be arrested for attempted murder.

ABOUT HALFWAY DOWN the driveway, there came another blare of a horn, and I turned, half hoping and half expecting to see that Annie had come back, perhaps having forgotten something, perhaps deciding that crawling back into bed with me and seeing what Turner Classic Movies had to offer for the day on television sounded more appealing than a campaign rally, but no, I wasn't that lucky.

A blue Mercedes-Benz convertible had stopped at the parking lot, and a man came out, clad in a long gray winter coat, gray slacks, and wearing black leather gloves. He waved and I waved back. I stopped, putting my hands in my coat pocket, as the man quickly made his way down my driveway. Any other guy wearing those kind of dress winter shoes would have taken his time walking down the slippery driveway, but Felix Tinios isn't what one would call any other kind of guy. He came down to me, nimble as a mountain goat, and gently slapped me on the shoulder as he came up to me.

"Lewis, good to see you," he said.

"And the same. Did you give anybody a wave back there?"

That confused him. "From the parking lot? Why?"

"Dumb joke, that's all. The Lafayette House has seen a number of its guests lose radios and other stuff from parked cars over the past several weeks. Rumor has it they now have the lot under surveillance."

"Then I would have dropped trou, if I knew that."

"A lovely sight to some, I'm sure. What brings you by?"

Felix said, "Was heading down to Boston and gave you a call. No answer on your end, so I thought I'd swing by and see what's up."

"I was seeing somebody off. Didn't hear the phone."

Felix grinned, cocked his head. "The lovely and talented Annie Wynn?"

"The same."

"Good for you. C'mon, it's too cold out here. I need a quick chat."

"What for?"

"Need your advice, that's what."

I looked at the smooth-shaven face, the thick mat of black hair, the cocky confidence in his brown and happy eyes. Felix was originally from the North End of Boston, and told people he didn't know that well that his occupation was security consultant, but I knew him well and I knew him better. I folded my arms and I said, "You feel that?"

"Feel what?"

"Felt like the Earth was spinning off its axis. Because I thought I heard you say you needed my advice."

Felix grabbed my upper arm with a firm grasp and said, "Come on. Maybe this will be a day full of surprises."

IN MY HOUSE I made us both a cup of tea, and though I should have been hungry, I wasn't. We sat at the kitchen counter and Felix had his coat off, revealing a black turtleneck sweater and the usual bulk of his shoulders. He clasped the hot mug with both of his hands and I said, "Advice. What in hell kind of advice can I give you? Spelling? Grammar? How to get an agent?"

He looked hurt by my comments. "I'll have you know that when I was in seventh grade, at St. Mary's Academy, I won a rosary for a spelling bee."

"A rosary? Do you still have it?"

"Of course."

"And do you say your rosary?"

He lifted up the mug, smiled. "Every goddamn night. Look, here's the deal. I've got a job lined up for the next couple of weeks, and I want to make sure that it won't cause any difficulties with you and yours."

"What kind of job?"

He took a slurp. "Working for one of the presidential candidates."

"Which one?"

"Senator Nash Pomeroy. From our fair sister state to the south."

I took a sip from my own tea, grimaced. The nausea down there was perking right along. Two thoughts: I hoped I didn't have food poisoning, because it sure as hell would mean Annie would have the same problem. And I sure as hell hoped it wouldn't keep me from this afternoon's rally.

"I knew the senator was in trouble when he lost the Iowa caucuses, but now his campaign must be really collapsing."

"Why's that?"

I resisted an urge to burst out laughing, because Felix had such a serious look on his face. "My God, Felix, your background…I mean, no offense, but how many times have you been arrested?"

"No offense taken, and trust me, I don't particularly care about the number of arrests. It's the number of convictions that matter. And that number is quite, quite low. Just so you know."

"Maybe in your world arrests don't matter, Felix, but this is politics. Any hint of scandal with the campaign and…well, hell, it can't matter to them, because you've said you've been hired."

"That I have."

"Doing what? Security? Driving around the candidate?"

"Nope." Another sip of tea. "Oppo man."

"What?"

"Oppo. Opposition research. You've heard of that, I'm sure."

"Sure. Digging up dirt on the other guys. Sounds beneath you, Felix."

"Maybe so, but it's good money…and can I tell you a secret?"

"Sure."

He made a point of looking around, and again, I was going to laugh, but that look on his face…It was a different look, a hesitant one. "Here's my secret. Tell anybody and…well, I know you. You won't tell anyone. Thing is, Lewis, I don't know why, but this winter is slowing me down. Get up in the morning, the usual aches and pains I got, they don't disappear like they used to. Working out…the thought of starting up a cold car and driving out to the gym in the morning, when it's so goddamn dark…I don't know, maybe I'm getting old. More often than not, I stay home instead."

I tried to keep my voice innocent. "Getting old is the secret I should be keeping?"

"No," he said, his eyes flashing at me. "Slowing down is the secret you should be keeping. And a lawyer acquaintance of mine, we were talking a couple of weeks ago, said that the Pomeroy campaign needed some help. Wondered if I could do it, and he mentioned the money, and it's good money for work that mostly involves talking. This winter, talking I can handle. The other stuff…well, there's always spring."

"Yeah, you can count on that. So. What's the advice you're seeking?"

He put the mug down on the counter. "Okay. Maybe it isn't advice. Maybe it's just reassurance. I like Annie. I like you and Annie together. It's a good thing, something good you've needed for a while. But I don't want her pissed at me—and through me, you—because she's working for the Hale campaign and I'm working for the Pomeroy campaign."

I nodded. "A sweet attitude, but I don't think it'll make a difference…except, well, there's two other candidates besides Hale and Pomeroy. Congressman Wallace and General Grayson. Who will you be doing the opposition research on? If it's Wallace or Grayson, I doubt she'd care. If it's Hale, she might be pissed no matter what I say."

That made Felix smile again. "I'm doing oppo research on Senator Pomeroy."

"Hold on. The campaign that's hiring you, they want you to dig dirt up on their own guy?"

"Sure," he said.

Despite my nausea, I had to smile. "Come on, you've got to tell me more. It doesn't make sense."

"On the contrary, it makes a lot of sense. Nobody—especially a guy running for president—wants to come forward and expose his warts and imperfections. They hide, they shade, they ignore. Just ask what happened to McGovern back in 1972 when he went shopping for a vice presidential candidate, and his first selection turned out to be a guy who went through electroshock therapy treatment for depression. And people who back candidates—the guys with money, the guys with power—they don't want surprises. When you're this close to getting nominated for the most powerful office on the planet, they want to make sure everything is vetted. They don't want something to blow up in their faces at the very last minute, ensuring that their investment has gone for nothing. That's what I'll be doing. Working as if I were one of Pomeroy's opponents, instead of coming from his own campaign."

"You've been reading up on political theory?"

"Theories I learned came from the streets, my friend." He finished off his tea and said, "So. We okay?"

"Yeah, we're fine. Go ahead and do your oppo research. And by the by, here's one bit of advice."

"All right. I'm in a good mood, I'll take it."

I raised my tea mug in his honor. "Make sure you get paid in advance, or at least on a regular basis. In politics, bills sometimes get lost, sometimes get ignored, and more often than not, never get paid when the campaign is over. There's lots of horror stories about car rental agencies and photocopying centers and other small businesses still looking to get their bills paid years later. Make sure you get paid first, Felix."

"Thanks for looking out for me."

"Nice to be on the other end for a change."

FELIX DECLINED MY OFFER to walk him back up to his car, which pleased me, because by the time he left my home, I wasn't feeling so hot. My face felt warm and the tea seemed to slosh around in my stomach, and even though I had skipped breakfast and didn't feel like lunch, I still wasn't hungry at all. Instead I was achy and I took a couple of aspirin, chased then down with a swallow of orange juice, and went back to the living room. I started up the fire from last night and stretched out on the couch, a thin comforter across my legs. I picked up a copy of *Smithsonian* magazine and started to read, and when my eyes felt thick, I decided to rest them.

For only a while, I thought. For only a while.

I SLOWLY CAME TO later, feeling groggy, feeling out of place. When I saw the living room ceiling, I realized what had happened and sat up, and then held on to the couch cushions for support. My head was spinning and then it calmed down. Well.

I stood up, checked the time.

It was 1:40 p.m.

The campaign rally for Senator Hale was at two. If I was lucky, it would be a fifteen-minute drive to the Tyler Conference Center and I wouldn't be late. If I was lucky. It felt like a mighty big hope. I coughed, headed out to the closet to get my coat. I supposed I should have stayed home, but I promised Annie that I'd be there, and my plan was to drive out to the rally, slide in and stand in the rear, applaud at the proper places, wave to Annie if possible, and get home and get to bed.

Some plan.

The Tyler Conference Center is on the west side of Tyler, almost right up to the border with Exonia, home to Phillips Exonia Academy. It's a small hotel with conference rooms, within a five-minute drive from Interstate 95, and it serves as a convenient meeting place for businesspeople out of Porter and Boston and Nashua who need to meet without fighting a lot of traffic jams and traffic lights.

But the fight seemed to be here today. Once I got within a half mile of the center, traffic had slowed, bumper to bumper, and I felt like I was suddenly transported into downtown Boston on a Monday-morning commute. I couldn't remember the last time I had been stuck in traffic in Tyler, except during the middle of summer at the beach. But not at this end of town. There were plowed mounds of snow on each side of the road, and I checked the dashboard clock and saw I had exactly five minutes to go before the official start of the campaign rally.

Some cars in front of me were pulling off to the side, and I decided to give up, too. I managed to squeeze into a spot and got out, locking the Explorer behind me. The cloud cover was still there, there was a sharp bite to the air, and my throat and chest hurt. Just slide in and slide out, I thought. Enough to make an appearance, and then time to go home. And then let my bed and sleep work their magic.

I slogged my way to the conference center, a four-story hotel with a low-slung building off to the right, a banner saying WELCOME SENATOR JACKSON HALE AND SUPPORTERS flapping in the breeze above the main entrance.

And the supporters were there. Scores of them. The parking lot was full of people holding up campaign signs, most of them for Senator Hale, but there were a few brave others working for his three opponents. These folks were getting jeered at by some Hale supporters, but in a relatively good-natured way. Three large buses were by the rear entrance of the building, diesel engines grumbling, Senator Hale signs hanging off their sides. I moved through the crowds, working my way to the entrance, and I stopped. The crowd was just too damn thick. Some people were chanting, "Go, Hale, go! Go, Hale, go! Go, Hale, go!" Their voices were loud in the cold air. I moved away from the crowds by the entrance, about ready to give up, when there was a tug at my arm.

"Looking for something, Mr. Cole?"

I turned, smiled. The voice and face were a welcome sight. It was a woman about my age from the Tyler Police Department, wearing green uniform pants, a knee-length tan winter coat with sergeant's stripes on the sleeves, and the typical officer's cap, which looked very out of place upon her head.

"Detective Sergeant Diane Woods," I said, raising my voice. "How very nice to see you."

"The same."

"Out of uniform today?" I asked, making a sly joke, since I hardly ever saw her in her official dress uniform.

"In uniform, on detail, making a nice piece of pay per hour. What's up?"

"Trying to get into the rally and not having much success."

She smiled. "Didn't know you had such a burning interest in politics."

"Well…"

The smile remained. "Perhaps you have a burning interest in someone involved in politics."

"Perhaps," I replied. "But right now, I have a burning interest in getting inside to the rally. But that crowd isn't moving."

"That's right. But why go through the main entrance?"

"Excuse me?"

She reached up and gently tapped me on the cheek with a gloved hand. "Silly man. Lovemaking on a regular schedule is screwing up your mind. You're obviously not used to all that attention and it's scrambling your thinking process."

"Meaning?"

"Meaning you're a magazine columnist. You have a press ID issued by the New Hampshire Department of Safety. Go through the press entrance."

"Oh."

"Come with me."

I followed Diane as she maneuvered her way through the crowd and went to a side door that was offset by a set of orange traffic cones and yellow tape. There was an older, beefy man with a red beard at the door, holding a clipboard, and when I turned to say thanks to Diane, she was gone. From my wallet I took out my press identification badge, which has my vital stats and a not-so-bad photo of me taken a couple of years ago by the same people in the state who do driver's license photos.

The bearded man, who had the nervous energy of being part of a process that might make his boss the most powerful man in the world, looked at my identification and me and then the list. For just a moment, there seemed to be a flash of understanding on his face, but I was mistaken. He shook his head.

"You're not on the list."

"I'm sure I'm not. But why can't I go in?"

"Because you're not on the list."

I took a breath. For Annie, only for Annie. I said, "This is the press entrance, right?"

"Yes."

"And I'm a member of the press, aren't I?"

"Yes, yes, of course."

"Then," I said brightly, "it's all coming together, right?"

I pushed by him, he squawked some things at me, and after a brief walk through a narrow hallway, I was into the large conference room and into—

Chaos. Absolute and unfettered chaos. I moved so that I was standing against a wall. Near me was a raised wooden stand. There, almost a dozen cameramen with their cameras on tripods were aiming at the stage at the far side of the room. If the gatekeeper had followed me in, I had lost him in the crowd in a matter of seconds. And the crowd inside made the crowd outside look like a meeting of surviving World War I veterans. People were jammed up tight against one another; the room was hot and loud, the sound coming from rock music over a sound system and hundreds of people trying to be heard over the din. Balloons and bunting hung from the ceiling and walls. The stage was nearly empty save for a large JACKSON HALE FOR ALL OF AMERICA'S TO-MORROWS sign hanging at the rear. A lectern was in the middle of the stage, along with a number of empty chairs on each side.

I wiped at my face and my eyes. My heart was racing and my throat hurt and nausea was sloshing around in my stomach. A woman's voice, close to my ear: "Hey, Lewis. What brings you here?"

I turned. A young woman was standing next to me, wearing a thin down tan winter coat and a bright smile. Despite how lousy I felt, it was good to see her. Her ears stuck through her blond hair, and Paula Quinn, reporter for the Tyler *Chronicle,* one-time lover and now friend, and second-best writer in Tyler, stood there with a reporter's notebook in her small hands.

"Just getting a piece of the political world," I said.

"Yeah," she said, smiling knowingly. "A piece of something, I'm sure. How's it going?"

"Not too bad."

"Really? Don't take offense, but you look like crap. You coming down with something?"

"Sure feels like it."

She gently nudged me with her shoulder. "My, she sure is something, to get you here today."

"That she is. How's your day?"

She laughed. "Campaign rally here, another rally this afternoon, and another rally tonight. Rah rah, sis boom bah. The joys of primary season. Look. I'm going to get closer to the stage. If you feel better, let's do lunch later this week, all right?"

I nodded and tried to say something, but she had moved by then and the noise seemed to have gotten louder. I looked around the crowd, trying to spot Annie, and gave up after a few minutes. It was impossible. There were just too many people, too many signs, too many conversations, and as I stood against the wall, as the crowd flowed and ebbed around me, I could only make out quick snippets of the give-and-take.

"—latest polls show it's tightening up—"

"—can't believe we'd lose to somebody like Pomeroy, even if the moron is from Massachusetts—"

"budget deficit as a campaign issue is a loser—"

"—so I told her, if I don't get five minutes with the candidate, then—"

"—God, guns, and gays, how often have you heard that—"

The crowd was a mix of journalists, young, enthusiastic volunteers, and in one corner, a knot of well-dressed older men and women who talked among themselves like veteran campaign observers who had Already Seen It All. One woman with brown hair, wearing a dark blue wool dress, seemed to be the center of attention, and I found it amusing that a few of her companions were busy trying to hear what she was saying, instead of paying attention to what was going on elsewhere in the room.

I closed my eyes, my stomach rolling along. The music went to some sort of crescendo, and there was a burst of applause as people started filing across the stage, waving at the crowd. There were four men and two women, and I didn't recognize any of them. Was something odd going on?

I took a breath as one of the women—older and wearing a sensible pantsuit, bright pink—came out and adjusted the microphone on the lectern. Something went wrong and the squealing feedback felt like an ice pick stuck in my ear.

No, nothing odd, as the feedback went away. Just politics. The woman started speaking in a loud, breathy voice, and I quickly learned that she was the head of the county party organization, and that the people sitting behind her were candidates for local state representative openings, the governor's council, and county attorney.

As she started introducing each of these people, it quickly became apparent that the crowd was not in the mood to listen to the candidates for state representative, the governor's council, or county attorney. The respectful silence moved rapidly to low mutters and murmurs, but the head of the county organization kept plugging away, talking about the challenge facing the local towns and the county, and how all must work together. As she gamely went through her fifteen-plus minutes of fame, I wondered if the crowd would eventually revolt and charge the stage.

I leaned against the wall. Closed my eyes. Kept my eyes closed. It was so loud, so hot.

And then—

"…my honor and privilege to introduce the next president of the United States, Senator Jackson Hale!"

The crowd erupted with cheers and applause, long bouts of applause, which grew even louder as the senator came up on the stage, waving and laughing, pointing to people in the crowd. I had seen him, of course, on television and in the newspapers, but in the flesh, he seemed more fit, more tan. He was about six foot tall, with a thick thatch of gray black hair, and an easy, engaging smile that seemed to make everyone in the room think they were his very best friend. He waved and waved, and then motioned, and a slim woman joined him up on the stage, Mrs. Senator Jackson Hale herself, also known as Barbara S. Hale, and known to a few others, years earlier, as Barbara Scott, a name I knew her by back when I had dated her in college, so many years and lifetimes ago,

# THREE

THE APPLAUSE WENT on and on. Hale held up both of his arms like a prizefighter, finally getting to a place he belonged, a place that was soon to be his destiny, and then he went to the lectern, where he adjusted the microphone with practiced ease. Near me the cameras on the raised platform moved as one, scanning to one side as he made his way to the lectern. The applause began to ease and he bent forward, saying, "Thank you, thank you, thank you…"

I noticed that I was being watched by some of the people about me, staring at me with hostility, and I started applauding, too. No reason to upset the true believers in my immediate vicinity.

Senator Hale said, "Thank you so much for this lovely reception. I'm honored to be with you here today, among the good people and voters of New Hampshire, and I'd like to take a few minutes to…"

I looked around the room again, trying to find Annie, but gave up. It was impossible.

So I looked at the senator's wife instead.

Barbara.

She stood next to him, smiling widely, and something inside of me tingled just a bit. It had been a very long time since I had seen that particular smile in person. Her blond hair was different, of course, for in college she had worn it long and straight. Now it was cut more fashionably about the shoulder, and Barbara, whose idea of fashion in college had been tight jeans and a T-shirt, was wearing some sort of skirt and jacket combo that was probably worth more than my home computer.

Her husband said, "This election is about more than just me

and my opponents, it's about the direction we plan to take, the direction that all of us in this fine country will choose in the next several months as we determine what kind of people we plan to be, what kind of nation we intend to be…"

Barbara stood there and smiled and applauded at all the right points, and I wondered what was going on behind that bright smile of hers, that smile that years ago I had found so relaxing and inviting. When I had known her in college, we were both majoring in journalism, both of us planned to be investigative reporters, and both of us planned to change the world. Corny, I know, but when you're that young and that intelligent and that fueled with righteousness, well, it was easy to make fun, years later.

But it didn't mean I sometimes didn't miss that clarity.

So, years later, and here we were, together again, separated by a few dozen feet and so many years of experience and relationships and moves on both our parts. I had never changed the world and had long ago given it up as a goal. I wondered if Barbara still thought about doing it, and if so, if she planned to do it with her husband's help. That would make some sort of sense, though when I had known her, the thought of her trying to achieve some sort of goal on the basis of one's marriage to a powerful man would have gained me a hefty punch in the arm and a sharp and to-the-point comment.

The senator said, "…Just last week, we made an important start in this process, with our victory in Iowa…"

The news of his unexpected victory in that Midwestern state caused the room to erupt again. More cheers, more applause. Barbara applauded right along with the crowd, laughing and smiling, even though she probably knew the speech and the applause lines by heart. And as she applauded her husband's words, she kept on looking at the people in the crowd, looking at all of the supporters, looking—

At me. She looked right at me.

And I looked back.

Her face froze, just for a moment, and for a quick flash, she was no longer the senator's wife, the possible next first lady of the nation, but a woman with whom I had spent some lovely months, years and years ago, arguing about writing and style and poetry and Faulkner and Orwell and—

My stomach rolled. The heat was just too much. The noise was too much. It was all too much.

She quickly recovered, going back to her role as supporter and possible first lady. She was no longer looking at me, which was fine, since I was no longer looking at her but for the exit. I elbowed my way through the crowd, through my fellow members of the press, through the true believers, through the short hallway and outside into the crisp, cold, and clean air.

I took about five or six steps, leaned over, and vomited in the parking lot. The usual cramps and coughing and drooling followed, but in a manner of moments, I was sitting on the rear bumper of a Honda Accord, wiping my face with a handkerchief, feeling my arms and legs tremble. I looked around the lot for a moment, embarrassed that somebody might have seen my discomfort, but this part of the lot was blessedly empty, save for the parked vehicles and nearby news vans.

And being on that car bumper, wiping my face with a soiled handkerchief, is how I came to miss the attempted assassination of Jackson Hale, senator from Georgia and probable next president of the United States.

THE FIRST SIGN that something was wrong was when a low "oooh" or "aaahh" came from the crowd inside the conference room, audible even out in my part of the parking lot, followed by loud yells and screams, which I could make out from the open door that I had just exited. More yells. More screams. I looked over and people were running out of the main entrance and the side entrance, holding on to one another, tripping, falling, and picking themselves up and running some more. Their faces were white with fear or anger or terror, and many glanced behind them, as if they were being chased by some evil force.

There were a couple of camera crews already out in the parking lot, and the crew members started shooting footage, no doubt not knowing what the hell they were recording, just knowing it was something important, something to be kept and interpreted later. I stood up, tried to get a better look at what was happening. Then the sounds of sirens cut through the cold air, and from the rear of the hotel a New Hampshire State Police cruiser roared out, followed by a black limousine with tinted windows and two dark blue Chevrolet Suburbans with flashing blue lights in their radiator grilles.

When the second Suburban hit the road, I saw that the rear hatchback window was wide open, and two Secret Service agents were sitting back there, leaning out, both holding Uzi submachine guns in their hands. War wagon, a memory came to me, that's what the heavily armed Suburbans were called. War wagons. Full of weapons, from submachine guns to Stinger antiaircraft missiles and everything in between, all to protect a president or would-be president.

A weeping young woman came by and I said to her, "What happened in there? What's going on?"

"Somebody…somebody shot the senator. The fucker. They killed him! They killed him!"

Jesus, I thought, not here, not now.

I thought of Dallas, I thought of Memphis, I thought of Los Angeles, I thought of all the places marked by so much history and death and shootings and assassinations and broken dreams and not here, not in my hometown, and I thought of Annie and Barbara and—

More people came out, and somebody was yelling, "He's okay! I just got a text message from one of his aides! Nobody got hurt! They missed! They missed!"

I wiped at my face again, legs quivering. More and more people were streaming out. They were now being intercepted by members of the fourth estate, whipping into action, and I suppose if I were a better magazine writer, I would have been doing the same thing. But I wasn't. I got up and started going through the crowd, looking for Annie, to see her and hold her hand and find out if she knew anything else.

But after long minutes when I thought I might get sick again at any moment on the feet or legs of the people near me, I still couldn't find her. I wanted to go back into the conference center, but the doors were blocked by state police officers, backed by serious-looking men and women in suits with half-hidden earpieces, and I gave up. I slowly walked back to my Explorer, dodging some of the traffic streaming out of the parking lot, and got in and started the engine and put my head down on the steering wheel for a moment.

I raised my head, saw that there was finally a break in the traffic trundling by. I got out onto the road and drove home. Along the way, from some of the homes on this stretch of road leading out from the conference center, residents were standing in their driveways, looking out at the traffic, no doubt knowing they were viewing some sort of historical event, and no doubt not knowing what in hell it was. Well, it wasn't my place to tell them, and like the rest of the world, they would learn what had happened back there soon enough.

Halfway back to Tyler Beach, I caught a bulletin on WBZ-AM radio out of Boston, which announced that the Secret Service and New Hampshire State Police were investigating the attempted assassination of Senator Jackson Hale, who was fine and was being protected at an undisclosed location somewhere in New Hampshire. After the bulletin was a series of live reports from shaky-voiced reporters at the scene in Tyler and at Hale campaign headquarters in Manchester and down south, in Atlanta. What followed were several minutes of prediction, analysis, and the ever-sorrowful what-does-this-attempted-as-sassination-mean-for-us-as-a-people.

By then I was home at my very disclosed location, probably feeling no better or no worse than poor Senator Hale. I parked in my shed and trudged through the snow to my front door, and before going inside, doubled over again in another bout of vomiting, this time just bringing up some harsh bile. I kicked some snow over the mess I made and went inside, straight to my telephone. I placed a call to Annie Wynn. Her cell phone dumped me into her voice mail and I said, "Hi, it's me. I was there at the rally…couldn't find you…hope you're okay…call me or come back here…I'm coming down with something and I'm going to lie down…"

Which is what I did, stretching out on the couch and resisting the urge to turn on the television, knowing that everything I saw now would be repeated later, and so I just stayed there, comforter up to my neck.

And despite everything that had just happened, I was feeling so lousy that I did fall asleep.

I WOKE TO THE SOUND of the door being unlocked and I sat up, as Annie came in, face red, eyes red. She dropped her bag and came right at me. I sat up on the couch and she sat there, now in my arms, and I held her tight as she choked and cried some and then cried some more. She then pulled back and rubbed at her eyes, and I said, "Get you something? Drink? Something to eat?"

She opened her purse, took out a tissue, blew her nose. "How about a new day? Can you do that for me?"

"If I could, I would."

She managed a wan smile, crumpled up the tissue in her hand. "Oh, Lewis, I never want to go through anything like that ever again."

"Tell me where you were. Tell me what you saw."

She took a deep breath, clasped her hands around her purse so tightly I could see her knuckles whiten. "I…I was backstage, with some of the campaign people. You see, most of us, the volunteers, what little compensation we get is the ability to be behind the scenes, to say hi to the senator and his people. A couple of times, though, I snuck a peek out to the crowd, tried to spot you."

I said, "I was near the press section. I couldn't see you. And I guess I'm lucky…I mean, I didn't see what happened. I got sick, had to get out of the building. Went out to the parking lot, dumped my guts on the ground, and then people started running out."

She closed her eyes for a moment, like she was trying to see again what had happened back at the conference center. "He came in…right on time…Hale time, you know? He's always on time. But he had to wait backstage. That dimwit county chair, she had to go on and on, practically introducing candidates for dogcatcher…but then he went out with his wife, and started his talk…"

"Yes," I said, now holding my hand over her two hands on the purse. "I was there for that."

She said, "You know, I've read his damn stump speech, and I've seen bits of it on TV, so it wasn't any surprise…but you know, seeing him in person, it was wonderful. It's a damn cliché and all, but he held me. He's a great speaker, Lewis, he really is…and about halfway through it there was a gunshot, and then another."

"Just two, then?"

"Yeah. Two too fucking many, if you'll excuse my language. The first time, I think we all froze, thinking maybe it was a balloon, but the Secret Service jumped ugly real quick, heading to the senator and his wife, and there was another shot, and people started screaming and running."

"Did anybody see who did it?"

"Nope. You saw how crowded that place was…Jesus, what a mess. There were two shots and then people started running, and the senator and his missus were practically carried out the rear…and that was that."

"Annie, I'm sorry it happened. Even more sorry you were there to see it."

She smiled, squeezed my hand back. "Sounds crazy, but there's no place I'd rather be…I had to be there, Lewis, and I'm damn glad I was."

"Any idea who or why?"

"Why? Take your pick…every position the senator holds, there's sure to be some sort of nut who opposes him. And who…no idea who the shooter was, but I heard a rumor that the cops and the Secret Service caught themselves a break."

"How so?"

"After most everybody bailed out, they found a gun on the floor of the conference center. There you go. Some of the cops tried to keep people from running away after the shooting, so they could be interviewed, but you saw what the crowd was like. Lucky nobody was trampled to death."

I squeezed her hand again. "That's a big break. It could mean a lot in tracing who in hell was involved. Look. You must be tired, must be hungry, why don't you—"

She shook her head. "No. Sorry. You're being a dear and all

that, and any other day, I'd love to sit here in front of the fire and veg out, but not today, not after what happened."

"You're going back to Manchester."

"Yes," she said, a bit of steel showing in her voice. "I've talked to others in the campaign. I'm going back to Manchester and make the phone calls and stuff the envelopes and crunch the numbers, and I and the rest of the crew are going to work twice as hard, after some asshole tried to take our candidate away. Our next president, Lewis. He can make it, he really can, and I'm not going to sit on my butt and be intimidated."

"And such a lovely butt it is."

On any other occasion, that would have brought a smile, but this wasn't any other occasion. She stood up, put her coat back on, and bent down and kissed me quickly on the forehead. "I'll call you, okay? Don't worry about me. I'll be fine."

"All right. Be safe."

And in a few seconds, she was out the door, and I was alone. I coughed some more and rolled myself up in the comforter, and thought again about turning on the television, but decided I needed sleep more than news. So sleep is what I got.

THE PHONE RINGING got me up, and I sat up, nose runny, throat raspy, my stomach still doing slow rolls. I answered the phone and there was nobody on the other end, and then there was a click and a bored female voice said, "Sir, good day, I'm conducting a survey of the presidential candidates, and I want to ask you a few questions if I may."

"I don't—"

"Sir, would your vote in the New Hampshire primary be different if you knew that Senator Nash Pomeroy accepted PAC money from gun manufacturers, even though he comes from a state that saw two of its favorite sons cut down by assassin's bullets?"

"Good try," I said.

"Excuse me?" came the female voice.

"I said, good try. This isn't a survey. It's a push poll. You're trying to drive up the negative poll numbers for Senator Pomeroy by asking crap questions like this. Who's paying the freight? Which campaign or PAC?"

Click. The mystery caller had hung up.

The constant joys of living in the first-in-the-nation primary state. Annoying phone call after annoying phone call.

I stumbled into the kitchen, washed my face, took a big swallow of orange juice that almost made me cough as the acidy juice slid down my throat, and then I started the stove to make a cup of tea.

Another ring of the phone. Another brief delay as the auto-mated computer connected me to a live person, a woman again.

"Sir, I'm calling from Alliance Opinion Surveys, gauging the mood of the electorate. On a scale of one to ten, with one being strongly disagree and ten being strongly agree, how would you rate orbital space-based weapons as a campaign issue this year?"

"Orbital space-based weapons?" I asked, looking for a clean tea mug and accompanying tea bag.

"Yes, sir," she said. "On a scale of one to ten, with one being—"

"How long?"

"Excuse me?"

"How long is this survey?"

"Sir, it's only fifty questions, and we find that most callers complete the survey in—"

Click. Now it was my time to hang up.

I usually find these types of surveys oddly amusing, but I guess that's just me. Being from Massachusetts, my dear Annie never receives such phone calls, and Diane Woods of the Tyler Police Department says she hardly gets any at all, since she has an unlisted number. Paula Quinn of the *Chronicle* follows the three-second rule, meaning that if nobody on the other end speaks up in three seconds, she hangs up before the computer can switch her over to a live operator.

All of us in this state have different strategies, but I guess I like Felix's best. He politely listens to the opening remarks, and then says he has one question of his own: Does the caller have any suggestions for cleaning fresh bloodstains out of clothing?

"Usually, they hang right up," he told me once. "And it really has cut down on the follow-up calls."

Now the water was boiling and I was about to pour it in my tea mug, when the phone rang again, and by now I was tired of all the attention. I picked up the phone and said, "I swear to God, if this is another survey, I'm going to trace this number and hunt you down and rip your phone out of the wall."

The woman on the other end laughed. "Can't do that, Lewis. I'm on my cell phone, right in downtown Manchester."

"Oh."

Annie said, "I feel bad about something and I need to tell you that."

"Okay, go ahead." I poured the water into the mug, liking the sensation of the steam rising up to my face. "Still upset about the shooting, I'm sure."

"No, it's not that."

"It's not?"

"No, and if you let me talk, I'll tell you all about it. Look. I came in and dumped all over you, and you gave me a shoulder and a few hugs and all that good stuff. But you told me you were sick, that you threw up in the conference center's parking lot, and I found you all wrapped up on the couch when I came to see you. I should have asked you how you were doing. I should have offered to help you. But I didn't. I'm sorry."

"No apologies necessary," I said. "You've had a tough day. Don't worry about it."

"Well, I did worry about it, and I wanted to let you know. Okay?"

"Okay."

"Good. I'm in front of the campaign headquarters now. I'll call you tomorrow. Hope you feel better. Bye."

"Bye right back," I said, and sure enough, even before I had the cup of tea, I was feeling better.

DINNER WAS A COUPLE of scrambled eggs and toast, and maybe my aggressive nap schedule was working in my favor, for I felt more human as the day dragged on. I caught a bit of the news at six-thirty and saw some of the shooting coverage, but missed the actual first footage of the shooting and what it looked like from inside the building. Still, most of the coverage was similar, with all channels showing a graphic of the interior of the Tyler Conference Center—I'm sure the management couldn't buy advertising like this, and I wasn't sure what they thought of this particular good fortune—and there were interviews with a cheerful Senator Hale, who did his best to shrug off the attempt on his life. Plus the usual and customary interviews with a variety of eyewitnesses, none of whom actually saw a damn thing, but heard plenty, or thought he did. This was followed by the typical stories of our violent society, and how we were all to blame for what had happened in Tyler this day.

When that coverage was over, I decided that I'd had my fill of politics for the day, so I channel-surfed for a while, and almost cheered my luck when I saw a two-hour documentary on one of the cable channels on the history of U-boat operations in the North Atlantic. I settled back on the couch, fire in the fireplace, comforter wrapped around me, and cherished a time when the conflicts were so clear, so finely drawn.

THE NEXT MORNING when the phone rang, I was washing my breakfast dishes, feeling much better, and I was surprised at the woman's voice on the other end of the phone: not my Annie Wynn, but my good friend Detective Sergeant Diane Woods. It sounded like she was on a cell phone.

"Hey," she said. "How are you doing?"

"Doing all right," I said. "How are you?"

"Well, got my fingers in a bit on this Senator Hale incident," she said.

"You do, do you? I thought the state police and the Secret Service would be all over this and pushing poor little you aside."

"I'm not poor, and I'm not little."

"All right. Point noted. And what part of the investigation has your fingers in it?"

She sighed. "You."

I folded up the dish towel I had been using. "Mind saying that again? I had the oddest idea that you just said 'you.' Meaning me."

"That's right."

"Why?"

Another big sigh. "I don't know, Lewis. All I know is that the Secret Service wants to talk to you about the shooting. They came to me, asked me if I knew you. When I said yes…well, here's the deal…"

I took the folded towel, wiped down an already clean kitchen counter. "They asked you to bring me in. Right?"

"Right."

"All right. What's the deal? You want me to meet you at the police station?"

"Um, no…"

Then I got it. "Where are you? Up the hill, at the parking lot?"

"Yeah."

"Okay. I'll be up there in a minute."

I hung up the phone, thought about making a phone call, but to whom? Annie? Her law firm? Felix?

No, nobody, not now.

I went out of the kitchen to the entranceway and grabbed a coat, and then went out the door and trudged my way up to the Lafayette House's parking lot.

THERE DIANE WAS waiting for me, standing next to an unmarked Tyler police cruiser, a dark blue Ford LTD with a whip antenna, engine burbling in the cold morning air. She was bundled up in a short leather coat with a cloth collar and dark slacks. I stood there and she said, "Sorry."

"No, it's okay. If I'm being brought in, would rather it be done by a friend."

She got in the front seat and I walked around and joined her. As in all cop cars, the upholstery was heavy-duty plastic and there was a police radio slung under the dashboard. She picked up the microphone and said, "Dispatch, D-one, coming in."

"All right, D-one."

She tossed the microphone back in its cradle, shifted the cruiser into drive, and in a matter of seconds, we were on Atlantic Avenue, heading south. Six months earlier or six months from now, the roadway would be packed, each parking space would be filled, and the sands of Tyler Beach would be packed with almost as many people who were set to vote here the following week.

But this was January. The road was nearly empty, and the temperature inside the car seemed to match the temperature outside.

After a few minutes I said, "Anything else you want to say?"

She looked troubled. "No, I'm afraid not."

"You know why the Secret Service wants to talk to me?"

"No," she said.

I stayed quiet for a little bit, and said, "Well, didn't you ask them?"

She turned to me for a quick second, exasperated. "Hell, yes, Lewis. I asked them. Over and over again. And all I got was polite and federal pushback. The attempt on the senator's life is a matter for the Secret Service, and the state police are assisting. I've been told by my own chief to cooperate, and that's what I'm doing. Getting your cheerful butt from your house to the station with a minimum of fuss. All right?"

I thought for a moment and said, "The Secret Service has already talked to me. Two days ago."

"Really?"

"Truly," I said. "Came by on what he called a routine check. Thing is, I seem to be on a list of 'persons of interest,' to be interviewed before the arrival of a president or presidential candidate. He came by, made sure I didn't have a bomb factory in the cellar, and left. Ten-fifteen-minute visit, tops."

Diane said, "Might be a routine visit then. Just to check your name off a list."

"Sure," I said. "Routine."

"Routine," she repeated, and as we pulled into the police station's parking lot, I was sure that neither of us believed that at all.

# FOUR

AT THE TYLER POLICE STATION, she parked in the rear of the fenced-in parking lot, reserved for police and other official vehicles, and she led me through the back door, where the on-duty dispatcher buzzed open the rear inner door after seeing Diane through a closed-circuit television. The building was the usual one-story concrete style of decades earlier, and one of these days, if the chief could convince three-fifths of the eligible voters in Tyler, he would get a new station built nearby.

Sure. One of these days.

We went through the booking room, past the empty holding cells, and through an open door marked interview. A tired-looking man with wavy black hair in a fine dark gray suit was sitting there. He stood up when Diane and I entered. There was a battered conference room table and four chairs, and the usual one-way glass mirror on the near wall. Diane reached over, squeezed my hand. "See you later, Lewis."

"Sure, Diane."

"Thank you, Detective," the man said in a quiet and firm voice. "Please close the door on your way out, will you?"

She said nothing, but did as she was requested. I sat down.

The man said, "Mr. Cole, I'm Glen Reynolds, Secret Service."

"Nice to meet you."

"Sure," he said, opening up a file folder. No hand was offered, and I wasn't offended. I had an idea of where this was going.

"Mr. Cole, I'm looking for your cooperation."

"All right."

"You can imagine what we're up to, trying to determine who shot at Senator Hale yesterday, and why."

"Yeah."

"So I'm going to ask you a series of questions. All right?"

I looked behind him, at the mirrored glass. I wondered how many people were back there watching us, and how many recording devices were listening to us.

"Sure. That'd be fine."

He grinned. "Nice to have a cooperative witness, for once in my life. All right. Mr. Cole, were you at the campaign rally yesterday for Senator Hale?"

"I was."

"And why were you there?"

"As a favor."

"For whom?"

I gave him points for grammatical precision and said, "A lady friend. Who works for the senator's campaign."

That brought a knowing nod from him. "Right. One Annie Wynn of Boston, Massachusetts. So. You have no particular political interest in the senator or his political positions."

"Not particularly."

That brought a smile. "If you're a New Hampshire resident who doesn't have much interest in politics, then you're one of the few I've met in my time here."

"I'm sure."

"So you don't have any grudge against the senator, or the United States government, am I right?"

A brief snippet of memory of when I was with the Department of Defense, younger and less cynical, until a moment in the high Nevada desert, a training accident that took everyone's life save mine.

"Fifty percent right," I said. "No grudge against the senator. Perhaps a grudge against the government."

A knowing nod. "Your time in the Department of Defense. I understand."

"I'm sorry, I'm not allowed to say anything about my time of service in the Department of Defense."

He smiled again. "Really, I'm not interested in that particular part of your past. I'm interested in other things."

"Such as?"

"Such as your enrollment in Indiana University in Bloomington. When you were romantically involved with one Barbara Scott, a classmate of yours. Who later became the senator's wife."

"And what's your interest?"

He shrugged. "Just wondering…if you're jealous of the senator. For being with the woman you were once intimate with."

"No. I'm not jealous."

"Really?"

"Yes, really. Agent Reynolds, may I ask you a question?"

"Sure," he said, grinning. "I've been monopolizing the conversation since you've gotten here. Go ahead. Ask away."

"Why am I here? I thought I had been cleared by the Secret Service agent who saw me two days ago. Agent Harris."

"Agent Harris?"

"Yes. Agent Spenser Harris. From your Boston office. He came to see me two days ago, since I'm on one of your lists…persons of interest, he said. He talked with me for a while and left. Said that everything was just fine."

"Mr. Cole, like I said, I'm not much interested in your past. It's your present time that interests me. Especially what you were doing at the rally yesterday."

"Again, why me? You're interested in me as a witness? Because to tell you the truth, I didn't see much when I was at the rally yesterday. I was there for most of the speeches and then I got sick to my stomach and went outside. Where I then promptly threw up."

"Point noted," he said.

"So why am I here?" I asked.

"You're here because your presence at the campaign rally was reconfirmed, leading us to a few questions."

"Reconfirmed? By whom?"

Agent Reynolds's voice seemed to sharpen. "By our very dear and closest friend in the agency. Mr. Forensics."

"Sorry, I don't understand. What do you mean, Mr. Forensics?"

He went back to his folder. "Mr. Cole, do you own a stainless steel Ruger .357 revolver, serial number 468723698?"

Something cold started touching the back of my neck and the

back of my hands. "I do own a Ruger .357 revolver. I don't have the serial number memorized."

"They never do. Well, let's get right to it, shall we?"

"Let's," I said, now deeply regretting I hadn't called anybody before coming here.

"Mr. Cole, have you lent or given away this revolver recently?"

"No."

"Have you sold it?"

"No."

"Then can you tell us why your revolver, with your fingerprints and your fingerprints only, was found on the floor of the Tyler Conference Center yesterday? With three unfired and two fired cartridges?"

I said not a word.

"Two rounds were removed from the stage wall at the conference center. Ballistics conclusively show that they were fired from your revolver. And you were there."

"But I wasn't in the room when the shots were fired. I was out in the parking lot, puking up my guts."

"You see anybody in the parking lot? Anybody at all while you were out there conveniently being sick?"

"No."

Agent Reynolds carefully closed the folder. "Are you sure you don't want to change any of your previous answers?"

"Positive."

"Because there's an opportunity you have, right now, to make everything right."

"How?"

"By telling me why you brought your revolver to the campaign rally yesterday, and why you tried to shoot Senator Hale."

My hands were underneath the table, clasped tightly together. "I was at the rally, but I wasn't armed. And I didn't try to kill the senator."

"And that is going to be your story?"

"No."

"Good," he said. "Now we're getting somewhere."

"No, we're not, because you're not understanding what I'm trying to say. That's not my story. Those are the facts."

He stared at me and then made a crisp nod. "Mr. Cole, in a few minutes we're going to place you under arrest for the attempted murder of Senator Hale. You're going to be transported from this police station to the county jail nearby, and from there, I imagine the nearest federal facility, which will be in Boston. It's your choice as to whether you will then wish to have representation. I imagine you will."

"You imagine right," I said. "And you'll find out in a very short while that I had nothing to do with that shooting."

"Why? Because you're telling the truth?"

"Of course I am," I said.

"Interesting thought," he said, standing up. "Especially since I'm stationed in the Boston office, and I've never heard of a Spenser Harris."

SOME HOURS LATER, I was in a cell at the Wentworth County jail, staring at the stainless steel toilet in the corner of my new little universe. While the processing in was efficient and proper, the ride over was anything but. After formally being placed under arrest and being handcuffed, I was quickly led out of the Tyler police station—not seeing Diane Woods in the process—and was taken to a dark blue van, pulled up to the entrance where I had earlier walked in as a free man. I was placed inside the van by two other agents, who carefully seatbelted me in. We then left in a little convoy; the van was led and followed by dark blue Ford LTDs, similar to the one Diane drove.

When we turned the corner of the police station parking lot, we drove through a phalanx of television cameras, reporters, and news photographers, all flashing their cameras, all taking notes, all sucking in bits of information. One of the Secret Service agents said, "Hey, you're famous."

"Lucky me," I said.

"Too bad the windows are tinted. Your face would be seen by half the planet in an hour or so."

I didn't say anything more, and the agents also kept quiet on the drive west. We got out to Route 101, and along the way, I could see that the media interest was chasing us all the way along the state road. Other camera crews were stationed along the side of the road, and there was a moment, hearing the steady thrumming of an overhead helicopter, that I knew that live camera shots of this little procession were being beamed out to the insatiable cable news networks. Some people dream all their lives to achieve such fame.

I've never been one of those people.

At the county jail—an old brick edifice, stuck out in the middle of a field in the small town of Brennan—another group of journalists were waiting as we pulled in. Getting in was a challenge, as Wentworth County deputy sheriffs did their best to push aside the reporters in a manner that allowed an opening, but didn't allow the trusty guardians of press freedom to charge police brutality. Still, some got close enough that I could see their cold faces, almost pressed up to the tinted glass, as they tried for more photos and shouted more questions in my general direction.

I said, "What are they thinking? That you're going to open up the door and hold a press conference?"

An agent sitting next to the van driver laughed. "The nature of the beast. It demands to be fed. Doesn't mean it's logical. It just means it's a beast."

And from there we went into a garage, and then through the booking area, and it was pleasurable to be standing up, handcuffs off, right up to the point where I was in my cell, alone, staring at the stainless steel toilet, just after making that always promised one phone call to someone far away.

I GOT UP FROM THE BUNK, walked around, and then sat down again. My belt was off and my footwear had been confiscated, leaving me with prison-issued paper slippers. My feet were cold. I stretched out on the plastic-covered mattress and waited, feeling okay, except that damn cold or whatever seemed to be coming back. Stress and lack of food, no doubt, but all in all, I had this serene sense of confidence while being held there. I guess I didn't expect to be in jail for long, for even if Agent Reynolds didn't believe me, I had been telling the truth. I hadn't tried to kill the senator. End of story.

I put my hands behind my head. All right. End of one story. There was another story, about Spenser Harris, or the man who claimed to be Spenser Harris. Who in hell was he, and what had been his purpose in questioning me?

So I stared up at the cement ceiling—almost as attractive a view as the stainless steel toilet—when a uniformed corrections officer came by.

"Cole?" he asked.

"That's right," I said, sitting up and swinging my legs over to the side.

"Your lawyer's here," he said. "Want to go see him?"

"Since I called him, yes, I would."

I knew that the tide had turned when I was let out of the cell, for handcuffs weren't placed on me, and the walk was a short one. I was led into an office area and then a meeting room—much better than the one at the Tyler police station—and I was pleased to see Attorney Raymond Drake was there, from Boston, a friend of Felix's and a mentor to Annie Wynn, and I was less pleased to see someone else in the room: Agent Reynolds.

But Agent Reynolds didn't look so happy, so that improved my mood.

I shook hands with Raymond and sat down. Raymond was smiling widely, I guess, at the thought and challenge of actually having an innocent client to represent, and a gold bracelet on his tanned wrist jangled a bit as he leaned forward. He was in his midfifties and owed a lot to Felix, back when he had ticked off one of Felix's relatives and was going on the usual and customary one-way trip out to Boston Harbor, before Felix had interceded. The conference room was warm, had no windows, but the chairs and table were almost brand-new, and there was a television with a VCR unit on a stand in the corner.

Raymond said, "Just to bring everyone up to speed, I'd like to show this news footage again."

Reynolds said, "There's no need for that. We can already stipulate that—"

It was like being in a courtroom, for Raymond had that

demeanor, a man in his role and enjoying it fully. From the tabletop he picked up a remote for the television and switched it on, and once the blue screen came into being, he pressed another switch and up on the screen was the parking lot of the Tyler Conference Center.

I'll be damned, I thought, and leaned forward to get a better view.

The tape had a running digital readout on the bottom of the screen, denoting date and time. Besides the vehicles in the parking lot, it showed the side entrance to the conference center. I had no doubt what I was going to see next.

There. A figure, stumbling out of the doorway. Looked familiar, though pathetic, and I watched the digital avatar of Lewis Cole come out a few steps, lean over and—

Well. Perhaps it's embarrassing to see oneself on a secretly recorded sex tape, but I would guess seeing oneself become violently ill for eternity ranks right up there in the embarrassment department. Still, I was happy to see it.

Raymond held up the remote again, froze the image. "I know I've said it before, Agent Reynolds, but I still love saying it. Check the time stamp of the recording from this Boston television station. A full two minutes before the shots were fired inside the conference center. My client did not attempt to shoot the senator."

Reynolds said, "Fairly obvious, but it doesn't explain how his revolver was used in the shooting."

My lawyer turned to me. "Lewis, do you have any idea who shot at the senator?"

"Nope."

"Do you know how your Ruger .357 ended up at the conference center?"

"Obviously, it was stolen."

"Any idea when?"

"No," I said.

"Any idea by whom?" he asked.

"No," I said, lying for the first time that day, which I was sure would disappoint the good agent, but I didn't care right then.

Raymond turned back to Agent Reynolds. "There you have it, Agent Reynolds."

He said, "We still plan to ask him more questions. Especially about that so-called Secret Service agent he claims visited him."

"I'm sure," Raymond said, reaching into his coat pocket and removing a business card, which he slid across the polished conference room table. "And if you desire to do so, please contact me directly. You're not to contact my client without my say-so."

Agent Reynolds picked up the card delicately, as if it had contagious defense attorney germs on it, and said, "I guess we're through here."

Raymond shook his head. "No, we're not."

"Excuse me?"

"Agent Reynolds, I expect that within the next several minutes, you're going to hold a press conference out there to the main entrance of the county jail. You're going to announce to the world that the arrest of my client was made in haste, that he is not a suspect in the attempted assassination of Senator Hale, that all charges have been dropped, and that the United States government and the Treasury Department offer their deep apologies to Mr. Cole for putting him through this terrible ordeal."

The Secret Service agent's face reddened. "That's not my call."

"It better be, or we'll take action."

Reynolds said, "What? A lawsuit? Go ahead and try. You won't succeed. Nobody ever succeeds in suing the federal government."

My attorney said, "Who mentioned anything about a lawsuit? Here's a hint, Agent Reynolds. Look at my business card. Look at my firm's name. Consider I'm based in Boston, consider the contacts we have in the United States Senate and the House of Representatives. Wouldn't it be a marvelous coincidence if during the next budget cycle, your offices are slated for renovation, and that you have to spend the next two or three years in temporary offices…say, modular trailers at the old Charleston Navy Yard? Wouldn't that be an amazing coincidence."

There was a pause and Reynolds said, "You got your press

conference. But your guy stays in the area, and you're cooperative if we want to talk to him again."

Raymond looked at me, I looked at him, and Raymond said,
"Sir, you've got a deal."

PROCESSING OUT WAS a heck of a lot more fun than processing
in, and the staff and deputy sheriffs were cheerful and polite in
getting my possessions back, after word had filtered through
that the arrest had been a mistake. Raymond led me out to his
silver BMW and we soon left the grounds of the county jail, and
I was surprised that the journalist scrum was gone from the gate.

But after we started driving out, it just took a moment to see
Agent Reynolds, standing on a set of steps by the main building,
talking to said scrum, and I said to Raymond, "Looks like he kept
his word."

"For now, and that's a good thing."

"Ask you something?"

"Of course."

"The television tape," I said. "Where did you get it?"

"Friends and favors owed, Lewis. I know how well covered
these events tend to be. Just our luck one television station from
Boston had a camera trained on the exit door that afternoon."

"Let's hear it for luck."

"Sure," he said. "How does heading home sound?"

"Home would be wonderful."

As we got back onto Route 101, this time heading blessedly
east, Raymond said, "Offer you a suggestion?"

"Absolutely."

"I don't have to remind you of the number of journalists
scrambling around your fair state, trying to get a different angle,
a different story on the primary. It's always a combination circus
and revival meeting, and this assassination attempt has just spun
out the reporters even more. Not to mention that little bit about
you having a relationship with the senator's wife back in college."

"That was a long time ago."

"Still, it's newsworthy, if it gets out. And knowing how dedicated these journalists are, I'm sure it will come out one of these
days, sooner rather than later."

"I know."

"Good. And you're going to see something else, Lewis. Despite that little show back there at the county jail, where you've just been set free on the side of goodness, you are now a story. Probably one of the biggest stories in the nation, right up to the time next week when the ballots get cast."

I said, "If you're advising me to keep a low profile and keep my mouth shut, consider it done."

Raymond said, "Good. I had a feeling you knew where I was going; glad to see my high opinion of you is based on something."

"Not disappointing my attorney, that's always been a goal in my life."

He laughed at that and said, "Right now we've embarrassed the Secret Service. They thought they had a shooter, and we've just blown that right out of the water. So don't be surprised if they come back at you with lots more questions, lots more attention, usually at a time and place inconvenient for you. Don't worry; we'll ride it out."

"Thanks."

Off in the distance I could make out the thin line of the Atlantic Ocean, and Raymond said, "Now, this was a change. Usually I come see you because of some…adventure involving Felix. But you've managed to get into trouble all by yourself this time. Not sure that's an improvement."

"I just went to a rally and got sick. That's all."

"More than that, my friend. You've got yourself caught up in an attempt to kill a leading presidential candidate. When you die, that will probably be the first line in your obituary."

The approaching ocean looked good. I said, "I don't plan that anytime soon. Besides, something else might be the first line in my obituary. First man on Mars, for example."

He laughed. "I won't hold my breath, but if you do do that, bring me back a rock or something."

"Or something."

Now we were crossing a long stretch of marshland, heading east to the ocean, and off to our right, squatting at the edge of the marsh, were the cement and steel structures of the Falconer nuclear power plant.

Raymond said, "Besides this campaign almost putting you in jail, it's lost me one of my best paralegals. How is Annie Wynn doing?"

"Doing well," I said. "Though yesterday was a pretty rough time. She's been taken in by the senator and his campaign. Question I have is, where is she going after the New Hampshire primary? She's made noises about going south if the primary goes well and if the polls improve for the senator."

"And how are the two of you doing?"

I eyed him. "Just fine, Counselor. Just fine."

That managed to keep him quiet. The road ended at Atlantic Avenue, which ran right along the edge of the coast, and he turned left, heading north. Empty parking spots flanked us all the way up to my home. I rubbed my hands across the tops of my legs. I knew I had just a few minutes left before we got to the Lafayette House parking lot.

"Raymond," I said.

"Yeah."

"I need to tell you a couple of things."

"Sure."

"I was set up."

He tapped a finger on the steering wheel. "That you were, son. That you were. Have you pissed anyone off lately?"

"Not that I'm aware of."

"Who do you think stole your handgun?"

"The fake Secret Service agent, that's who. He made sure I was going to be at the rally. And he knew me, knew about Annie…knew a lot of stuff. Which tells me he or his friends did their homework, did their research. They needed a patsy, and I was it. Lucky for me I got sick at the right time."

"Sounds good."

"Then how come that real Secret Service agent didn't press me?"

"Good question. I have a feeling Agent Reynolds knows a lot more than he was letting on. But I can tell you this, he does have his hands full. Trying to find out who shot at the senator, trying to find out who was impersonating a Secret Service agent. Just be glad you're not him."

"All right, I will."

He spared me a glance. "What's next, then?"

"What do you mean?"

"Not to worry, you're still under lawyer-client privilege, my friend."

I looked over at the wide cold ocean. "I'm going to find out who set me up. And why."

"Hell of a task."

"Don't think I've got much of a choice."

Raymond said, "You could let it drop. Let the professionals handle it."

"Not my style, Counselor."

He sighed. "All right. Just make sure you have my business card with you."

"Always."

The road rose up and went to the right and before us was the white Victorian structure of the Lafayette House, and across the street was the parking lot, the entrance to my house, and there was—

A mob scene.

The parking lot was a milling mass of reporters, photographers, news cameras, satellite trucks and vans, and assorted bystanders and passersby.

"Well," Raymond said.

"Understatement of the year, Raymond."

"Yeah."

He slowed down and I said, "You can let me out and—"

"Lewis," he said, his voice changing, sounding more like that of the guy who had gotten me out of prison a half hour ago. "I said I was going to take you home, and by God, I'm going to take you home. Just sit there, look straight ahead, and keep your face blank. Like you're holding a full house in a poker game with a motorcycle gang. All right?"

"Sure."

He made a sharp turn to the right, into the parking lot, and we moved forward slowly, like an icebreaker going through a mass of jumbled ice. I followed my lawyer's advice and stared straight ahead, as the enthusiastic members of the fourth estate pressed against the windows and sides of the BMW. We had a bumpy ride down to my house, and I felt a flash of anger as I saw another, smaller collection of reporters around the front door. Raymond said, "You let me handle this crowd, all right?"

"Sure," I said, thinking of the nice collection of firearms I have in my house, save for the one stolen two days earlier.

He pulled up and opened the door, letting in a burst of cold air and shouted questions, and he stood there for a minute or two, as the reporters gathered around him. He held his cell phone in his hand, smiled and said something, and after another minute or two, the reporters started going up the driveway. I turned and watched them trudge up the slight hill, and when they reached the parking lot, I got out.

"What magic words did you use to get rid of them?" I asked.

"Standard words. That they were all trespassing, and I was going to call the Tyler police to arrest their merry behinds. That's all."

I went up the door. Raymond followed and I turned and shook his hand.

"Thanks," I said.

"Not a problem. Just remember my advice. All right? And if you don't remember my advice…"

"I remember. And yes, I've got your business card."

"All right." He slapped his hands together against the cold and said, "I'm off. Give my best to Annie."

"Consider it done. And, Raymond?"

He was back at his BMW. "Yes?"

"Why don't you send me a bill this time?"

That made him laugh. "You're under the agreement I have with Felix, and with Felix, it's a lifetime of free legal services. It's taken care of, it will always be taken care of, and that's it. Now. Get your butt inside before you freeze it off."

"Sure. And get your butt back to Boston before some campaign up here hires you out."

"No chance, no chance, no chance," and with a smile and a

slammed door, he was back in his BMW, and heading up to the Lafayette House parking lot.

I went up to the front door, kicked the snow off my footwear, unlocked the door, and went inside.

Where I quickly determined I was not alone.

# FIVE

THE HOUSE WAS TOO WARM, there was a fire burning in the fireplace, and there was the low sound of music. The phone started ringing and I ignored it, knowing it was probably from one of the reporters up in the parking lot, checking in on me.

"Annie?" I called out.

"Yes, dear, I'll be right there."

But the voice sure as hell didn't match the sentiment. I went into the small living room, and in the kitchen, sitting at the counter like he owned the damn place, was Felix Tinios, a cup of coffee in front of him, his coat draped over a nearby chair. I suppose I should have been angry or upset that he had gotten in without telling me, but I knew how his mind worked. A friend of his was coming home from a stint in jail, so how could he not be here to greet me? The phone finally stopped ringing as I got to the kitchen.

He wore a thick green and black sweater and, I was a bit surprised to see, his shoulder holster and automatic pistol. "Carrying?" I asked. "That's a hell of an oppo research effort you're making."

He smiled, shook his head. "Not part of my oppo research job. Just part of getting into your house without having to answer lots of questions from those bottom-feeders out there in your yard."

"How's that?"

Felix toyed with the handle of the coffee mug. "Going to get all clichéd here and all, but most members of the press, they think the Constitution begins and ends with the First Amendment. They're not familiar with the particulars of the Second Amendment, and I've found that a flash of a shoulder holster and its equipment tends to shut them up. Oh, they bitch and moan about being threatened, but it's never come to anything. Funny how somebody who's brave enough to ask a mom how it feels to see her son drown gets all cowardly when he sees something made by Smith and Wesson."

"I see what you mean."

I sat at the counter, across from him, and he reached back and poured me a cup of coffee. I dumped in two spoonfuls of sugar and said, "I won't insult you by asking how you got in. Your usual skills, am I right?"

"Of course."

"I might have need of your other skills, if you can pull yourself away from finding out if Senator Pomeroy likes to surf the Net for big-breasted porn."

He said, "Somebody screwed you over."

"Correct. If it wasn't for the fact that I got sick at a certain time, I'd still be in prison, and I'd probably be going to trial in a few months."

"What happened, then? Just heard a radio report that a magazine columnist—you—had been arrested for trying to kill Senator Hale. Knew that you didn't have it in you. So what's the deal?"

"Deal was, two days ago, a guy came by to see me. Said he was from the Secret Service, was sent to my house to do an interview. Said I was on a list of 'persons of interest' and once he was satisfied that I was your run-of-the-mill nut, and not the kind of nut who blows up buildings, that was that. Wanted to know if I was going to the Hale rally the next day. Which I did. That's when somebody in the crowd took two shots at the senator, using my .357 Ruger. Revolver was left behind, with my prints and nobody else's. So I got arrested this morning and was released after your Raymond Drake came by and proved I wasn't in the building at the time of the shooting."

"How did he do that?"

"Got some television footage showing me throwing up in the parking lot of the Tyler Conference Center, about two minutes before the shooting started. Since I couldn't have been in two places at once, I was let go."

"You feeling better?"

"Better after having thrown up, or better after being released?"

"Both."

"Affirmative on both counts," I said.

Felix smiled. "Good old Raymond."

"That's not all. Right after I was arrested, I found out that the guy who was here talking to me the day before the rally wasn't really from the Secret Service."

Felix said, "This faux Secret Service agent. His name?"

"Spenser Harris."

"Show you ID?"

"Yes, he did."

He took a swallow from the coffee mug. "That's some serious scamming that was going on."

"I know. If I had been a bit more on the ball or suspicious, he would have been facing some hard charges of impersonating a federal law enforcement officer."

"Right. What else can you tell me about him?"

"Early thirties. Short black hair. About my height, though thinner and more muscled. Well dressed. Well-spoken. And… well. Yes."

"Yes what?"

"Yes, I'm sure that he's the one that stole my Ruger."

"Did he have a mysterious bulge in his pocket?" Felix asked.

"I wasn't looking for bulges, mysterious or otherwise," I said. "But I saw something I should have noticed. It was snowing when I came home and he was waiting for me. But his coat was clean. There was no snow on his shoulders. He had been in my house before I got here, long enough to steal my Ruger."

"Some setup," Felix said. The phone started ringing again, sounding sharp against my ears. I ignored it again.

I looked around at my small and snug and safe house, and while I was somewhat put out that Felix had let himself in, I really didn't like the thought of a stranger in here, a stranger who had gone through my belongings, looked at my belongings, stole one particular belonging as part of—

Part of what? The phone stopped ringing.

I said, "Setup. That's right. And look at what was involved. This guy knew me, knew my background, knew my relationship with Annie. He knew enough about my job with the Department of Defense to ask the right questions, look for the right answers. And he was confident enough to pull it all off, like he had help, somebody backing him up."

"More than one then."

"Yes."

"So. Who'd you piss off lately?"

"Excuse me?"

Felix said, "Look at the facts, my friend. Somebody tried to kill the senator. And not just any old run-of-the-mill senator. A guy who's trying to become president of the United States. And someone tried to pin that on you. More than one person. And if it's more than one person, ipso facto, it's a conspiracy. Organized. Smart. With resources. Not some nut lone gunman with a crush on a movie star or something equally stupid. So. Like I said, who's out there to get you?"

"Not a clue."

"Well, better get a clue soon, or next time you get set up, they'll do a better job."

"Felix, you're beginning to sound like bad late-night AM radio."

His eyes flashed at me. "Maybe so, but you should know better. You should look at things more closely, like you used to do, back when you were at the Pentagon."

"Really?" I asked.

"Yeah, really," he said. "Not that you've ever said word one about what you did back there, but I'm no idiot. I know what kind of things are looked at, what kind of things are researched. So research this. All these guys running for president—Senator Hale, Senator Pomeroy, the congressman, and the general—they're not out there on their own, with a stump speech and a smile. They've got people, lobbying groups, and corporations backing them, backing them with volunteers, phone banks, and lots of dollars. These people like power, they like to have power, they like to keep power. And when things get tight, like this primary season, things happen. Dirty tricks. Whisper campaigns. And maybe an assassination. So watch your back."

"I will."

"Good."

He finished his coffee, put the mug down, and said, "I need to be going. If you'd like, I'll see what—if anything—I can find out about your fake Secret Service agent. Usually I can sniff around and find out about strange men bearing firearms and identification that show up in my neighborhood."

"I don't think you'll find squat."

"Probably not, but it'll make me feel good, and hopefully, you, too." He stood up, retrieved his long coat, and put it on.

I said, "A couple of days ago, you came to me seeking advice. Today, you're talking about feelings. You still surprise me, Mr. Tinios."

"Good." He started to the door and said, "Meanwhile, I'd stay away from campaign rallies."

"All right, but I can't stay away from campaign volunteers. Well, one particular volunteer."

"I can see why," Felix said. "You be safe now."

"I will. You watch out for the media up in the parking lot, all right?"

"Sure. Not a problem."

"And…thanks. Thanks for coming by."

He grinned as he opened the door, and I stepped outside with him. "It's wintertime, there's not much to do, and days like this, Lewis, you make a fine, distracting hobby."

And when my friendly hobbiest left, I went back inside.

AT MY PHONE, the answering machine announced in little red numerals that there were thirty-six messages waiting for me.

How nice to be so bloody popular.

I grabbed a pen and a slip of paper, sat down, and started going through the messages. It didn't take as long as I expected. Four of the messages were from pollsters or campaigns, thirty-one were from various media outlets—only one of whom I intended to contact—and in the middle of the mess, one from Annie.

"Lewis, call me on my cell, all right? I've heard about…your troubles. Call me when you can."

I called her back. No answer. I left a message, and then looked again at the phone. I made the call, and there was the cheerful voice of Paula Quinn, my reporter friend from the *Chronicle*.

"Lewis," she said. "How sweet you'd call me back. I'd think you'd be angling to go on one of those cable round-table shows. Or a major network. Or an exclusive with *The New York Times*."

"I'm not friends with any of them," I said. "Just with you."

She laughed. "One of the few advantages of being a reporter in a small newspaper during the primary. Look. Are you up to talking to me?"

"Absolutely."

"All right, I'm leaving friend mode and now going into reporter's mode, all right?"

"Sure," I said. "And I'm going into source mode. Fair enough?"

I could make out the tapping of her computer keyboard. "Considering this is the biggest story in the Western Hemisphere today, you can go into any mode you'd like."

"Thanks. Look, everything and anything I say from now on, I'm not to be quoted by name or inference. Just say 'a source close to the investigation.' Does that work?"

"Works fine, and you're being a dear, but deadline is fast approaching. Can we get going?"

"Absolutely."

So I talked to Paula for a bit, answering the best I could, and despite my short answers, I think she was pleased that she was scooping the entire journalistic world with exclusive details on the attempted assassination attempt against Senator Jackson Hale. And to show her pleasure, she squeezed a lunch date out of me for later in the week, with a promise to pick up the check.

LATER IN THE AFTERNOON the illness that had saved me from a longer stay at the Wentworth County Jail rallied and assaulted me again. The nausea had returned, along with a set of chills that made me shiver every few minutes. I had called Annie twice more and had left her messages both times, the last one saying, "I'm feeling awful again, so I'm unplugging the phone and crawling into bed. Join me if you can."

Which is what I did, but before crawling into said bed, I went around and made sure the windows were locked, that the door was locked, and the sliding glass door leading out to my first-floor deck was locked. I also did a quick weapons inventory, and aside from the missing Ruger, my twenty-gauge shotgun, my eight-millimeter FN-FAL, and my nine-millimeter Beretta were all in place. I went upstairs and retrieved my Beretta from my bedroom, took a long shower to warm up my chilled bones, and then slid into bed. I read for a while and soon enough, the sounds of the ocean put me to sleep.

THE CREAKING DOOR from downstairs woke me up. I reached over to the nightstand, grasped my pistol. It was cold and awkward and yet comforting in my hand. I sat up, moist and cool, and knew my fever had broken. There were footsteps on the stairs coming up to my floor, and I aimed the pistol out toward the open door, waiting. Waiting.

The wind rattled the windows in my bedroom.

I waited and—

Damn.

I lowered the pistol and pulled the sheet over it, just as a figure appeared in the doorway. I called out, "Hello, Annie."

"Lewis," came the familiar and lovely voice. "Didn't mean to wake you up."

"You didn't, not to worry," I said.

She came in, and as she undressed, I tried my best to quietly put the Beretta back on the nightstand, and she said, "That's a new one, Lewis. Usually you can get me into bed with a soft word, not a weapon."

"The day I've had…sorry, I heard someone come in."

Annie came over, slid under the sheets. "But you invited me, didn't you?"

"That I did."

She cuddled up next to me and said, "You've been all over the news, but you knew that."

"Yes."

"Do you know why you are involved? Who did this to you?"

"Not a clue."

"Mmm…you intend to find out."

"That I do."

She said, "I…I cherish you, Lewis, but please. Please don't do anything to cause any more bad publicity for the senator. All right? I believe in him. I really do. And…I just want him to win next week. Okay?"

I stroked her hair. "Is this my Annie talking, or campaign Annie?"

"It's me talking, that's who."

"I understand, dear one, I do. Whatever I do, it'll have nothing to do with the senator. I just want to know how and why I was set up."

She touched my forehead. "How are you feeling?"

"Tired. Drained. Whatever I had before the rally seems to be going away."

"Good."

She kissed me chastely on the cheek and said, "You've had a long day. I've had a long day. Let's…let's just sleep, all right?"

"Fine. That'll be just fine."

She moved some more and in an instant was asleep. I held her for a bit, and then gently disentangled myself and rolled over. I lay there, listening to her breathing slow and deepen, until it almost matched the rhythm of the ocean's waves.

I AWOKE WITH wet hair in my face. Annie was there, fresh out of the shower, it seemed, and she raised herself up. "You okay?" she asked. She was already dressed, and knowing Annie, breakfast was either ready or already consumed.

"Feeling better. I think."

Another kiss. "I've got to run. Campaign staff meeting in forty-five minutes, and I'm only going to be on time if I speed my pert little ass over to Manchester. I'll call you later, all right?"

"Sure. Thanks for coming by. It…it meant a lot."

"Meant a lot to me, too. Especially when you didn't shoot me."

I raised up and kissed her, and she smiled, and then she was gone.

I lowered myself back to bed, yawned, and thought about what I should do next, and when I looked at my bedside clock—

keeping company with my nine-millimeter Beretta—I saw that
another hour had passed.

Time to get up and get going.

GETTING DRESSED AFTER my shower, I felt like I hadn't eaten
well in days, so I treated myself to a coronary-encouraging breakfast of scrambled eggs, bacon, toast, and some shaved potato bits
that passed as home fries. I left the television off and switched
on the radio to a classical station out of Boston that never broadcast news or political commentary, and with that comfort, I ate
well.

After a quick wash of the dishes, I felt better than I had in
days. I went out to the entranceway to get my coat, and then to
walk across the way up to the Lafayette House, to get the
morning papers, and then—

Something was on the floor, by the door.

An envelope.

I picked it up. An interview request, no doubt, from some enterprising news media type who had snuck down my snowy
driveway. It made me think about Felix and his direct way of
dealing with the news media. I thought about wandering up to
the driveway with my eight-millimeter rifle strapped to my back,
and decided that was going against my lawyer's advice to keep
what snipers call a low profile.

I opened up the envelope, and a heavy piece of stationery was
inside, folded over in threes. I undid it and there were handwritten words penned there.

> A clean, well-lit place with books and companions and
> soft chairs. What more can anyone want?
> At eleven?

The sentiment and the handwriting were familiar. I could not
believe it. I could not. But there it was.

I carefully put the paper back in the envelope, went upstairs,
and placed the missive in a desk drawer. Saw the time. Just past
10:00 a.m.

I sat down in my chair, looked about at my collection of

books, until I saw the ones I was looking for, old and unopened for so many years. There were four of them, large and flat and on the bottom of the farthest bookshelf.

I suppose I should have gone over there and pulled them free, to reminisce about what was and what might have been, but instead, I waited.

As the time passed, as the time always did.

JUST BEFORE ELEVEN—and after successfully driving past the lonely remnants of the media mob that had greeted me yesterday—I was in downtown Tyler, the small collection of office buildings and stores about a five-minute drive west of Tyler Beach. The beach is just a village precinct within the town of Tyler, and the two have always had a rocky relationship, like that of two brothers, one a bar-hopping ne'er-do-well, the other a sober, churchgoing type. But while the beach has much more to offer than the town proper, the town has one advantage the beach doesn't: a bookstore.

It's off Lafayette Road, on a small side street called Water Street, and, oddly enough, is called Water Street Books. It's in a two-story brick building with small green canvas awnings. I walked in. There was a large area in the center, lined with bookshelves after bookshelves, and before me was a display with a current *New York Times* bestseller. I walked past that collection of books, with the eyes of Mona Lisa following me, and to the rear of the store, which had padded chairs and coffee tables.

There was a small table with fresh-brewed coffee and tea and some snacks that operated on the honor system, and I poured myself a cup of coffee, dropped a dollar bill in an overflowing straw basket, started browsing. It was, as described, a clean, well-lit place with books and companions and soft chairs.

I found her at the farthest end of the bookstore, curled up with a coffee table book about Shaker furniture. She was sitting in a large easy chair, windows behind her overlooking a small park, and she had on designer jeans and a dull red turtleneck sweater. A matching red knit cap was pulled over her head, her blond hair tucked up underneath, and as I approached, she looked up and smiled right through me.

"Lewis," she said.

"Barbara."

She stood up and I automatically came forward, and we exchanged hugs, the touch and scent bringing back old college-aged memories, memories I didn't even know I had anymore. She kissed me on the cheek and I returned the favor, and then we sat down, holding hands, just for the briefest and most delicate of moments.

"You look great," I said.

"Right."

"No, I mean it. You look like you just left the Student Union, heading out to McGrath's Pub."

She smiled at the name of the old pub back at Indiana University, where we had spent long hours drinking cheap beer and solving the problems of the world, and she said, "You look good, too."

"Now you're the one who's lying," I said. "Face not as smooth, hair not as thick."

The smile was still there. "I like your face. It's got character. It's got life to it. Are you all right…with everything else?"

I nodded. "I am. I had nothing to do with the shooting."

"Of course. My staff tried to brief me last night and I told them not to bother. I knew you could have never done anything like that."

"Thanks. And was it your staff who delivered your note this morning?"

She nodded, the smile…oh, that smile. "Yes, an eager intern who knows how to keep her mouth shut, and who loved pretending to be a reporter, begging you for an interview by sliding that envelope under your door."

I looked around the nearly empty bookstore. "Speaking of staff…how in hell did you get here without a media mob following you?"

The smile took on an icy edge I had never seen before. "One of the advantages of being the wife of the senator, and a possible first lady. The staff have their demands, but they also know I have a long memory, a memory of who's been helpful and who's been a pain in the ass, a memory I'll bring with me to the East Wing.

And if I need a chunk of time here and there for personal time, without handlers, without staff, even without Secret Service protection, then that's the way it's going to be."

"I see."

Then the ice disappeared from the smile, and the old Barbara was sitting there before me. "Listen to me, a cranky and confident bitch on wheels. When I get to the East Wing. If I get to the East Wing, my old friend. There's a lot ahead, and New Hampshire's just the second step."

"How's the senator doing?"

"With the shooting? Jack's shrugging it off. That's one of his many admirable qualities. When he is focused on a goal, on something he desires so much, he won't let anything get in his way. His opponents in Georgia. Members of his own party who thought he should sit this one out. Or one deranged shooter."

"I saw you at the rally. You must have been scared."

The barest of shrugs. "It happened so fast…I don't think I had time to think about anything. The first shot sounded like a firecracker going off, but the Secret Service…they move very, very fast. I have bruises on my arms where they grabbed me. They don't fool around."

"I'm glad."

She shifted her legs in the chair. "What I found amazing was that I saw you in the audience. That was a surprise and a half. How did you end up in New Hampshire?"

"Long story," I said. "Quick version is that I ended up here after working for a while at the Department of Defense. I had some old memories about being a kid here on the coast, before my mom and dad moved us out to Indiana. And now I'm a columnist for a magazine."

"*Shoreline.*"

"That's right."

Barbara reached out, touched the back of my wrist. "Congratulations to you, at least. You and I, back at school, we were going to be great writers. Journalists who make a difference. To report from D.C., from conflicts in Asia and Africa. Struggle and fight to bring out the truth, to change the world."

"Not much change comes from a monthly column."

"Maybe, but at least you're still writing. Me...I'm lucky if I get to edit some of Jack's speeches. When he's in a good mood, that is."

I put my coffee cup down on the table between us. "Last I knew, back at school, you went out to D.C. on an internship."

Her voice was flat. "And never came back to Indiana. And never wrote or called you. I know. It's been a long time. I hope you've forgiven me since then."

I looked at her. "I have."

"Thanks. I mean that, Lewis. Thanks." She sighed. "Such a story. Went out there, just for a semester. Interning at Congressman Reisinger's office. Not supposed to do much of anything but answer phones and sort mail...but there was a vicious flu season that semester. Bunch of staffers got sick. So I got pushed into service, got myself noticed, and as time went on...I didn't want to go back to Indiana. And I didn't want to report the news. I wanted to be on the inside, making the news. So I transferred out to George Washington University, stayed and worked on Capitol Hill, and eventually, I got noticed by another congressman."

"The Right Honorable Representative Jackson Hale."

That made her giggle. "Such a mouthful, right? And if you had told me that I was going to marry a Southern congressman, a guy from Georgia, I would have told you, you were crazy. But I did...and you know why? Because I could sense he was going places. That he was going to make lots of news, and besides the fact that I was attracted to him, I wanted to be a part of it. So I got used to breakfast meetings, fried catfish, grits in the morning, and learning who races what kind of vehicle in NASCAR. Along the way, a wonderful son and a wonderful daughter. And here we are. All because of a bad flu season, all those years ago."

I made a point of looking around the store. "Yes. Here we are. A clean, well-lit place with books and companions and soft chairs."

"What could be better?" And then she looked down, as if suddenly fascinated by the cover of the book in her lap.

There was just the quickest of moments there, I think, when we were both in our early twenties, full of energy and good intentions, and recalling our shared love of bookstores, and our solemn vow to each other that if our relationship continued, that if we made it that much more, that we would always have to live in a place that had a fine bookstore.

Old promises.

She looked up and said, "My story. And what's yours? How did you end up at the Pentagon?"

"Senior year," I said. "I had done my own internship the previous summer, at the *Indianapolis Star*. I was getting ready to apply there for a full-time gig after graduation, when I saw this little ad in the campus paper. Something about did you think you were smart enough to work in an intelligence agency for the United States government. I don't know why, I just thought it was a bit of a goof, a bit of a challenge. So I applied, got a response, took an intelligence test with a few score other college students, and after a bunch of interviews and more tests, there I was, working on the inside."

"Regret not staying in journalism?"

"Not at the time," I said. "Later…yeah, there were regrets. But at the time, I thought I had the best job in the world. I was on the inside. I knew things that would never appear in newspapers, would never appear in print. I could spend the day reading, spend the day talking to people, following leads and tips, and then write reports. That's it. One week, a report prepared for one person, another week, a report prepared for the Joint Chiefs. That was my job. And at the time, I loved it."

"Now?"

"It's…the past. Some good memories. One very bad memory. And here I am."

"Why did you leave?"

My throat felt just a bit thick. I wanted so much to let it all go, but yet… "I'm sorry Barbara. I can't say. When I left, I had to sign a nondisclosure agreement. It…it was tough. But here I am."

"Married?"

"Nope."

She smiled. "A woman friend?"

Somehow, a tinge of guilt. Why? "Yes. A dear one. In fact, she's working hard to see your husband get elected."

"Good for her."

Barbara looked at her wristwatch, a delicate gold item that must have cost the good senator a chunk of change, some time ago. "Lewis…I've been here as long as I can. It's…it's been good to see you."

"The same."

She stood up and so did I, and there was another embrace, quicker this time around, and she said, "I just wanted to see you. Funny, isn't it? I saw you at the rally…and, well…you look good. I'm glad you came." The old smile. "If we're lucky, I'll make sure you get another invite. To the inauguration, next year."

"That'd be great."

Another touch of her hand to mine, and then she was out the door.

I stayed behind for a while, browsing through the books, enjoying this time in a clean, well-lit place with books, all by my lonesome.

# SIX

BACK HOME, I passed through the dwindling crowd of news media, out there freezing for the dubious possible privilege of talking to me, including one enterprising type who wouldn't move from in front of my Ford Explorer. Considering I had gotten enough law enforcement attention already—and not wanting to dent the fender or hood of my Explorer—I let the driver's side window down and waited. The man was thickset, balding, with steel-rimmed glasses, and he said, "First things first, Mr. Cole. I'm not a reporter."

"Bully for you," I said.

He passed over a business card. "My name is Chuck Bittner. I'm with Tucker Grayson's presidential campaign. I'd like to talk to you."

I tossed the business card on the passenger's seat of the Explorer. "Sorry, Mr. Bittner. The feeling's not mutual."

He tried to lean into the open window. "Mr. Cole, look, General Grayson is what this country needs, and I'm dedicated to seeing him elected. Just a few minutes of your time, and I'm sure you'll agree with me, and agree to help his campaign by—"

I raised the window and kept on driving, and when I got down to my house, there was yet another visitor, standing outside the front door. I had an urge to keep on driving, to see if I could make my visitor run into the snowbank, but I was a good boy and turned into the garage.

I parked my Explorer, got out, and said, "Last time somebody stood there, he claimed to be a Secret Service agent. Glad to know your credentials seem to be in order. Or at least I hope."

Secret Service Agent Glen Reynolds didn't smile at my little gibe and said, "Do you want to see them again?"

"Nope."

He said, "I'd like to talk to you for a few minutes."

I scratched at my face. "Thought my attorney was pretty clear, Agent Reynolds. You weren't to talk to me without his say-so."

"Maybe I tried to call him. Perhaps I didn't reach him."

"Perhaps," I said.

"Or maybe I just wanted to see if I could talk to you without your hiding behind your attorney."

"I'm not sure if 'hiding' is an appropriate term, Agent Reynolds."

A quick nod. "My apologies then."

"All right. I guess we can talk away."

I stood there, and he stood there, and he said, "Well?"

"Yes?"

"Can we go inside?"

"Oh. Can you say the magic word?"

A slight grimace. "Mr. Cole, can we please go inside to talk?"

"Sure," I said, smiling at him.

I unlocked the front door, went inside, and dumped my coat on a nearby chair, and Agent Reynolds followed me and sat down on my couch. From inside his coat he pulled out a section of newspaper, which he tossed on the coffee table. I saw the familiar layout and typeface of the Tyler *Chronicle*.

"This article is not helpful," he said.

"Really?"

"Really. Not helpful at all."

"Then I suggest you talk to the reporter. Who was it?"

His voice got sharp. "You know who wrote it."

"So talk to her. Why talk to me?"

"Because of what she said in the story. Lots of juicy information and quotes about the shooting at the conference center, all of the quotes anonymous. None of them from me, none of them from the state police or anybody else officially involved in the investigation. So it was you. Why?"

"Seemed to be the right thing at the time."

"To interfere with the investigation?"

"Some investigation," I said. "You thought you had it wrapped up in a nice little package with my arrest. A one-day investigation, with everything all confirmed and concluded, no more work to be done. Right?"

His face flushed. "We followed the leads that were there. Beginning with your weapon, your fingerprints, your presence at the campaign rally. To do anything else would have been foolish."

"Well, it seemed foolish to me."

"Then consider yourself lucky that you don't have to worry about such things."

"All right, I'll do just that."

Reynolds said, "The investigation is continuing, Mr. Cole. Both into the shooting at the campaign rally and this supposed Secret Service agent who saw you the other day." He gestured to the newspaper on my coffee table. "Question I have is this. Do you intend to keep on interfering with our investigation?"

"Guess it depends on your definition of interfering, Agent Reynolds."

"All right. Here's my definition. Talking to the press again about what happened at the campaign rally. How's that?"

"Fair enough," I said. "And just to let you know, my press appearances have officially ended. That sound good to the Treasury Department?"

"That sounds excellent, Mr. Cole."

"Glad to be of service."

"Now, about this Spenser Harris. Do you have any information as to who he is, or where he came from?"

"No," I said. "Do you?"

He paused for a second, like he was debating what to tell me, and he said, "No, not a whit. We've done a canvass of what passes for a neighborhood around here, talked to the people at the Lafayette House and other nearby hotels and motels to see if someone by that name was registered. Nothing."

"Sorry to hear that," I said.

Reynolds said, "I'm sure it won't come as any surprise to you that we now believe this fake agent was connected with the shooting at Senator Hale's campaign rally."

"No, it's not a surprise."

"And you'll let me know if you find out anything about who he really is?"

"Of course."

"Thank you," he said, picking up the offending piece of news-print and putting it back into his coat. He got up from the couch and I walked with him to the door, and before he left, he said, "One more thing, Mr. Cole."

I had to grin. "You know, there's always one more thing, isn't there. You learn that at the training academy or something?"

His smile didn't look particularly inviting. "Here's the deal. I'm in no position to tell you what to do with your personal life, but I think it would be a very good thing if you stayed away from the senator's wife over the next several days. Some of the senator's staff and supporters…well, they may make your life difficult if such news were to be made widely known."

"Really?"

"Really. Even if you both do enjoy spending time at the local bookstore. Have I made myself clear?"

"Quite."

"Good."

And then he left, and I went back into my house.

I CALLED ANNIE and got her voice mail and then I sat on the couch and just brooded for a bit. Somewhere out there was Spenser Harris and his friends, and I so wanted to talk to him again, to find out who they were and why they wanted me to be their patsy. But where to start? Felix was out there, sniffing around, and I knew he would do a better, quicker, and more thorough job than I could imagine. Plus, trying to poke around on my own to find out who Spenser Harris was, coupled with the publicity tagged on me with the assassination attempt, that would pretty much take care of my promise to Annie not to do anything to disturb the Hale campaign.

So instead of spending the rest of the day on the couch, thinking useless thoughts, I went upstairs and tried to decide what kind of column I was going to write for the June issue of *Shore-line*. It being January, it was hard to get in the mood to write for an issue of the magazine that would be published in bright sunshine and warm nights. Part of the fun challenges of being a magazine columnist: your writing clock is always three or four months off.

The phone rang and I picked it up, waiting for my old and trusty Apple iMac to boot up. "Hello?"

"Mr. Cole?"

"Yes."

"I'm calling from CNN and was wondering—"

"Sorry, not interested."

I hung up the phone, opened up my word processing program. Looked at my blank computer screen. I suppose I could write about the annual migration of tourists to the beach communities of New England, and how their presence changed the atmosphere of these little towns, and how this caused tension between the tourists and the year-round residents. I started writing down a few thoughts but then stopped. Practically every other newspaper or newsmagazine that covered this region did the same outsiders-impacting-the-locals story, and who was I to inflict another such story upon the long-suffering readers of *Shoreline?*

The phone rang.

"Hello?"

"Mr. Cole?"

"Yep."

"Mr. Cole, I'm calling from *The New York Times.*"

"Really?"

"Um, yes, I'm from *The New York Times* and I was wondering—"

"Well, thanks for calling, but I get the paper from across the way. At a local hotel. It seems I can't get a subscription to my residence. Why's that?"

"Ah, Mr. Cole, I'm not calling from the circulation department. My name is George Mulvey, I'm a reporter from the *Times,* and—"

"Oh, a reporter. I apologize. I thought you were trying to sell me a subscription. But I guess you want to talk to me about a news story."

"Yes, I do, and I'd like to know—"

"Sorry, not interested."

I hung up.

Before me was the screen, still very much blank.

Why not a story about the islands of the New England shore-line? Too often my columns had been about the actual coastline of New England, about the communities and fishing villages, and why not expand it a bit? Across the way was the Isles of Shoals— All right, maybe not those islands, they'd been written about more than enough times. But there was Block Island down in Long Island…nope, overwritten as well. Nantucket and Martha's Vineyard? Please. How many forests had to die to churn out copy about those two special places every year? Long Island sound again, but Plum Island had been claimed by a well-known and well-regarded novelist a few years back, and there were the islands off the coast of Maine, all one or two hundred of them, and how could I choose, and—

The phone rang.

"Mr. Cole?"

"The same."

"Mr. Cole, it's Chuck Bittner again, from the Tucker Grayson campaign. Look, I really think it would be in your interest to talk to me, so that your story can get the proper attention it deserves, about your relationship with the—"

"Mr. Bittner."

"Yes?"

I turned in my office chair. "You're an oppo researcher for the general's campaign, am I right?"

That seemed to make him pause. "Suppose…suppose I say no?"

"Then I'm not going to talk to you for even a second."

There was a sigh. "All right…yes, yes, I do perform opposition research for the general. But each campaign has such researchers, and I really need to talk to you, about you and the senator's wife. It's a story that really needs to be fleshed out, and—"

"Nope."

"But you said you'd talk to me!"

"No, I said I wouldn't talk to you if you denied being an opposition researcher," I said. "But you know what? I'm still not going to talk to you, even if you did admit to being an oppo researcher."

Then I hung up the phone. I was getting pretty damn good at it.

All right, back to the patient and blank computer screen. Maybe it was time to think outside the box. Maybe I could do a column about odd aspects of history that had happened along the New Hampshire coastline that not many people knew about. Like the evidence that Vikings had settled here more than a thousand years ago. Or the case of the German U-boats that had been interned at the end of World War II up at the Porter Naval Shipyard. Or—

Or give it a rest, I thought. Who'd want to read offbeat stories like those two?

Another ring of the phone.

"Hello?"

"Lewis? It's Annie. How's that sickness treating you?"

"Sickness seems to be bored with me and is leaving. How are you doing?"

There was pause, and I wondered if she hadn't heard me, and there was the briefest of sighs. "Lewis… I was talking to some senior staff in the this morning. About you. And the shooting. And one other thing that somebody slipped out, a big-ass secret that only a few in the campaign know about."

"Yes?"

"Lewis…I've come to know you're a man with secrets. You've not told me much about the scars you have. Or what you did at the Pentagon. Or how you ended up in a prime beachfront home on a magazine columnist's salary. You've joked and fooled around and have really never answered my questions directly, and I've put up with that. Your other…your other assets have outweighed whatever questions or concerns I've had."

My hand tightened on the telephone receiver. I knew where this was going.

"So, having said all of that," she went on, "would you mind telling me why you've never told me about you and the senator's wife? Barbara? Why you decided to keep that little secret from me? Good God, I can't believe the news media have picked up on it already…her former boyfriend being initially charged in the shooting. So far, its only the staff who knows this."

"We knew each other in college," I said. "Just for a while. It was…I didn't think it was that important, Annie."

Another sigh. "I'm working on a campaign for a man who might be the next president of the United States, and you used to date the future first lady when you were in college. And you didn't think to tell me?"

"I was…it just didn't…well, to tell you the truth, I didn't think Senator Hale was going to make it this far. So I didn't think it was worth bringing up."

Annie said, "Nope. Not good enough. I think there's something else. And once you figure it out, do me the favor of telling me. All right?"

It was my turn to sigh. "Sure. Look, there was no secret agenda, it was just—"

"Lewis, you're a man with secrets. Most times it's charming. This isn't one of those times."

"I hear you."

"Thanks. Look…we'll be pretty busy over here tonight. I don't think I'm going to make it over to your place later."

"Oh. I see."

"No, really…we're busy. I'll see if I can't come over tomorrow. All right?"

"That would be great."

A few more words here and there, and then she hung up.

Before me again was the blank screen.

The hell with it.

I was done for the day.


THE NEXT MORNING I went for a quick walk across the street to the Lafayette House to get my morning newspapers. Being in such an isolated location, newspaper delivery was out of the question, and since I got my mail from a post office box—which meant the usual drive into town—I most always got my newspapers from the gift shop at the Lafayette House.

The air was sharp and crisp as I walked up my driveway. Hands in my pockets, I carefully made my way up to the hotel's parking lot, trying to decide what to say to any die-hard members of the fourth estate who might still be on stakeout duty. But when I reached the parking lot, I hated to say it, but I was disappointed. No one was waiting for me. The reporting hand, having writ, had obviously moved on to another story.

I took in a deep breath of the fresh sea air. Some other story was no doubt out there, being chased by the dedicated men and women of the news media, and I was now content to be left alone.

I went across Atlantic Avenue, up to the white colossus that was the Lafayette House, and then strode into the marble and glass splendor of its lobby. To the left was the gift shop, and I left a few seconds later, with five newspapers under my arm, after exchanging the usual pleasantries with the gift shop manager, a retired air force chief warrant officer named Stephanie Sussex. She had short gray hair, old-fashioned black-rimmed glasses that were bowed like cat whiskers, a black turtleneck adorned by a simple gold crucifix, and the same old joke.

"Still reading for five people?"

"Looks that way, doesn't it."

She rang up my purchases and said, "Least you could do is make 'em pay for it. Have a good one."

"Thanks," I said. "I'll try."

I liked the feeling of the newspapers under my arm. I know that we are in a new world of computerized information, with most of the world's newspapers now available with the click of a keyboard or a mouse, but I still like the feel of newspapers in my hands. It just feels more real. Besides, the computer geniuses who brought us to this brave new world still haven't come up with a way of devising a personal computer that you can easily carry into the bathroom when the need arises.

I WENT THROUGH the parking lot on my way back, seeing a panel truck at the north end of the lot. JIMMY'S ELECTRICAL SERVICE, FALCONER, it said on the side of the truck, and I felt bad for Jimmy, having to hump his equipment up to the hotel.

Down the driveway I went, and back home, there was someone waiting for me at the doorsteps to my house, sitting there, legs stretched out, looking quite comfortable. It looked like the fourth estate hadn't given up quite yet in their quest to interview me. I came down the driveway, focusing on my footwork, making sure I didn't slip and knock my skull against a piece of rock outcropping. I looked up once, and my visitor was still there, sitting patiently. Well, he could be as patient as he wanted. I certainly wasn't going to say much when I got to the doorway. I was done with the news media. The primary election was just a few days away, and I was going to keep my head down, ignore the senator's wife, and make nice with Annie Wynn after our last discouraging phone call.

When I got to my house, I stopped, as if the snow about my feet had suddenly turned into ice, keeping me still.

For before me was Spenser Harris, fake Secret Service agent.

I stood, waiting to see if he would say anything, but that didn't seem possible.

For he was dead.

# SEVEN

I GINGERLY WALKED AROUND, checking to make sure he was as dead as he looked. He was on the snow-covered ground next to the doorsteps, leaning up against the stone foundation. His legs were out in front of him, his hands were folded primly in his lap. His eyes were closed. Thank God for small favors. I looked to the side of his head and saw a mass of blood and torn flesh and splintered bone just behind his right ear. He seemed to be wearing the same coat and necktie and slacks combination from his first visit to my home.

I stepped back, taking a breath. I didn't like him, and didn't like what he had done to me, but still…I didn't like seeing him dead on my doorstep.

Another breath.

There were things to do, procedures to be followed, phone calls to be made.

I unlocked the door and went inside.

I left the dead form of Spenser Harris behind me.

I DROPPED THE NEWSPAPERS and went upstairs, taking the steps two at a time. Into my office, up to a small closet. Opened the closet, went through some boxes of papers and files until I saw a small, multicolored box stuck in the rear. I ripped the box open, tearing a bit of finger skin in the process, and sat on the floor, going through about twenty pages of instructions in English, Spanish, French, and German, and then tossed the paperwork aside.

Before me was a prepaid cell phone, about the size of two credit cards together. I had gotten it as a Christmas gift the previous year from Detective Sergeant Woods, when she had told me that in this new age of ours, it was customary to be accessible through instant communications. I replied that I rather liked being inaccessible. And she had smiled and said next time I was driving in East Overshoe, New Hampshire, tracking down a story, it would be nice to have a cell phone in case my car died or I ran into a moose.

I had agreed, and had promptly put the phone in my closet.

Until now.

It had no charge in its little battery so I managed to plug it into a free receptacle in my office. I fumbled through a few more minutes of trying to figure out what in hell to do with this marvelous instrument, when I started punching in the numerals.

By now, I guess shock was coursing its way through my system, for my hands were shaking.

But I still managed to dial the number.

I waited as it rang.

And waited.

Conscious that a body was cooling itself outside my front door.

The phone was answered.

"Yeah."

"Hi, it's me."

"Oh. What's up."

"Got a situation," I said.

"A situation?"

"Quite the situation."

"Go ahead."

I said, "Remember that joke you told me a couple of months ago, about the difference between a friend and a true friend?"

"Yeah."

"I need a true friend. Right now."

"Where are you?"

"Home."

"You injured?"

"Nope."

The voice was as brisk and as professional as it had been from the first greeting. "Be there in under a half hour. Don't touch a damn thing."

"I won't."

"Good."

I hung up the cell phone. The joys of being accessible.

And somewhat untraceable. I wasn't sure just how untraceable this phone call would be, but there was no doubt that using the old landline telephone in my home would have been as visible as elephant tracks in the snow. Maybe this call would be harder to trace.

Maybe. I sure hoped so.

Then again, maybe I was just fooling myself.

However, after seeing what had been out there in the snow, I was probably in the mood for being fooled.

I tossed the cell phone across the room, and went back downstairs.

I STOOD OUT THERE in the cold, hands in my coat, trying to ignore the body nearby. Hell of a thing. But I couldn't do it. I looked over at Spenser Harris. Still dead. Lots of questions and no answers were rattling inside my head. I toed a piece of ice-encrusted snow.

Just stood there. My breath was visible in the cold air. The sound of the waves just a few feet away were always there, and always ignored, until one listened. I was listening. The waves were constant, were a part of the background.

Toed another piece of ice. Waited.

Another noise.

I looked up. A dark green Honda Pilot was maneuvering its way down the driveway, its four-wheel drive making the sloppy trip look easy. Something tight in my chest started to ease. I took my hands out of my pockets.

The Pilot stopped. Felix Tinios got out, looked at me and my uninvited guest. From his dark wool coat, he pulled out two sets of rubber gloves, tossed one set to me, which I caught with one hand. Damn, wasn't I good?

Felix said, "All right. Time for talking is later. Time for action is now. Got it?"

"Gotten."

He put on his gloves, and I followed as well. Instantly my

hands felt warm and clammy. Felix went to the rear of the Pilot, opened up the hatchback. With the middle row of seats folded down, there was plenty of room back there. Felix reached in and pulled out a black rubberized body bag, and my stomach did a slow flip-flop, realizing once again what kind of man Felix was: the kind of guy who had ready access to body bags.

But I sure as hell wasn't complaining.

Felix made his way to the body of Spenser Harris, flipped the bag out on the ground. There was a heavy-duty zipper that started at the top, went down the side and then to the bottom, like a garment bag designed for undertakers. Felix zipped the bag open, the noise sounding obscene in my tiny front yard, and opened up the flap. He looked up at me, his face serious.

"Can you give me a hand? You going to be all right with this?"

"Yeah."

"All right, let's move him. You get the legs."

Felix went to the rear of the body, reached under his arms, lifted him off the steps, and I grabbed the legs. The phrase "dead weight" rang through my mind as we moved the body over to the open bag. I slipped some in the snow and dropped Spenser's legs, but Felix had it under control, and got most of the upper body over the bag. I maneuvered the legs in and then Felix flipped the cover back over, zipped the damn thing shut. Suddenly it just felt better. There was no longer a body in my front yard. There was just a lumpy thing inside a bag, something without a face.

"Okay. Handles on both sides. Let's get him in."

As he always is, Felix was correct. Heavy black web handles were on each side of the bag, and we both grabbed on and got him off the ground. A handful of steps later, we had him in the rear of the open Pilot. Felix went forward to the passenger's side door and dragged the body bag in. When he had moved the bag far enough, I slammed the hatchback door shut. By now Felix was in the driver's seat and the engine was running. I joined him and he said, "You don't need to be here. I can handle it."

"You may think I don't need to be here, but I do. Let's get going."

"Sure."

Felix maneuvered the Pilot about in my yard, and then we were heading back up the driveway, to the parking lot of the Lafayette House, and in a minute or so, we were heading south, away from my home, away from Tyler Beach. We both pulled off our rubber gloves. My hands felt moist and soft.

I was feeling just a little bit better.

But only a bit.

WE DIDN'T GO FAR, only to Salisbury, the first town over the Massachusetts border. We took Route 1-A—Atlantic Avenue—all the way south. I was conscious of how tight my chest was as I sat next to Felix.

He said, "All right. Good job back there."

"Thanks. Coming from you that's a hell of a compliment."

"Do you know who he is? Or was?"

"Yeah. The fake Secret Service agent who scammed me a few days back. Spenser Harris."

"No shit."

"True. No shit."

Felix made a show of looking back at the shape in the rear, and turned back. "Strange world, isn't it. Last time we were together, I said I'd do a little digging, see what I could find out about this guy, and now he ends up dead on your doorstep. Sorry I wasn't quicker finding him."

"You're forgiven."

"Gee, thanks. Well, I'll keep on digging, but having your Spenser Harris show up dead puts a damper on things."

"I guess so. And when did he become my Spenser Harris?"

Felix shrugged. "He was in your front yard. Possession being nine-tenths of the law, it seemed to be a logical assumption."

I told him what he could do with his logic, and that made him smile.

Traffic was light as we went by the deserted buildings of Tyler Beach, approaching the drawbridge that led into Falconer, the southernmost town in New Hampshire. Stuck in almost every snowbank was a campaign sign. HALE FOR AMERICA'S TOMORROWS. WIN WITH WALLACE. POMEROY/PRESIDENT. GRAYSON FOR

PRESIDENT. Lots of signs, all with the same color pattern. Red, white, and blue. True imagination at work. It was good to look at the signs. It didn't require me to think of the body riding back there in the rear.

"His body hadn't gone into rigor yet," Felix said. "Figure he's been dead only an hour or so. That sound right?"

"Yes, it does. I was out at the Lafayette House, getting my morning newspapers. I was out maybe fifteen, twenty minutes at the most."

"Any idea who did it?"

"Not a one."

We went over the drawbridge spanning the small harbor of Tyler Beach. Off to the right were the concrete buildings of the Falconer nuclear power plant, quietly producing power, with nary a protester in sight. We were in Falconer for about a minute or two, and then we were in the Commonwealth of Massachusetts, in its northernmost community of Salisbury. For some reason I turned again and looked back at the body bag.

Felix said, "Any idea why this guy was killed on your front lawn?"

I turned back. The body bag hadn't moved a bit.

I said, "Have an idea or two. Main idea is...well, I think whoever did it wanted me to take the fall for trying to kill Senator Hale. When that didn't stick, they wanted another try by dumping Spenser Harris's body in my front yard."

In Salisbury, Felix maneuvered the Pilot through its nearly empty streets. "For what reason? If they wanted you to get arrested for Harris's death, why not keep an eye on the place and make a phone call when you arrive?"

I folded my arms. "They were probably counting on my civic duty. A phone call to the cops, the arrival of the cops and the state police Major Crimes Unit, followed by another media circus, all just before the New Hampshire primary."

"Then why didn't you do your civic duty, Lewis?"

"What?"

Felix said, "You're one of the more civic guys I know. Any other guy found a body in his yard, the call would go to the cops.

Especially since you have such a fine relationship with the local constabulary's lead detective. So why no call?"

I said, "You can probably figure it out."

Felix grinned. "Women. Aren't they something? If this dump was from opponents of Senator Hale, wanting to give him another bucketful of bad publicity just before the primary, then you didn't want to give them that publicity, did you? All for your girl Annie."

I sighed. "That's as good a guess as any."

"Works for me."

I turned to him. "I suppose if the Pomeroy campaign was up to something nefarious like this, you'd let me know."

Felix laughed. "From what I know of the Pomeroy campaign, Lewis, they couldn't spell 'nefarious,' never mind knowing what it means."

Now we were in an industrial part of Salisbury, near I-95, and the buildings were one-story concrete and brick structures—printing plants, small businesses—and, there, just ahead, a barbwire enclosure, a self-storage business called, aptly enough, the Space Station.

The gate was open and Felix drove in and went down into one of the open lanes to the right, flanked on both sides by one-story buildings with roll-up steel doors. At the end of the building on the right, the doors were big enough to let a vehicle pass through, Felix stopped the Pilot at the stall at the end of the lane. He got out, undid the combination lock at the side of the door, and rolled it up. He flicked on the interior lights for the now open storage unit and got back inside.

"Where did you get the Pilot?"

"A business associate. Let's leave it at that."

"Some business associate."

Felix slowly backed the Honda into the storage room. "Didn't think I could use my Mercedes. And I didn't want to use your Ford. And when we're done with the Pilot, it's going to get steam-cleaned and detailed. Just to be on the safe side, which is a side I love being on. Come on, we've still got work to do."

We both got out on the concrete floor of the storage room, and Felix went to the entrance and lowered the steel door. It was now quiet and it felt good to be inside with the door closed, away from any curious neighbors. I followed Felix as he went forward. There were storage lockers on both sides and, at the end, a large top-opening refrigerator. He propped open the cover to the refrigerator and said, "He'll fit."

"How come I get the feeling you've done this before?"

While there was humor in his voice, there was no humor in his expression. "Don't make me answer dangerous questions, Lewis. Deniability is a wonderful gift."

Back to the Pilot we went, and up went the rear hatch. Felix reached in said, "I want to open up the bag for a moment and examine our guest."

"I'm not going to stop you, so go right ahead."

The interior was roomy enough so that Felix knelt down and opened the bag up, the zipper sounding better here than at my house. He worked for a while, his hands busy inside the bag and the clothing of the dead man, and he looked at me, his face impassive. "Dead people are hard to work with. Frozen, not moving, resisting."

"Yeah, well, we've all got problems."

"At least we're doing better than your friend here."

"Not my friend."

"If you say so."

He worked for a couple of minutes more and said, "Lewis, he's been cleaned up. No driver's license, no money, not even a scrap of paper. Very professional."

I thought about a promise I had made the day before to the very real Secret Service agent Glen Reynolds. I had promised to let him know if I found out the man's true identity. So far, I hadn't, so at least that was a promise I could keep.

"Thanks for looking," I said. "Can we get this wrapped up?"

"Sure."

The zipper went shut and Felix came back out and started pulling at the body bag, and I followed suit. A few steps later, the body of Spenser Harris went into the refrigerator, and the lid shut down.

Felix looked at me. "You okay?"

"Sure am. Could use a drink, though."

He smiled. "Damn it, man, it's not even ten in the morning."

"What does that have to do with anything?"

He shrugged. "Not a damn thing. Let's go get those drinks."

WE HAD A LATE BREAKFAST at the Lafayette House, in the main dining room, with coffee and Belgian waffles and eggs Benedict and mimosas in tall, cold glasses and bacon and sausage. With each passing minute in the luxurious comfort of the hotel, I felt the tension slide away, like a solid block of ice exposed to the warm April sun. We were in a part of the dining room that had a fine view of Tyler Beach, the parking lot, and if you looked real hard, the top of the roof of my house. Another reason I felt good is that the parking lot had the standard collection of vehicles belonging to hotel guests and visitors. There were no police cruisers or television vans out there, looking to record Lewis Cole's next misadventure with the criminal justice system. Nothing at all. Quiet is a wonderful thing.

Felix said, "What now?"

"I find out who the hell's drawn a big bull's-eye on my back, that's what."

"Going to be hard to do, with your only link to them now resting comfortably in Dallsbury.

"I'll think of something, I'm sure."

"And then what?" Felix asked. "Make them stop?"

"Sure. I'll appeal to their better nature. Or something."

"Or something."

I took a swallow of my mimosa, enjoying the mixed sensation of orange juice and champagne in my mouth. "Ask you a question?"

"Ask away."

"Why store him in the refrigerator? Why not the ocean? Or the proverbial shallow grave?"

Felix thought for a moment and said, "You dump a body, you can never get it back. Keep it in a safe place, you need it for something down the road, no matter how nutty or off the wall, you can get it."

"What in hell do you think we might need that body for?"

"You never know."

I took one last swallow of the mimosa. "So. If this goes south on us, what kind of troubles are we looking at?"

"The usual and customary. Concealing evidence. Obstruction of justice. Illegal transport of a dead body. Hell, maybe even suspicion of income tax evasion when it's all said and done."

I toasted him with an empty glass before putting it down on the tablecloth. "At least we have the best in legal representation."

Felix said, "You know, the night I saved Raymond Drake from a one-way trip out to Boston Harbor was the second-best investment I've ever made."

"And what was the first-best investment you've ever made?"

Felix picked up the check, a nice surprise. "Some secrets should stay secrets, my friend. Let's go. I've got a Honda to clean up."

We walked outside to the main parking lot, and Felix said, "What's up for the rest of the day?"

I had to smile. "It's been a full day already. I think I'm going to take it a bit easy, but first I'm going back to the Lafayette House for a moment."

"What for?"

"Just to follow up on a hunch, that's all."

He held out his hand, and I gave it a firm shake. "Thanks. And thanks for the joke. It paid off."

"Sure," Felix said. "So. As a reminder: What's the difference between a friend and a true friend?"

And like clockwork, I answered, "A friend will help you move. A true friend will help you move bodies."

Felix laughed, slapped me on the shoulder. "Good job. Let's see if we can't keep this joke to ourselves for a while. You take care."

"You, too."

I stood in the parking lot and watched Felix drive out in his borrowed vehicle. No police vehicles followed him in pursuit. No helicopters descended with SWAT teams at the ready to intercept. Felix drove off, unimpeded.

I turned and went back into the Lafayette House.

# EIGHT

INTO THE GIFT SHOP I went, and Stephanie was waiting on a couple that spoke English with a heavy German accent, and I wondered what would bring someone from Europe to my little corner of New Hampshire in the middle of winter. When they left I went up to Stephanie and she raised an eyebrow at my approach.

"Drop your newspapers in the ocean already?"

"Nope. Not yet. German tourists?"

"I wish. Belong to some German television network. Here for our quadrennial circus. If you think local news media are goddamn divas, try those from Europe. Who the hell ever heard of copies of *Der Spiegel* ending up in a gift shop like this? Jesus…So. What's up?"

"Wondering if I could ask you a question."

"Sure."

"Who's the manager nowadays?"

"Paul Jeter."

"What's he like?"

"Truthfully?"

"Yeah. Truthfully."

She smiled. "Truthfully, he's a prick."

"Please, Stephanie, don't sugarcoat it."

"Well, that's how it is. Don't know any way around it. Used to be, under the old management, how this shop was run was mostly my business. If I made a nice little profit each month and there were no complaints from the customers, then I was doing all right and I could be left alone. Now…don't get me going. Some days, I think that man counts the number of toilet sheets in each stall just to keep track for tracking's sake and nothing else."

"Think I could talk to him?"

"Sure," she said. "For a prick he's open to seeing people. But, Lewis...don't confuse being seen with being helped."

I thanked her and went to the main desk at the lobby, asked a perky female clerk if I could see Paul Jeter, and in a few minutes, I was ushered into his office, on the same floor and with a stunning view of the side parking lot and assorted Dumpsters. I guess hotel management wasn't all it was cracked up to be. Jeter was about my age, heavyset, wearing a dark gray suit, white shirt, and dark gray tie. He had the look in his eyes of the kind of guy who couldn't walk past a mirror without checking his appearance. I passed over my business card, identifying me as a columnist for *Shoreline,* and he passed the card back.

"What can I do for you, Mr. Cole?"

"I was hoping for a favor from a neighbor."

"A neighbor?"

"Yes, I live across the street. At the old lifeboat station."

His eyebrow lifted just a bit. "Ah, yes, the writer. The one we allow to use our parking lot as an entry to his house."

"That's right."

"And what kind of favor would you like? Free towels? Free hotel room? Gift certificate to the restaurant?"

So far, Stephanie had been dead on in her description. Not that I had doubted her. I was just being hopeful.

"Nothing like that. I've heard that the past month or so, there's been a series of break-ins among guest cars across the way."

He seemed to take that in for a moment, and said, "If one has a large number of cars, there will always be some incidents of vandalism or theft. That's just normal. Why do you ask? Do you know anything about who might be breaking in?"

"No, I don't."

"Well...no offense, what do you know then, Mr. Cole?"

"I've heard that the hotel might have set up a camera surveillance system in the parking lot. To see who might be doing the break-ins."

Jeter shifted just a bit in his seat, enough to make the leather creak. His already chilly mood cooled even more. "Perhaps. Perhaps not. And what's the favor?"

It was my turn to be a bit cool. "The favor is…somebody came to my house this morning. I'd like to know who it was."

"Did the person break in? Commit some other offense?"

"He didn't break in. But in a manner of speaking, yes, he did commit an offense." Well, that was certainly one way of putting it.

He folded his hands across his chest. "Then I suggest you contact the police. If they are interested in what kind of surveillance system the Lafayette House may or may not have, then I'll have my lawyer talk to them."

I leaned forward a bit. "You see, that's where the thought of doing a favor comes in. I don't want to involve the police."

"No police. I see. But you'd rather involve the hotel in whatever you're trying to prove involving your visitor this morning. Thereby opening up the Lafayette House to certain legal liabilities. And I don't see why we should do that."

"All I want to do is look at the surveillance tape from this morning. That's all."

There was the shortest shake of the head. "I'm sorry, Mr. Cole, I'm forced to decline. While, of course, neither confirming nor denying that such a surveillance system exists."

"I see. So much for being neighborly."

The cool factor seemed to be enhanced by another ten-degree drop in temperature.

"Neighborly is allowing you to continue using the Lafayette House parking lot as a gateway to your driveway. Not being neighborly would be putting up a concrete berm at that end of our lot. Catch the difference?"

It was time to leave, so I stood up and said, "Difference caught."

IN THE LOBBY of the Lafayette House, I was ambushed by a guy with a familiar face. Chuck Bittner of the Tucker Grayson for President campaign stood in front of me and said, "Mr. Cole. Please. Just five minutes. That's all I ask."

I wasn't in the mood but I was also tired of being stalked by him, and with the primary just a few days out, defusing him now might save me some aggravation later on.

If I was lucky, but Lady Luck seemed to have been taking a vacation lately.

"Five minutes," I said. "Three hundred seconds. Make them count."

We sat in a secluded corner of the lobby, in nice, comfortable chairs, and he leaned across a glass-topped coffee table and said, "You're a New Hampshire resident, so I won't insult you by asking if you know anything about General Grayson and his career. We've been publicizing his career very heavily these past few months."

"Career United States Army, former head of NATO, roving ambassador to the Mideast and Southeast Asia, or wherever else the current administration believes a firestorm can be snuffed out by his charming presence."

"Very good." He suddenly smiled, which I found disquieting for some reason. "There are those who hate your little state, hate the fact that it has such impact every four years. Every four years, the same arguments. Your state is too rural. Your state is too white. Your state is too rich. So forth and so on. But you know what? Your state takes its presidential primary role seriously. That's what I love. Retail politics, right on the ground. Candidates forced to think on their feet in living rooms and town halls, to answer questions from real voters. Quite refreshing. Suppose we gave the first-in-the-nation primary to Michigan or Ohio or California. What then?"

I said, "Might give us a break from all the attention and accompanying nonsense. Like dozens of phone calls every day, mailboxes filled with flyers. That sort of thing. Though I'd imagine the restaurant and hotel owners might complain."

"Maybe so," he said. "But a campaign that would start anywhere else but New Hampshire wouldn't be a true campaign, a true way of sorting out the best candidate possible by going to the people. It would be an airport tarmac and television studio campaign, that's what. And the only way the average voter would meet a candidate, or vice versa, would be through a television screen."

I said, "You're using up your precious three hundred seconds, Mr. Bittner."

He nodded. "I'm former U.S. Navy. Tend to get into briefing mode, and it takes me away from the point sometimes. So let me tell you this. You're an educated voter. You're a resident of this state. You have an important background."

"What kind of background?"

He looked about the lobby and lowered his voice. "Your time in the Pentagon. In the Department of Defense. In a little research group that you and your fellow people called the Marginal Issues Section. Researching and analyzing issues that fell through the cracks from the bigger boys in national intelligence."

I said not a word. The bastard had gotten places so very few had ever done. He seemed to note the look on my face and said, "You, more than many others, know what kind of president we need for this country, Mr. Cole. Someone who won't rely on paper treaties, won't rely on world organizations, won't rely on the supposed good nature of our adversaries. We need somebody with sharp elbows, who doesn't mind trusting as long as it's matched with verifying, and who's had experience making life-and-death decisions. In short, this country needs General Grayson."

I cleared my throat. "So far, it seems the majority of voters in Iowa and probably New Hampshire would disagree with that assessment."

"Perhaps, but that assessment can change. The right words from you, a former research analyst with the Department of Defense, who has, shall we say, an intimate familiarity with the senator and his campaign, could go a long way to taking the steam out of the Senator Hale campaign. And boost General Grayson's chances of making a respectable showing."

Out in the lobby there was a flare of light, and I looked over, saw a well-known television correspondent from one of the major networks doing a stand-up. He was wearing a suit coat, tie, and dirty blue jeans and wet boots. But who cared? The camera would only capture his serious tone and nature from the waist up.

I turned back to my inquisitor. "You seem to forget that a few days ago, I was the leading suspect in the attempted assassination of Senator Hale. Anything else I might say would probably be seen as the ravings of someone with a grudge against the senator."

A chilly smile. "So what? It means publicity, bad publicity for the senator, and a chance for you to contribute something to this country again."

Suddenly I stood up, my legs trembling, and I pulled up my coat and shirt to reveal a scar on the side of my abdomen. "I have five others like this on my body, and the chances of more appearing in the future, thanks to something that happened to me while in service of my country. I've already done my part. Don't ask me again. You and your general will have to do it on your own."

I stalked out, with Bittner calling after me, "We can still make a fuss, Cole, with or without you! It's your choice!"

I WENT OUT OF the Lafayette House, fists clenched, trying to forget Bittner and trying to focus on my original intent in revisiting the damn place.

I stopped for a moment, looked up at the elaborate design of the building, a Victorian appearance from the times of the grand hotels at the turn of the twentieth century. I examined the windows, turrets, and moldings, looking for some telltale sign of some sort of recording device, and then I gave up. Surveillance cameras were no longer the big, bulky units that looked like they came from a 1960s science fiction movie. They could now be the size of one's thumb—or even smaller—and there were so many different places to hide them, up there in that elaborate building design.

Of course, allowing for the fact that they even existed, a particular fact that the hotel's manager was in no rush to confirm.

My hands went back into my coat pockets. The wind was coming up from the ocean at a stiff clip, and I walked away from the lobby entrance, across the bare pavement of Atlantic Avenue, and made my way through the parking lot again. As a joke, I counted the number of bumper stickers on the cars at rest in the lot. There were two for Senator Jackson Hale, five for Senator Nash Pomeroy, and one for General Tucker Grayson.

There was none for Congressman Clive Wallace. Most of the

good congressman's voters and supporters didn't have the financial means to spend a night at the Lafayette House, which didn't mean much, since neither did I.

AT HOME I HESITATED outside my front door. There was a disturbance in the snow where Spenser Harris had rested, and where Felix and I had worked to get him bundled up and out of here. I went up to the stone foundation and the dark gray clapboards of my house. They were clean of any blood spatter, brain tissue, bone fragments, and clumps of hair. The mess had all been in the snow where he had lain, and Felix had taken care of that. A nice small gift. I stood up, breathed in hard. I guess I should have been thankful for small favors, but my thankfulness quotient was pretty damn low.

I went inside, glad to be inside and away from my front lawn.

THE DAY DRAGGED BY and as it got dark, I was thinking of dinner—which usually meant rummaging through the pantry and the freezer to see what was available—when the phone rang. I almost ignored the damn ringing, for it would probably mean a poll, yet another inquiring remark or the charming Chuck Bitther from the Tucker Grayson campaign.

I went to the phone and picked it up. Damn, it wasn't time yet to cower here.

"Hello."

"Good evening, sir," came a familiar female voice. "Was wondering if you had time for a brief survey."

"Sure," I said, sitting down on the couch. "Yes, yes, no, yes, and briefs."

Annie laughed. "Just what I was looking for. How are you doing?"

Hell of a question, considering what had gone on that morning, and I told her the truth. Or at least part of it.

"I'm doing fine. And you?"

"Great. Look…I was hoping I could combine my two passions tonight. Interested?"

I looked out the window, into the darkness. "Go on. You've definitely got my interest."

She took a breath. "Before I get into that I just want to say I…I felt bad, the way our last talk went. I…I just want to go on with you, my dear one, all right? Just go on, don't bitch and moan about the past or whatever you did or didn't do with the senator's wife back in college. So I want to focus my attention on two passions, you and this damn campaign, and I've come up with a way to balance both."

"Quite a job. Maybe I should call the campaign manager, give him a glowing review. If that'd help."

"Hah. Who knows. All right, here's the deal. Senator Hale is holding a private reception, up in Wallis, with some of his money people tonight. Free food, free booze. You and I get a chance to eat something nice, maybe chat and grope each other in a deserted corner…and you get to see the senator up close. Lewis…I'm working so hard to help him become the next president. It's important to me…and I want you to see why."

I cleared my throat. "The news media will make this a horrible circus, you know. The senator's alleged assassin, perhaps coming back for another round. Have you thought about that?"

She laughed. "Of course, silly. Which is why this reception is going to work. It's media free, and I've already cleared it with the higher-ups. Your name will be on the list. What do you say? Dinner, drinks, a talk with the next president of the United States, and if you're really, really lucky, I'll come back to your place for some constituent outreach. Just show me you care by staying away from his damn wife."

I looked out the window again, at the rise of land that went up to Atlantic Avenue and blocked the view of the Lafayette House. I couldn't see the hotel but I could see the glow of light that represented its presence, in all its high-priced glory. I wanted to be up there tonight, doing illegal things, but important things, to see if the damn place had what I needed to find out why and how Harris had ended up dead in my front yard.

I needed to be up there tonight. Had to.

The phone receiver was still in my hand.

But there were other needs as well.

"Sure, I'll be there," I said. "I'd love to."

# NINE

WHICH IS HOW TWO HOURS LATER, freshly showered and dressed in clothing that included one of my three neckties, I found myself driving up to one of the mansions that are scattered along the shores of Wallis, two towns north of Tyler Beach. While Tyler Beach is all cottages and condos and hotels and restaurants and nightclubs and T-shirt and souvenir stores, its sister town to the north—called in a burst of imagination some decades ago North Tyler—is like a junior partner, with a couple of state parks, some cottages, no hotels, and few stores and restaurants.

And to the north yet again, in some sort of example of declining sprawl and increased property values, was the town of Wallis. Along this particular stretch that I drove, the home values started in the low millions and worked their way up with each passing mile, and the homes were set back a way from the rocky shores, with long driveways flanked by stone and metal gates.

In other words, it's about a fifteen-minute drive from a booth that sells fried dough to Massachusetts tourists to a home whose owners had probably never touched a piece of fried dough in their lives. Sometimes quite a shock to the system to those who, for the first time, drive the coastal route along my fair state.

I turned into a driveway that was reached by going through an open gate supported by two stone columns, each with a brass numeral 7 set in the stone. On either side of the gates were Wallis police officers, providing crowd and traffic control, and a small knot of reporters and supporters from the Hale campaign and the other campaigns as well, waving signs and banners at one another. I was processed forward and about fifty feet up into the driveway, I ran into a more formal checkpoint. Smart work. That way, traffic wasn't backed up on Atlantic Avenue from the arriving guests, such as we were.

The checkpoint was manned by a uniformed Wallis cop—no doubt on paid detail—and a Hale campaign rep, a young man who checked my name on the clipboard. There were portable lights set up on a pole and a kerosene heater at their feet.

"Cole, Lewis Cole," he said, shivering a bit in the cold, holding a clipboard in one gloved hand, holding a small flashlight in the other. "Yep, you're on the list."

"Thanks."

"Hey—quick question, if you don't mind. You're not the Cole who was arrested a few days ago, are you?"

I decided the truth wasn't in my favor. "Nope. That was my evil twin."

"Oh." I guess the guy wanted to ask me more questions, but headlights were appearing behind me, so I kept on driving.

Up ahead, the driveway curved to the left and I parked among a host of other high-powered, high-priced SUVs to the side of an expansive two-story brick home with black shutters and a white-columned entrance. One vehicle was parked right near the door, a black Jaguar XJ8 with vanity plates: WHTKER. Based on the parking lot population, I guessed the topic tonight wouldn't be alternate energy sources or our never-ending reliance on Middle East oil. Outside it was bitterly cold. Inside, I was glad to be someplace where the cold didn't make my nostrils seize up, and I dumped my winter parka on a long counter in a foyer that was serving as a coat check.

Before me was a wooden table, manned by yet another collection of eager volunteers, and after making sure I was on the all-powerful list that either allowed me entrance with a smile or a curt dismissal with a sneer, they passed over a contribution folder with an attached envelope for the good senator. A nice picture of the senator and Barbara was on the outside of the folder. Inside were some stock paragraphs from his campaign speeches, and little boxes one checked off to make a donation. The smallest box was a hundred dollars, the largest—due to campaign financing restraints—was one thousand dollars. I shoved the envelope in my pocket and walked away.

I grabbed a Sam Adams beer from a young waitress with dark skin, and went into the main dining room. Unlike the last campaign rally, this one was smaller, more manageable, and I didn't feel sick to my stomach. A good combination. The hall was wood paneling and high ceilings and wooden chandeliers, and it looked like the place had been magically transferred from medieval England. Around me, talking and drinking and eating, were what passed for high political society in Wentworth County. Annie wasn't here yet. To say I felt out of place was like calling the sinking of the Titanic a minor setback for steamship travel.

I took a swallow of my beer and looked around the dining hall, went over to a bookshelf that had a collection of leather-bound volumes. Some history books, a few biographies, and a collection of seafaring tales from Edward Rowe Snow, a New England historian who had a flair for storytelling that made a lot of young men and women—including a writer from *Shoreline*—fall in love with this region.

"Admiring my first husband's collection?" came a voice.

I turned and there was a woman, dressed in a fine light blue wool dress with a string of pearls about her throat. Her dark brown hair was carefully coiffed, and her skin and face were those of a woman in her late fifties, perhaps midsixties, and even early seventies, depending on the light. But her eyes were that of a young woman who could not believe that her girlish spirit was still trapped in a body determined to grow old. I had the oddest feeling I had met her before.

"Yes, I was," I said. "A nice collection."

She held out her hand, which I briefly squeezed, and she said, "My name is Audrey. Welcome to my home."

"Thanks for having me," I said. "I'm Lewis."

"Are you part of the senator's campaign staff, or a local?"

"A local."

She cocked her head in a little display of amusement. "I'm afraid I haven't seen you at any party functions these past several years. Are you a newcomer to politics?"

"Hardly."

"And what, may I ask, is your political persuasion?"

I sipped from my Sam Adams. "I'm a drunkard."

She laughed and laughed at that one. "Oh, that's a good one. The great line from Rick Blaine, in *Casablanca.* Of course, he was asked about his nationality, not his politics…. Still, such a wonderful, wonderful movie, filled with classic lines. That was George's favorite movie…George being my first husband. You know, he always thought he had the rakish charm of Bogart, when he wasn't too busy making money…such charm."

She seemed lost for a moment, and smiled again. "Charm brought him a long way, especially in business. But charm is what killed him, because of his hobby."

"His hobby killed him?"

Audrey nodded. "Yes. George loved to fly. Owned a small plane that he kept at an airport up in Rochester. He charmed his way through flight school and pilot licensing and all that, but the night he was trying to get to Nantucket and his instrumentation failed…well, the sky and the ocean weren't impressed with his charm."

"I'm sorry," I said.

She shrugged. "It happened a long time ago…and now I'm married again. To Henry, over there in the corner."

I looked to where she was pointing, at a great stone fireplace that was roaring right along. A man about ten years Audrey's junior with a red face and too fine blond hair and wearing one of those funky navy blue jackets with a crest over the breast pocket was holding court with a couple of young, attractive women dressed in cocktail dresses that looked more suitable for June than January. Even with the low roar of conversation in the room, I made out the sigh of disappointment from my newfound conversationalist.

"Henry doesn't have as much charm, but he is a fair companion…though you can probably guess about his particular hobby. But I'm of an age and condition that I don't particularly care. But what I do care about is giving back."

I nodded and she said, "And I've been entirely too rude, prattling on and on about my personal life. And you, Mr. Lewis. Where are you from?"

"Tyler Beach."

"And what do you do?"

"I'm a columnist for a magazine. *Shoreline*."

The smile on her face froze just a tad. "The understanding, of course, is that tonight's event is entirely off the record, and not open to members of the press. I'm not sure how you gained entrance."

"I'm sure it is off the record, and I guarantee you, I don't consider myself a member of the press. I write about the seacoast of New England and its history. I don't write about contemporary politics. And I gained entrance through the good graces of a woman friend who works on Senator Hale's campaign."

The frozen smile defrosted back to its original state. "That's fine…. I once considered becoming a reporter, back when I was in college, in the Stone Age, when writers worked on manual typewriters and television crews used real film in their cameras…but I decided life was too short and too grand to be just an observer. I wanted to participate, to be in the arena, not in the audience."

"I see."

"Mmm…perhaps not. I believe I think you see an old, rich, idle woman, throwing a party for her equally rich friends, all for the privilege of seeing another lying politician up close." She leaned into me, her voice crisp. "But that's not the case. I can't sing, dance, or run for office. But what I am do is write checks, and convince my friends to write checks, to men and women and causes that I believe in. And tonight, I believe in Senator Hale. And I hope you do as well."

"We'll see," I said, feeling light now as Annie approached me through the crowd, smiling, wearing a tan turtleneck sweater and a long black skirt.

Audrey saw where I was looking, and she touched my wrist. "So glad to meet you, Lewis. Enjoy yourself…and someday, why don't you come play with us? It can be so much more fun than kibitzing from the sideline."

She moved into the crowd and Annie came up to me, we kissed, and she squeezed my hand and said, "I get here a few minutes late, and already I see you're trying to bed one of the wealthiest women in your state."

"I was?"

"Certainly. The former Mrs. George Whittaker, whose late husband was a developer who cheerfully raped the southern portion of the state and built lots and lots of malls and strip housing developments, and who ended up in the bottom of the Gulf of Maine some years ago. His wife has his fortune and not his politics, and she's been a heavy hitter and king-maker—or queen-maker—during the last three New Hampshire primaries. Having her in Senator Hale's corner has been a real break for him."

I now knew who owned the impressive Jaguar parked outside. I saw Audrey Whittaker pause and talk to some people, and then it clicked. I had seen her before, at the campaign rally where the shots had been fired. At the Tyler Conference Center, she had been holding court as well, but even though I now knew where I had noticed her before, something odd was niggling at me.

Annie squeezed my hand. "I'm starved. Let's get something to eat."

"And the senator?"

"Another thirty or so minutes out. We've got plenty of time."

Still holding my hand, she led me through the crowded dining room and through a set of swinging doors that led into a kitchen, which looked like it belonged in a small restaurant. A catering crew was working there, and lots of pans and pots were being banged around, and steam was rising up from a couple of cooking stations. Annie let me be and came back a few minutes later, carrying two Sam Adams by their long necks, and two full plates, which she managed to balance on her wrists. I grabbed a plate and a beer and kissed her on her nose for her effort.

"Nice balancing act, Counselor," I said.

"Old waitressing trick. You never quite forget them, no matter how old you get. Let's find a quiet place."

Which we did. From another door we went into a small hallway leading to a breezeway that looked like it headed out to a garage or some other outbuilding. The breezeway had tall windows with recessed padded window seats, and we shared one while balancing the plates on our laps. Annie, knowing me so well, had filled my plate with scallops wrapped in bacon, slices of prime rib, rice pilaf, and a chunk of salad for roughage. I raised my bottle in salute.

"Thanks for dinner."

"Don't thank me, thank your new friend, Mrs. Whittaker."

"If I can, I will." I looked around the paneled walls and fine wooden floor and said, "How do you know your way in and around this place so well?"

Annie was being good in her food choices tonight, with lots of salad, lots of rice, and a couple of small pieces of haddock and a fine collection of steamed vegetables. Murmuring through her first bite, she said, "Been here a few other times for fund-raisers. Get to know the lay of the land after a while. Mrs. Whittaker is a real sweetheart in lending out her home to the campaign."

I ate some and said, "Ask you a campaign-related question?"

She delicately dabbed at her lips with a napkin. "As opposed to asking a bosom-related question?"

"That can come later. I was just wondering…how many fund-raisers can one person like her support? I mean, I thought the federal limit on making campaign contributions is one thousand dollars per person. There must be a limit on one's pool of friends."

Annie smiled at me and raised up her bottle in a mock salute. "One of these days, you really need to show me that cabbage patch you were raised in, my dear."

"What do you mean?"

"Yes, campaigns are limited to what they can receive. But not, quote, independent political action groups, unquote, which can get as much money as they want to pump up any message they want. Especially if said message by some wonderful coincidence manages to complement a certain campaign's message. Tonight's soiree is being held by something called the American Fund for America's Future. Or some such nonsense. But what it does is raise oodles and oodles of cash to help Senator Hale, without being constricted by the Federal Election Commission. Because it's a so-called independent committee, it can attack the other candidates and make them look bad without being an official part of the Hale campaign. Is this a great country, or what?"

"I don't know if I ever had political virginity," I replied, "but if I ever did, I think you just took it."

She gave me a wicked smile. "Keep on hanging around with me, and we'll see whatever forms of virginity are up for the taking."

WE FINISHED OUR MEALS and dropped off our dishes with the busy catering staff in the kitchen, and went out to the main dining hall, which was now even more crowded. There was a hum in the atmosphere, something anticipatory and electric, and I looked at all the young and old eager faces, all sizes and shapes, male and female, all of them looking forward to that one moment in time, the one in which they shared a room with the next president of the United States.

At the far wall was a doorway and a crowd of campaign officials, and I recognized one of them: the red-bearded gatekeeper who had tried to keep me out of the last disastrous campaign rally. Not wanting to encounter him yet again, I moved to another side of the room, just as Annie got swept up by a couple of her friends from the local campaign office and managed to wave at me as she was dragged away. I found myself standing by the bookcase as the door at the far wall opened and the cheers and applause began.

Senator Hale came into the room, accompanied by his lovely bride, and I took a breath, for seeing Barbara again rekindled those old thoughts and memories, and though I did my best to ignore them, they were still there. I was angry at myself for thinking of the times we spent in her apartment or my dorm room, the young and eager lovemaking and long, wonderful conversations that never seemed to go anywhere but always seemed so important, and both the conversations and the lovemaking had an energy to them that I had forgotten even existed.

And even though I knew that the passage of time was a great editor, that my memories had been enhanced and cleaned up like some old photograph, the memories were still there, and I was surprised at how powerful they still were.

I looked for Annie again. I couldn't find her. That made me feel guilty for a moment, and then there was more movement and it was time for the politicking to begin.

I folded my arms and listened to Senator Hale go into his

stump speech, as Barbara stood by his side. As he spoke, his face animated, his eyes lively, the gaze he gave out as if each and every single person in the room were his friend, I realized that he had it, the almighty "it" that separated mere mortals and mere politicians from those who would be president. There was energy and confidence and strength in his voice and his presence, and though the words on paper would most likely be the same clichés that other politicians, future and past, have used ("strength at home and abroad," "a compact with our old and young," "a nation with more than just friends, but true partners"), his gift brought them a certain power. The words seemed to roll over me with their strength, and I thought about the contribution envelope in my pocket and how now it seemed quite right to make a campaign donation.

I shook my head, no longer thinking about a possible contribution. I kept my focus on the senator from Georgia, seeing the light in his eyes. It must be a strange and horrible thing to have such a gift, for once your goal of being president is in sight and almost in hand, would anything else ever be as worthwhile, ever again?

The applause startled me. His speech was over, Barbara still at his side, and right then and there, in the close confines of this magnificent home in Wallis, I knew two things: I was looking at the next president of the United States, and I was being used by someone to prevent that event from happening.

# TEN

THE CROWD JOSTLED and people moved around, and in the movement of people about me, I started looking for Annie. Somebody bumped me hard, propelling me between two older women, and before I had a chance to apologize, Senator Jackson Hale was there, right before me. He smiled and I found myself smiling back, and I shook his hand as he said, "Thanks for coming tonight, appreciate it."

I said not a word as he moved past me, and then, I found myself facing his wife. She had a bemused smile on her face as she shook my hand as well.

"So nice to see you," Barbara said.

"Me, too," I said, as I felt a slip of paper pressed into my hand.

She joined her husband and maybe the smart or rational thing would have been to drop the piece of paper on the floor.

Instead, I slipped it into a pocket, and went to find Annie.

I FOUND HER IN A CORNER, talking to a couple of energetic young men, and they looked closely at me as I approached, as if I were her father, ready to collect her after the junior high school dance. It was good to see her work, good to see her fulfilling her passion, her dream, and that little surge of affection seemed to drive away the thought of Barbara and the mysterious slip of paper. As I got closer to her and her friends, she said, "…and that's why importing a lot of out-of-state talent to knock on doors, day after day, doesn't work. Just pisses off the voters. The locals don't want to be told how to vote by a lot of eager out-of-staters who think they're smarter than everybody else."

As I came up to her she squeezed my hand and turned and said, "Get me out of here, will you?"

"Sure," I said.

As we walked away, I said, "Must be nice to be so popular."

"Yeah, right," she said, "I've been with the Hale campaign for six months, and that makes me an old vet."

I thought of something and said, "Saw a familiar face tonight. Guy with a red beard. He was running media interference at the conference center rally. Who is he?"

"Hah," she said. "You've got a good eye for imported assholes. That's Harmon Jewett, campaign flak for the senator. From Georgia, a true believer but with a temper that can curl paint off the side of a house from fifty yards. He was with Hale when Hale was just a state senator, and helped manage his congressional campaign. Said ten years ago, if you can believe it, that Jackson Hale would be the next president and he'd kill his own grandmother to make it so. And that little story has made more than one reporter look into the circumstances of that poor woman's death."

"So why is he up here in New Hampshire?"

Annie grimaced for a moment. "One of the senator's least best traits is loyalty, combined with forgiveness. He's never forgotten that Harmon got him started in politics and managed to usher him through some very tough campaigns. So the senator keeps him on, even in a job as simple as a media gatekeeper. But that temper…once it lets go it could really hurt the senator. Any other guy would have cut Harmon loose years ago. But not our Jackson."

We gathered our coats from the official coat drop-off place and stepped outside, Annie also carrying a bulky over-the-shoulder leather bag. I think we both shivered at about the same time as we went down the stone steps. It was damn cold, but the stars sure looked fine. I stopped to admire my favorite constellation, Orion, rising up in all his glory in the east, the mighty hunter, his club-holding arm still there, at the ready, thousands and thousands of years later.

Annie nudged me in the side. "Come along, star boy. I want to get to your place before some of my favorite—and your favorite—extremities start freezing."

I looked around the rapidly emptying lot. "Where's your car?"

"In Manchester, silly. I got a ride from some of the staff. You don't mind bringing me back to Manchester tomorrow, do you? Please, pretty please? I'll be your best friend...."

And then I knew that bag she was carrying contained a change of clothes and other essential items. Sometimes even when I was being observant, I could be as blind as a chaplain at a cathouse.

My Annie, always thinking.

I tried to keep thoughts of the Lafayette House and the mysterious piece of paper, weighing down my coat like a chunk of lead, out of the way. I leaned over, kissed her. "I'd take you to Manchester, England, if that's what you'd like."

"What I'd like," she said, her voice just a touch curt, "is to go someplace warm."

And someplace warm is where we ended up.

AT HOME I BUILT A FIRE and went to my liquor cabinet—all right, the space next to the handful of spices and condiments that I have managed to collect over the years—and pulled down a bottle of Australian sherry. I poured some in tiny sherry glasses and set them on the counter. Annie was on her cell phone, talking campaign talk yet again, and when she moved to the sliding glass doors that led out to the deck, I went back to the fire and looked at what Barbara had handed me.

It was a slip of notebook paper, from the Center of New Hampshire hotel and conference center in Manchester, with a short note: *Room 410, between 8 a.m. and 9 a.m. B.*

I reread it and tossed it into the flames, where it curled up and disappeared. Annie's voice rose a bit and then she said, "Fine!" and snapped her cell phone shut. "Asshole," she murmured, and she came into the living room and said, "You might not like this."

"All right, try me," I said.

"There's an all-hands meeting tomorrow at seven a.m. Which means—"

Ugh. "It means getting up early. That's all right."

She raised the glass of sherry. "Take our drinks and go to bed?"

"Absolutely."

WE CLIMBED INTO BED after tumbling out of our clothes, and as I held my sherry glass, Annie leaned against my shoulder. I said, "Your feet are cold."

"Tell me something new."

"I mean really, really cold. Were you eating ice cream with your toes before going to bed?"

In response, she moved her feet briskly up and down my shins, causing me to shiver. "There," she said, "take that, you insensitive man."

"My legs are now insensitive," I said. "Not sure about anything else. Hold on while I try to warm up."

I took a stiff swallow of the sweet sherry and Annie said, "I ever tell you the two types of campaign people?"

"No, but I think you're about to."

"Meanie," she said.

Annie knocked her sherry back with one swallow and said, "Two types. Type one is the true believer. He or she really believes in his or her candidate, will follow the candidate around the country, will work for free pizza and a place to crash on the floor at two a.m. These are the ones who man the phones, stuff envelopes, and go door-to-door handing out campaign brochures, and will stand outside in a polling place on primary day, holding a sign, in the pouring rain, sleet, or snow. They can be a bit nutty but you can't run a campaign without them. They get teased, they get overlooked, but you can't kill them. They're like those blow-up clowns that you can punch in the head. They always bounce back."

"I think I know who the second group are."

She nuzzled my ear. "Then you've been paying attention these past months, Grasshopper. But let me remind you. The second type are the professionals. The poll takers, the money men and women, the consultants. They parachute in and try to stitch things together so that the true believers don't run things into the ground. Sometimes they believe in the candidate and sometimes they hate him or her. A lot of it depends on who's paying the most…and in a campaign, a lot of times, a lot of energy that should be spent on the actual campaign is spent on gossip, revenge, and bitching over who has the biggest office. You would not believe some of the war stories I've heard since I've been with the campaign."

"And what does this have to do with the meeting at seven?"

"Oh, one of the pros wants to rein in us amateurs. Stop playing around and focus on winning the damn primary, and don't be so pie-in-the-sky, trying to be everything to all voters. We have a candidate who is hungry for this win, despite his wife, so knock off the amateur hour. Blah, blah, blah."

I carefully put my now empty sherry glass on the nightstand. "What do you mean, despite his wife? I thought she wanted to be come first lady in the worst way. And that she didn't make any secret of it."

Annie laughed and rolled over. "Lewis, I don't know what she was like in college, but Mrs. Senator Hale is one prime bitch diva, and coming from one who admires prime bitch divas, that says a lot. She hates campaigns, hates campaigning, and most days, she's a goddamn drag on the campaign."

"I see."

She finished her own sherry and said, "So…do tell me. What was she like in college?"

"Barbara?"

"No, silly, the mysterious woman who lives in your basement, that's who."

"Oh," I said. "Very fair question. We worked on the student newspaper, which is where we met. Typical student paper for the time. Lots of long hours into the night, writing and composing and pasting up. Sometimes you'd skip classes to be able to work on the newspaper. I'm sure I lost a point or two on my grade point average due to all the time I spent there."

"What was the name of the newspaper?"

*The Indiana Daily Student.*

She laughed. "Such an original name. What else can you tell me about her?"

"Typical college student, I guess. Full of energy and the feeling that once you get out, you can do anything…Long story short, we dated for a while, and then summer came and we went off to our respective internships. I did one at *The Indianapolis Star.* She wanted to dabble some in politics, so she went to D.C.

to work for a congressman. I came back to Bloomington and she stayed in D.C. End of story."

Well, sort of, I thought, thinking about the note I had received earlier.

"She break your heart?"

"At the time, yeah."

"Bitch," Annie said, and we both laughed and Annie then sighed and said, "Dear one, do cuddle me and keep me warm, will you? I'm about ready to fall asleep, and it'll be so much better if you're holding me at the time."

I turned the light off and rolled over, holding Annie in the dark. We nuzzled and kissed for a while, her warm body—now even including her feet—in my grasp, and I held her for a time in the darkness, hearing her breathing deepen and slow, as she fell asleep.

It took me a long while to join her.

TO GET FROM TYLER BEACH to Manchester is pretty much a straight shot, from Route 101 all the way west to the interior of our fair state. It's a trip of just under an hour, and we both skipped breakfast before we left, though Annie did find time for a quick shower. Her fine red hair was still wet as we joined the other travelers on the two-lane highway, the rising sun shadowing us as we raced west. I listened to a bit of the morning news as I drove, hearing about a snowstorm heading our way this evening, and then I got a look from my companion, and switched the radio off, as she dug her cell phone from her purse.

For most of the time we drove, Annie was on the cell phone, checking with her staff, coordinating the logistics of a luncheon meeting later that day, and basically juggling about a half dozen questions, concerns, and complaints. It sounds odd but while any other man may have felt ignored or slighted at the lack of attention, I felt a sense of pride. She was damn good at what she was doing. The highway raced through mostly open rural areas that were only developed with homes and service stations at the different exits, and though the speed limit was sixty-five and I kept my Ford Explorer at seventy, I was passed on several occasions.

It was something to see her work, but what pleased me most was that during one break in the call, she reached over and gave my thigh a quick squeeze. "Thanks for the drive in, and a promise for better things later," she said.

I returned the favor, squeezing something else, and she laughed and returned to her cell phone as the buildings of Manchester came into view. The state's largest city, it's a mix of poor neighborhoods and office buildings in the center of town. New immigrants from Latin America and Asia jostle for jobs in places where the accents were once Irish or French-Canadian. The headquarters for Senator Hale were on Elm Street, the main drag for Manchester, and I pulled in next to a fire hydrant. Highly illegal, but I planned to be there only for a few moments.

Annie dumped her cell phone in her purse and reached behind her for her overnight bag. I kissed her a few times and she said, "Thanks, dear one. I'll see you later."

"Bad weather coming tonight," I said. "Are you coming back to Tyler, or are you going to stay here?"

"Stay here, I'm afraid," she said. "But look at it this way. Less than a week to the primary, and then you get me all to yourself."

"Lucky me."

She made a wrinkling gesture with her nose. "I'd like to think I'm lucky as well. Take care."

"You, too."

She walked into the storefront, each and every window obscured by HALE FOR PRESIDENT signs, and already she must have been in campaign mode, for Annie didn't turn and wave at me as she went inside.

But that was okay. I drove away and in a matter of minutes, I was in a parking garage that was adjacent to and serviced the Center of New Hampshire.

I WAS EARLY SO I BOUGHT a *New York Times* and *The Wall Street Journal* and settled down in a lounge area next to the check-in counter, and I surprised myself by letting the papers go unread. There was a floor show going on near me, and despite myself, it was fun to watch. Guests and assorted hangers-on were moving about the lobby, talking and arguing and speaking into their cell phones. Camera crews were stationed by the doors, gear piled at their feet, like soldiers on a long campaign. The reporters from different organizations came to and fro, and I recognized a few network and cable television correspondents. They always had the best skin. The reporters made it seem a point of pride to wear their IDs and credentials around their necks, as if they were some well-bred species of animal that had been awarded a number of blue ribbons.

It was amusing to see the looks on the faces, to hear the snatched bits of conversation, and in some way, it was like a high school reunion, as old relationships were started up again. And more than a few times, I heard, "See you in South Carolina!" knowing that was the next big primary after New Hampshire's.

And before I knew it, it was time.

I gathered up my newspapers and walked to the bank of elevators.

AT 8:01 A.M. I knocked on the door to room 410, and it opened quickly, as if she had been waiting for me. Before me was the wife of the senior senator from Georgia, barefoot, wearing blue jeans and an Indiana University sweatshirt.

I went in and she kissed me on the cheek and said, "Old reliable Lewis. I know you'd be here if you could, right on the dot."

"Thanks, I think," I said, and followed her in, and I was surprised at how small the room was. It was a typical hotel room with two double beds and a television and bathroom and small table with a chair, but for someone like Barbara, the possible future first lady, it seemed all wrong. She sat on the bed and curled up in a familiar pose that made something inside me ache with memory, and I took the chair across from her.

I said, "Another way to keep your sanity, above and beyond sneaking out to bookstores when no one's looking?"

"You know it, Lewis." She rubbed her face and said, "When you are where I am, you're constantly on. You're surrounded by staff, by consultants, by campaign workers. They all demand and expect the perfect candidate's wife, the perfectly scripted fembot, the perfect arm candy for the next president. I have a room here

paid for by the campaign that's the size of my first damn apartment. This one's been rented in the name of my mom. It's nice
to slip away and wear old clothes and watch television programs
that aren't news shows, and know that the phone won't ring."

"Sure is." I looked at her and she looked at me, and I recalled
what I had done less than an hour ago, dropping off Annie at her
place of work, and I tried to keep my voice even and gentle.
"Barbara, what's up?"

It was amazing, seeing the look on her face change from that
of an old college friend to that of a candidate's wife, morph from
relaxation to cool hostility. For a moment I felt a flash of
sympathy for this woman who could never be quite comfortable
with new acquaintances, could never know if someone wanted
to be her friend because of who she was, or because of her
position and power.

"I'm not sure what you mean," she said.

"Barbara…this has been wonderful, catching up with you
and our times back in college, but in less than a week, the primary
will be over and you and your husband and the campaign will
be heading to South Carolina. I'll still be here, in Tyler Beach.
In the meantime, you and I are playing 'remember when,' and
the only thing I can do is damage the campaign. Some smart
reporter, still wanting to know how and why I might have been
involved in the shooting, might decide to tail me for a bit. And
can you imagine the headlines if a story comes out that you and
I have been seen together?"

"Sounds cool and logical."

"It sounds right, Barbara, and you know it. So. What can I do
for you?"

"I need your help," she said.

"How?"

She folded her arms tight against her chest. "I…I need you.
I need you…because I think someone's trying to kill me."

And then she started weeping.

I WAS ON THE BED with her, holding her, the scent and touch
bringing back memories of college years so hard it made me feel
light-headed for a moment, and there was that sour tinge of

regret, of what might have been, how our lives would have been diffcrent if she had come back from D.C., if I had been more aggressive in tracking her down, in finding out why she had gone east and had never come back.

Old regrets, still feeling fresh.

She turned to me and said, "All right, all right, maybe I'm being a bit hysterical…but, Lewis, I don't know who to talk to, who I can trust."

"What's going on?"

"There's been two attempts. The first was a month ago, outside Atlanta. I was driving our Lexus and I got in a car accident. Flipped right off the road and into a drainage ditch. Almost broke my damn nose when the airbag popped open. It was at night, a light rain…but no reason why it should have happened. The Georgia Bureau of Investigation kept Jackson and me informed through their investigation…managed to keep most of it out of the newspapers. Seems like my Lexus was sabotaged. Brake lines were cut, the tires were underinflated, making it easier to roll over."

"Who did it?"

She smiled, though her eyes were full of tears. "Who the hell knows? The Georgia Bureau of Investigation are still investigating and Jackson…he just nodded at the right places and told me that the professionals should handle it, and by then, the Secret Service were with us, and there was a campaign to run."

"The car accident was the first attempt. What was the second?"

"You should know," she said. "You were there."

"The campaign rally?"

Barbara nodded. "Nothing I can prove, Lewis. But I managed to see a preliminary report from the Secret Service on the shooting. From where the bullets impacted the wall behind the stage, it was apparent that I was the target. Not my husband. Me."

"Why?"

She rubbed her arms, as if the room had suddenly gotten cold. "Despite all the polls and predictions, the Hale for President campaign is a hollow shell. We're running on credit and optimism. We need to nail down the New Hampshire primary for another round of funds and campaign people to come streaming in. You see, there comes a point in any campaign when the well goes dry. And it remains dry unless the landscape changes. A scandal in another campaign. Some string of good news. Other things."

Now I felt cool as well. "Other things…like the shooting or killing of a candidate's wife just before the primary."

A sharp nod. "You have no idea…politics is a dirty business. Not as dirty here as in other places…but when certain people and certain groups have an idea and confidence that they are going to be part of the new crew come next inauguration, then they can get a bit crazed. They get so close to those centers of power and influence that they do things they wouldn't otherwise do."

"So if a candidate's wife is wounded or killed…"

"My God, an orgy of publicity…can you imagine it? The sympathy vote would roar right in, the funding would increase, they'd have to drive away the excess volunteers with a fire hose…and those people backing Jack would be very, very happy."

Having her in my arms now seemed to be quite wrong, but I couldn't move, couldn't disturb the moment. "All right…having said all of that, Barbara, what can I do to help?"

She sighed. "I'm not proud of what I did, Lewis, but after seeing you at the bookstore, I wanted to know more…wanted to know more about what you did after college. So I had you checked out."

"Lucky me."

"Your time at the Pentagon is still in deep black, but not what you've done with yourself afterward. You write a snappy column for *Shoreline* but you've been involved in some criminal matters over the years, poking around, asking questions, working as an investigator without a license. And that's what I need."

I squeezed her gently with my arms and got off the bed and back into the hotel room's chair. "What you need is beyond what I can offer, Barbara. You have the Secret Service, the Georgia Bureau of Investigation, the New Hampshire State Police, probably even the FBI at your fingertips. You don't need me."

"Right. And in any one of those agencies, there might be

people supporting one of the other candidates, who'd take great pleasure in leaking a story about a crazed wife, who's gotten paranoid and thinks someone's trying to kill her."

"And what can I do?"

"What you've done in the past. Poke around. Ask questions. See what you can find out from the locals, from the cops to the party organizations. I know I'm grasping at straws, Lewis, but…"

I looked into those familiar blue eyes, listened to the soft cadence of her voice, and I knew I couldn't do a damn thing. The election was just a few days away and my contacts were limited, no matter what Barbara thought about my talents. There was no way I could find out who was trying to hurt her—if, in fact, somebody was trying to hurt her—before the primary election. Not a chance in hell.

So I should gracefully decline, and get out of this room, and let her go on with her life with her maybe soon-to-be-president husband, and in less than a week, she and her husband would be gone from my state and my life.

Just a few days.

I looked at her again. It looked like she hadn't gotten a good night's sleep in days. If I told her no, I knew what would happen. More stress, less sleep…And maybe this whole thing was why Annie and the others thought she was a diva. No wonder they had the impression that Barbara hated the campaign, if someone was actually trying to hurt or kill her.

And if I said yes…perhaps a chance at some peace and relaxation over the next few days. Then she would leave, go to South Carolina and beyond, and in the crush of campaigning that would follow, other issues would rise up, other demands on her time, and I think she would eventually move on. And maybe I would get an inaugural invite sometime next year.

Maybe.

"Okay," I said. "I'll do it."

She held her hands up to her face and then lowered them. She swung over a bit to the nearest nightstand, scribbled something on a piece of paper. "My private cell phone number. Call me if you have anything, all right?"

"Sure."

She came over to me and I took the number from her hand, and I looked at her and she looked at me, and it was like the flow of water, reaching its natural state. She just sat in my lap. The smell and the sense of her being there…I put my arm around her still-slim waist and pulled her close. A bit of her hair tickled me. I kissed her and she kissed me back, and before it got any further, I said I had to leave.

Which wasn't much of a lie, but it worked.

I got out of the hotel room and a few minutes later, left to go home.

BY THE TIME I GOT BACK to Tyler Beach, an hour later, clouds had rolled in, thick and gray and threatening. I listened a bit to the radio as I drove back east; we were going to have a nice dump of six to eight inches of snow overnight. Of course, given the time of year, most of the weather report was centered around campaign speculation, over who it might help and who it might hurt. As I went up Atlantic Avenue, heading to my home, I had a thought of what the snow might achieve, in terms of cover, and I was thinking so hard that I missed the turnoff to the Lafayette House parking lot.

And as I made an illegal U-turn to come back, I had another thought. I went into the short-term parking area and after parking my Explorer went inside to the gift shop, where Stephanie Sussex was at work, handling a small crowd of people. Before me was a group of Japanese visitors, talking slowly and with great precision to Stephanie, and I waited in an area of the small store that had Tyler Beach T-shirts and sweatshirts for sale, as Stephanie carefully packed up the group's purchases.

When they left I walked over and Stephanie placed my morning ration of newspapers on the glass-topped counter. "You're late," she said.

"Yes," I said. "And good morning to you, too."

That brought a laugh and as she rung up my purchases, she said, "There's a lesson there in the passage of time, if you saw it, Lewis."

"What's that?"

"That little overseas group. From a Japanese television

network. NTK or something like that. The woman reporter, the one who does the on-air work, she was talking about a visit she had up to Porter. We tend to forget that's a very important place for the Japanese."

"Some forget, others don't. The Russian-Japanese peace treaty. Where Teddy Roosevelt got the Nobel Peace Prize for manhandling Japan and Russia into a peace agreement, about a hundred or so years ago."

I paid her and she passed over the change. "Good for you, Lewis."

That bit of history got the two of us talking, and she mentioned that her father was a naval aviator in World War II. Barely made it through the war alive. And I told her that my dad flew Wildcats off the *Enterprise* at about the same time. That's when we both realized our dads may have shot at each other once or twice. We both laughed, but you know what? A funny world, isn't it, how sworn mortal enemies, more than a half century later, can have their children share a moment without trying to slit each other's throats.

The newspapers were now under my arm and I said, "History sure is a funny thing. Ask you a question?"

"Sure, go ahead."

I made a quick scan of the store, noted that we were alone, and said, "The parking lot break-ins, last month and before."

She looked cautious. "Yes?"

"They've mostly stopped now, haven't they."

"So I've heard."

"Is it because of the surveillance system, keeping an eye on the outer parking lot?"

Stephanie took a bottle of glass cleaner and sprayed some of the blue stuff on the counter. "Well, I've got to give you that. That was a question. I guess your visit with our local insufferable prick didn't pan out. So is it now dumped in my lap?"

"What's the problem?"

She tore off a sheet of paper towel, started wiping down the glass. "The problem is, it's how the Lafayette House has changed the past year. We used to be an overpriced white elephant, charming and fun with waterpipes that banged in the middle of the night. Sort of a genteel snobby place, pretending to be one of those old New England upper-class resorts. Hung on by our teeth, year after year, until a sharp little hotel investment group from Switzerland took over and brought in Paul Jeter to run things. Which meant a new regime. A new approach. And new rules."

"What kind of new rules?"

The paper towel was now wadded up in her fist. "Rules that change the nature of this place. No longer are we the shabby, overpriced place where your parents and grandparents once stayed. Now we are trying to appeal to the very upper reaches of wealth, to offer them an experience that they can't get anywhere else. And part of that experience is anonymity and privacy. So if a guard for the Boston Celtics allegedly has a permanently rented room here, where he keeps his two mistresses—"

"Two?"

"Allegedly, he has big appetites…and as I was saying, if this supposed basketball player knows he can stash his two mistresses here, away from the eyes of the Boston news media, he'll pay dearly for that privilege. And the word will get out to other folks in similar circumstances, who wish to keep their hobbies and tastes secret. So the Lafayette House develops a nice little reputation for quiet and discreet service. Publicizing the supposed fact that the parking lot is under surveillance doesn't help that reputation, now does it?"

"No, it doesn't. Where…where might this alleged surveillance system be set up?"

Stephanie threw the wadded paper towel away. "That's why you wanted to see Paul Jeter yesterday, right?"

"Right."

"Something happen over your place that morning, you looking to find out what's what?"

"You could say."

Her face was firm. "Lewis…I'm sorry." There was noise at the entrance of the gift shop and a couple of kids tumbled in, wearing swimsuits, carrying towels, and expressing joy at the pleasure of being able to swim in a heated pool in January.

"I see."

She shook her head. "No, you don't. I need this job. It's relatively easy, pays reasonably well, and I get nice benefits. Nice benefits to help support a sick husband and help me do things for my church. That means a lot to me and…I'm sorry, I can't help you."

I managed a smile. "No problem, Stephanie. No problem at all."

And so I left, newspapers under my arm, leaving her behind with her job and her history.

# ELEVEN

AT HOME I WAS in my upstairs office, looking out the window, watching the snow start to tumble its way down. Up above the rise of land stood the Lafayette House, and somewhere in there was the surveillance tape of the nearby parking lot. I had an idea of where it might be, and I also had a couple of ideas of how I was going to get it.

But there were other things to do, as well.

From the Internet, I was able to call up a story from *The Atlanta Journal-Constitution* and found out that yes, the good senator's wife had been in a car accident the previous month, while driving to a political function outside Atlanta. The story rated about four paragraphs and mentioned minor injuries on the behalf of Barbara Hale, and the usual and customary, "the accident remains under investigation."

All right, I thought. Step one complete. Time for step two.

In the bad old days, before information got digitized, to find out about the Georgia Bureau of Investigation would have meant a call to directory assistance, a phone call to a central number, and maybe a half dozen more follow-up phone calls, as you navigated the bureaucracy and killed most of an afternoon. Yet now, it was all there, at your fingertips; it took only a few minutes before I got a public information officer's name and phone number from a quick Internet search.

Of course, this bit of information revolution didn't necessarily mean you got your information faster. Sometimes it just meant you hit the roadblocks that much sooner.

The public information officer's name was Samantha Tuckwell, she sounded like a charming lady from the Deep South, and while she would give me the time of day in Atlanta,

Greenwich, and no doubt Murmansk, that's about as far as it went.

"So, tell me again what you're lookin' for, Mr. Cole?" came the sweet voice from some office park in Atlanta.

"As I said, I'm a writer for a magazine based in Boston. Called *Shoreline*. I'm looking for some additional information about a traffic accident involving Senator Hale's wife, Barbara. It happened about a month ago."

"And this story…all about a traffic accident?" Although there was a fair sprinkling of Southern charm and hospitality in that silky voice from hundreds of miles away, there was also about a ton of skepticism.

"Not just the accident. A profile piece about the senator and his wife…and the accident's just part of the piece. A bit of human interest, that's all."

"Well, hold on, will you?"

"Certainly."

I held on as instructed and looked out at the heavy snow and the increasingly dark sky. I wondered what the weather was like in Atlanta. My Apple computer was humming along contentedly in front of me, and it would just take a few keystrokes to find the exact temperature and nature of Atlanta's weather, but I decided not to. Sometimes, mysteries are best left mysteries.

"Mr. Cole?"

"Right here."

"Mr. Cole, that accident took place on Tuesday, December twelfth, at six ten p.m., on Interstate Twenty. Mrs. Hale was the sole occupant of her automobile, a Lexus. She received minor injuries and was treated at the scene. The vehicle had to be towed away. The accident remains under investigation."

"I'm sure it does," I said. "But it's been over a month since it happened. What was the cause of the accident?"

"I can't rightly say, Mr. Cole. It remains under investigation."

I switched the phone from one ear to the other. "Yes, I know. But could you get an update for me, please."

"Why?"

I pondered what to say, decided to go for broke. "Well, Miss Tuckwell—"

"Mrs. Tuckwell."

"Sorry, Mrs. Tuckwell, I would think that it would be your job. To answer questions from legitimate news organizations and writers."

"And your question is?"

Could someone be so dense, or so crafty? I said, "I'm looking for an update on Barbara Hale's traffic accident. To see if a cause of the accident was determined."

"Oh," she said, her voice cheerful again. "I certainly can find that out for you."

"Wonderful. When do you think you can get back to me? Later today? Tomorrow?"

"How does next Wednesday sound?"

"Wednesday? Next Wednesday sounds awful. Why so long?"

A soft chuckle, and I felt a bit of admiration that I was being played so well by this fine example of Southern womanhood. "Mr. Cole…you seem to be a bright fella, and I've really enjoyed talking to you, but I'm sure you can figure out all on your own why I'm gonna give you a call next Wednesday."

"Because it's the day after the New Hampshire primary."

"Right," she said, almost purring. "That is entirely one hundred percent correct."

"But I'm not going to do anything—"

"Mr. Cole, I've been on my job for a while and know all the ins and outs of dealin' with the news media. That means the rest of this conversation is off the record, and I'll ever deny saying it, but here it goes: we're awfully proud of our senator, we would love to see him in the White House, and we don't like the fact that your pissant little frozen state is gonna have a key part in whether or not our man gets there. Understand? And you may be doing an innocent story and all that, but it sounds like bad publicity to me, professionally speakin'. And even if it is bad publicity, I'll still be doin' my job by callin' you back. But I'm just gonna be doin' it next Wednesday. All right?"

"All right. I understand completely. And Mrs. Tuckwell…"

"Yes?"

"You're very good at what you do."

A throaty laugh. "Why, thank you, Mr. Cole. And you have yourself a real good day, okay?"

"Sure."

After I disconnected from this underpaid public servant, I stared for a while at the computer screen. In doing a search for Barbara Hale and her car accident, other links had come up as well. Including one involving the actual shooting at the Tyler Conference Center. I had been inside the conference center, I had seen the shooting's aftermath from the parking lot, and I had missed some of the news coverage.

So I had never seen the actual shooting footage.

I moved the mouse and double-clicked a few times.

That was going to change.

THE FIRST LINK DIDN'T WORK, because my Apple software—being old and being Apple—couldn't read the movie file. But the second link worked, and I felt the back of my neck tense up. I was back there in the conference room, feeling sickly and warm and—

The footage went on, and there she was, up onstage with her husband. She was standing next to him at the lectern just as I recalled. The speech went on and even though I knew what was going to occur in the next few moments, I had a dark sense of something bad about to happen. It was like the very first time, so many years ago, when I had viewed the Zapruder film of JFK's assassination. You wanted to stop the film. You wanted to shout out a warning. You wanted someone in the crowd, somewhere, to look up at the right time at the Texas School Book Depository.

And you felt so powerless.

A round of applause, the sound coming out quite nicely from my computer's dual speakers. Senator Hale was smiling. Barbara was right next to him, applauding along, and then she moved to the right a few feet, still applauding, and the applause died down and Senator Hale said, "Who among us—"

The gunshots were loud and rapid, and the crowd screamed and shouted, and Senator Hale flinched, and in a matter of seconds, a crowd of Secret Service agents were upon Senator

Hale and Barbara and they were gone, just like that, as the camerawork got jerky, out of focus, and—

My breathing was rapid. I swallowed.

Barbara.

I shut down my computer and went downstairs.

DINNER WAS A HAM and cheddar cheese omelette, and I sat on the couch and balanced the plate on my lap as I ate. I ate with Annie in mind and watched some of the cable television shows, all of them with breathless reports of who was up in the polls, down in the polls, when the next poll was going to come out, and what was going to happen then. There was shouting, there was yelling, there were accusations, and there were talking heads from the Hale, Pomeroy, Grayson, and Wallace campaigns.

I watched for about an hour, and in those entire sixty minutes, if anyone had talked about what was going on in our corner of the world, what was wrong, and how we could work together to improve it, I must have missed it.

AFTER WASHING THE DISHES and putting them away, I was planning to take a walk across the way, when there was pounding at my door.

I was in the living room and the sudden sound made me jump. Usually my visitors announce themselves through a phone call or such, and I don't like surprises. I thought quickly of securing my .357 Ruger—usually kept downstairs in a kitchen drawer—but remembered that it was still in the possession of the Secret Service. My nine-millimeter Beretta was upstairs, but the knock came again and in that particular moment, I was tired of being afraid. So I left my weapons where they were and went across the living room.

I opened the door to a burst of swirling snow and a young man and woman wearing Clive Wallace campaign buttons on their damp coats. "Good evening, sir," the young man said. "Can we have just a few minutes to talk to you about Congressman Clive Wallace?"

Any other time, I would have politely said no and would have closed the door. But this wasn't any other time. The snow was quite heavy, and while the young man had spoken to me, energy and confidence in his voice, his companion had stood there, a brave smile on her face, but from the light from the living room, it looked like her lips were turning blue, and she was shivering.

"Sure," I said. "Come on in."

They came in, snow coming off their arms and shoulders, and they politely stomped their feet on the doormat. I closed the door. They were in their early twenties, energy just radiating from them, and they wore what I guess was called "protest chic," cargo pants and heavy boots and tweed coats, and those popular wool caps from South America with earflaps and long strings. He had a thin, stringy brown beard and she had long black hair that had mostly escaped her hat.

In their thin gloved hands, they held pamphlets, and the young woman passed one over to me. "My First Sixty Days, by Congressman Clive Wallace," and on the back was a photo of the congressman, who looked to be about the same age as his volunteers.

"The name's James," he said, "and she's Julia. We're campaigning for Congressman Wallace, and I hope we can count on your support."

"I'm Lewis," I said, getting a brief handshake from the both of them. "And before we start talking politics, let's talk practicals for a moment. How did you two get down here to my house?"

"We walked," Julia said, her voice a bit reproachful. "We were dropped off at the beach at ten this morning by our Tyler coordinator to canvass the neighborhoods, but nobody knew that most of the places here are closed for the winter. So many empty cottages and buildings…it was spooky as hell."

"Where are you from?"

James said, "I'm from Pennsylvania, and Julia's from Florida. We're taking a year off from Amherst to campaign for the congressman. Sir, if you'd take a moment to look at the pamphlet and understand where—"

But I was still paying attention to his friend, who had unbuttoned her coat and was looking around my house, and I thought I saw a furtive sniff. I thought of what she had said and I asked, "When did you last eat?"

James, a bit defiant, said, "We had lunch, some sandwiches and—"

Julia looked right at me and said, "We're starved."

He turned to her and said, "We still have some canvassing to do and—"

I opened the door for his benefit. "Look out there," I said. "See that snow? You try to walk back up my driveway, there's a good chance you'll wander off and fall into some rocks or boulders. Maybe even get drenched by a wave. And this time of night, there's not many locals out there who are going to want to talk to you."

"Sir," Julia said, "if we could stay for just a bit, we'd be very grateful."

About two minutes earlier I had known where this was going, but it still didn't make me feel particularly happy. I was doing the right thing, but as I closed the door, I also knew the Lafayette House was not in my plans tonight.

WE SPENT A WHILE in the kitchen, as I went through what I had in the pantry, freezer, and refrigerator, and as James took charge and vetoed almost everything and anything that was meat-related, dairy-related, or was processed in some way. Finally, Julia said, "Oh, for God's sake, just shut up and let the man feed us. If you can make us a veggie omelette or something, that would be great."

James started to ask me whether the eggs were free-range or not, when I heard a thumping noise, and turned to hide a smile, knowing Julia had kicked her companion from underneath the countertop.

As my omelette pan made its second appearance of the day, James kept up a running conversation about his life, about volunteering for the Congressman Wallace campaign, and about his goals for his life and that of the congressman. From his talk I knew he was an intense young man, with a passion for what he was doing, for not once did he mention Julia or inquire about my own political beliefs.

Even while they were eating, the fairly one-sided conversation continued, and once, while James was swallowing part of his meal, I caught Julia's attention and winked at her. That earned me a smile, a fair exchange.

But James had missed it all.

"The way I see it," he said, wiping up his plate with a piece of toast, "once the congressman gets to the White House, he's going to need us volunteers to move down there and keep the pressure up. That's the only way things will change. It will be a permanent campaign, day after day, week after week. We volunteers will move to D.C. and keep visiting the offices of the senators, and the congressmen, and the lobbyists, and we'll tell them that enough is enough. That change is coming, whether they like it or not."

"That sounds like a good idea," I said carefully. "But you're going to need to win a primary or two before you get there."

James smiled. "Don't you worry. We're going to win here next Tuesday, and win big, and that'll be the story of the year."

"The polls seem to say otherwise."

"The polls," James said. "Ha. First of all, they call people based on whether they've voted in the past. They don't count new voters. That's a good chunk right there, because Congressman Wallace has inspired hundreds and thousands of people who've never voted before. The pollsters also ignore those people who have cell phones, who are off the regular phone grid. Those people never get counted. And third, most polls are owned and operated by the big news media corporations. It's in their best interest to underestimate the support of Congressman Wallace."

"Why is that?" I asked, picking up the dishes.

"Because they know if the word gets out that Congressman Wallace's campaign is catching fire, is gaining support from the real people in this country, then the secret powers in this country, the corporations and their bought-and-paid-for politicians, will realize their time is over. That there's going to be big changes, real big changes, after the election. Read the pamphlet, Lewis, it's all in there. Sixty days. That's all he'll need to change this country."

Julia was keeping quiet, and I had the sense she had listened to this earnest screed about a half million times before. I started washing the dishes and James, taking my silence for encouragement, went on. "Sixty days after the inauguration. Two months, and at the end of two months, we're going to eliminate all forms of racism and sexism and ageism and ableism in government. We're also going to bring all the troops home, have free health care for everyone, free education, right up to college and graduate school, a new energy policy that considers people before profits, and a revised welfare program for the young and the old, and everyone else in between."

"That sounds great," I said. "How do you think it'll get paid for?"

"Taxes," he said. "That's the way all societies take care of their people."

"I see," I said. "And do you pay taxes?"

James said, "Ha! To this oppressive regime? The hell I do. Besides, there's other ways to pay for what the people need. If we bring all our troops home, then we won't be instigating other peoples to hate us. Then you don't need a military. There's billions of dollars right there. And then there's the space program."

I paused in my dishwashing. "What about the space program?"

He made a dismissive noise. "Billions and billions…spent for what? To send military pilots in space? To get pretty pictures? To find out what kind of rocks are on Mars or the moons of Jupiter?"

I guess it's a tribute to the way I was brought up by my parents that the young man continued to sit at the counter, and wasn't trying to breathe snow while having been tossed headfirst into a nearby snowbank. Julia looked at me and I could tell that she knew her companion had hit home with that last remark, and she said, "There's other causes Congressman Wallace is fighting for that don't mean money being spent."

"Sure!" James said, still charged up. "There's laws that need to be passed as well. Lots of different laws, like a law to eliminate heteronorminism, for example."

While this new recitation was going on, Julia came around the counter, wordlessly picked up a dish towel, and started drying the plates and silverware.

"I'm sorry," I said, also picking up a dishcloth. "I didn't recognize the last word you used. Heteronorminism."

"Sure," he said, as if eager to teach an oldster like myself something new. "You see, society and the way it projects itself in the media and advertising promotes the lifestyle of heterosexuality as the only acceptable sexual lifestyle there is. Heteronorminism. That leads to oppression and hate crimes and discrimination. What the congressman and others propose to do is to ensure that advertising and other media outlets do their part in recognizing other sexual identities, through a quota system. That way, by educating people as to what's really out there, you remove the fear. Remove the fear, you remove discrimination and the possibility of hate crimes."

I opened the cabinet, started putting the dry dishes away as Julia handed them over to me. "So…if gays make up five percent or ten percent of the population, you'd require that five or ten percent of advertising depict gay people in the commercials?"

He laughed at me. "See! Right there, that's a perfect example of heteronorminism. You automatically assume that sexuality is divided into two classes: heterosexuality and homosexuality. But there's so many others…transgender, preop transgender, transvestism, gender-neutral, and of course, the different classes within the leather community. It's a very diverse subject."

"Of course," I said, fighting hard to keep my face straight. "And your role is to educate the voters in New Hampshire as to the congressman's position regarding advertising and the different classes within the leather community."

"Among other things," James said. "No offense, Lewis, and really, I hope you don't take offense, but it's amazing that such a small, overwhelmingly white and reactionary state like this one has such an enormous influence in choosing our next president. It really is outrageous, once you think about it. And it makes our job so much harder."

I dried my hands and Julia went back around to the counter, and I said, "Well, lucky for us white reactionaries that you and so many others have volunteered their time to educate us correctly."

Julia raised a hand, to hide a smile, I'm sure, and James nodded and said without a trace of irony, "You are so right, Lewis. So right."

BY NOW THE SNOW WAS really coming down, and the wind off the ocean was making the windows rattle. I went to the door and managed to open it a bit, and the cold wind was sharp on my face and hands. Visibility was about three feet, if that. "No offense, guys, but I really think you need to spend the night here."

James said, "Don't you have a car or SUV that can get us up that driveway?"

Julia said, her voice tinged with sarcasm, "You're being silly, James. Would you really ride in that? What about your core beliefs?"

"All I'm saying is that—"

"James."

I closed the door and said, "Look. I'll build a fire in the fireplace, unfold the couch into a sleeper, and in the morning, after the storm breaks and the plows have gone out, I'll give you a ride to your Tyler canvassing coordinator, or anyplace else you'd like."

Julia smiled. She had faint dimples, and if I had been James, I would have ditched the Congressman Wallace for President campaign in a second for the opportunity to see that smile again.

"Thank you," she said. "That'll be wonderful."

But James didn't seem that happy. "Well…if I can use your phone, I guess that'll be all right."

So A FIRE WAS BUILT and I folded out the couch, and brought down blankets and sheets and pillows, and Julia was quiet again, and I offered to turn on the television and James proudly said, "Haven't watched television in sixteen months and don't plan to start up again tonight," and I left them to figure out sleeping and other arrangements.

Upstairs I washed up and went to my own bed, and looked out the window for a moment. I supposed I could wait until they fell asleep and then sneak out of my own house, to make my way in the storm to the Lafayette House.

But…there were now too many variables. How to explain to these two volunteers why their host was trudging out in the middle of a storm? And how to explain my sudden presence at the Lafayette House, when every other sane person was sticking close to home? And I hadn't been exaggerating when I'd told the two how dangerous it could be, to try to walk out at night so close to the ocean and the shoreline. Two winters before, during the Super Bowl, a drunk football enthusiast, not wanting to stand in line at the Lafayette House to use the men's room, had stumbled outside to do his duty. He was found about a month later, wedged in some boulders a half mile up the coast, no doubt still legally drunk but also quite dead.

So another day would have to pass. I got undressed and slipped into bed, and picked up my trusty biography of Winston Churchill, and wondered if I had ever been that dense or idealistic when I had been James's and Julia's age.

Idealistic, perhaps, but I hoped never that dense. I read for about a half hour, listening to whispers and once a loud giggle from downstairs, before switching off the light and going to sleep, quickly wondering how Barbara and I must have sounded to our professors and older acquaintances, way back then in college.

THE VOICE WOKE ME UP. "Lewis?"

I rolled over, sat up in bed. In the dim illumination of the clock and small night-light in the bathroom, I made out the form of someone at the foot of my bed.

"Julia?"

"Can...can I come over for a sec?"

"Sure."

Julia came over and sat down on the edge of the bed. I rubbed my face and said, "What's wrong?"

"It's...it's...oh, I'm sorry," and she started sobbing.

"Hey," I said, touching her shoulder. "Hold on, hold on, what's wrong?"

She wiped her eyes and said, "I'm sorry to dump this on you. Really. But can you help me?"

"What do you need?"

She sobbed. "Oh, Lewis, I want to go home!"

"Shhh, it's okay," I said. "Campaigning not working out for you?"

"Oh God, you don't know what it's like," she said, almost

blubbering. "We sleep on floors or chairs…the food is awful…and I've never been so cold in all my life, and we spend so much time outside. The staff work us so hard and so many people hang up the phones or slam the doors in our faces or throw our pamphlets on the ground…and there's always more to do…and I should be home, getting ready for second semester…and I…want to go back home. I don't want to do this anymore."

"So why did you come here in the first place?"

"James," she said, practically hissing the word. "He made it sound so special, so romantic, so idealistic. Be part of an awakening movement, a community to change the world…He didn't say anything about cold pizza and no hot showers and dirty bathrooms. And he's…well, you saw how he is. So full of himself. So righteous. I mean"—and she giggled, a welcome change—"educating the average New Hampshire voter about Congressman Wallace and the leather community…he didn't even know you were making fun of him."

I looked at the time: 1:00 a.m. "I shouldn't have done that, but the temptation was too great. So. Why not go home? What's stopping you?"

In the faint light I saw her fold her arms, and she seemed to shrink into the frame of a twelve-year-old girl. "I told you he was idealistic…he can also get very angry if he doesn't think you believe in anything. That you're willing to compromise. And I get scared when he gets angry. I…I really get scared, and I don't know what he might do. Once I was upset that we went a whole day without eating and I told him that I wouldn't do that anymore…and he tugged my arm something awful…It hurt for two days. Do…do you think you can help me?"

I scratched the back of my head. "Across the way is a hotel called the Lafayette House. There's a shuttle service that'll take you into town tomorrow, to a newspaper store that's the local Greyhound stop. You can even buy the bus ticket at the hotel so there's no waiting at the store. And in an hour's time you'll be in Boston. From there I'm sure you can catch a flight or a bus ride home. That good enough?"

"Yes, yes, it is…but what about James?"

"You let me worry about James. You just worry about getting home. Got enough money?"

"Yes, that's not a problem."

"How about belongings? Luggage?"

"Everything important is in my bag. Other than that, it's just a bunch of smelly clothes I can do without."

"Then you'll be all set. I promise."

The sniffles came back. "Oh, Lewis,…thank you, thank you so much."

"Not a problem. Look. It's late…why don't you get back to sleep."

She leaned over and kissed my forehead, and I guess I was a bit stunned at the unexpected attention.

And if I was just a bit stunned, then, a moment later, I became fully stunned.

Julia said, with a touch of shy hesitation, "Would…would you like me to spend some time here with you?"

I touched her shoulder again. "Any other night, any other time, I'd be honored. But go back downstairs, Julia. It'll be all right. I promise."

Another whispered "thank you" and she got up, and at my bedroom door she said, "You know. I haven't gotten a good night's sleep since I've been to New Hampshire. He snores and sounds like a washing machine…and he denies it! Can you believe that? He thinks I'm imagining it, night after night."

"Nights like these," I said, "I can believe almost everything."

# TWELVE

In the morning I let them loose in my kitchen to fix whatever kind of breakfast suited them, and I shoveled a bit from the front door, and from the sliding door to the shed that served as a garage for my Ford Explorer. The snow wasn't as deep as I had expected, and I knew my Ford would plow us right up and out into the parking lot and Atlantic Avenue with ease.

I went back into the house, warm from my exertions. James was standing there with Julia, dressed, munching on a piece of toast. It wasn't whole wheat or whole grain or harvested from a cooperative in Baja, California, but I guess hunger trumped politics, at least this morning. I also figured that since James hadn't come out to help me shovel the way clear, he was saving his energies for something more important. Julia looked quiet, shy, and I said, "Ready to leave?"

"Sure," James said. "Our campaign guy, he's staying at the Redbird Motel, on Cromwell Street. I just called him and he's waiting for us. Can you drop us there?"

"No problem."

They joined me outside and in the open garage, James went ahead of Julia and climbed into the front passenger seat. I started up the Explorer and backed out into the snow-covered driveway, and started going up the slight incline. James was talking to Julia about what they were going to do that day, how they would probably have to skip lunch because of the time lost due to last night's snowstorm, and how they would really have to redouble their efforts because the corporate-controlled media and rival campaigns would—

"Excuse me for a sec," I said, driving across the street to the Lafayette House, a quick and easy task due to the lack of early morning traffic. "I need to run an errand and then we'll be on our way."

I parked in an area marked for guest drop-off and I put the Explorer in park, shut the engine off, and said, "Julia? Care to come with me for a moment?"

"Oh, thanks, I will," she said quickly, and before James could say or do anything, she was outside in the parking lot, and fell in step with me as I went up to the front entrance of the hotel. We went into the lobby and I made a left to the gift shop. Julia leaned into me as we went into the gift shop and said, "Thanks. Thank you very much."

"You're quite welcome. You have a good ride home, and a good semester."

Inside the gift shop, Stephanie was behind the counter and looked up from a sheaf of invoices that she had been examining.

"Morning, Lewis. What can I do for you?"

I said, "This is my friend Julia. She'd like a Greyhound ticket to Boston, and a ticket to the shuttle uptown."

"Oh, I think we can do that," she said, pulling a ledger and ticket book from underneath the counter. "You're in luck. The next shuttle leaves in about five minutes."

Julia started going through her purse and she and Stephanie started with their business arrangement, and I waited, looking out the gift shop window, as the women worked and information was recorded and currency was exchanged. My Explorer was in view and then James, probably realizing at last that something was amiss, got out of my Ford and started up the short walkway. I moved around and as Julia and Stephanie finished their transaction, James strode in.

"Hey, what's up?" he said.

I smiled at him. "Julia's heading home."

"You're joking."

"Nope."

He tried to get past me, and I moved in front of him. "Tell you what," I said. "We'll stay here for a minute or two, and then I'll give you a ride to the Redbird Motel to meet up with your campaign guy. How's that?"

He said something with lots of syllables that probably

wouldn't endear him to the League of Women Voters, and he called out, "Julia! What the hell is going on here? C'mon, don't you care anymore?"

She kept quiet and grabbed her tickets, and walked by, heading toward the lobby and the outdoors, and James stuck a hand out to stop her and I moved it back, saying, "Let's be polite, all right?"

Two words, one being "you," and the other not being "you," and he tried to follow Julia out of the gift shop. He said, "Julia, don't you leave me! Damn it, don't you leave me! I'm not going to let you—"

Then he shut up, real quick, since as he went by, I grabbed his right hand, tightening my grip on his thumb, and then pulled it around and tucked his arm up toward his back. My friend Detective Sergeant Diane Woods had taught me this move—called a come-along—some years ago, and rarely have I ever felt such pain.

"Oooh," James said, stopping, his legs getting weak. I leaned in, whispering in his ear, "Don't move, don't say a word, or your thumb gets shattered. If I have your attention, say yes."

"Yes," he whispered back.

"Good," I said. "Now. You and I are going to stay in this lovely little gift shop, and we're going to admire their sweatshirt collection, and you're going to be a good boy. All right? Say yes again if you understand."

"Yes," he murmured.

"Nicely done," I said. Stephanie stood behind the gift counter, taking it all in, and her face had no expression. She was letting me be, which made me quite happy, for I wasn't sure what she would do about what was going on here, despite our casual friendship. And the lack of customers to see what was happening made me even happier.

Outside I saw Julia, standing by herself, and she stood there and I stood in the gift shop, holding the hand of a male college student from Massachusetts, and I thought that was a pretty odd way to start one's morning, no matter how you looked at it.

Then a white passenger van pulled up, and Julia quickly

walked into an open door. I waited for a moment, to see if she was going to wave good-bye or look back or somehow acknowledge that I was there, which would have been sweet, but no, the door to the van was shut by the driver and it drove away. So much for sweetness.

I let James go. "There. Feel better?"

He turned, rubbing his hand, face red, and he said, "You son of a bitch, I'll have you arrested! Right now! See how that makes your day!"

I shrugged. "Give it a go. You're young, a college student, and a college student from Massachusetts. I live here, I know all the cops and most of the lawyers. We'll see who'll have the better day."

Another rub of his hand and another string of curses, and I felt disappointed in the caliber of today's college youth, since I had known all of those curses years ago when I was his age.

When he was finished with his latest outburst, I said, "Come on, let's go."

"What the hell do you mean, let's go?"

"You need a ride to the Redbird Motel. I said I'd give you a ride. Ready?"

Another two-word exclamation and he said, "No way in hell I'm getting a ride from you! Asshole...I'd rather walk!"

"Fine," I said. "Have a good day canvassing."

"Sure! And another thing...I made a half dozen phone calls last night from your phone. Long distance. Take that, sucker!"

He charged out of the gift shop, and I called after him—though I doubted he heard me—"Not to worry, I've got unlimited long distance. For just thirty bucks a month."

Stephanie finally said something, but started off with a loud laugh. "Oh, that's a good one."

I turned to face her. "Enjoy the show?"

"In a way, yes," she said, pulling together my morning newspapers. "You did well."

"Glad I could provide you with entertainment."

"Better than none. Here's your papers."

"Thanks," I said, pulling out my wallet, but Stephanie

laughed. "Nope. On the house. You go along and read your papers, Lewis. Have a good one."

I put the papers under my arm. "I'm going to try, if the gods let me."

BUT THE GODS MUST have been otherwise occupied, for once again, in the lobby of the Lafayette House, I met up with Chuck Bittner, the rep from the Tucker Grayson campaign, who stood there, arms crossed, his pudgy face glowing.

"Mr. Cole," he said.

"Mr. Bittner," I said. "What, you live here?"

"As a matter of fact, I do. For the duration of the campaign."

"I hope the Lafayette House is charging you full freight."

"I'm sure they are," he said. "Last time, you gave me three hundred seconds. May I request half of that this morning?"

I shifted the papers from one arm to another. "All right. One hundred fifty seconds. Go ahead."

He looked at his watch. "At this time tomorrow, if you haven't agreed to make a statement on behalf of the Grayson campaign, we're going to publicize your Pentagon background and something new as well, something that has just come to our attention."

"And what's that? My unpaid parking tickets from the city of Boston?"

"No," he said, his voice triumphant. "A revelation about your background with Barbara Hale. Your choice. Either the word comes out and it comes from you, or it comes from us. And you get some very nasty news media attention. You come out in support of General Grayson, and you don't have to say anything about Mrs. Hale. Just your support of the Grayson campaign would be enough."

I thought about that, thought about what it might do to the Hale campaign, how Barbara would feel, God, how Annie would feel…

Remembered Annie's plea. No more bad news, please, she had said. No more bad news about you and Hale.

"No," I said.

"No, what?"

"No, I'm not going to say anything tomorrow, and no, neither will you."

He laughed, unfolded his arms. "Or what?"

"Or you'll regret it."

A smile was still on his face, and he reached over and grabbed my upper arm, squeezing it hard. "Mr. Cole, I may be retired navy, but I'm still in shape. Much better shape than you, I would guess. If anyone's going to be hurt, it's going to be you. And if you think you can threaten me, prevent me, stop me from doing what's right for General Grayson's campaign, then I just have three words for you. Bring it on."

I pulled my arm free, nodded, and walked past him. "Consider it brought."

Outside the sun was still shining and it looked like the day might improve, when I got to my Ford Explorer and saw that some thoughtful person had keyed both sides of my vehicle. On the passenger's side it was just a series of scratches, but on the driver's side, inspiration must have set in, for scratched in the paint was pig.

Not very imaginative, but the point had been made.

I got in and went home.

AT HOME I WENT THROUGH the papers and made two phone calls to Felix Tinios, but he wasn't home or reachable through his cell phone. I got his to-the-point message twice: "Leave your name and number," which I did. An attempt to reach Annie was also equally unsuccessful.

Usually I like to take my time going through the morning papers, contrasting and comparing the different coverage and editorials, but this morning, well, there was too much going on. I had a late breakfast and even later shower, and as I was putting on a pair of socks, the phone rang.

"Lewis?"

"Hey, it's the soon-to-be-famous Paula Quinn," I replied.

The expected laugh didn't come from the Tyler *Chronicle*'s best reporter, but what she said next made me close my eyes in embarrassment. "Not famous enough, if you forgot our lunch date today. I'm all by myself at the Harborview Restaurant."

I said something that James had said just that morning, and then said, "Ten minutes," and I finished dressing and got the hell out.

BY THE TIME the check arrived and I had passed along my credit card to the waitress, overruling Paula's earlier promise to pay, Paula's mood had improved. Some time ago we had shared a brief romance that hadn't panned out, and after some rough patches, we were doing well. Odd, but I didn't have that vaguely uncomfortable and queasy feeling with her that I had with Barbara Scott Hale. Maybe it was because Barbara was married and Paula wasn't, or that there was still a sense of unfinished business with Barbara and me and none with Paula, but I didn't want to think too much about it. Instead, I just sat and enjoyed lunch with her, admiring her little upturned nose, her smile, and the cute way her ears would sometimes poke through her blond hair.

Despite its name, the Harborview was in the center of Tyler proper, and only by standing on the roof and holding on to the fake cupola could anyone see a view of Tyler Harbor. Still, it's a popular place with the locals and tourists, and today, even in January, it was fairly busy. We sat in a booth that overlooked a mound of plowed, dirty snow in the parking lot, the cars and SUVs out there lightened by a faint white sheen that comes from the salt dumped on the roads to keep them clear.

I looked around and said, "I get the feeling most of these people won't be here come the day after Primary Day."

"So true," she said, sipping at her second iced tea. "You know the musical and movie *Brigadoon?*"

"Sure. About a mythical Scottish village that only appears to the rest of the world every hundred years or so."

"That's right. And this little state of ours is like *Brigadoon.* For three years in a row, we're just a little backwater, the prickly state north of Massachusetts that is mostly ignored by the rest of the world. Then…in that fourth year, something magical happens. This little state of just over a million people becomes power central. Pretty funny, isn't it. This little state of tax avoiders and sensible-shoe wearers and independent cusses plays a prominent role in who the quote leader of the free world unquote is going to be. If anyone had a question of whether God had a sense of humor, our little state and how we pick the president should settle it."

"And how are you doing?"

She smiled. "I love it. Honest to God I do. You know why?"

"Access," I said.

She stuck her tongue out at me. "Show-off. Yes, absolutely, access. The candidates need to get their message out to the locals, and the locals don't trust the big media, even the not-so-big media from Boston. So us little folks get all the attention from the candidates and their campaigns. When most times some local police chiefs enjoy their power trips by not calling us back in a day or so, it's wonderful to have media reps calling from Washington or Manhattan, wanting to know if we'd like to have a private, one-on-one lunch with the candidate that day. It's delightful."

The waitress came back with the check, and when she left I said, "So. Primary Day next Tuesday. Who's going to win?"

Paula said, "Well, of course, that depends on who you talk to, or who's going to spin what. The easiest prediction is that the junior senator from our southern neighbor, Nash Pomeroy, should win it in a walk. Favorite son and all that. And that's what his campaign is pumping…then there's Senator Hale. A Southern boy who one wouldn't think would do well in New Hampshire, but he just won in Iowa, and people love a winner. So it depends on whether, one, the voters want to vote for a winner, or two, vote for somebody else to shake things up so that New Hampshire isn't taken for granted."

"You hear anything about the Hale campaign?"

She made a face. "Considering who you're spending time with, I'd think you'd have an inside track on that."

"Maybe yes, maybe no. What do you hear?"

"Me? Usual stuff. Campaign in chaos, moving forward on momentum, need a win here in New Hampshire to bring in more big bucks for the Southern primaries. But even if he comes in second—or third, which I doubt—he'll stay in it for a while. He's from the South. Lots of primaries coming up in the South."

"That's it? No other gossip or dark tales or rumors?"

"If there is, I haven't heard it."

"How about General Grayson? Or Congressman Wallace? How are they going to do next Tuesday?"

She finished off her iced tea. "In a purely logical, mathematical sense, they will lose. But I'll predict here and now, my friend, each will declare himself a winner, no matter the outcome. They'll play the expectations game. Each side will tell pollsters and columnists and reporters that their internal polls only have them winning five percent of the vote, so when they actually win ten percent of the vote, all these sober-minded reporters can write inspiring stories of how they did better than expected, and how this has breathed new life in the struggling campaign of blah, blah, blah."

I reached behind me for my coat. "So. Who do you think's going to win?"

Paula made me laugh by lowering her voice, pretending to be some sort of television anchorman, and announcing, "Well, Lewis, the American people will win next Tuesday, of course...."

OUTSIDE THERE WAS no breeze and the thin January sunlight felt good on my face. I walked Paula to her car and she said, "You and Annie...how's it going?"

"Goes well, between campaign meetings and appearances."

She grabbed my hand. "Good. You make it work, or I'll hurt you. Understand? She's good people, and I like what she's done to your mood."

"Thanks for the advice. And how's the town counsel, Mr. Sullivan, treating you?"

She looked embarrassed and suddenly ten years younger. "He's...he's fine...and you know what?"

"What?"

She touched her left ear, just for a moment. "He...thinks I should get my ears done. Flatten them so they don't poke out like they do. What do you think?"

I kissed her cheek. "I think he's a bonehead, that's what I think."

AT HOME I TRIED to spend some productive time in front of the computer, to come up again with a snappy column idea for June, and after a half hour or so of false starts, it just wasn't happening. Then I logged on to the Internet, to see what nonsense was being written about the primary and my home state, and after some time slogging through stories written by reporters who think it's charming as all hell that most of the small towns here still have white clapboard churches around grassy town commons, I spent some time searching for something about Barbara Hale and her famous husband.

I didn't find much. Through the magical powers of the Internet, I found some old file stories written when Hale was first elected senator, and a nice profile in the *Washington Post*'s Style section, written after Hale had announced his candidacy, but not much else. It was odd to call up a search system on the Internet, and see dozens and dozens of photos of a woman who you once were intimate with, knowing that your mind's eye had clearer and better photos than what existed in the digital universe.

I also viewed some video clips as well, Barbara appearing with her husband, almost stuck to his side, as he appeared at campaign rallies in Iowa and Michigan and, yes, of course, New Hampshire. And in those clips, I saw her smile, saw her enthusiasm, and saw her devotion to her spouse, and something just didn't seem right.

Why would anyone want to kill her? What would be the point? Was she overreacting, and the real attempt had been against her husband, like everyone else thought?

And for God's sake, what in hell was Spenser Harris's role in all of this, and who had killed him and dumped him in my yard?

I looked at the clips, again and again, and there was a little tickling at the back of my skull, just the barest hint that something was wrong, and whatever it was, it was gone, the minute the phone rang.

"YES?" I answered.

"You rang?"

It was Felix Tinios, and I spun around in my chair and put my feet up on the nearest windowsill and said, "Thanks for calling me back. Sounds like you're at a hog-calling festival or something equally charming."

He sighed. "I wish. Days like this, you get a better class of people at a hog-calling festival. Nope, I'm at O'Hare, ready to come home in an hour."

"Chicago? What in hell are you doing there?"

"My new job, son. Oppo for the Pomeroy campaign."

"A Massachusetts senator, and you're in Illinois?"

"The world of the oppo researcher travels far and wide. Especially when your subject has some interesting hobbies, none of which I'm going to mention over an open line. What's up with you?"

"You going to be tired when you get home?"

"Probably."

"Feel like a job?"

"A job? From you?"

"Yep."

Felix said cautiously, "It's…it's not a moving job, is it?"

"God, no," I said. "I've had enough of those to last a lifetime. Nope, something else. Tell me, ever see the movie *All the President's Men*?"

"Sure. Dustin Hoffman and Robert Redford. You got a newspaper job lined up for me?"

"Nope. Something else."

"Oh…okay, I got it. What time suits you?"

"Flying into Boston or Manchester?"

"Manchester. Just after eleven."

"How about if I pick you up and we go on from there?"

"Fine." And then he laughed. "Looking forward to it, if you can believe it. It'll be a nice change after digging up dirt all these days."

And after another minute or two of receiving flight and arrival information, I hung up and made another phone call.

IT TOOK SOME maneuvering, but I got through to the Hale for President campaign headquarters in Manchester, and actually got somebody on the line who knew Annie Wynn. "Hold on, I'll see if I can get her," and I could hear the phone clunk on a tabletop, and in the background, there was the noise of voices and keyboards being slapped and a television program, and then there was a clatter, and the phone was picked up.

"Annie Wynn."

"It's Lewis. How are you?"

A sigh. "It's been one of those days…look, I can't talk much. Did you ride out the storm all right?"

"I did, and when I see you next, I've got a funny story to tell you."

"My friend…it won't be tonight, I'm sorry. Maybe tomorrow."

It seemed like the noise in the background grew louder. "Well, how about dinner? I could drive out to Manchester."

Another sigh. "Cold pizza is what's ahead of me, Lewis. A wonderful thought, but I can't leave here tonight. There's too much going on. Look, I've got to run. I'll talk to you tomorrow. Deal?"

"Deal," I said, and that was that.

I put the phone down, stared at it for a bit, and then picked it up and did some additional calling.

TWO HOURS LATER, I was in Manchester, wearing my best suit and best wool overcoat, and even shoes that matched. I parked about a block away from my destination, and walked gingerly along the slippery sidewalks. Snow piles were still on the sides of the street, and they were sprinkled with campaign signs from all the campaigns, like candles on a soggy slice of ice cream cake, melting on a plate.

Over my shoulder I carried a wide leather bag that bumped against my hip, and which was warm to the touch. I tried not to think too much of what I had in there as I made my way to the well-lit storefront that announced HALE FOR PRESIDENT. Inside I wiped my feet and took in the scenery. There were rows and rows of battered metal desks manned by men and women, mostly young and intense-looking. Phones were ringing, photocopying machines were humming, and hardly anybody was paying attention to the four television sets in one corner, all of them turned to a different cable news channel. Posters of Senator Hale were taped to the walls, and there was the constant movement and hum of people at work.

I stood there, just taking it all in, when a woman spotted me and came over, her sweater festooned with Hale buttons, and carrying a clipboard. She was about ten years younger than me, pudgy, with a no-nonsense attitude about her.

"Can I help you?" she asked, looking past me, as if counting down the seconds as to when she could pass me off to somebody else lower on the food chain.

"You certainly can," I said, removing a thin leather wallet from inside my coat. I flashed it open and quickly closed it. "The name's Cole. I'm from the FEC. I need two things, and I need them now."

Well, that got her attention. She was no longer staring over my shoulder. "What's the problem?"

"There is no problem," I said. "And it'll remain that way if I get what I need right away."

"What's that?"

"A private office, with a door, and a campaign worker you have here. One Miss Annie Wynn."

She seemed to hold her clipboard tighter. "Can you tell me what this is about?"

I stared at her. "Are you Miss Annie Wynn?"

"No, I'm not."

"Then that's all you need to know. Now. Am I getting that office and Miss Wynn?"

She seemed to struggle for a moment, but maybe the exhaustion and the looming deadline of the upcoming primary, and the fear of anything bad, overtook whatever common sense the poor dear had, for she nodded and said, "Follow me, then."

# THIRTEEN

I DON'T KNOW who the office belonged to but it had a nice round wooden table adjacent to the desk, the door that I required, and I carefully removed the piles of files and papers from the table and placed them on the floor. My leather case was now open on one of the chairs, and I was about to get to work when there was a soft knock on the door and Annie came in, carrying the no-doubt-required clipboard.

She started by saying, "What can I do for…Lewis, what the hell are you doing here?"

From the open leather case, I took out a small white tablecloth, which I spread over the table. "Feeding you dinner."

"Dinner? You're…damn it, Myra said there was somebody from the FEC here to see me, the goddamn Federal Elections Commission!"

I started taking out plates and wineglasses. "I never said I was from the Federal Elections Commission. I said I was from the FEC. Many, many years ago—unless my memory is wrong, which is distinctly possible—I joined an organization called the Federation of Employed Consultants. Or something like that. They never sent me a renewal notice, so I guess I'm still a member in good standing."

Annie said, "Myra said you showed her a badge!"

Plates, silverware, wineglasses, and a little vase with a rose, made from plastic, unfortunately. I smiled. "Yes, I did. It was a junior detective badge I once got from Diane Woods at the Tyler Police Department. I'm quite proud of it, and love showing it off. I hope she didn't mistake it for something else."

Annie was trying to be angry and not laugh at the same time, and I wasn't sure which would succeed. "Lewis, I told you I didn't have—"

"Annie."

"It's a madhouse here, and it's going to be—"

"Annie."

She looked at me, tired and quiet. "What?"

"You said you couldn't leave. So you're not leaving. You need to have dinner, and why not a good one? And why not a dinner where you can talk about something else besides the campaign? You can have some quiet time, a fine meal, and go back to work on the Hale campaign, full of vim and vigor."

She wrinkled her nose as she smelled what was coming from the open leather bag. "I know what vigor is, but what the hell is vim?"

"Beats me. What do you say we eat before it gets cold?"

I could sense the struggle going on inside her campaign volunteer mind, and finally she smiled and dropped the clipboard on the floor. "Wonderful. I'm starved."

So I DUMPED MY COAT and brought everything out, and dinner was chateaubriand for two, already sliced in generous portions, with garlic mashed potatoes, small salads, and asparagus spears in a cheese sauce for Annie. There was also a half bottle of a Margaux wine from France, which I poured for the two of us. As I spread everything out, she practically clapped her hands in glee at the spread of food.

"How in hell did you manage this?"

"I managed it by not cooking it," I said. "There's a new restaurant here in Manchester. Called Soundings North."

She picked up a fork. "Yeah, I've heard of it. But I didn't know they did takeout."

"They don't"

"So how did you get this?"

I picked up my own fork. "By a charitable contribution."

"A bribe?"

"Quiet, woman. Eat before you start drooling."

And she took a bite, and then another, and gave a soft sigh of pleasure, and that was dinner.

I MADE SURE we didn't talk much about politics, but I also didn't press my luck. We ate, and ate well, and for dessert I had some sliced strawberries with heavy cream and some brown sugar, and hot coffee from a thermos bottle. She ate quickly and as I cleaned up, she said, "The best I've eaten in a very long time, Lewis. Thank you."

"You're quite welcome."

She looked up at the wall, noted the time, and said, "I hate to eat and run, but…"

"You've got to eat and run."

"Wait…you said something earlier about a funny story."

"It can wait," I said.

"You sure?" she asked.

"Unless you want to start telling me about Senator Hale's position on the various members of the leather community, yes, it can wait."

"I'm glad it can wait," she said, "though it does sound like a hell of a story."

"You can't imagine."

Annie stood up, retrieved her clipboard from the floor, and I admired the view and how she filled out her tight black slacks. She turned to me and said, "Next Wednesday."

"I know. It comes after Tuesday."

"Smart-ass. No, what I mean is this…next Wednesday, it changes for the better. The primary will be done. I promise. After the primary I'm going to move in with you for a day or two and…catch up with things. If you don't mind."

"Best offer I've had all year."

She laughed. "And the year has just begun! No, Lewis, I need to tell you something. I've been asked to join the campaign in South Carolina when this is over…and I've been thinking about it. I believe in Senator Hale and what he wants to do when he gets in the White House. I truly believe in that…but I also don't want to stop seeing you…you mean a lot to me."

"Likewise from here, dear one."

"So, when Tom next talks to me, I'm going to tell him that South Carolina is off the table. New Hampshire still needs more work."

"As a resident of New Hampshire, I thank you."

"And I thank you for dinner. And delightful conversation. And the lovely dessert. And coffee."

I went forward and said, "How about one more helping of dessert?" and I pulled her toward me.

That brought a giggle and a few minutes of kissing and ca-ressing, as we stood before the closed door, and she whispered in my ear, "You better stop now, or I'm going to do you right on the floor of Tom's office."

"And why's that a problem?"

"Tom is sort of my boss, and I want to be able to see him in the future without blushing about what the two of us did in his office."

I reluctantly let her go and gathered up my belongings, placing them back into the leather case. "Thanks," I said.

"For what?"

"For going along with dinner. For not tossing me out on my ear when you first saw me. For the smiles and good times."

She opened the door. "Come along, FEC-man, while I try to come up with an explanation of what we've been doing the past twenty minutes."

Outside it was the usual chaos of ringing phones and raised conversations, and there were some curious glances tossed our way. Annie leaned into me and said, "This. This is what I believe in. What do you believe in, Lewis?"

"I believe I must be going," I said. "That's what."

"Thanks," she said. "I'll call you tomorrow."

"That'd be great."

She walked away and was quickly corralled by some workers, and I went to the front door, where I slipped on my coat and grabbed my now lighter leather carrying case. I was about to open the door when a loud woman's voice got my attention. I and about thirty other people turned to look at a closed office door, about ten feet away from me, when it slammed open and the woman's voice now said, "—keep on ignoring me, you'll see what'll happen, you'll be goddamned lucky to come in third place next week!"

A well-dressed and well-coiffed woman stormed out of the

now open door, and she blew by me like I was a piece of garden statuary, something to be ignored and perhaps defiled by small birds or dogs, but not anything that counted.

Which sort of disappointed me, since I had enjoyed talking with her the other night at her home.

The door outside flew open, cold air rushed in, and I caught one more glimpse of Audrey Whittaker, wealthy woman from Wallis—how's that for alliteration?—who seemed pretty angry at the Hale campaign.

I followed her out, perhaps just to say hello or to find out what had gone on, but the cold January sidewalks were empty by the time I made it out there.

So I trudged my way through the darkness and got to my Ford Explorer—still marked with pig, visible from a nearby street-light—and got in and started her up.

ABOUT TWENTY MINUTES LATER I was at the Manchester airport. Not so long ago, according to Felix and others, the airport had been a sleepy little regional facility that had about a dozen or so flights a day, with a parking lot next to the terminal building that charged two dollars a day for parking, and which wanted people to pay on the honor system by putting their money in a little brown envelope and mailing it in. Some place. I wish I had gotten to know it before it so drastically changed, after fliers—fed up with the continuous horror show that is Boston's Logan Airport—started streaming out to Manchester and Hartford and Warwick, Rhode Island.

Now the airport is bigger, there's a three-story parking garage, but any airport that has a stuffed moose in its arrival area still has some of its old New Hampshire charm. I put the Explorer in short-term parking and made a ninety-second walk to the sole terminal building. Arrivals were on the second floor, and I did a quick check of the status board and saw that Felix's flight was on time.

So I sat down and people-watched for a while. I thought about the campaigns and the upcoming primary and other things, and I still thought about Barbara and our little make-out session in her hotel room, and I thought about the videos I had seen with her and her husband, and now I felt guilty, thinking about kissing a married woman, even one I had been intimate with all those years ago, and then, thankfully, the status board said Felix's flight had landed, so I could stop thinking so damn much.

I stood up. I would be so glad when next Tuesday would be here and over. Barbara would be gone from my state, to be with her husband, where she belonged, and I would stay here, and, delightfully, so would Annie.

From the arrival gate, people started to stream through, and I liked seeing the happy reunions among them as the plane emptied. Landing alone at night in a strange airport can be such a soul-deadening experience, seeing other people's laughs and smiles and hugs. I waited and I waited, and pretty soon, the departing stream of people dwindled down to a trickle.

No Felix.

I double-checked the status board. It was the right gate, and it was the right flight. I then had that niggling feeling at the back of my skull, the one when you think you either made a dumb mistake or, worse, that something bad has happened to the one you are waiting for, and—

There, strolling along like he owned the damn place, was Felix, wearing black slacks and a dark gray woolen coat that went down to his knees, carrying a soft black leather briefcase, and keeping up an animated conversation with two flight attendants, one on each side. The women were laughing at something that Felix said, and he garnered a quick kiss on the cheek from both of them as he stopped before me. The women went on, their wheeled cases being pulled behind them, and the one on the left, a brunet, gave a quick wave to Felix when she was sure that her companion wasn't looking.

"Hi there," I said. Whenever I come back from a trip, I always feel like taking a long shower and brushing my teeth and changing clothes and dumping them in the washer, but Felix looked so fresh and relaxed, it was like he'd had a private cabin, all to himself, on the flight from Chicago.

"Hi, yourself," Felix said, looking at the slim forms of the departing flight attendants. "Need to know something real quick. You still with Annie?"

"As of a few hours ago, yes."

"Ah. And this little job you have for me…is that still on?"

"Yes, again."

Felix tore his glance away from the women. "Ah, a pity. If both questions had been in the negative, I would have quickly followed those fine airline employees, and such a night you and I would have had. Such a night."

I started walking toward the stairs that led down to the main floor. "And what kind of night would that be?"

"Sorry, I don't want to tease you with what you might have had."

"Really?"

Felix laughed. "One of these nights—not any time soon, but one of these nights—you're going to wake up at 2:00 a.m. with a snoring wife next to you, and maybe a squawling baby in the room next door, and a heavy-ass mortgage dragging you down…and you're going to wake up and say, 'Damn, I should have dumped everything and gone out with Felix that time in Manchester.' And that night *will* come."

We were now on the main floor, heading to the exit doors. "If and when that night ever comes, I'll make sure to call you."

"That doesn't sound fair."

"What the hell does fair have to do with it?"

We went through the doors and out into the frigid night air, and in the parking lot I said, "How in hell do you look so refreshed?"

"Clean living?"

"I sure as hell doubt that."

Felix said, "Then it must have been the first-class accommodations, out there and back again."

"First class? I'm not sure if I were a contributor to the Nash Pomeroy campaign that I'd be thrilled knowing they were paying for first-class airfare."

He shook his head as we approached my Explorer. "Lewis…I will make a prediction, here and now. Sometime in the next several weeks, Senator Nash Pomeroy of Massachusetts is going to drop out of the race due to health reasons, and if some enterprising reporter or blogger starts digging, stuff will be found about Senator Pomeroy that will make my first-class tickets look as scandalous as stolen pens from somebody's desk. I made an oral report to some of his campaign staff and that's the feeling I'm getting. You know, it's a queasy thing, to listen to a grown man cry, a man who's pinned all his hopes and dreams on a candidate that has such a background…. Now, what's this?"

Felix pointed to the pig scratched on the driver's side door. "Local outreach from the Clive Wallace campaign," I said, unlocking the doors.

He shrugged as he went around the front of the Ford. "Well, that's one way of getting a voter's attention, but I sure as hell don't recommend it."

SHORT-TERM PARKING was a whopping two dollars, but Felix insisted on paying for it and getting a receipt. "It's so rare that I'm doing something this legitimate, it's pretty much a new experience for me. Expense reports. Can you believe that?"

"Sure, I can," I said, and in a matter of minutes, we were heading east, on Route 101, about an hour out from Tyler. Felix stretched his legs and stretched his arms and said, "Okay, kid. What's the job? Based on your movie reference, I'd guess it's going to be a Watergate-type activity."

"I think so, but without the publicity and the book deals."

"God, now that's a hope. Who's the target?"

"There's an oppo researcher for the General Grayson campaign. His name is Chuck Bittner. Ex-navy. He wants me to make an announcement tomorrow endorsing the general and criticizing Senator Hale and his family."

Felix said, "No offense, my friend, but for a day or so, you were the lead suspect in the shooting involving the senator. Does this Bittner character really think having your endorsement is going to be a good thing?"

I checked the speedometer. Seventy miles an hour, just five miles an hour above the limit. Traffic was very light. We would make good time. "It's not the endorsement part they're excited about. It's the criticism aspect they're more interested in."

"Wait a second. You said something about the senator and his family. What do you know about the senator's family?"

I gave him a quick glance. "Keep a secret?"

"Ha-ha," he said, his voice flat. "Very funny. What's the big secret?"

"Well, it's an open secret among the Secret Service and some members of the Hale campaign, and a few others. Luckily, so far, it hasn't reached the news media, though give them some more time, I'm sure they'll get it. The senator's wife, Barbara Hale?"

"Yes, the blonde. What about her?"

"I dated her in college."

That got his attention. "You're kidding me."

"Not for a moment."

Then he laughed. "Lewis, you...you are so full of surprises, and this one, this one really tops the list. Dated the future first lady of our great land. I never knew you had it in you."

"Not sure what kind of 'it' you mean, but that's the deal. Tomorrow I'm supposed to endorse Grayson, criticize Hale and his crazed, power-hungry wife, and all will be right in the world."

"Knowing you, I know that's not going to happen. So what else?"

"The 'what else' is that if I don't go out and make this all public, Grayson's campaign will do it without me. It's a win-win for them. I go out and endorse Grayson, the media buzz will hurt Hale. I don't go out and endorse Grayson, and Grayson's campaign makes a big deal about the alleged shooter being an ex-spook with a mysterious past, connected romantically to Hale's wife, and the media buzz hurts Hale. And with just a few days before the primary, there's not enough time for Hale to recover."

"Knowing you and how you feel about Miss Wynn, I think hurting the Hale campaign is definitely off the plate."

"Definitely," I said.

We stayed silent for a few minutes, as Route 101 made its way through Epping, the self-proclaimed center of the universe. "This Bittner character...where is he tonight?"

"At the Lafayette House."

"How convenient. What can you tell me about him?"

"Arrogant. Assured. True believer in Grayson's campaign."

"What else?"

"Seems strong, in shape. Threatened me."

"Threatened you how?"

"Just said he was in better shape than me, and tried to break my upper arm to prove a point."

"Tsk, tsk," Felix said. "How childish. And what would you like me to do?"

We were now approaching Exonia, home to Phillips Exonia Academy and an obscenely high population of writers. I said, "Your usual and customary approach to making otherwise reluctant people see the error of their ways."

That brought a good laugh. "You've been with me so long, my friend, that I'd think you could do it yourself."

"I could, but I need you."

"Why, thank you. Always nice to be needed. But don't sell yourself short, Lewis. You can be a strong fellow when the circumstances require it."

I passed a lumbering semi going up a slight incline. "It's not strength I'm worried about. It's something else."

"What's that?"

"You'll do it right."

"Meaning you would do it wrong?"

I gave the top of the steering well a small slap. "Yes, I'd do it wrong. I'd go at it wrong, take it to wrong places, and probably go too far. You won't."

"Why do you think that?"

"Because…because for you, it's professional. For me, it's personal. He wants to use me to hurt the Hale campaign, hurt someone I had fond feelings for and someone I currently have fond feelings for…and he brought up my past service and tried to use that against me. Ticked me off big-time. So, yeah, Felix, for me, it's quite personal. I know you'll do what has to be done, and I'll be there as well. But I trust you and your abilities. Which is why I need you. And why I thank you in advance."

"And you're welcome, too. In advance."

There was another moment of silence as we went over I-95, fairly busy at this late hour, and Route 101 had shrunk to two lanes, and the marshlands and frozen sands of Tyler Beach were now beckoning us.

Felix said, "Need to ask you something else."

"Go ahead."

"The fake Secret Service agent. The one . . . the one dumped in your front lawn."

I sighed. "Yeah, I was thinking the same thing."

"If this Bittner character is desperate to use you to stop the Hale campaign, then there's a good chance this isn't their latest try. Maybe Bittner—or somebody connected with him—was behind the whole deal. Getting this Spenser Harris character to talk to you. Lifting your .357 Ruger. Hoping and planning that you'd be at the Hale rally that day. Makes a rugged sort of sense, you know."

"I know. If we have time, maybe we'll chat that point up with Mr. Bittner."

I could see Felix's grin from the glow of the dashboard lights. "Then that's a plan."

"Just curious, is our fake Secret Service agent still where we left him?"

Felix chastised me. "He's your fake Secret Service agent, and yes, he's still where we left him. And I know I said I would try to find out something about him, but in my spare time I've come up with squat."

"I suppose getting his fingerprints and trying to have Diane Woods do something with them is out of the question."

"Please," he said. "Detective Sergeant Woods already has a very low opinion of me. Why should we reinforce that?"

"All right."

Now we were racing along the clear asphalt of Route 101, approaching the few lights of the low buildings before us that were the heart of Tyler Beach. From the marshland the road then tightened up, narrowed on both sides by rental cottages closed up for the season, and there was not a single lit home or cottage about us as the road rose up to intersect with Atlantic Avenue.

I certainly hoped my new friend James from the Clive Wallace campaign was out there on this dark street tonight, trying to talk to whatever voters were huddled by themselves in the cold and dark.

We stopped at the intersection, crept forward through some

parking areas. The Ashburnham House hotel and restaurant was to our right, and it was the only open place within view. I made a left and we went up Atlantic Avenue, heading north, about eight minutes or so from the Lafayette House.

Felix looked at the shuttered homes and businesses, the empty parking lots, the deserted side streets, and he said, "This time of year, and this little slice of paradise, looking like this, could make almost anybody slit their throat. How bloody depressing."

"Buck up. In six months this place will be packed with cars and tourists, and the primary will be a distant memory."

"Yeah, but it'll come back again, in winter. The great desolation. Empty streets, empty buildings. Like we suffered through a plague year or something. Blah. Enough to turn most guys to religion or legitimacy."

"Most guys?" I asked, trying to keep my voice innocent. "Like you, Felix?"

"That's why I said most guys. Keep quiet or you'll miss our turn."

Which was doubtful, since the Lafayette House was now before us, in its white Victorian splendor, but I guess Felix was tired of showing his metrosexual side, and that was fine with me. I turned left and was able to find a space, which pleased me. We got out and I left the doors unlocked—if we had to leave quickly, fumbling to unlock said doors could cause problems—and then Felix asked for a moment to go through his bag.

"Of course," I said, as he rummaged through his leather carrying case, and then he said, "Ah," and placed something in his coat pocket. I caught up with him as we went toward the entrance, and said, "As a matter of record, sir, are you carrying?"

"Yep."

"And what kind of weapon do you have?"

"This," he said, and he showed me what he had just placed in his coat. I looked at him and looked at the object, which quickly went back into his coat.

"Tape?" I asked. "Duct tape?"

"Absolutely."

"And why duct tape?"

Felix said, "Ever tell you the tale of my uncle Julius?"

"Nope, but I have a feeling you're going to."

"That's right. Uncle Julius was a disappointment to some family members, since he ran a small, legitimate hardware store in the North End, down in Boston. A little of this, a little of that. Everything from pipes to tools to small appliances. Was proud of showing people how to make small repairs around their homes and apartments. He told me once that most people could get away with two things in their home repair kit."

"And what's that?"

"WD-40 lubricant to make things go, and duct tape to make things stop."

I had to laugh. "Good for Uncle Julius. And you have the tape because…"

"Because someone's being a pain in the ass to you, I'm going to make it stop. That all right?"

"That's perfect."

"Good."

We went into the lobby of the Lafayette House and I saw that the gift shop, the site of my earlier triumph that day, was now closed. There were just a few people in the lobby but the lounge looked pretty well attended, with someone playing the piano, and a few drunken souls were trying to sing along in such a manner that I couldn't even identify the tune. I found a house phone and after a moment or two with the hotel operator, got the room of Chuck Bittner.

"Yeah?" came the foggy reply.

"Chuck, it's Lewis Cole."

"Lewis Cole…Jesus, man, do you know what time it is?"

"No, I don't, and that's not the reason I called you. I'm…I'm ready to make an announcement. I just need to run something by you."

Now he didn't seem so asleep. "Good. Where are you?"

"In the lobby."

"Room 312," he said, and that was that.

I hung up the room phone and Felix fell in step with me as we headed to the bank of elevators. As we waited for an elevator, Felix said, "All right with you, I'll take the lead here. Okay?"

"Sounds fine."

"Way I see it, you want a promise from him to leave you alone, not to bring you into the campaign. Correct?"

"One hundred percent. But Felix…"

The indicator light dinged and the door slid open. We went in and he said, "Yes?"

"He's going to be a tough one," I said. "Ex-navy. Full-time campaign worker for General Grayson. True believer in the general's cause. He might not roll over for you like other guys you've…encountered."

Felix gently pushed the button for the third floor. "Don't fret, son. Don't fret. You forget how I do love a challenge."

"So you do consider this a challenge?"

Felix had a faint smile on his face and then the door opened up, and he said, "Hush. Just let your uncle Felix make it all right."

# FOURTEEN

WE WENT DOWN the soft-lit hallway, found Room 312 with no difficulty, and Felix said quietly, "Okay, you stand in front of the door, so he can see you through the peephole. Make sure you're standing there, nice and still, and when the door opens up, you take two steps to the right, wait, and then follow me in. Once you're in—and this is important—don't touch a damn thing. Got it?"

"Yeah. Stand in front of the door. Nice and still. Two steps to the left and—"

"To the right, moron, to the right, didn't you hear what I just said?"

I gave him a smirk to let him know he wasn't the only one playing games here tonight, and he shook his head and I stood before the door to Room 312 and gave it a sharp knock. From inside I could make out the low murmur of a television set and then the sound of someone approaching the door. I stood still and quiet, but out of the corner of my eye, I made out Felix to my left, standing flat against the wall, and now he was wearing thin black leather gloves. Damn Felix. I hadn't even seen him do that.

The sound of the door unlocking almost startled me, and then I took two steps to the right and—

Felix moved whip-snap fast, going right into the room, one hand on the shoulder of a very surprised Chuck Bittner, wearing a white terry-cloth robe and—

A heavy, meaty sound as Felix punched him square in the nose, and—

I followed in, the door shutting behind me. Chuck was on the ground, and Felix quickly tore off a strip of duct tape, slapped it over Chuck's mouth, and Chuck scrambled to move away from the pain and the attention, and Felix got up and rolled Chuck over on his side. Chuck then tried to take advantage of that, by clambering up on his hands and knees, but like some damn wrestling move from TV, Felix slammed into him with his whole body weight, falling onto the man's back with his knees, and that must have hurt like hell.

Chuck collapsed with an "oomph" and a groan, and in the fast mess that followed, Felix worked quickly again, binding Chuck's wrists together with duct tape. Felix got up, breathing just a bit hard, and then he grabbed Chuck by his upper arms and maneuvered him onto an unmade bed. Chuck hit the bed on his side, another moan following, and he looked at me and I looked at him. Blood was streaming from his nose, trickling down the shiny gray duct tape. Felix looked to me and said, "Glass of water, if I may? And don't forgot what I said about touching things."

I went into the open bathroom, got a small drinking glass, holding it with a white washcloth, and filled it with water using another washcloth on the tap. I came back out into the room and the television was just a bit louder. Felix took the glass and drank it all, and then put the glass in his pocket—no use leaving DNA evidence behind—and came back over to the bed. Chuck looked at me and looked at Felix, and started making grunting noises from behind the tape.

Felix shook his head, took a chair and sat across from Chuck. Felix said, "Before we begin, my apologies. I have the utmost respect for men and women in and out of uniform who've volunteered to serve. I might have been in the service as well, except for a juvenile record that made even the most aggressive recruiter turn gray with dismay. So. Having said that, my apologies for breaking into your room, sir, and causing you pain and discomfort."

I stood there, waiting, and Felix leaned over and said, "But apologies aside, sir, I have loyalty to that gentleman standing by the wall, a loyalty I take quite seriously, and before the two of us leave here tonight, we're going to reach an understanding. If I make myself clear, just nod your head."

There was no nod, just a vigorous shaking of the head, and violent grunting noises that, if they had been decipherable, were no doubt laced with a host of obscenities. If this bothered Felix, he didn't show it. He didn't have to. There were other ways.

Another strip of tape appeared in his hands, and this time, it was shoved against his bleeding nose. There was a muffled howl as Felix worked the tape, blocking both nostrils, and Chuck's chest started heaving. Felix leaned in again and said, "Nothing works one hundred percent, so I'm sure you're getting some oxygen into your system…but is it enough? We'll see…. In the meantime, stop flailing around and give me a nod that you understand what I'm saying, and the tape comes off your nose."

Chuck's fleshy face started changing colors, and then, movement stopped and I thought he had passed out, but no, he nodded. Briefly and quickly, but he nodded. And true to his word, Felix removed the tape from his nose, and there was a hoarse, rasping sound as Chuck started panting through his nose.

Felix, his voice now soothing, said, "Ah, now, that wasn't hard, was it? Just a little nod and you started breathing again. A wonderful thing. We're very proud of you, sir."

The breathing became more normal, but there was anger behind those eyes, a deep and abiding anger that made me want to look away, but Felix would not move, would not flinch, and he stayed right there, right in the man's face.

Felix said, "I don't think I need to tell you, but I'm going to remind you of what's next. I can take the tape off your mouth and you can start in on how my friend and I broke in here, assaulted you, and how you're going to have us arrested and ruin us and sue us and take all our money and our homes. It's what I'd expect from a man in your position. I've heard it before. And you know what? It doesn't mean a damn thing. So let's not waste each other's time with such nonsense. We came in here for a specific reason, one specific goal, and once that goal's been achieved, we'll all move on. Do you understand what I'm saying? If so, do favor me a with another nod."

I waited, wondering how far Chuck would go in fighting Felix, but there was just the faintest of head movements. Felix took it and there was such pleasure in his voice, I almost expected him to start clapping.

"Very good again, sir," Felix said. "So. Let us begin. Here's the agreement we're going to reach. You and the Grayson campaign are going to leave Lewis Cole alone. You're not to contact him or bother him in any way. You're not going to even mention his name in your staff meetings. You're not to leak information about him to any friendly press or Internet blogger. In other words, you are going to forget his name, his appearance, his life, his background, his very existence. Now. Have you understood everything I've said? Have you? How about a little nod for the home team?"

The eyes were still burning with hate and anger, but there was that faint nod. "Good. Now, having gotten that out of the way, I'm sure you're wondering, what's in it for you? What possible benefit do you gain from having agreed to all that?"

Felix carefully crossed his legs, clasped his hands over his knees. "A smart and legitimate question. And here's the answer. We depart. At once. Never to bother you again, never to cross paths again, never even to breathe the same air in the same room. We depart, you depart, and after the primary next Tuesday, you and the general move on to South Carolina and all is right with the world. Do we have an agreement?"

The air seemed heavy in the room as we waited. I suppose I should have felt guilty or embarrassed or upset at what Felix was doing to this man, but I remembered Bittner's touch upon my arm, and the words he spoke about my service in the Department of Defense. I had lost dear ones many years ago that were close enough to be family, especially one woman (ah, Cissy, came the quick and sharp memory), and having this man before me try to use that service and those memories for political purposes...it was like someone urinating on the altar at Notre Dame at the height of a sacred Mass.

Not to mention the threats that would have impacted both Barbara and Annie.

So I felt fine. But still, I waited.

Chuck looked at me and then looked at Felix, and there was the nod.

Felix unfolded his legs. "Ah, good. Now that we have this agreement, I guess I can take the tape off and we'll be on our way...."

Was that it? I wondered. Was that going to be it? But I guess I knew Felix better than I thought, for when he leaned forward to remove the tape, he suddenly stopped and sat back down in the chair.

Another few moments of waiting, and Felix quickly shook his head. "No. It's not going to work. I mean…we're all men here, men of the world, worldly men…how can any agreement we reach last when you're under such duress? What would stop you from calling the police after we leave? I mean, Lewis here would probably skate, being such good friends with the local gendarmes, but not me. As you could probably deduce, I've had my share of police attention over the years. No, I'm afraid this isn't going to work. I'm going to have to come up with something else. Lewis?"

"Yes?"

"Any ideas?"

"Fresh out," I said. "But give me a few minutes or thereabouts. I'm sure I'll come up with something."

Felix turned back to the former navy man and said, "So, that's the quandary we're in. You see, if you were anybody else, I wouldn't have any problem. Pain and the threat of pain are wonderful motivating factors. A few minutes with an exposed lightbulb and some tweezers, you'd be ready to sign over the title property to your home to make me leave. But once we start down that path, well, there're no good choices available to us. You can still go back on your promise to us…even more, if pain is involved, because no matter what pull Lewis might have with the police, it won't go very far if pain is involved. So it has to be something else. Something else that matters to you, something that will ensure that whatever promise you made here to leave Lewis alone actually sticks."

Felix then got up and walked around the room, looked at the television set—which was broadcasting a C-SPAN program about the day's speeches from the different primary candidates—and then grabbing the remote, he sat on the bed with Chuck. Felix patted him on the shoulder and then started flipping through the channels, and then he toggled a switch on the remote that brought up a menu selection guide on the television.

"Time for a little contemporary history lesson," Felix said, stretching himself out as Chuck kept his hateful stare on me. "Do you know what the single largest entertainment source—in terms of money made—is on cable and satellite television nowadays? Do you? Oh, I'm sorry, you can't reply. Well, it's not much of a challenging quiz. The answer is, of course, pornography. Hard to believe, but it's true. All these large hotel and motel corporations, and legitimate cable and satellite television networks, they all have a hand in promoting and trafficking hard-core pornography. Oh, this type of investment doesn't get much play in the news media—especially since some of the very same news media have a hefty stake in porn—and some conservative groups try to embarrass them to keep them from doing such kinds of business, but you know what? Even in the most conservative states, there's a healthy demand for it. And when there's demand, business will follow. Such that even in a quaint New Hampshire resort like Tyler Beach, the most high-grade hotel, the Lafayette House, will offer to its adult consumers a wide range of pornographic delights that even thirty years ago might have gotten you some serious jail time in any major city across the nation."

I tried not to smile. I had an idea where Felix was going. Felix went through the menu choices and said, "Each man to his own poison, I say, and to each man his taste in porn. Lord knows I have no halo over my head…so let's take a look at some of these titles. Hmmm…*Locker Room Studfest, Saturday Night Cruising Delight, Buns and Rods of Steel,*—not really *Casablanca,* but they sure do offer a varied sort of entertainment. Don't you think?"

Felix rolled off the bed and his voice got sharp. "So this is how it's going to be. I'm going to remove the tape. You're going to say in a nice, clear voice that nothing is required of Lewis, that nothing is going to happen to Lewis. And if I remove the tape and I don't hear those words, then the tape goes back on, and your television starts displaying the latest and greatest in gay male pornography. Lewis and I stay here for a while. Order lots of room service. Play the television really, really loud, so when management comes and kicks us out…well, the story the next day, just a few days from the Tuesday primary, is that a campaign adviser to General Tucker Grayson entertained two men in his hotel room while watching well-muscled men have their way with each other on the television. All programming, of course, recorded on the room bill. Do we have an understanding now, Mr. Bittner?"

A quick nod this time. No hesitation. "Good," Felix said. "I'm going to remove the tape and wait for those magic words."

Chuck winced as the tape came off—some skin was probably caught in the adhesive—and he breathed in some and said, "You have my word."

"Glad to hear that," Felix said. "But let's put some more meat into that."

Chuck closed his eyes and said, "What you said…nothing is going to happen to Lewis Cole. No news story, no news leak. Nothing. You have my word on it."

Felix turned to me and said, "Satisfied?"

"Almost," I said. "One other thing."

Chuck cursed and said, "Changing the rules of the game already, are we?"

"No," I said. "Just being political for a moment. I'm sure you know the drill."

"Fine, asshole," he spat out. "What else?"

"Spenser Harris," I said.

"Spenser who?"

"Spenser Harris. Is he an operative of yours?"

He shook his head, licked his dry lips. "Never heard of him."

"Perhaps under another name. He's in his late thirties. Trim. Black hair, a few streaks of white on the sides. Tanned skin. Fit. Likes to dress well. Occasionally he pretends to be a Secret Service agent."

Another shake of the head. "Look, I don't know the name, don't know the description. You can blackmail me all you want, do whatever you want, but I don't know Spenser Harris, and I don't know anybody like him."

Felix was still looking at me, raised an eyebrow, and I shrugged. Felix rolled Chuck over on his side and like magic, a folding knife appeared in Felix's gloved hand, and after a moment or two of sawing, the tape at Chuck's arms was cut free.

Felix stepped back and I got up. Chuck rolled over and looked at me, the hate still in his eyes.

I said, "We'll be on our way, but I'll leave you with one more thought, Chuck. This is our turf. Our field of battle. Even if you check out of here tomorrow and think of doing something funny with me, we have friends with the management here, friends that owe us favors. So don't think that coming up with an invoice showing your porn movie rental can't be arranged in a very short period of time. Enough to impact this primary, or any other future primary we choose. Got it?"

"Asshole," Chuck said, sitting up in bed, tearing at the strips of tape around his wrists, fingers fumbling some.

"Probably, but you invited me to bring it on. Which is what I did."

He rubbed his face and said, "Pussy boy. You had to come in here with muscle to do your dirty work. What kind of fucking wimp are you?"

I was going to say something but Felix was quicker. He said, "Truth be told, sir, I'm the wimp."

"What?"

Felix put the knife away. "Lewis told me about his past encounters with you and your threats. He told me what he had planned for you. Trust me on this, I'm the wimp in this equation. I managed to calm him down, for if he had come up here by himself, you'd now be in that bathtub, bleeding, still bound with duct tape but missing a few inches of flesh that I'm sure you're awfully fond of."

He said, "Get the fuck out. Now."

Felix said, "Ready?"

"You got it."

So we got up and we left.

ONCE WE WENT DOWN in an elevator and made our way through the lobby, outside the cold air was refreshing and it felt good to be out of that room. We paused in the parking lot and Felix said, "You okay?"

"I'm fine. And you?"

Felix brought his hands together, up to his face, blew warm

air into them. "Always nice to practice one's skills, to see that you still got it. And tonight, I still got it. Makes me feel good about myself. You sure you're okay?"

"I'm all right…though I have to admit I feel guilty."

"Guilty? About what?"

I started walking to my Ford. "Guilty about lying to Chuck."

"When did you lie to Chuck?"

"When I said we were friends with management. Maybe you are but I'm not. I think management here is a jerk. But it made sense to tell Chuck otherwise."

I'm not sure Felix realized the joking nature of my comment, for he took it seriously. He said, "Well, we all have compromises we have to live with. I'm sure you'll get over it."

"Yeah."

At my Ford I turned and looked back at the Lafayette Hotel. I had Felix here at my side, and with his skills and talents, I'm sure we could have returned back to the hotel and have gotten to work, and might have been quickly successful breaking in and finding that surveillance tape.

Yet…

We had been lucky tonight, getting in and doing our business and getting out with an agreement that pleased me, for not only protecting my sorry butt but also removing a potential embarrassment for a political candidate I didn't have particular allegiance to, but who was important to someone very dear to me. So, all in all, it had been a productive night. I didn't want to push it.

"Lewis?"

"Yeah?"

Felix looked over at me from the passenger's side of my Ford. "You okay?"

"Sure," I said, opening the door. "Just daydreaming for a second."

"That's fine," he said. "But how about daydreaming your way to getting my tired ass to home and to bed."

"No problem," I said, and in a matter of moments, we were on our way north, back on Atlantic Avenue.

FELIX LIVES IN North Tyler, on Rosemount Lane, a street that juts off to the right and which has fairly nice views of the ocean. There are six homes on Rosemount Lane, and five of them are clustered together near the road's entrance. Felix's stands alone, on a slight rise at the end of the road, and though he has never come right out and said it, I know he likes the location of the house. Homes like his are easy to defend.

I drove into his driveway and he said, "Coffee? Drink? Further conversation?"

"I thought you wanted to get to bed."

"Hell, Lewis, I may be getting old, but I'm not ready to be buried."

"Neither am I, but I've had a long day. Thanks for your help. I owe you one."

He grinned. "We've gone beyond determining who owes whom anymore, Lewis. You just take care of yourself."

"I will. And are you finished with the Nash Pomeroy campaign?"

"Oh, probably," he said, retrieving his leather bag and putting it on his lap. "Let's be honest. When you're sent out on a research trip like this, to find out oppo stuff on your candidate, the people who hire you are hoping for the best. They've heard the rumors, they've looked for the facts, and now they want to know the truth. It's like the guy who hires a private investigator to see if his wife is cheating on him. Deep in his heart he knows, but he wants to grasp at the straw and hope that it's all a mistake. Well, the guys who hired me…tomorrow they're going to fire me, no doubt about it, once I submit my written report. But I've already been paid in advance, my job is done, and there you go."

"A nice, professional attitude, Felix. You'll go far."

"I'm sure. And speaking of going places…you do well by that Annie girl, okay?"

"What makes you say that?"

"Just a thought. You back her up. I know she's working long hours and doesn't have much time for you and all that happy crap, but she's doing something important. And it can't last too much longer. So you don't screw this one up. She's…she's made you a better person, my friend. You smile more, you talk more, and you don't walk around anymore like the weight of the goddamn world is on your shoulders. So. Got it?"

"Got it, Dr. Felix," I said. "You go on and let me sleep."

"That I will," he said, opening the door. "You just have fun not sleeping alone, all right?"

"Good night, Felix. You want I should walk you to the door?"

"Damn it, like I said, I'm not dead yet."

He slammed the door shut and maybe it was just the way the night had gone, but I did wait until he got up to the door and went inside, and the lights came on. He didn't need my protection or my backup, but still, I wanted to make sure everything was all right.

A hell of a goal.

I backed out and went home.

AT HOME THERE WERE four messages on my answering machine, three from groups reminding me that in the event I had been living in my cellar for the past six months, that next Tuesday was indeed Primary Day, and that my vote was sorely needed so that the forces of darkness and Satan would not emerge to march upon the land, sowing war and pestilence in their path, or something like that. I deleted them all.

The fourth message was from Annie, and was to the point: "Lewis, you wouldn't believe how much grief I got from my bosses about your little dinner stunt tonight. In fact, Tom wanted to punish me by sending me up to Colebrook, right then and there, until cooler heads prevailed. So, yeah, your little dinner idea really caused some heartburn tonight…."

Her voice dribbled off some and I waited, not breathing, just listening, when she laughed and said, "And you know what? It was worth it, worth it very much. Thanks again. You're the best, my dear, the very best. Sleep well and I'll talk to you tomorrow."

I smiled at that and went into the living room, watched some of the late night cable news, and interspersed among all the talking heads, I saw a fresh clip of Senator Hale and his lovely wife, Barbara, at a campaign event way up north, in a mill city called Berlin. At the rally I saw the confident look of the senator, and the loving look of his wife, who was at his side throughout his remarks, and when that bit of political news was over, I shut the television off and went to bed.

THE NEXT MORNING I hesitated at the door, before embarking on my usual routine of getting my morning newspapers from Stephanie at the gift shop across the way. It had been my routine for months, and save for those times when the weather was really rotten, or I was ill, I had never skipped it, not once. But this morning was different. I wasn't sure if I wanted to be there, on the off chance of running into Chuck Bittner after our little adventure from last night. I was not sure how an encounter like that would be, but I had a feeling it wouldn't be a particularly cheerful one.

So maybe I wouldn't go today.

Maybe.

I thought about it some more and then grabbed my coat. The hell with it. I was going to keep to my routine and not let anything bother me. That was my decision, and shortly thereafter, I was trudging my way up the packed snow to the place where my newspapers awaited me.

Funny thing about decisions. The simplest ones sometimes can have the most deadly and far-reaching consequences, for if I had skipped getting the papers that morning, my, how things would have turned out differently.

So differently.

THE GIFT SHOP WAS crowded and Stephanie had to wait on a practically UN General Assembly of guests—I heard German, French, and something that might have been Korean—before she came to me. She looked around the store and smiled and said, "Tell you something, if you've got time."

"Sure, I've got time."

"Ever tell you where I grew up?"

I thought for a moment. "Someplace in Pennsylvania, I believe."

"That's one way of putting it. Yes, someplace in Pennsylvania. Foley's Corners. Tiny little place that shouldn't have existed, except there was coal in the hills, coal that was easy to get to. But by the time I came around, the coal was gone, the coal company was gone, and there wasn't much left for the people there."

Truth is, I didn't have that much time to talk to her—I hadn't called Annie yet and there was still that damn magazine column to finish, along with other pressing issues—but this was the most Stephanie had ever said about her past, so I stood there, polite, and nodded in all the right places.

She went on. "Those people included my dad, whose own father and grandfather had managed to support a pretty big family on a coal company's salary. But by the time he got married and had me and two other daughters, well, jobs were mostly part-time work, stitched together here and there. Some fathers adjusted, some fathers rolled with the punches. My dad wasn't one of them."

She took a breath and I saw that her hands were trembling. "My dad…well, I don't know if it would have been different, if the coal were still there…but all I remember are the shouts, the alarms, the broken dishes and the empty beer bottles, piled up in the rear yard by the toolshed. Lots and lots of empty beer bottles."

"Must have been rough," I said. "I'm sorry."

She nodded, bit her lip. "I'm sorry, too. Sorry that I'm going on so long, telling you this. But there's a point, Lewis, if you just give me a few more seconds."

"Absolutely."

"Point being…Dad was a bully. And when he wasn't hitting my mom, he was hitting me, or hitting my sisters. The hitting went on right up until I joined the air force, and when I came back from Texas, after basic training, that night…it stopped. I dragged him out to the rear yard and I…well, I made it stop. I know it sounds pathetic, a daughter beating up on her old, drunken father in the family's backyard, but I don't care. He never hit my mom or my sisters again. Not ever."

With that, she reached under the counter, pulled out my morning newspapers. This morning, unlike any other morning, they were folded over and held together by a rubber band. I left the money on the counter. She handed them over to me and I almost dropped them, from the unexpected weight.

I looked into her face, now content, now relaxed. "Lewis, I've always hated bullies, especially bullies who pick on women. And what you did yesterday for that college girl…it was special. And I had to pay you back for it. Just so you know."

I hefted the weighted newspaper, my hand tingling with anticipation, knowing exactly what was in there. "Stephanie… thanks. Thank you very much."

She shook her head quickly. "It's nothing. I should have done it for you earlier. I really should have…but I was scared. Scared like I was when I was a girl, before leaving home. And I don't like being scared like that."

I started out of the gift shop. "I'll get it back to you, soon as I can."

Stephanie smiled. "I know you will."

# FIFTEEN

IF IT WASN'T FOR THE SNOW and ice still on the ground, I would have trotted back to my house, but cracking my skull or losing the videotape in a snowdrift wouldn't have been too bright. So I took my time and I got into my home safely, dumped my coat on the floor, and was unsnapping the rubber band from the newspapers as I entered the living room. The newspapers fell away and there it was, a standard black VHS tape. I turned it over and there was a white label with neat printing—PARKING LOT SUR-VEILLANCE—followed by beginning and end dates. I turned on my television and VCR and got to work.

I was surprised at how easy it was. The view was of the parking lot, all right, in shiny black and white. There was a fishbowl effect with the lens, skewing the view at the edge of the screen. At the lower right hand side of the screen was a time and date stamp, which was helpful since it wasn't a continuous video. It was more like a series of snapshots, one every few seconds. But after a few minutes of rewinding and playing, I got it down to the moment that morning when Spenser Harris had made his last visit to my home.

I leaned forward on the couch, to get a better view, I suppose, and I let the tape play through that special morning. Everything looked quiet. Two sedans and an SUV were parked at the south end of the lot. Very normal. Very quiet.

There. Movement to the left of the screen, the north end of the lot, near my driveway, and I froze the tape—

And shivered.

Sure. I recognized that figure, all right.

It was me, heading up to the Lafayette House to get my morning newspapers.

I don't know why, but seeing myself on the television screen, in not-so-living black and white, creeped me out. The little form there, in electrons and bits and bytes, that was me. Innocently going up to a hotel to get reading material, not knowing, not even imagining what was ahead of me. It was like a time machine, glimpsing back into the past. Almost as weird as seeing that tape of myself the other day, vomiting so magnificently in the parking lot of the Tyler Conference Center.

I shivered again, let the tape play through.

The electronic Lewis Cole left the screen. Another car parked. Then a white panel truck came in, parked at an angle at the north end of the lot, where my driveway was. A guy came out carrying a large leather bag. I remembered the truck. An electrician's truck, if I was right. Yeah. Some guy named Jimmy. Could Spenser and his killer have gotten to my house that way?

A few more frames clicked through.

Nope.

A black car appeared, maneuvered its way to the north end of the lot. The car had black tinted windows. The way it was parked, the driver's side was obscured by the panel truck, but the passenger's side was clear enough. The door opened up.

And a living, breathing, talking Spenser Harris got out.

"I'll be damned," I whispered, leaning even farther toward the television. I reversed and played the tape again. A black luxury car, and Spenser Harris, stepping out.

So far, so good.

I let the tape play on.

Spenser leaned into the open passenger door, talking to the driver, it looked like, and then he stood up. The door was slammed shut. Spenser moved off to the left, disappeared from view.

I waited.

The phone rang, making me jump. I let it ring and ring and went back to the television, my own little time machine.

Even though it was partially blocked by the panel truck, the driver's side door then opened up. Somebody got out. A figure in a coat. That's all I saw. Couldn't tell if it was male or female. But the driver went to the left, too, following Spenser.

I waited.

Then the figure came back, opened the driver's door, leaned in and—

Got in, closed the door.

But there was something there.

I stopped, rewound, played.

Stopped, rewound, played.

And again.

The driver and no-doubt shooter was wearing a white trench coat of some sorts, the belt tied at the waist, and black gloves.

I rubbed my chin.

Couldn't see a face, couldn't see a head. Was there anything else?

I let the tape play again.

Oh yes, there was something else.

Stopped, rewound, played.

And saw the car maneuver its way out of the spot by backing up, going forward, backing up, and then leaving the lot.

The car was now recognizable. It was a black luxury car, made in Great Britain, the latest model of the Jaguar XJ8, and I could see that the front license plate was New Hampshire, that it was vanity, and though I couldn't make out all of the letters, I was positive what the front plate said.

WHTKER.

I shut off the television, ejected the tape, and got the hell out.

NORTH OF THE CENTER of Tyler, Route 1 widens some, allowing a depressing series of mini-malls and strip stores to fester and take growth. Paula Quinn of the *Chronicle* once told me that it was like the malignancy that had grasped so many of Massachusetts's North Shore communities had infected Tyler, and who was I to disagree?

Stuck between an auto parts supply store and a sub shop was a tiny place called Mert's Electronics, about a hundred yards north of Tyler center. Parking wasn't a problem so early in the morning and so early in the year, and inside the store, I breathed in for a moment, taking in the view and the scent. The scent was of burned wire and dusty radio tubes and old ways of communicating, and the view…old television sets piled up next to CB radio gear next to cardboard boxes of circuit boards and radio tubes, and shelves and shelves of dusty gear that looked old when Marconi had retired.

At the rear of the store was a waist-high counter, and an older man was sitting back there, eyeing some papers as they came out of a computer printer, and he nodded at me as I approached.

"Lewis," he said.

"Mert."

Mert Hinderline was retired navy after thirty years in the service, with mermaids tattooed on his forearms as a constant reminder, and a ready smile and dapper little mustache that wouldn't look out of place on a 1940s film star. He was smart and affable and knew electronics, and his store wouldn't last anywhere else, I guess, except for Tyler and its collection of eccentrics. Like me.

"What can I do for you?" he said, putting another piece of paper down.

I held up the tape. "Need something duped. Two copies, if that's all right."

"The whole tape?"

"Just ten minutes' worth. Got it cued up right where I want it to start."

He held out a beefy hand. "Pass it over. Can do it right now and you can stick around as it dupes, if you'd like."

"Sure," I said, dragging over a metal stool. "I can wait."

He went to the rear of the store and out of view, and I heard movement and switches being thrown, and I looked to the printer, to see what he was doing. Next to the printer was an old Apple computer, and displayed on its monitor was a page of a Web site dedicated to a political action committee opposed to the current administration that used the words "storm trooper" and "fascist" and "book burner" a lot. The printer still ground along, and I saw what Mert was doing: He was printing off screen shots of the Web page.

Seemed like a waste of time and paper, and when Mert came back and said, "All right, ten minutes and we'll be through," I asked him about the printing.

"Looks interesting," I said, pointing to the stack, "but I never thought of you being interested in politics that much. Especially fringe politics."

"Oh. That." He scratched his ear and said, "I'll tell you, but you've got to promise that you're not going to laugh at me."

"That's not a problem, Mert," I said. "Last summer, when my VCR croaked, the manufacturer said dump it and buy a new one. You got it up and running again in fifteen minutes with a fifty-cent part. So, no, I'm not going to laugh at you."

Mert grinned and picked up another sheet from the printer tray, and put it in a separate pile. "I'm a volunteer. Belong to some thing called the Gutenberg Society. We're preserving our historical record for future generations."

"Oh."

Mert said, "I know what you mean by that. What does that have to do with printing off Web site pages and e-mails and other electronic stuff? Quick answer is, everything. You see, in this wonderful and wild electronic age we're in, it's actually easier to do research on the Eisenhower administration than this administration and its immediate predecessors. Too many documents are now in an electronic format. The older presidents, they did everything on paper. Stored properly, paper can last hundreds of years. Electronic files? Who knows? There are gigabytes of information stored on electronic files that can no longer be read, because computers and their operating systems have surged ahead, leaving older files useless."

From beneath the counter he pulled out a framed photograph, a black-and-white picture of a young man in a sailor's uniform standing on a ship. He said, "My dad. Was a quartermaster aboard the USS Converse in World War II. A hundred years from now, this photo will still look like this. Same thing with my wedding day picture of me and Cathy. But there's color pictures of me, taken in the 1980s aboard my own ships, that have already faded and will be blank in fifty years. And don't get me going on digital cameras. All these wonderful photos, and who knows if they can still be viewed in ten or twenty years when new operating systems are being introduced."

I nodded. "Read something similar to that about authors and

their books. Used to be, researchers could look in the papers of a writer from fifty or a hundred years ago. Could look at the various drafts, see the handwritten notes, the sections that were crossed out, the inserts that were made, and could see the process of how a writer reached the final version of a novel. But now...so many authors edit on-screen, and make changes right up to when the book is finished, so all that's in the records are the final versions. There's no record of how the author got there."

"Exactly," Mert said, and he gestured to the computer screen. "So that's what we do in our little volunteer group. Digital information can be manipulated, can be changed, can disappear. So what we do, we make hard copies, as much as we can, so that future generations can have an idea of who we were and what we did. And not have to worry about the final record being cleaned up and edited."

From the back room came a ding as a kitchen timer sounded, and Mert got off his stool and went to the rear of the store and came back with three tapes. He handed them to me and I thanked him and said, "How much?"

"Oh, let's say five bucks for the cost of the tapes. Sound fair?"

"More than fair. Sounds pretty damn generous."

I handed him a five-dollar bill and he said, "Well, there was a discount. For two things."

"What's that?"

"For not laughing at me, and for listening to me."

I picked up the tapes. "My pleasure."

Mert smiled and sat down next to his busy printer. "Just remember what I said, Lewis. Digital information is wonderful. But it can be manipulated."

"Just like people," I said.

He nodded in agreement. "Just like people."

WITH TAPES IN HAND, I drove south about ten minutes to the Tyler post office, where I mailed something out and then checked my incoming mail. My box was chock-full when I pulled it out, and I went over to one of the counters and sorted through everything. I had fourteen pieces of mail.

One was my checking account statement from the Tyler Cooperative Bank, and another was a mailing from the National Space Society. The rest of the mail was brightly colored flyers divided as so: pro-Hale, pro-Grayson, pro-Hale, anti-Hale, anti-Nash, anti-tax, pro-tax, anti-gun, pro-Grayson, pro-Wallace, pro-gay marriage, and anti-Grayson.

I gathered them up and tossed them in an overflowing trash can, also filled with similar messages of democracy.

Just another day in the land of the first-in-the-nation primary.

A QUICK STOP back at the Lafayette House, and I walked quickly up into the lobby and to the gift shop. Stephanie was using a label gun to put price labels on Tyler Beach sweatshirts, and I went over to her and handed back a copy of that day's *New York Times,* wrapped around the original surveillance tape and held again by a rubber band.

"Sorry," I said. "You must have given me an extra paper this morning, Steph."

Her smile looked relieved. "Thanks for taking the time to bring it back."

I looked at her, a smile on my face as well. "I owe you one."

She put the paper and surveillance tape under the counter. "No, no debt, Lewis. It's all taken care of. I hope it helped."

"More than you know," I said, and I got out of there as quickly as I got in.

A PHONE CALL LATER and I was in the office of Detective Sergeant Diane Woods, south of the Lafayette House, and I said to her, "Well, I'm pleased that I can get you on a Saturday, but I'm not sure how pleased you are."

She shook her head, leaned back in her chair. "Not very, and neither is my sweetie Kara, but primary season will be over in three short days, and that will be just fine. I love making detail money but you know what? It's a nice little bundle that's going to pay for a vacation to Cozumel next winter for the both of us, but I'm getting sick of all the candidates and their precious little staffs. 'Why can't the traffic go there instead of here?' 'Can't you do something about the news helicopter overhead?' 'Can't you put the protesters over there behind a fence?' Bah. Four years from now, let Vermont have this little circus."

Diane's office is in the rear of the one-story concrete cube that is the Tyler Police Station, and her desk was reasonably clear. I always told her that a live camera feed depicting her desktop could tell an alien species what season it was in New Hampshire: a clean desk meant it was winter, and an overflowing desk of papers and files meant it was summer. Diane had told me at the time that any aliens that existed no doubt spent their summer at Tyler Beach, and they could all go to hell, and that was that.

She was dressed in civvies today, heavy brown turtleneck sweater and well-worn blue jeans, and as she leaned back she had her hands behind her head, like a prisoner giving up, except I don't think Diane has ever given up anything for anybody.

"What's going on with you?" she asked. "The Secret Service treating you well?"

"I don't think they're treating me like anything, and for that I'm thankful."

Her face looked a bit somber and she said, "I hope you don't have bad feelings about that day I took you in to meet Agent Reynolds. I was doing you a favor, Lewis, though I'm sure as hell it didn't seem like it at the time. I wanted to bring you in nice and quiet, without them charging into your house and knocking things over and slapping your wrists in handcuffs or something like that. What I did seemed to be the best alternative."

I smiled to show her there were no hard feelings, and I said, "If one has to be arrested by the Secret Service, getting there through the actions of a friend is as good a way as any."

"Why, thank you, Mr. Cole. Nicest thing anybody's said to me today. And besides the Secret Service, how are the chattering classes of the fourth estate doing? Leaving your ass alone?"

"Ass is very much alone and belonging to me."

"Good. So. Now that we're all caught up and everything, what's going on?"

I took a breath. "Audrey Whittaker."

She tilted her head a bit. "Audrey Whittaker. Socialite lady for whatever passes as society on the New Hampshire seacoast. Very wealthy, working on her second husband, quite active in political affairs. Believe she's supporting Senator Hale from Georgia. Why the curiosity?"

"What else can you tell me about her?"

Diane dropped her hands and let the chair move forward some. "What else do you want to know?"

"Has she…has she ever been the subject of interest from law enforcement circles?"

Diane now stared at me for long seconds, and I knew exactly then how she got suspects to talk, with that firm gaze and clear eyes. "That's a hell of a question, Lewis. Especially the way you just put it. Mind telling me what's gotten your attention?"

"Something involving a column I'm working on," I said.

"Oh. That makes it clear then. One of your famous columns that never seems to make its way into print. All right. I can tell you from my own personal experience that Audrey Whittaker, to the best of my knowledge, has never been—as you so delicately put it—the subject of interest from law enforcement circles. But…"

My ears got quite sensitive at that last word. "Yes?"

She said, "Like I said, from my own personal experience, nothing. But it doesn't mean that something hasn't gone on that I don't know about. Which means a records check could reveal something. But there's something you've got to know before you ask me to do that."

"Which is what?"

Diane carefully picked up a pen and moved it from one side of the desk to the other. "It's like this. Used to be, in the wild and woolly days when I first became detective, you could do a records search for no other reason than to satisfy your curiosity. Those days are gone. Records of inquiries are kept, and questions can be asked. Like, why are you so interested in so-and-so, Detective Woods? Is there an official reason for this inquiry? If not, why? And what prompted you to make such an inquiry if there's no official reason?"

"I see."

"Good. Because I'll do a records search for you, Lewis, if it means something important for you. But you should know that if something about Audrey Whittaker becomes public knowledge in the next week or month or something like that, some people might want to know why I was doing a records search on her, and for what reason. So, having wasted about half your Saturday morning, I just want to know this: Lewis, do you want me to do a records search on Audrey Whittaker?"

I looked back at her, and thinking of our friendship and our past and favors done and favors expected, I took a breath.

"No," I said. "I don't want you to do a records search on Audrey Whittaker."

Her mood instantly changed, and the atmosphere in the room seemed to lighten right up. "Fine. I'm very glad to hear that. And here's a bit of advice from an old detective who's seen an awful lot. Ready?"

"Go ahead, ma'am."

"Leave Audrey Whittaker alone. She's old, she's rich, and she has a lot of time on her hands. A very dangerous combination. Focus on Annie Wynn. She's good for you, Lewis. Very good for you. And take it from someone who's an admirer of the female form and function."

"Glad we have something in common."

"More than you know. Now, if you'll excuse me, I've got some case folders to go through, and my better half is promising me dinner and entertainment, and since I've been lacking in the home-cooked meal and homemade entertainment departments lately, get the hell out."

I wished my old friend the best, and did as I was told.

IT TOOK SOME TRACKING on my part but by the time late Saturday afternoon rolled around, I had finally found Paula Quinn. She was at a campaign rally for Senator Nash Pomeroy of Massachusetts, and after promising at a volunteer desk that I would work my local polling station on Tuesday, bring five friends to the polls, wear a Pomeroy button on my coat and a Pomeroy bumper sticker on my car, and commit ritual suicide if he didn't win on Tuesday, I was allowed in.

The rally was at the MitchSun electronics plant in Tyler Falls, owned by an eccentric entrepreneur called Eddie Mitchell. Eddie was a firm believer in the electoral process and took a major hit in his productivity every fourth January by inviting candidates to stop by and talk to his employees. For the employees, it meant an extra-long meal break—especially for those doing time-and-a-half work on Saturdays—and for the candidates, it meant a captive audience of about a hundred potential voters.

Inside the plant's cafeteria, I found Paula at the rear, hiding a yawn with one hand, typing away on a laptop with the other. The light green tables were occupied by workers in white coats and slacks, not bothering much to hide their bored expressions, while on the far side of the room, Senator Pomeroy—a product of prep schools, Harvard, and district attorney work in Massachusetts—gave a talk in which he left no doubt that he'd rather be back in Washington than talking to his lessers here in—horror of horrors—New Hampshire. He was standing behind a portable lectern that had a POMEROY FOR PRESIDENT sign taped to its front, and even the gaggle of cameramen and reporters off to one side looked almost as dispirited as the candidate and his audience.

I sat next to Paula and she looked over at me, and then looked over at me again with surprise and said, "What are you doing here?"

"Looking for you."

"Well, that's flattering. You need something, is that it?"

There was a not-so-nice edge to her voice and I said, "Well, I was going to trade you something. Information for information. How does that sound?"

"Newsworthy?"

"Quite."

"Very newsworthy?"

"Oh, you know it."

"Newsworthy in a presidential primary sense?"

"Wouldn't waste your time otherwise."

She grinned and turned away from her laptop. "Oh, you better not be teasing me."

"Haven't teased you in months, and you know it."

"Lucky me. Okay, you go first. What do you need?"

"I need a quickie bio on Audrey Whittaker, and I already

know she's rich, she's married twice, and that she's active in political events. What else can you tell me?"

Paula said, "Knowing how you operate, I'm sure you don't care much about her charitable activities."

"I'm looking for something a bit more edgy."

"Hmmm," she said. "Edgy. How come she's gotten your attention?"

"You know my methods, Paula."

That earned me another smile. "Another quest from the mysterious Mr. Cole…how can I deny you that?"

"You've denied me before."

"On other things, my friend. All right. Audrey Whittaker and edgy. Here's the story I've been told, and you can't tell anybody else where you heard this story, because I'll deny having told you. Lord knows, I wouldn't touch it with a ten-foot pole. Or even a twenty-foot pole. Nasty stuff, it was."

I touched her hand. "I knew I could count on you."

"Ha. How sweet. Look, here's the deal. Word is, this particular event happened two, maybe three years ago. She lives in one of those so-called summer homes up in Wallis whose construction costs can support a school for a year. Nice place, of course, and across the street, there's a tiny little strip of beach. I mean really, really tiny. Most of the shoreline up there is nothing but rocks and boulders, but from what I've found out, over the years, she and her minions—God, I wish I had a minion on days like these—would secretly and quite illegally improve that tiny section of beach. Nothing blatant, just a few boulders removed, year after year, and a little sand dumped in the right places. Pretty soon, Audrey had the only private beach on the oceanfront in New Hampshire."

I said, "No such thing as a private beach in New Hampshire. State law."

Paula laughed. "Look who's talking, the gentleman with his illegal No Trespassing signs outside his house."

"The signs are a suggestion, not an order. Besides, we're talking about Audrey Whittaker."

Up forward, Senator Pomeroy seemed to pause in that part of

his speech that said, *Pause, wait for applause,* and when no applause came forth, he pressed on.

"Yes, we are, aren't we. Anyway, Audrey—from what I was told—loved to bundle up a picnic lunch, chair, umbrella, and thermos full of martinis, and walk out her front door, down the majestic front lawn, across Atlantic Avenue to her private little beach, and spend the better part of a day there. Pure delight, for a woman like her. Her own private beach, her little stretch of paradise, which she didn't have to share with members of the working class."

"What happened then? Someone from the state tried to kick her off?"

Paula shook her head. "Nothing so official. One day she went there and found some people on her private beach. Three families, up from Massachusetts—Lawrence or Lowell, still a bit murky—and they were having a grand old time partying and playing loud music, little barbecue grills, the usual stuff. Audrey told them to leave. The families told her no, in so many words. I guess they had gotten the word that there are no private beaches in New Hampshire. More words were exchanged, Audrey left, and when the families left…well, they and their friends never came back. Not ever."

"Why?"

Paula tried to laugh, to lighten her mood, but it didn't seem to work. "Lewis, from what I hear, she went back to her house and got to work—with her minions lending a hand, I'm sure— and soon enough, she found out who those three families were and where they had come from. She picked one family, randomly, probably, and she destroyed them."

"Destroyed them? How?"

"From what I hear, the father worked in maintenance for the Lawrence school system. His wife worked in the system as well, as a secretary. Within a week, both of them were out of work. Then they were evicted from their apartment. Their children got into trouble at school and were suspended. No matter what they did, no matter who they talked to, their lives were ruined. They even packed up from Lawrence and moved to New York. And like some curse or something, she followed them there as well.

Last I heard, the parents got divorced, Dad is serving time at Concord-MCI, Mom is on welfare, and who knows what kind of future the children will have. All because they were on her beach. And didn't leave when they were asked."

Above us, Senator Pomeroy's face was turning a light shade of red, as he did his best to work the crowd into a frenzy. Near me, a woman of about thirty was looking up at the senator while she worked on her nails.

I said, "Appreciate the history lesson."

"That was the lengthy lesson," Paula said. "Here's the short lesson. Don't piss her off. She's a wealthy woman with time on her hands who can afford to see her whims, no matter how nasty they are, be fulfilled. I'd hate to see you become one of her whims."

"Point taken," I said.

The young lady next to me started working on her other hand. Paula said, "So, that's what I've got for you. What's your side of the deal, my friend?"

I thought for a moment and leaned into her and said, "Take in this scene well."

"What scene is that?"

"Of Senator Pomeroy, running for president."

She turned to me, face now serious and inquisitive. "Say that again."

"Senator Pomeroy. He won't be a candidate in a few weeks."

"He's dropping out?"

"That's what I hear."

Now her tone matched the look on her face. "Lewis…this is Paula from the *Chronicle* now talking to you. This isn't Paula your bud…got it?"

"Got it."

"All right then," she said. "What do you have for me?"

I chose my words carefully. "An informed source connected with the Nash Pomeroy campaign has confirmed that due to personal reasons, Senator Nash Pomeroy will withdraw from the presidential primary race within the next few weeks."

Her hands seemed to fly across the keyboard. "How good is

this source? Not some volunteer who's upset that they've run out of bumper stickers."

"Nope, a well-paid consultant."

"Okay," she said. "The personal reasons. What do they involve?"

"Something involving the senator and events in Illinois."

"Illinois? Far from home."

"Away from your fellow scribblers and other prying eyes."

"Can you tell me what happened in Illinois?"

"No, I'm afraid I can't," I said.

"And this is good information?"

"Solid," I said.

"Real solid? I mean to put this out in the Monday paper…and it's going to cause a hell of a crapstorm with the Pomeroy campaign and the other news media, my little paper breaking a story like this."

"Solid as a rock."

Paula finished typing and then gently scratched one of her delightfully protruding ears. "You know, this is the kind of story that's going to need another source before going to press. No offense to you and your mysterious informant."

"No offense taken."

She grinned. "My dear Mr. Sullivan, that's who."

"The Tyler town counsel? Your better half?"

"The same," she said. "He has connections to the Nash Pomeroy campaign. Once I get out of this wake, I'll give him a call. Man, that's going to tick him off something awful."

"Think he'll talk?"

The smile got wider. "If he wants to continue to be lucky with me, he'd better talk, and better give it all up."

"If he's smart, he'll do just that."

Senator Pomeroy then wrapped things up by saying, "…and I look forward to your support next Tuesday. Thank you, thank you so very much!"

Some steady applause that dribbled out after a number of seconds, and she put her mouth up to my ear and said, "Thanks, Lewis. A scoop like this…well, it'll make all this weekend and night work this past month worth it."

"Glad to hear it," I said, standing up.

She stood up as well, gathered her laptop, and looked at Senator Pomeroy, gamely shaking the hands of those few voters who came up to him.

Paula shook her head and said, "You know, there are times, like I told you back at lunch, when I think this primary season is so special. And then I look at what we have here. The endless cattle show. The endless droning recitation of canned speeches. Candidates who hate what they're doing, and hate being here. Makes you wonder how this fair little country of ours stumbles along. Lord knows candidates like Lincoln or FDR or JFK or even Ike couldn't survive what goes on now, with the cable networks and all the background investigations. So what do we end up with? Bland candidates with bland backgrounds who try to be everything to everybody…that's what we get."

"You know what Churchill said," I told her.

"What? About fighting on the landing fields and beaches?"

"No," I said. "Something about democracy being the worse political system ever devised, except for the rest."

"Sounds right," she said. "I just hope the people, God bless 'em, never decide to put that statement to the test and try something else. Thanks again for the tip, Lewis. Gotta get going."

"Me, too," I said,

I went out of the cafeteria and spared a quick glance back. Senator Nash Pomeroy was navigating a crowd of reporters and news photographers, the harsh light from the television cameras making his face look puffy and red. Paula was right. It was a hell of a process.

But so far, the only one we've got.

# SIXTEEN

AT HOME I BUILT A FIRE and checked my messages. Another baker's dozen, of which I deleted twelve. It got to the point where I knew to delete the message when I heard nothing for the first few seconds; it usually took that long for the automated message to begin its spiel, allowing me to avoid yet another heartfelt automatic plea to either vote for somebody or vote against somebody. There was also one live message, from a very real person—Annie—which I returned, and I was pleased that it went right through.

"Oh, Lewis, it's you," she said, and I sensed the exhaustion in her voice.

"Sounds like you're running on caffeine and energy," I said.

"Lots of caffeine, not much energy. Oh, we're getting close, my dear, so very close."

"What's going on?"

"Latest round of polling shows the damn race is still fluid," she said. "Hale still holds on to a lead, but that hold is damn slippery. All it'd take is one bit of bad news, one bit of controversy, and it could sink us…but if we hang on till Tuesday morning, then we can make it. And then it's on to South Carolina."

"South Carolina…with or without Annie Wynn?"

She laughed. "South Carolina…here's your answer about that. All right if I move in with you Wednesday morning? Take a vacation?"

"Where do you want to go?"

"Mmm," she murmured. "No goddamn where, that's where. I want you to unplug the phone and your computer, and I want a fire in the fireplace all day and night, and I want all of my meals served on a tray on my lap. And the only thing I want to see on television are old movies. Cary Grant. Gregory Peck. Audrey Hepburn. Katharine Hepburn. Spencer Tracy. Think you can arrange that for me?"

"Consider it done."

Another sigh. "But I have something for you, if you'd like."

"What's that?"

"Monday night," she said. "You free?"

"Of course."

"Good. We're having an old-fashioned wingding of a political rally for Senator Hale, at the Center of New Hampshire. Free food and drinks…music…lights, camera, and action. One last big-ass rally before voting begins the next day. I'd love to have you there, right with me, holding hands, as the campaign wraps up in New Hampshire. Tell me you'll say yes."

I looked at the dancing flames, thinking, Just a couple more days, that's all, just a couple more days. Then this damn primary and its problems be over.

"Yes," I said. "Of course, yes."

"Thank you, dear," she said, and I made out voices in the background, and she said, "The campaign calls. See you Monday night, 5:00 p.m. The Center of New Hampshire. Come to Room 110, all right?"

"Room 110, 5:00 p.m., Monday night. It's a date."

She chuckled. "It seems like ages since I've heard you say that. A date it is. Bye, now."

"Bye."

After I hung up, I looked at the flames again for a while, before getting up and making a simple dinner of corn beef hash, fried up in a big black cast iron skillet. Feeling particularly bachelorish, I ate from the pan to save some cleaning up. Annie would have been horrified to see me and that made me smile, to think of her face. After I ate I made a speed clean of the kitchen and decided it was time to go to bed. Tomorrow was going to be a long day, and I know it was arrogant of me to say so, but I had no doubt what I was going to do on Sunday would have an impact on who the next president of the United States would be.

Despite of all that, I slept fairly well.

SUNDAY MORNING I went over to the Lafayette House for my daily dose of newspapers, and Stephanie wasn't working that day, so I got out with my heavy load of reading without any serious conversation. I was also pleasantly surprised at seeing a familiar face while leaving the lobby; Chuck Bittner, campaign operative for General Grayson, who looked at me and pretended he didn't know who I was. The pleasant surprise, of course, was not in seeing him; it was in his ignoring me. I guess our little visit was already working. I returned the favor and walked back home.

It was a brisk morning, a faint breeze coming off the ocean, the salt smell good to notice. Out on the horizon were the lumps of rock and soil marking the Isles of Shoals; and I made out a freighter, heading north to the state's only major port, in Porter. There was a nice winter contrast to the snow and ice on the ground, the sharp darkness of the boulders, and heavy blue of the water that reminded me again of how nice it was to live here, even in the dark times of winter. Even when the quadrennial circus was in town, bringing with it all sorts of problems and headaches.

Like a dead man in my yard. And a former college lover, probably destined to become the next first lady, and my poor Annie, working so hard, working so diligently, for something she believed in. I shifted the papers from one arm to the other, glanced at all the big headlines predicting what might happen here come this Tuesday.

At home I made a big breakfast of scrambled eggs, sausage, toast, tea, and orange juice, and plowed through most of *The New York Times* before I decided it was time to get on with the business of the day. I washed the dishes, went upstairs and showered and checked my skin, as always, and got dressed. Usually getting dressed means finding whatever's clean in my closet and bureau, but this time, I decided to do it right. I put on a clean dress shirt, white with light blue pinstripes, a new pair of heavy khaki slacks, and a red necktie. Sensible winter footwear, of course, and a dark blue cardigan. I looked at myself in the mirror before heading back downstairs and said, "Dahlink, you look marvelous."

Downstairs I grabbed my coat and a duped copy of the Lafayette House surveillance tape, and in addition to my cell phone,
I thought about bringing something else. I hesitated, and then
shrugged and went back upstairs. Better to be safe, and I thought
Felix would approve, though I'm not sure about Diane. From my
bedroom I grabbed my nine-millimeter Beretta and shoulder
holster, and slid it on underneath my cardigan. The heavy weight
on my shoulder felt almost comforting. I then went downstairs
and outside to the crisp January morning. Freshly showered, fed,
dressed, and armed, I felt like I was ready to take on the day and
win.

My Ford Explorer started right up and in a matter of moments,
I was heading north. My plan was a simple one. I was to see
Audrey Whittaker and see her I would, for there was no doubt—
with the primary just two days away—that she should be either
home or somewhere reachable. Then, I would show her the tape,
and tell her my demands: lay off. Just lay off whatever the hell
she was doing. For I was doing this for two women in my life,
one past, one present, each of whom was hoping for the very
same thing. For Barbara, and for Annie, I would ensure that
things would be quiet, at least, for this upcoming primary, so their
man would have a clear shot at the White House.

After Tuesday…well, I'm not sure but I thought I would
probably be an accessory to covering up a crime. I had no doubt
about the circumstances of Spenser Harris's death, or whoever
he was. I just wasn't too upset about it, since he had been part
of something that was going to put my butt in jail, and if his body
was to be dumped on the side of a road in rural Massachusetts
sometime this spring, well, I'd let the professionals sort it out.

In the meantime, it was a glorious Sunday and the road was
clear on my drive to Wallis and the home of Audrey Whittaker,
and I was going to take care of everything. And tomorrow night
I'd be at that party with Annie, and wish good luck to Mrs.
Barbara Hale and her husband, and after Tuesday, everything
would be back to where it should be.

In any event, that was my plan.

And as the old joke goes, if you want to make God laugh,
make plans.

I LOOKED QUICKLY to the right before I turned into Audrey Whittaker's house, to see that little stretch of beach that had caused such heartache to a Massachusetts family that didn't like being bossed around by an old New Hampshire lady. I wasn't too worried about what she might do to me—even if she did shoot Spenser Harris—for I was fairly independent and relied on almost no one else for my health and livelihood. And I was also sure that we would reach some sort of understanding, for it was in her interests, as well, to keep up her appearance as the grand dame of New Hampshire politics. And if it was going to take a bit of time to reach an agreement, the Beretta within easy reach would ensure that I wouldn't end up like Spenser Harris.

There was no checkpoint at the driveway entrance so I sped right up, and noted a couple of SUVs in addition to the Jaguar with the WHTKR vanity plate. I parked my Explorer and got out, and shook my head again at the pig scraped into the paint. I would really have to get that fixed, one of these days.

Up at the massive oak door, I pressed the doorbell but didn't hear a thing. Maybe it's a sign of being rich and powerful, that you can't hear your doorbells from outside, so I pressed it again.

This time, the door opened up.

I waited, duped tape in my hand.

"Yes?" came the woman's voice, and I hesitated, disappointed, for it wasn't the right woman.

Instead of Audrey Whittaker, there was a young, strong-looking woman, wearing black slacks and a black turtleneck shirt, and her blond hair was cut quite short, and seemed to be a dye job.

"I'm looking for Audrey Whittaker," I said.

"Is she expecting you?" she replied, and her voice had a slight Hispanic accent. I thought I had seen her before, perhaps the last time I had been here.

"No, but it's urgent that I see her. My name is Lewis Cole."

She smiled and shook her head. Now I was sure. She had been with that catering crew that night, no doubt one of Mrs. Whittaker's employees. "She's not here, but if you come in, I'm sure I can get somebody to help you."

"Thanks," I said, walking in and letting the door slam shut behind me.

I was in the large reception area, and it looked so different from the last time I was here, with the people milling about, the HALE FOR PRESIDENT signs, the check-in table and the coat area. Now, the place looked like it really did, wide and open and almost sterile. My house was old and small and was cold in the winter and too warm in the summer, and beach sand sometimes got into the sheets and the sugar container, but at least it was a home. This was an estate, and I decided I didn't like it.

Voices, out in the large hallway that led into the house, and I turned at the sound of a male voice, a male Southern voice, as the man said, "I was just leaving, but maybe I can help you. Mr. Cole, you said you wanted to see Mrs. Whittaker?"

I turned and saw a man with a red beard there, a man I had seen a couple of times before, here and at the Tyler Conference Center, what was his name, it was…Harmon. Harmon Jewett, that was it. Longtime loyal Jackson Hale supporter, a man who wanted to see Hale elected president no matter what, a man who, as Annie said, had a temper that could curl paint off the side of the house…

And a man who was walking toward me, carrying his coat and gloves in his hands.

A belted white trench coat.

And black gloves.

Like the driver and shooter in the videotape I was carrying in my hand.

I looked at his clothing and looked at him, and said, "No, I'm all set. I'll come back later."

Harmon shrugged. "Suit yourself."

I turned and before me was the door leading out of this large and empty and cold house, and as I went to the door, to safety, something powerful struck me at the back and brought me down.

I THINK I SCREAMED. Or yelled. Not sure. But one thing was for sure: I bit my tongue and struck my head when I fell. My body was out of control, was moving on its own, my legs trembling and flailing, my arms and hands spasming. The floor was cold and harsh against my skin. I tried to roll over and step back up but it was impossible; my body had suddenly short-circuited, had failed me, and I managed to look up and Harmon was standing there, looking satisfied but grim.

"So glad you came by," he said. "Saved me and Carla here from having to fetch you, you dumb fuck."

Something in his hand crackled and there was a black plastic object, blue lightning flowing between two electrodes, and he knelt down and shoved it in my back, and I screamed again, flailing.

He pulled his hand back, smiling. "Amazing how ten thousand volts can get somebody's attention. Carla, c'mon, we don't have much time, what do you have to tie 'im up with?"

Carla replied in Spanish and Harmon said, "Fuck it, we'll make do with what we got here. Damn jerk threw us off schedule. I'll take care of him, you see what the hell's on that tape he brought. Must be something important if he was holdin' it like that."

Hands worked at my necktie and my belt, and my hands and ankles were tied together, and I tried to talk but my tongue had swollen up and it didn't seem like everything was working well. Carla left my field of vision and Harmon patted me down and pulled out my Beretta and laughed in my face.

"What the hell were you going to do with that, boy?" he asked, waving it in front of my nose. "Threaten that shriveled old bitch with it, make her wet her adult diapers? Christ on a crutch, boy, she lets me and others in the campaign use her home and her food and her car to further the career of one Jackson Hale, you think you were going to do anything with this to change her mind? Or scare her? Stupid bitch thinks she's gonna get a slow dance next January twentieth with Jackson, and nothing like you can do anything about it."

Carla appeared, a bit breathless. "Saw the tape, jefe. Looks like you're on it, the day Spennie got whacked."

Harmon laughed and said, "Okay, destroy it, and when I say destroy it, melt the little fucker so nothin' can get salvaged off it. The way they can reconstruct tapes nowadays, there's no way

I'd take a chance on that. I'll take care of our friend here. Lord knows, we're gonna need him tomorrow."

Carla left my view again, and then Harmon grabbed my legs, started dragging. My mind was foggy, my legs and arms still twitched, and there was a metallic taste in my mouth, from where I had bit myself.

As he dragged me, he kept up a little chat, like he was happy to hear his own voice. "We had you set up months ago, pal, to do what had to be done. All that hard work, plottin' and plannin' in the shadows. Thought we had every angle figured out. But how the fuck was I gonna plan on you tossin' your cookies so you didn't get arrested at the shooting and get us all those lovely headlines? Fool…But good plans always have Plan Bs, and you're gonna be nice and set for Plan B."

My head hurt, from having fallen and from having been dragged across the cold tile. Somewhere a door opened, the creaking hinges sounding so loud it made my head hurt even that much more, and Harmon knelt down again. "Here's the set. Old bitch Whittaker, her first husband drunk so much she didn't want a sloppy drunk living with her again, so she cleaned out first hubbie's wine cellar, so it's empty now, and I hope you're not thirsty, 'cause that's where you're gonna be kept for a while…oh, and one more thing. You be a good boy or I'll come back down there to visit you. Unnerstand?"

Again, I moved my mouth, but nothing came out, not even a whisper.

*Crackle, crackle,* came the noise, and I screamed once more, quite loud, arching my back, as the stun gun was shoved into me again. Harmon got up, breathing hard. "Didn't hear a word from you, so wanted to make sure I made my point. Okay, pal, here you go. Watch that first step."

Some first step. He dragged me through the door and shoved me down some stone steps, and my head struck the stone again, and my jaw, and the back of my head, and I yelled or screamed again, and there was the slam of the door, and then, darkness.

Darkness, where everything seemed to hurt.

I WAS OUT OF IT for a while, not sure of the length of time. I think it was for a long while. But eventually I became aware of some things, like my arms and wrists aching, and my feet falling asleep, but most of all, the taste of copper in my mouth and the deep, throbbing, aching pain along the side of my face. I gingerly moved my jaw, and though it didn't seem broken, it sure as hell had been dinged up some.

I then was aware that I was on my side, on a stone floor. I breathed some and exerted and breathed, and managed to sit up. That seemed to have been a mistake. My head spun and nausea rippled through my stomach and saliva gurgled up in my mouth, and it took some long minutes of deep breathing before I didn't feel like throwing up.

I blinked my eyes a few times. At first I thought the room was pitch black and as dark as the interior of a tomb, but there was light coming in from somewhere. I moved my head about and made out two tiny windows, about ten or twelve feet off the ground, off to the right. I looked around a bit more and took in the small wine cellar. It looked like there were empty wooden shelves along the stone walls, fit for hundreds and hundreds of wine bottles, and not much else. Behind me was the stone stair-case that Harmon had so thoughtfully tossed me down some time ago.

I tried to straighten my legs out, but I didn't have much success. I took a deep breath, tried to propel myself up, and my feet slipped and I fell back and struck my head on the stones, and all was darkness again.

WHEN I CAME AROUND the light was even dimmer. I looked to the tiny windows and saw that whatever light was coming through had to be from an outside spotlight or something. Which meant it was evening, though I didn't know how late it was. But New Hampshire winters produce pitch darkness after 4:00 p.m. or thereabouts, so who really knew. All I knew was that I was in one serious world of hurt.

I moved around some and this time, I got my legs straightened out. Took a breath. Took stock. Arms and wrists still aching, feet and hands tingling from lack of circulation. Jaw and head one big throbbing mess of a headache, but still, no apparent broken bones. Took another breath. Started to think.

Harmon Jewett. Annie had told me how he was utterly devoted to Jackson Hale, would do anything and everything to further Hale's career. And I remembered what Barbara had told me, the last time I had seen her, in Manchester. About how some crazed people in a campaign would do anything to see their man elected, even up to and including the attempted shooting and killing of the candidate's wife.

Harmon Jewett. Looked pretty damn crazed to me. Had set me up for the shooting at the Tyler Conference Center, and from his talk about Plan B, I was going to be set up for something on Monday, the day before the primary.

I didn't know the how and where, but I was sure of the why: to get his man elected.

And maybe he would get elected. I don't know. But I did know that I hadn't volunteered to be part of anybody's damn plan, and I was going to do something about it.

I moved. Ouch, damn it, and I whispered, "Pretty bold talk for a man all bound up."

So. Time to get unbound.

By now my eyes had adjusted even better in the darkness, and I saw that except for the shelves, the place was pretty damn empty. It was about fifteen feet square and cool, and I started to move out in the center of the room, by folding and unfolding my bound legs like some overgrown centipede. I had moved about halfway out into the room when I had to stop. I was breathing so hard it made my jaw and head ache even more, and I was afraid the pain would make me pass out again. So I stopped, looked at where I had come from.

Just a plain stone staircase, hugging the far wall, heading upstairs. No bannister. Just plain cut stone. Not much to work with there. There was also no handy-dandy workbench, with saws, files, or other sharp tools hanging down for easy access. Nothing. I moved my head. Three walls, all with the framed shelves for holding pricey bottles of wine. And from what I could tell, each shelf was empty. Just me and the stone and the dirt and the staircase and the shelves, and the two tiny windows.

My heart rate eased some, as did my breathing.

Time to get back to moving.

Stretch, constrict, stretch, constrict, and as I moved, I saw the pieces of what had happened slide into place. The shooting at the Tyler Conference Center. I was to have been the patsy, the nutty former lover, trying to kill the senator's wife. But the bullets missed and I'd got sick, and that story didn't pan out. Then there was Spenser Harris, the faux Secret Service agent. Killed and dumped in my yard to do what…make me lash out? Make me run to Barbara Hale for another setup?

Who knew.

But I did know one thing. I had to move faster.

Stretch, constrict, stretch, constrict. Something in my coat pocket was pushing against the small of my back, hurting it like hell, but it wasn't going to stop me.

More movement. Now I was hungry, too, and thirsty.

Stretch, constrict, stretch, constrict.

And I still hurt like hell.

Stopped for a moment. Almost there. Looked up at the windows. There was light now coming in, strong light, fresh light.

It was Monday morning, a day before the fine citizens of this state would help choose the next president.

I shook my head and kept moving, and then, when my bound hands touched the smooth wood of the wine shelves, I stopped and took another long break, breathing hard, head throbbing and aching. A long, hard slog. A very long, hard slog.

And not over yet. Not by a long shot.

I MOVED MY FINGERS ABOUT, searching for a piece of sharp wood, a protruding nail, or even a bit of metal framework, anything that could cut through the necktie holding my arms still.

Nothing.

Just smooth wood and stone.

I moved to the left, my bound hands still underneath the bottom shelf of the empty wine rack. Moved along, moved along, still feeling nothing but smooth rock and stone. From overhead, there were heavy footsteps up on the foyer floor. Up there, movement, up there, people at work, planning and plotting, waiting for me to fulfill my role.

The hell I would.

Now I was at the end of the shelves. Nothing. I looked back to where I had started. About halfway back across the room. Another section of the shelves remained. I took a breath, started inching back like one bruised and tired inchworm. Back to the shelves, moving along, my hands searching and poking, probing, feeling along and—

Something sharp.

Something sharp bit at my hand.

I froze.

Didn't dare move, just waited.

Moved my hand again.

Whatever was there had moved.

Closed my eyes. Took a breath.

Moved my hand again…

Nothing.

Upstairs, more footsteps, the murmur of conversation.

I moved my hand. Still nothing.

I wiggled around, shoved my hand under the shelf, grunting in the process, scraped some skin off my wrist and—

Sharpness again.

My fingers were numb, tingling with lack of circulation, but I held on to whatever was there.

I moved forward, my hand tight against the sharpness, and I felt it and I thought I smiled, there in the darkness.

A piece of glass. Part of a broken wine bottle.

For this had been a wine cellar for quite a number of years, and I had a thought, a prayer, really, that somewhere along the line, a bottle would have been dropped, would have broken, and a piece of glass would have been overlooked as whoever had done the dropping would have had done a sloppy job in cleaning up.

I felt along the piece of glass. A sharp edge. I moved back against the shelf, lodged the glass against the wood, and started moving my bound wrists against the glass. Up and down, up and down, and—

The glass slipped.

Cut against my right wrist.

"Shit," I said, feeling the glass drop, feeling my wrist burn with the cut, now replaced with warmness as the blood started trickling down.

Reached and groped and got the glass.

Back again, cut and cut, and I felt the fabric of my necktie start to fray and break away. More cutting, more cutting, and I started moving my wrists and—

Everything tore away.

My wrists were free.

Freedom.

I was free.

I rubbed and rubbed my wrists, the blood roaring back into my fingers, tingling and tingling, more rubbing.

I leaned forward, started working on the leather belt around my ankles, my fingers numb and my wrist bleeding, and I tore a fingernail or two getting it off, but off it was, and I stretched my legs and rubbed out the cramps, rubbed some more, and yes, I was free…

I looked up at the staircase, the locked door, the two tiny windows.

Some freedom.

# SEVENTEEN

I WENT THROUGH MY POCKETS, wanting to find out what in hell had been poking at me, and I felt a small square of plastic and metal, and I pulled it out, and almost shouted with glee at what was there.

My hardly used cell phone, tiny and overlooked.

I pulled up the tiny antenna, switched it on, and started punching in the number of the Tyler Police Department. Diane would help me, Diane would know what to do, and—

Nothing.

Nothing at all.

Looked at the tiny display screen.

In tiny little letters that felt twelve feet tall.

NO SERVICE.

Of course. Why should anything be easy?

I stood up, swaying, almost fell down again. Stretched and gasped as cramps rippled through my legs, and then I moved, rubbed again. I went up to the stone staircase, gently moved up along the steps, trying to keep the noise down, until I reached the top. Just for the hell of it, I moved my hands along the wall. No light switch. And I tried the doorknob. Locked, of course.

Cell phone in hand, I tried again.

The phone flickered into life, swinging between SERVICE and NO SERVICE. Close…so very close.

I looked around the cellar, saw the light streaming in through the two small windows.

Maybe…just maybe.

I quietly went down the stone steps, almost fell as another series of cramps went running through my legs, and I went over to the shelves, looked up. About eleven, twelve feet. A hell of a thing. Blood was still trickling down my right wrist and I made a sloppy bandage with my handkerchief.

And then I started climbing.

The wood had sharp edges against my hands, and I winced as I made my way up, the shelves groaning under my weight. About halfway, my foot broke through one of the slats, making a loud crack that I was sure could be heard as far away as Porter, and I murmured another series of expletives when the cell phone dropped from my hand. I looked down in the dim light and almost passed out when I saw the piece of metal and plastic split apart when it hit the stone floor.

I made my way slowly down to the floor, went and gathered up the pieces, and went to the center of the cellar, where the light was best. I put it back together as best as I could, and then went back to the wine rack, putting the cell phone back into my coat. Something must have loosened from my previous attempt, for the wood groaned and I felt the shelves move away from the wall.

"Close," I whispered. "So damn close."

I moved back up the shelving, taking it slow, knowing that by going slow, I wouldn't slip but was leaving open the chance of the damn thing collapsing under my weight, and I let that cheery debate run itself out as I got higher and higher, right up to the top, right by one of the two windows. The window was built into the stone foundation and couldn't be opened, and in any event, it was too small to crawl through…but what I wanted to get through the window wasn't made of proteins. It was made of protons. Or something similar. My grasp on science right at that moment was pretty damn fuzzy.

Hanging on with one hand, I got the phone out of my coat, pulled the antenna out with my teeth, and held it up to the window, pressed the keypad.

There. I'll be damned.

SERVICE.

But another message was blinking at me.

LOW BATTERY.

I guess my phone was one of those newfangled ones, for there was a digital countdown letting me know exactly how many seconds of usable power I had left, and I saw the number thirty become the number twenty-nine, become the number twenty-eight…

Who to call?

Back in my coat pocket again, looking and finding…a slip of paper in my hand, up to the window and the light, and there, the one call I would make. A call to warn her, a call to let her know, to go into hiding, to prevent her husband's defeat tomorrow, to call the Secret Service and do what had to be done…

I punched in the numbers and waited, imagining the little digits running their way back to zero, and—

From upstairs, I heard a phone ringing.

What a coincidence.

An odd counterpoint, this phone ringing, the upstairs phone ringing—

A click. It was answered. A hesitant voice. "Hello?"

"Barbara?"

And everything got quite cold, as I realized the phone upstairs had, had…

Had stopped ringing.

"Lewis? Is that you?"

And in the background, a very familiar voice, one I had heard the day before, as he was thumping me with a stun gun.

"Here? The sumbitch phoned you here?"

She hung up. I looked at my phone, now dead, and let it gently fall out of my hand and drop to the floor.

I slowly and carefully made my way back down to the stone floor, and feeling like the floor itself was being carried on my shoulders, I went over to the bottom of the stairs and looked up at the closed door.

And waited.

I didn't have to wait long.

THE DOOR OPENED and the lights came on, blinding me for a moment. I raised up a sore and bloody hand to my eyes to shield them. Harmon Jewett yelled down, "You wanna come up here, boy?"

"Do I have a choice?"

He laughed and a woman murmured behind him, and then he

came down the stone steps, smiling widely, holding out the stun gun in his hand. Behind him was someone dear and familiar, and with each step she took downstairs, she broke my heart again and again. For a moment I was that college-aged boy, wondering and wondering why she had left me and had never called or written.

"Barbara," I said.

"Lewis."

She came down to the bottom of the steps and was now standing close to Harmon, standing right close to him, and with her arm through his, her head lowered. I flashed back to what I had seen, what I had remembered, about her and Jackson Hale. Over the past several days I had seen numerous videos of Barbara with her husband-candidate, and in each video—save one—she had been the devoted spouse, standing right next to the senator, smiling with him, laughing with him, applauding at each appropriate applause line. In each and every video, save one.

The one from the Tyler Conference Center.

And in that snippet of history, I remembered seeing Barbara with her husband, standing apart from her husband, standing very far apart from her husband…

…because she knew.

She knew gunshots were going to be fired.

She knew.

She always knew.

Harmon said, "Hands where I can see 'em, boy."

I held my hands out, and Harmon chuckled. "Glad to see you're bleeding. Helps everything else as well."

I ignored him, stared at the woman I had once loved so long ago, and before me…before me was a stranger.

I said, "I guess first lady wasn't that attractive to you, was it."

Her head snapped right up and the sharpness of her eyes and her tone chilled me. "When did I ever have a choice? When did I ever have the right to say no? When did I ever have a voice in what was going on? When? It was all assumed. It was all planned. And if I hated being a senator's wife, being first lady to this nation of clowns was going to kill me. Was going to absolutely kill me…"

"And killing your husband was going to change things?"

Harmon said, "Not kill 'em. Just wound him. Except that damn Spenny couldn't hit the broad side of a barn…and our planned patsy was busy pukin' his guts instead of being inside the building and takin' the fall. So instead of a wounded candidate and a scandal over his wife's former lover, we got a bump in the fuckin' polls, if you can believe it."

Now I looked to Harmon. "This is what you do when you're marginalized, when Jackson Hale won't fire you? When he keeps you on his payroll?"

Harmon spat something on the ground, his voice as sharp as Barbara's. "His payroll. His gratitude. Damn him, if it weren't for me, he'd still be some little state senator cutting ribbons at Piggly Wiggly openings. I made him, and now I'm gonna unmake him, and steal his woman in the process."

He leered at me and squeezed Barbara tight, and in looking at her and looking at him, I could not imagine what had brought them together, what they hoped to do, and then I gave it up. Trying to fathom who they were and what they were doing was like trying to understand quantum theory with a third-grade math education. It just made my head hurt.

And the time for thinking was over.

"Barbara…"

She didn't say anything. My throat thickened and I said, "Just the other day, some smart man warned me of the danger of manipulation. I just wish I had appreciated how smart he really was."

Still no answer.

With a touch of impatience, Harmon said, "Upstairs, friend. Now."

"Or what? Plan to shoot me and dump my body with a rifle in my hand in front of Hale campaign headquarters?"

"Nope. Or I take my stun gun and shoot ten thousand volts into your private parts, then drag you upstairs. Either way, you're going upstairs."

Barbara's head was lowered again, as if that earlier outburst had tired her. "So…is that it? That's all it's been since you've been here? Me as a tool so you can spend your days with…with this creature?"

Her voice soft, she said, "He loves me, Lewis. He will do

anything for me. Anything. And he will save me from going back to D.C. anymore…so I can stop wearing that damn happy wifey mask."

She turned and went up the stairs. Harmon grinned at me, like a good ole boy sharing a joke with another equally good ole boy. I started up the stairs and Harmon gave me a wide berth, and as I got to the top of the stairs, Barbara was there and I had a quick thought of making a break for it, but the other woman—Carla—stood there with a wary expression on her face, a nine-millimeter automatic pistol pointed in my direction.

Harmon joined us and said, "Permit me to introduce my companion, one Carla Conchita Lopez. Carla was once a member of the Guatemalan People's Army…or the People's Army of Guatemala…or some damn thing, until she got a taste for capitalism and headed north. She got caught up in an immigration sweep in Atlanta couple o' years back…and long story short, my cousin from INS dumped her in my care. Old Spenny. Old stupid Spenny, couldn't hit a target to save his life, and he sure as hell didn't. Jesus, you were supposed to call the cops when you found his body in your yard. Why the hell didn't you do that, boy?"

"Guess I forgot."

"Where is he now?"

I said, "In a safe place. You want to trade? His body for my freedom?"

He grinned. "Not much of a trade. Sorry."

Harmon went to a pile of clothing by the door and said, "The cuffs, babe. Toss him the cuffs."

With her free hand, Carla reached into a pocket in her slacks and pulled out a set of handcuffs, which she tossed to me. I caught the jangling pieces of metal and looked over to Harmon.

"Put them on," he said, "or I tell Carla to shoot you in your kneecap. Either way, it don't matter to me, 'cause the cuffs will be where they belong. Carla's one tough bitch, buddy, and some of the stories she told me about down south would make your balls ache. So do what you're told and don't fuck with her."

I was still looking at Barbara, still trying to remember those magical days in Indiana, at the university, and then giving up. No more time for the past. None. I had to focus on the here and now, as hard as it was. Barbara stood by Harmon, and she was still not looking at me.

"The handcuffs, Lewis. Now."

I slowly put one cuff on one wrist, and then the other on the second wrist. The clicking sounded as sharp as a sliding saw hitting a bone. "All right," I said. "Your patsy is ready. So? Shoot me now, or shoot me later? And do you trust me with a gun?"

Harmon walked over to the small pile of clothing on the floor. "Who said anything about a gun? Carla, keep an eye on 'im."

He bent down, picked up what looked to be a cloth vest, and my aches and pains and cramps went right away as I saw the wires leading up from tubes of material, fastened to the outside of the vest. He held it up like a fisherman proud of the trophy he had just captured and was about to bring home.

"Carla here, when she was active in her little revolutionary movement, developed some nice skills, including bomb making. And what's gonna happen here, Lewis, is that you're puttin' this vest on…and in about twenty minutes, ol' Senator Hale is coming here for what he thinks is goin' to be a quick campaign stop to say thanks to that ol' bitch Audrey Whittaker, who is over in Concord expectin' the senator to have a drink with her…and when he comes up that driveway, why, you're gonna run out to meet him. You see, for the past half day, you've been holdin' the three of us hostage, which we're gonna swear to the investigatin' authorities. Plus, in that vest is some love letters you've written to Barbara…love letters that come from your computer that we didn't have a chance to use the first time around…and that little scandal will defeat that little bastard tomorrow."

The cuffs were cold and made my bleeding wrist sting even that much more.

"If stopping him is so important, why not put the word out about me? If that's the scandal you're looking for."

Harmon said, "Who humped who twenty years ago—so what?—but a crazed stalker, tryin' to kill the senator over a long-ago love affair…so much juicier, so much juicier that you dumb Yankees up here, who hate scandal so much, will give the nomination to somebody else…and give me and Barbara a good laugh when we're done, just to see what we managed to pull over that numb Jackson."

I said, "Just so you know, Harmon, there's another copy of that surveillance tape. A copy I mailed to a trusted friend. Let me go and we can settle this…settle it so nothing else happens, nobody gets hurt."

Harmon said, "Carla? The tape?"

She shook her head. "Can't make out your face. Can make out the license plate of the car. That's it."

Harmon turned to me, triumphant. "That ol' biddy lends her car, her house, and sometimes what's left between her legs to people she wants to help. So by the time investigators try to figure out what's what—especially with no body for Spenny— whoever's president will be working on his second term."

Barbara had moved next to Harmon like an obedient puppet. She was by the door, Harmon standing next to her, and Carla, in turn, standing next to him. All three of them standing in a row, looking at me.

I said quietly, "Barbara…you know what's going to happen. If I go out there wearing that vest, he's going to trigger it by remote control. Barbara, he's going to kill me. He's going to kill me. In the next few minutes, Barbara."

She said nothing. Just reached out and sought Harmon's hand, which he gave her. He was holding the vest with one hand, squeezing her hand with the other.

"Now, Lewis. Put the vest on now."

I lowered my head and moved forward, gauging my steps, and when I got close to Harmon and Barbara, the vest now held out to me, I tried to catch her eyes, tried to look at her, tried to make her see the man who was in front of her.

But she was studiously ignoring me.

And so I went up to Harmon and Barbara, and slugged her in the chin with my left elbow as hard as I could.

# EIGHTEEN

BARBARA YELPED AND FELL to the ground, still holding on to Harmon, and he stumbled and Carla shouted, and I grabbed the doorknob with my cuffed hands and opened the door and ran outside, almost tripping on the slippery steps, but I ran and ran and ran out onto the driveway. I was moving quick and thinking even quicker, and I knew the grounds would hold no shelter for me, not with the snowbanks of the driveway and the snow-covered lawn. I would slow down instantly in the thick snow and be a quick and easy target, so I stuck to the curving driveway, running and running, hoping that its gentle curves and the high snowbanks would hide me for a few seconds, for I was sure Carla was right behind me, with a shoot-to-kill order, and some-where back there, both she and Harmon and yes, damn it, Barbara, had a Plan C to take care of everything.

It was cold and windy but I didn't mind. I was moving quick, the cramps and discomfort in my legs and arms now overlooked, the open entrance to the estate now before me, wide open, and as I ran toward the opening, I had a fearful thought that perhaps there was some automatic system back at the house to close the gates, but nothing happened as I approached the stone columns and the silent cast-iron gates.

There. Right through. Now I was at Atlantic Avenue. Look to the left, look to the right. The road here was fairly straight.

No traffic.

None.

Ah, hell.

Then the sound of an engine.

Look, look, look, a voice inside me started screaming.

A dark blue pickup truck came around the corner, heading in my direction. I ran toward it, holding my arms up, yelling, pleading, and—

The truck sped up and passed me by, the older driver grimly staring ahead, pretending I didn't exist.

Of course.

Who in hell would stop for a crazed man with no coat, standing in the middle of the road, wearing handcuffs?

The sound of the gunshot spun me around, broke my stillness. Carla was running down the driveway, followed by Harmon, and I looked again at the roadway.

Nothing. Just an empty road, both sides with high snowbanks.

Can't go back. Go down or up the road, and be exposed like a fumbling ant on a kitchen counter.

Can't wait for another disinterested driver to intercede.

Only one place to go.

Forward.

So I ran across the two-lane road, hands still cuffed before me, and I scrambled up the snowbank and down the other side, feet digging into the crusty stuff, my legs and back now wet through from the snow. I now had cover, for a minute or two, and I was panting and shuddering, for it was still cold, still windy, and before me were snow-covered rocks and boulders, and the waves of the Atlantic Ocean, coming in, like they always do, nasty and gray-looking.

Plans. I had very grand plans. To stay alive and maybe move south, move among the rocks and boulders, keep some cover between me and my pursuers, and if I was very, very lucky, I could make some good progress, until…

Until what? Saved? Rescued? No one knew I was here, and sure, maybe tomorrow or the next day, Felix would receive the Lafayette House videotape that I had mailed him, but I didn't have tomorrow or the next day.

All I had was right now, and right now was pretty damn grim.

I went down the first set of rocks, looked at the place where there was a level snowbank, not much else, and I thought that must be where Audrey Whittaker's illegal—and to a certain Massachusetts family, dangerous—beach was hidden. Right now, it didn't look dangerous. Just looked empty. Audrey. One of these days, maybe I'd offer an apology to her for having thought she had something to do with this mess.

I moved across the slippery rocks and boulders to the south, scrambling as best as I could, hands cuffed before me, lungs burning with heavy breathing, my back suddenly feeling itchy and exposed, not letting the thoughts of betrayal overcome me. There would be plenty of time for that later. Right now I had to move, had to hide, had to—

Another gunshot. I ducked, glanced behind me, saw a figure up on the snowbank, saw that it was Carla, and I slipped and fell, striking my right knee on an exposed piece of rock, making me snap my jaw in pain. I got up, my bare and handcuffed hands red-raw from being dunked into the snow, and I kept on moving, weaving, thinking that if only I could get more rocks and boulders between me and my pursuer, and if that campaign convoy from Senator Hale finally got up here, even Carla might not want to be running around with a weapon in the midst of all the Secret Service and news media and—

Good thoughts, great thoughts, right up to when I got up on a piece of New Hampshire granite, slippery cold with ice, and fell into the ocean.

THE COLD FELT LIKE a telephone pole being swung against my chest, and I raised my head, coughing and sputtering, completely drenched, salt water in my mouth and nose, and my feet flailed about until I got traction and stood up, and I tried to slog my way back to shore, and I made one step and two—

The waves rolled in, banged me against a couple of rocks, and then dragged me out. The shock to my system made everything look gray, like some sort of veil had been pulled over my eyes. I moved my feet again, this time feeling nothing under me, and the weight of my wet clothes was starting to drag me down. The part of my mind that was still thinking rationally knew that in January in the Atlantic Ocean, I had just a handful of minutes left before hypothermia closed its cold fist around my heart and killed me. That's it. No appeal, no good nature, nothing. Just the cold facts.

I coughed and gasped and raised my head again. I hated being in the ocean even on the hottest days of the year, and in January…there was no coastline before me with open, inviting, sandy beaches and on-duty lifeguards looking for swimmers in trouble, swimmers like me. No, except for that strip of land converted by Audrey Whittaker, this was rocks and boulders and fissures and—

A wave was coming in. I moved with it, hoping the momentum would carry me far enough, and it did. Maybe I was wave riding or something, letting the wave carry me, and if it carried me far enough, I could get traction and—

The wave petered out. I coughed and choked from the salt water. My legs moved again, scrambling, and there was nothing to stand on, and the waves dragged me back, even farther away from safety. I was shivering wildly now, teeth chattering, and I rolled over, tried to get on my back, maybe floating on my back would give me a better chance of getting to shore and…

On my back, my handcuffed hands on my chest, the hands lobster-red raw, wondering if I could swim somehow, even with my fastened hands, or maybe kick my way to shore, if I was very, very lucky. But I was so cold and my wet clothes were dragging me down and my teeth were chattering and my legs and arms were numb, and I began to imagine things. Imagining I was warm, imagining I was in the desert, that's right, back in the Nevada desert so many years earlier, when I was younger and dumber and full of vim and vigor and energy, fighting the good fight from the Department of Defense, and—

Oh yes. The desert. When my intelligence section was accidentally exposed to something horrible and illegal, and the helicopters came, the helicopters came, and everyone died, everyone save for one poor fool, one poor fool named Lewis…

Now I was certain I was hallucinating. For I was quite warm, warm indeed, and the ocean felt as warm as it did in south Florida, and the sound of the helicopter was quite loud, chattering and overwhelming everything, and I closed my eyes and floated and things felt light indeed before there was nothing else there. Nothing at all.

THE VOICE SAID, "Are you all right? Can you wake up?"

I shifted my weight and winced from the pain in my right knee and—

The pain in my knee.

I opened my eyes and wiped them with my warm and dry hands and—

I sat up. I was in a bed and I looked around and it wasn't a hospital, but it was a hotel room. That was my very first big surprise. My second very big surprise was sitting next to me, in a hotel chair.

Secret Service Agent Glen Reynolds.

"I'm awake now," I said, my voice just barely above a whisper. "And I don't know how all right I am. I hurt like hell...but I'm alive. I suppose I have the Secret Service to thank for that."

"You do."

"Very well. Thank you. Thank you very much."

I sat up in the bed, put a pillow behind my back, winced again from the pain in my leg, and said, "The senator?"

"He's fine. Just gave a hell of a campaign speech a while ago."

"His wife?"

"Standing right next to him like a good wife and the possible first lady she might become. All nice and normal."

I looked again at the room. A funny world. It seemed like we were in the Lafayette House. How bloody ironic.

"And Harmon Jewett? And his woman companion?"

Reynolds shrugged. "In custody, talking to us. And they'll probably be in custody for the foreseeable future."

"I see."

I moved again in the bed and the pain wasn't as sharp this time. Goody. I was making progress. I looked at Agent Reynolds and remembered the last time we met, and what he had told me about staying away from the senator's wife and bookstores. I said, "You've been following me, right?"

"Of course. Off and on, here and there. We would have been remiss if we hadn't. For a few days you were the chief suspect in the attempted assassination of a leading presidential candidate. You were subsequently cleared of that attack, but just because you were cleared for that doesn't mean you were cleared for doing anything stupid in the future."

"Thanks. I think."

"You're welcome, Mr. Cole. You see, you have an odd and dark background, which we couldn't get into, no matter how much we dug," Agent Reynolds said pointedly, as if it had always been my fault. "So yes, we kept an eye on you. Right up to the point when you went for a swim earlier today after your visit to Mrs. Whittaker's home. Lucky for you, we had an airborne asset in the area, and we were able to reel you in after you took that swim. Any longer…they would have reeled in a corpse."

"How in hell did you bring me here?"

He shrugged. "Through a service elevator. So things would be nice and quiet without all that nasty publicity."

I rubbed my wrists and saw that one was bandaged, the one I had cut on the glass shard back in the basement. I looked at him and his calm appearance, and I said, "You guys are up to something, aren't you."

"Define 'something.'"

"So far, you haven't threatened me with arrest. Or anything else. We're having an adult, intelligent conversation. No mention of Harmon and the senator's wife conspiring either to have him killed or to lose the election. All the while using me as their handy-dandy nut with a grudge."

Reynolds held his hands together in his lap. "That's sheer speculation and idle chitchat, Mr. Cole, and you know it. If Harmon and his friend do face the music, it will be on violating federal firearms and explosives statutes, and probably homicide, if we're lucky and we find the right evidence."

"Homicide?"

"Of course. Mr. Jewett's companion, Carla, claims that Mr. Jewett killed his cousin, one William Spenser Harrison, aka Spenser Harris, just a few days ago. Carla wants a deal before saying anything else about the circumstances or location of his death, and right now, it's in the lawyers' hands. Which is fine. We don't like people pretending to be Secret Service agents, and since it looks like this fake Secret Service agent met a demise that he so richly deserved, I'm quite content to let others take care of matters."

"I see."

Reynolds said, "You wouldn't happen to know where Mr. Harris is currently located, would you?"

I said carefully, "I've not spoken to him since that day before the attempted assassination."

"So you say."

I changed the subject and said, "What about Barbara Hale?"

"The senator's wife?" he said. "I imagine that she will be traveling apart from the senator during the rest of this campaign… and I also imagine that her movements, conversations, phone calls, and e-mails will be strictly observed just to make sure that any future unpleasantness doesn't occur."

"The senator…he knows?"

"Of course."

"And…"

"What do you think?" Reynolds asked. "At this moment, do you think he's going to dump everything to try to have her arrested? Be real, Mr. Cole. He's within a few months of getting his party's nomination. If that means believing that his wife is slightly unbalanced, and that she and her troubles can be kept under wraps and control…well, that's what's going to happen."

The room seemed to vibrate just a bit, as if something were about to spin free and shatter, and I guess it was just a reaction to my deep-January swim. I shivered suddenly and pulled the thick blankets closer to me.

"So it's a cover-up. Why's that?"

Now Reynolds smiled. "Cover-up is such a loaded phrase. We prefer…we prefer a reality check."

"A what?"

"Reality check. And the reality is…well, I know a bit about your background, Mr. Cole, which is why we're having this kind of conversation. In your previous life you had a very high security clearance. That's why I think I can trust you with what you said earlier, about having an adult conversation."

"Go on," I said.

"For the past several years and campaign cycles, the Secret

Service has become a modern-day Praetorian Guard. We've been putting our elected officials in a safe, quiet bubble, where never is there a disquieting word to be heard. We've been on our way to losing our professionalism, and becoming just another part of the political process. You know, the sane, noncorrupted, noncynical political process that makes this country so great and admired."

"I see."

He shook his head. "We got a new administrator two years ago. And he put the word down. We were going back to our roots, as a protective force. We weren't going to be adjuncts of an administration or a campaign. We were going to serve and protect. That's it. Mr. Cole, you served some time in government. What's the worst thing that any government agency fears?"

I thought about that for a moment, and was going to say budget cutbacks, when something else came to mind. "Public humiliation or embarrassment."

He gently clapped his hands together. "Exactly. Embarrassment, which leads to headlines and news stories and the death of a thousand cuts from the news media and the Internet."

I thought it over and said, "So... the public release of information from the Secret Service that the wife of a leading presidential candidate is having an affair with a political operative in the campaign, and who may have a role in the shooting attempt on the senator himself…that's not going to happen, is it?"

"Not from us," he said. "You're a bright fellow. Imagine the uproar that would cause. The day before the New Hampshire primary, having a story like that make the front pages of all the newspapers and every minute of every cable show. We'd be accused of trying to influence the election. Of favoring one candidate over another. Of being the power behind the throne of whoever might become the next president." Reynolds shook his head. "Not going to happen, not this time."

I said, "By keeping quiet, you can be accused of the same thing."

"Maybe so. But we keep quiet about a lot of things. About which presidential candidate's spouse has a drinking problem. Which presidential candidate has a fondness for bisexual pornography. Or which child of which candidate has a problem of assaulting women. Not our job to make that stuff public. So here we are."

I was feeling warmer, though my right knee was throbbing like the proverbial son of a bitch. "So here we are," I said. "Is this the point in time when you tell me to keep my mouth shut, or else?"

Reynolds smiled and said, "No. It isn't the time. Not sure if that moment will ever come, no matter how many bad movies you've seen or bad books you've read. But it is the time when I tell you it's your choice to do what you will about what happened to you. And that you should think carefully about the choice you make."

"How's that?"

He said, "In a manner of minutes, I'm going to leave this room, Mr. Cole. A doctor is going to come in to give you a final check-over. The room is yours for the night, if you'd like. And after I leave, you can do whatever you want. Stay here. Depart. Call up CNN and tell them everything you know…However…"

"Yes?"

"What you need to think about is this," Reynolds said. "You have it in your power to destroy or damage the candidacy of Senator Jackson Hale. You. And it's up to you to decide if it's worth it…for some sense of justice or getting back at a woman who apparently used you and betrayed you. For what it's worth, a fair number of people want Hale in the White House. Do you want to keep that away from them?"

"I don't know," I said. "But if I do talk, it'll make things hell for you, won't it."

"We've been through hell before. Like November 1963. We'd survive. Question for you…I know you like your privacy. Would you survive?"

I looked at that professional face, the face of a man sworn to throw his body in front of an assassin's bullet for a man or woman who might not even be worth it. Some sort of man, some sort of dedication.

I burrowed back into my blankets.

"Sure, I'd survive," I said. "But there's more to everything than survival."

Reynolds stood up. "Ain't that the truth." He reached inside his coat pocket, took out a business card and passed it over. "Here you go. My card. Business and cell phone and home phone numbers…call me if I can do you a favor, or something."

I looked at the card and said, "How about now?"

He shrugged. "Sure. Go ahead."

"My…my friend Annie. She's involved with the Grayson campaign. I want to make sure that…well, if Barbara Hale can't get at her husband, I want to make sure that nothing bad happens to Annie."

A quick nod. "Sure. I'll make sure it happens. Anything else?"

"Not at the moment."

He started for the door. "If that's the case, Mr. Cole, well, it's been a bit of an adventure getting to know you. Look forward to the adventure ending tonight."

"Back to Boston?"

"I wish. Off to South Carolina, for the next stop on this crazy trip we call choosing a president."

Damn. I turned and looked at a small digital clock on the nightstand and the coldness returned and I said, "That time right? Is it really that late?"

"Sure is," he said, now at the door, "and I've got to get going."

So he left and I looked at the clock again. It was just past 9 p.m.

I was supposed to have met Annie Wynn, in Room 110, more than four hours earlier.

I picked up the phone at my side—and, by the way, confirmed that I was at the Lafayette House—and called her cell phone. Went directly into voice mail. I left a long and heartfelt message, and then I called home to check messages on my answering machine. Eight messages, all reminding me to vote tomorrow.

None from Annie.

I called her cell phone again.

And went straight to voice mail again.

Damn.

There was a knock on the door and I called out, "Coming!" thinking that maybe some magic had been worked, that Annie was here to see me, but no, no such luck on this cursed day. I went to the door and opened it and a sour-looking man in an ill-fitting brown suit said, "Mr. Cole? Frank Higgins, on contract with the Secret Service. I'm here to see that you're breathing and all that."

He looked me up and down. "And I can tell that you're at least doing that."

I went back inside the room. "Nice diagnosis, so far."

"Yeah, well, the night's still young."


ABOUT A HALF HOUR LATER, I was hobbling my way through the lobby of the Lafayette House, my right knee in a brace, leaning on a metal cane, the metal cold and uncomfortable in my stiff fingers. The lobby was crowded with all sorts of campaign people, press types and the usual hangers-on, some passing out press kits or leaflets, grabbing almost everyone and anyone trying to get his or her message out before the big day tomorrow.

I went past the gift shop and then made my way in, looking for a familiar or friendly face, and found neither. There was a young woman I didn't recognize behind the counter, dressed in black and with a hoop through her left nostril, leafing through a copy of *Rolling Stone* magazine that had a nightmarish cover depicting all of the candidates currently traipsing through my home state.

I went up to her and said, "Is Stephanie off tonight?"

She looked at me and said, "Hunh?"

"Stephanie Sussex. The gift shop manager. Where is she?"

"Oh," the young woman said, flipping through another page. "She don't work here no more."

It was like I was back in the ocean again. "What?"

"She don't work here no more. I guess she got fired."

"Fired? Why?"

She shrugged. "Heard she pissed off the boss. Which isn't hard to do, if you know what I mean."

I said, "I do. I really do."

Damn. I turned around. What a perfect way to end a perfectly miserable day.

# NINETEEN

GETTING HOME was challenging, with my bum knee and the rubber-tipped metal cane slipping on the snow and ice. Usually, the sight of my home at night is welcoming. Seeing that small place of refuge and comfort by the water's edge after the past forty-eight hours I had just experienced should have cheered me up, but it didn't. It looked dark and brooding and I thought that if it wasn't for my hurting knee, I would have turned around and gone back up to the hotel, to take Agent Reynolds up on his offer for the free stay.

But instead I made my way inside, checked again for messages—none—and turned up the heat. I poured myself a big glass of Bordeaux and stretched out on the couch, wincing at the pain, pulling a down comforter over myself. I called Annie three more times on her cell phone. The phone wasn't picked up, not once.

I drank my wine and if I had had the energy, I would have built a fire, but the energy just wasn't there. To torture myself, I guess, I turned on the television and went through the various cable channels, catching the headlines of the evening, a few hours before the start of the New Hampshire primary. The campaigners were scrambling and the polls were in disarray—not one of them agreeing with another—and I saw just one thing that made me smile, a story that Senator Nash Pomeroy was trying hard to kill: the junior senator from Massachusetts was about to drop out of the race over the next several weeks. The spokesmen and spokeswomen for Senator Pomeroy seemed halfhearted in their denials of the story, which had been first reported in a small newspaper based in Tyler, New Hampshire, and later broadcast across the world.

Good job, Paula, I thought, thinking that here at least was one place where I hadn't carpet-bombed to dust my relationship with someone dear to me.

I finished off the wine and pulled the comforter up and watched television until I fell asleep.

THE PHONE CALL from a woman came late that night, just before midnight.

I scrambled some in the darkness on the couch, reached the phone and put it on my chest and said, "Hello?"

"Lewis?"

A woman's voice, but one I didn't recognize. "Yeah. Who's this?"

"Lewis, my name is Angie Hawley. I'm an assistant for Barbara Hale, Senator Jackson Hale's wife."

I rubbed my eyes in the darkness. "Good for you. Must be a hell of a job."

She ignored my little editorial comment and said, "I have something I need to pass along to you."

"You do? What's that?"

"Mrs. Hale wants to—"

"Wait."

I sat up, rubbed my eyes again.

"Sir?" she asked. "Are you there?"

"Yeah. Hold on. Are you telling me that you have a statement for me? From Barbara Hale?"

"Well, it's not really a statement, it's more like a—"

"Wait, just one more time. Is she there?"

"No, it's just me."

"So she doesn't want to talk to me one-on-one. She wants you to read a statement to me. Am I right?"

She stopped, like she was trying to figure out how to appease me, and she said, "Partially right, sir. But—"

I said, "Sorry, not interested," and I hung up.

And surprisingly enough, it didn't take too long to fall back to sleep.

THE RINGING PHONE woke me from a dream in which I was sinking into the ocean, icebergs around my feet, and a woman said, "Hello?" and I said, "Annie?"

"Um, no, sir, this is the campaign of Congressman Wallace calling, to see if you need a ride to the polls today, and—"

I hung up. Scratched my chin. Checked the time. Almost nine o'clock. Sweet God.

I picked up the phone again, dialed the number that was burned into me.

Nothing.

Damn.

I switched on the television and made a light breakfast of tea and toast, and ate while sitting on the couch. I had a bit of a smile in seeing that the thriving metropolises of Dixville Notch and Harts Location, up in the northern regions of the state, had opened and closed their polls overnight, thereby casting the very first votes in the very first primary state, said votes totaling about a dozen. I suppose it was a testament to the depths that the news media and the campaigns had sunk that these few votes were interpreted and analyzed for most of the morning by people who should have known better.

I was washing my meager dishes when the phone rang again, and I hopped over and picked it up and sat down and said, "This better not be a solicitation of any sorts."

The man on the other end laughed. "Hell of a way to start Primary Day."

I sat on the couch. "Felix. What's up? Thought you'd be at Pomeroy headquarters."

He laughed again. "After what I found out for them, I took their cash and practically went into hiding. It's going to be a rough week or two for all concerned before the plug gets pulled on the campaign. What are you up to?"

"Sitting. Watching. Waiting."

"You vote yet?"

I looked out the window, at the cloudy sky. "Nope."

"You going to?"

I said, "Wasn't planning to."

"Why the hell not? Sure doesn't sound like you, not at all."

I looked at the brown brace holding my knee together. "Well, I banged up my knee yesterday."

"What happened?" Felix asked.

"I'll tell you later. Right now, it hurts like hell and I don't feel like moving."

Felix said, "Man it up, nancy-boy. I'm coming over to get you to the polls."

"Hey," I said, but by then, I was talking to a dead phone.

TRUE TO HIS WORD, Felix rolled in about fifteen minutes later. He came through the front door without knocking and whistled when he looked at my knee brace and the metal cane that I was using.

"What does the other person look like?"

"A hell of a lot better than me," I said.

"Care to tell me the story?"

"Promise to keep quiet?"

His face fell a bit, like I had insulted him, and he said, "After all these years…"

"Oh, for God's sake, put away that hurt puppy look and help me get out of here."

In a flash, his ready smile returned and he said, "Point noted. Sometimes I like to practice the hurt puppy look. You wouldn't believe the places and the women it's gotten me."

"I can imagine."

He laughed. "No, you can't."

I grabbed a coat and made my way to the front door. Felix was driving a black Toyota Highlander with dealer plates, and as he helped me down the steps, I said, "What's going on here? You've been raiding a local dealership?"

"No, just partial payment for a favor done, that's all."

We went around to the passenger's side door, and Felix opened the door and helped boost me up, and I felt slightly ashamed, like I was suddenly old and needed help to get around. Before Felix closed the door, I said, "What kind of favor?"

He said, "There's a dealership in Porter where I get my Mercedes serviced. The service manager had a problem with his daughter. Or, more to the point, the daughter's boyfriend. The daughter was no longer interested in the boyfriend. The boyfriend had other ideas and was quite determined in his other ideas. The police did what they could, but the boyfriend…well, he was persistent. When I found out what was going on, I had a talk with said boyfriend and showed him a better way of living. Case closed."

"Really?"

He gave a slight shake of his head. "Young men like that, they really need to learn how to channel all that excessive negative energy, especially when it comes to relationships. So I gave the young man an opportunity to redirect his energies away from trying to win back his old girlfriend to something more productive."

"Which was…"

A wide smile before he closed the door. "Teaching himself how to be left-handed for the next month or two, after growing up right-handed."

ALONG THE WAY to the polling station, I said, "You know, I've never really seen this part of you, Felix."

"Which part is that?"

"The civic part, interested in voting and all that. Doesn't quite…fit."

Felix said, "Oh, my friend, it does fit, and fit very well."

"Really?"

"Oh yes."

We were on Atlantic Avenue, heading south, and then he turned north on Winnicut Road, one of the direct routes into Tyler proper. We passed through an area of homes and subdivisions, and a fair number of homes had campaign signs out in the snowbanks. The last day, I thought, the very last day. And then the signs would magically disappear overnight and New Hampshire would once again return to its usual state of peace, harmony, and understanding among all peoples.

Yeah, right. In a month some of these signs would still be there, the paint faded, the sticks cracked, still waving in the breeze like the banners of a defeated army, stuck in the mud of some forgotten battlefield.

Felix said, "My grandfather's fault, I guess. Mikos Tinios. Grandpa Mikey is what we called him. A short guy, spoke passable English, had a thick white handlebar mustache and loved to play tricks on his grandkids. You know what I mean. Pulling nickels out of our ears, making cards disappear, stuff like that. Lots of laughs. Seemed like the happiest guy you could ever meet. And one day…oh, I don't know how old I was, I was maybe eleven or twelve, he was in his backyard—about five yards to a side, but he was so damn proud of that little plot of earth—sunning himself. I still remember what he was wearing, these old khaki shorts and beat-up sneakers, and he was under a beach umbrella, drinking ouzo or something, and I saw these old, old scars on his chest and belly. And, being the inquisitive little squirt that I was, I asked him about it."

"And what did Grandpa Mikey say?"

Felix's voice was quiet, almost somber, a tone I usually don't associate with him. "At first, he tried to make a joke about it, about being a circus performer and being mauled by lions and tigers, but I didn't believe him, not for a moment. I mean, the old boy used to tell me stories about gypsies and Greek gods and ghosts, so I didn't believe the circus crap."

"So suspicious at such a young age," I said.

"Yeah, well, blame my environment. Anyway, so I pressed him and pressed him, and finally, the story came out. Old happy Grandpa Mikey, he with the big booming laugh and love for his family, was a partisan in Greece during the 1940s. Some of the scars, he told me, came from the Nazis…and others came from the communists, during the civil war after World War II, and then he changed the subject. Even my dad didn't say anything to me about it, it was my mom who told me the rest. Grandpa Mikey was a famous partisan fighter, famous for going behind enemy lines—whether they be German lines or communist lines—and doing the killing that had to be done. With a knife. Never a firearm. Too noisy. With a knife…And when something approaching peace had finally come to Greece, Grandpa Mikey came to America…and you know what? I think he was happiest here, in the States. And not once did he ever forget to vote. Not once. When I got older and he got older, and getting him to vote meant bundling him in a wheelchair and carrying an oxygen tank along, he told me that it was a blessing to be in this land, where you settled your arguments at the ballot box, and not with a knife blade or a bomb."

Now we were at the polling station for the town, the uptown fire station for Tyler. Felix found a parking spot near the rear and said, "So I make it a point to vote, and I've not missed an election yet. All for Grandpa Mikey. In his memory."

"Good story," I said.

"Wasn't a story," he said back. "It's the real deal. So, go ahead and do your part, all right? I'll be waiting for you. And maybe later you'll tell me about that knee of yours."

"Okay," I said, stepping out, wincing as my right foot hit the ground and my banged-up knee flexed some. I walked across the plowed parking lot to the front of the fire station, where the town's uptown fire engine and ladder truck had been pulled out to make room in the equipment bay for the voting stations.

A mass of people were outside the door leading into the fire station, all of them holding signs or placards for their various candidates. There was nothing else on the ballot today save presidential candidates, and sample ballots were pasted up at the doors leading into the fire station. I spared them a quick glance as I hobbled up to the doorway.

On one ballot, there would be one name listed, that of the current president, who was running unopposed. And on the other ballot, besides a host of minor candidates, the list would include those names that I had become so familiar with these past months. Senator Jackson Hale, Senator Nash Pomeroy, Congressman Clive Wallace, and retired general Tucker Grayson. The volunteers were laughing and talking and were trying to make eye contact with us few voters as we trickled in, and they all stood behind orange tape, strung along some sawhorses on loan from the Tyler Highway Department.

Among the people were two Tyler police officers, making sure that the campaign workers kept their distance—New Hampshire is very strict on anyone hassling voters as they enter their polling stations—and one of them turned and said, "Hey, Lewis. What in hell happened to your leg?"

It was Detective Sergeant Diane Woods, of course, and I went over to her and said, "A slip and a fall. Nothing too serious. How are you?"

She was smiling. "Great. Voters are fine, the campaign folks are minding us and keeping behind the barrier, and I'm making some good detail time. Man, the money I made off these people this year…Kara and I are going to have fun trying to spend it all."

"Glad to hear it," I said.

I was going to say something else but she gently grasped my upper arm. "Would love to chat with you some more, friend, but I have to at least pretend I'm working."

"Understood."

She said, "Anyway, it's good to see you. Lunch next week?"

"Sure," I said, and as I went into the fire station, I think Diane called out, asking me how Annie was, but I pretended not to hear her.

Inside was the low murmur of people working, of democracy in action. On a table to the left was a large blowup of two sample ballots, and overhead were two cardboard signs. A-N, one said, O-Z, the other said, each with an arrow pointing in opposite directions. I got in the A-N line and moved forward, as the line went up to a table where three older women of a certain age sat, with large bound volumes before them. The supervisors of the checklist, making sure that only registered voters got to play at democracy today.

When I reached the table, one lady, wearing black-rimmed eyeglasses with a gold chain hanging from the stems, said, "Name?"

"Cole, Lewis Cole."

She opened up the book and with a ruler in hand went down the list of names. She stopped and looked up. "Address?"

"Mailing address is Box 919, Tyler. Physical address is Eight Atlantic Avenue, Tyler Beach."

She nodded and said, "Mr. Cole, you're listed here as an Independent. That means you can either have a Democrat or Republican ballot. Which do you want?"

I told her and she passed the ballot over and said, "Step over there, and one of the poll workers will assist you."

"Thanks," I said, and as I made my way out, she said, "By the way, I love your magazine columns."

I almost froze in my tracks. It had been many, many months since I had heard anything remotely like that.

"I'm glad you do," I said, and I meant every word of it.

In the equipment bay of the fire station, voting booths had been set up, made of a metal framework and covered with stiff canvas, the material being painted red, white, and blue. An older man of a certain age, wearing a VETERANS OF FOREIGN WARS cap, waved me along to an empty booth. I went in with my ballot. Before me was a metal counter that didn't seem too sturdy, and a pencil attached to the booth with a length of string and some tape.

I held the ballot on the counter, examined it, and in the space of five seconds made my mark.

I opened up the curtain and went down to the end of the equipment bay, where a large wooden box, almost the size of a steamer truck, had been placed on yet another table. The hinged box was locked and four or five sets of eyes watched me as I slipped my ballot inside an opening at the top.

There. I had voted. And in the simplicity that is Tyler, New Hampshire, the ballots would be hand-counted in front of election officials and representatives from all the campaigns, and the number of ballots would be matched against the registrar's tally of how many voters had come in. A simple arrangement, and one that didn't lead to conspiracy theories about manipulated electronic voting machines, or, God help us, hanging, pregnant, or swinging chads.

It was a method that had been used in Tyler for two hundred years—that same old wooden box—and I hope it would still be in use two hundred years hence. I went back to the registrar's desk and ensured that my voter affiliation went back to Independent.

And then I took a last glance and listened to the soft murmurs of the people coming in and out of the fire station, the voters here in this small town, one of scores of small towns in my quirky home state, and it felt all right.

Even with the events of the past week, with what I had learned about Senator Hale and his wife, and what I had learned about me and Annie, and the oppo research guy for General Grayson and Felix's own work, and the signs and the phone calls and the mailings, it was all right. This is what counted. Free people coming in for a free election, in a small step to choose our next president. It was loud and unpredictable and vulgar in so many ways, but it ended up working, more often than not.

Near the exit at the rear of the fire station was Paula Quinn, reporter's notebook in hand, and I smiled at her as I approached.

"I thought all you nasty members of the fourth estate weren't allowed inside this sacred precinct," I said.

"Maybe so, but I have pull with the town counsel, as you know. And I'm being very polite, asking a handful of typical voters what they thought of today's primary."

I waited and said, "Well?"

"Well, what?"

"Aren't you going to ask me anything?"

She laughed. "Didn't you hear what I said? I'm looking for a typical voter. You are anything but typical."

"Maybe so, but look who's talking. How's the Nash Pomeroy campaign treating you?"

"The death threats have subsided just a bit, but my word, I owe you a big thanks for that tip, Lewis. It's really worked out for me."

"How's that?"

"You name it—CNN, NBC, Fox—I've been on most of the cable and news channels talking about my story. Millions of people saw me, Lewis. Millions! And just this morning, I got a phone call from a publishing house in New York wanting to know if I can do a quickie book about the primary and its history. Is that fun or what? My very first book."

"Sounds like lots of fun, Paula. I hope it works out for you."

Another smile, a touch on my arm. "I owe you. Big-time."

"Just make sure I get an autographed copy, and we're even."

"Deal."

So I left the fire station and went out in the cold, where an earnest young man who wouldn't take no for an answer claimed to be working for the Voter Resource Group, or something like that, and forced an exit poll questionnaire in my hand. I didn't feel like arguing or fighting, so I took a few minutes to fill out the form on a table set up in the parking lot, and put it in a box to be counted, tabulated, and presented as a story during tonight's evening newscasts on the primary and exit polls, where various pundits would try to decipher the results and explain the Meaning of It All.

As I put the survey form in the box, I hoped other Tyler voters and voters in the rest of the state took my lead, for I told the poll takers that I was a gay woman, between fifty and sixty years of age, making less than ten thousand dollars a year, and that my most pressing concern this election year was deep sea fishing rights. Oh, and to wrap things up, I told them that I had voted for a dead man: Gus Hall, head of the Communist party of the United States.

Democracy in action. Sometimes it ain't pretty, but it sure can be fun.


A FEW MINUTES LATER, I caught up with Felix, who was standing outside his borrowed Highlander. He was talking to two young women whose campaign signs were hanging by their sides, ignored and forgotten, while he chatted them up. They both had long hair—one blond, the other brunet—and he looked at me and said something to the young ladies, and they went back to their assigned tasks.

I got inside the Highlander and Felix joined me, and I said, "What is it with you?"

He laughed. "Just keeping my skills in shape. That's all."

He closed the door and started up the engine, and I said, "Hold on for a second, will you?"

"Sure."

I looked at the voters coming out of the fire station, two or three at a time, and I thought about what it had been like inside. People voting, people coming together, people doing what was right, what had to be done…

There. There it was.

Something small in the grand scheme of things, but something, if I was lucky, could be accomplished before the end of the day.

I turned to Felix. "Feel like keeping other skills in shape?"

"Depends. What do you have in mind?"

"I need to make something right. I'll need you, and I'll need somebody else."

"Who's this somebody else?"

"Someone you've met before."

"Oh," Felix said. "Does he know he's being volunteered?"

"No, but I don't think he cares."

"Where does he live?"

"Right now, in a cooler in a storage facility in Massachusetts."

Felix's face was impassive and stayed that way for a bit, and then he grinned. "See? Always told you that a body could come in handy. What do you have in mind?"

"Head south and I'll tell you," I said. "And another thing. You're going to get a videotape in the mail, either today or tomorrow."

"I am, am I," he said, pulling out of the parking lot. "And what's that about?"

"I'll tell you that, too," I said. "Plus how I got my leg dinged up."

Felix said, "Damn, you better speak fast. It doesn't take that long to get to Salisbury."

"I'll do my best," I said, and then I began talking.

SEVERAL HOURS LATER my hands were sore, and my knee was throbbing like a son of a bitch, but I was back in the Lafayette House, and back in the office of Paul Jeter. He didn't look too happy to see me, and I knew that his displeasure was going to deepen in the next few seconds or so.

"Well?" he said. "I agreed to see you because you said you had something to tell me, something of great importance to the Lafayette House. Get on with it."

"Sure, but first I need to know something from you. What's happened to Stephanie Sussex?"

"Who?"

Oh, so he was in the mood to play games. "You know who she is. Your gift store manager."

"Our former gift store manager."

"Why is she your former gift store manager?"

"I would imagine that's none of your business."

"Probably. But as a friend, I would really like to know."

"And I would really like to know why you're here. Mind telling me?"

"All right, I will," I said. I took a cell phone out of my pocket and flipped it open, manipulated a button or two, and passed it over to him. He held the cell phone with distaste, like I had pulled it out of a sack of dung, and then his expression really went south when he looked at the cell phone, and then looked at me.

"What's the meaning of this?"

"Recognize the room?" I asked.

"Of course. It's one of our suites. And who is this…man?"

I now held my cane in my hands, to have something to do with them, I guess, or to prevent my hands from shaking. I said, "Who the man is doesn't really matter. What matters is the room that he's in. The room is registered to a Michael Marone. You and I both know that that name is a fake. The room actually belongs to a star Boston Celtics player. I don't have to say any more about that, now do I?"

Now his face was alternating between the paleness of shock and the redness of anger. It was an amazing thing to watch.

"You…you…who the hell is this man?"

I reached over and took the cell phone out of his hand. It belonged to Felix and I had promised him I would bring it back to him, right after he had made some phone calls to contacts in Boston to find out certain bits of information that were turning out to be quite helpful.

"I don't know who this man is," I said. "But what I do know is this. He's dead. Quite dead. And he's in your hotel, and he's in the room of a star guest. All I need to do is to make a single phone call to a friend of mine in the Tyler Police Department, and a storm of publicity is going to descend upon this hotel like nothing you can imagine. Add in the fact that because of the primary, we have a large portion of national news media representatives in the area…you can just imagine what will happen. That Celtic's career will take a major hit. Any other prominent guests you have here will want to take their business elsewhere.

And all this negative attention will no doubt mean the Lafayette House will be looking for a new manager before the end of the week."

I could see the emotions struggling underneath that expression, and it was vaguely repellent, like seeing two caged scorpions fight it out. Finally he seemed to catch his composure and he said, "How did you get that body up there without being seen?"

"Trade secret," I said.

He pondered that for a moment and said, "What do you want?"

"I want Stephanie Sussex to have her job back at the gift shop. I want her to get a nice little raise. And I want her job protected, so that in a month or six months or a year, she doesn't get laid off because of some sort of restructuring. You agree to that and the body is out of here within a half hour, and nobody has to know anything. How does that sound?"

"How do I know I can trust you?"

"Because I'm such a quiet and considerate neighbor. Most of the time."

It looked like he wanted to spit at me but instead he said, "You have a deal, you bastard. Now get out of my office and get the hell out of my hotel."

I got up, leaning on my cane. "My pleasure."

I WAITED OUT in Felix's borrowed vehicle, in the rear service area of the Lafayette House, and eventually Felix came out with a laundry cart, whistling, it looked like. He maneuvered the cart to the rear of the Highlander and opened it up, and I stared straight ahead while Felix did his work back there. I wished I could have helped him, but I was still too damn sore. There was a thumping, and the sound of something being dragged across the carpeting of the vehicle, and then Felix climbed in and said, "What now?"

"Can you…can you place him somewhere?"

"Sure."

I handed over a business card. "Good. And when you're done, make a call from a pay phone…maybe in Maine or New York, if you're paranoid. Just let the guy on the other end know what you've done and where Spenser can be found."

Felix took the card. "You sure?"

"Yes."

"This is the Secret Service agent who arrested you last week, right?"

"Right," I said. "But he's also the Secret Service agent who arranged to have me pulled from the ocean yesterday."

Felix pocketed the card. "Consider it done."

FELIX MADE THE SHORT DRIVE to take me home, and riding in the rear, nice and quiet, was the mysterious Spenser Harris, ending up who knows where. I asked Felix just that question and he said, "Let me worry about that. All right? You'll see it in the newspapers soon enough, I'm sure. Just remember this. Uncle Felix knew best…never throw away a body unless you know you don't have a need for it."

"But at the time, I didn't know that."

"Which is why I know best," and he glanced back for a moment, adding, "though I sure as hell didn't think this poor son of a bitch would be traveling so much."

"I'm sure he's not complaining."

Felix said, "You think? Now. Here you go. Need a hand getting inside?"

"Nope," I said, opening the door to the cold air and the sound of the ocean and the sight of my home. "I can make do."

"Glad to see that. Now it's time to go home and see who the hell won today."

I turned and smiled before shutting the door. "Don't you know who won today?"

"No, I don't. Do you?"

"Sure," I said, and as I closed the door, I called out, "The American people."

WHEN I GOT INSIDE, I found that there were five messages on my answering machine, four of which were frantic calls from the various campaigns to make sure I had voted, and if I hadn't voted, a quick call would mean I could get a ride to the polls, right up to the last minute. Not a problem at all, Mr. Cole, so please do call us if you can, they all said. I deleted all four of those messages, and I took my time listening to the fifth one, the one that meant very much to me. The phone message had poor quality, like it had been made in a very loud and very empty space, and as it started, it turned out that my guess was right.

"Hey, Lewis, it's Annie," her tired voice began. "I'm at the Manchester airport. Things are closing down here at campaign headquarters, and you know what? I've changed my mind. I'm off to South Carolina after all."

I closed my eyes. Her voice had gotten a bit shaky at those last few words. Even amid the ambient noise of the airport terminal, I could hear the intake of breath as she went on with her message.

"Don't take offense…and please, believe me, it has nothing to do with you not being with me last night at the rally. I know something important must have happened, and I know you want to tell me all about it…but I don't want to talk things out. I'm tired of talking. I like doing things. I like accomplishing things. And I helped accomplish a lot here in the state these past few weeks. And to see everybody pack up and start preparing for the next battle…I didn't want to abandon them. Oh, hell, I do want to be with you, but these people…I'm part of something now, something I want to see through. And…well, it's like this, Lewis. I'm going to South Carolina because I believe in something, something very important to me. Something that I'm ready to give up my schooling and my career…and other things…for, to do what I have to do. As for you…I don't know what you believe in, Lewis. I just don't know. Do you? Do you believe in something?"

She coughed and her voice quickened. "Well. They're calling my flight. You take care…and I'm sure we'll talk sometime. And I know I'll be back to see you soon. Just not now. Bye."

I held the phone for a bit, and hung it up, and just looked outside at the wide and unforgiving ocean.

What do you believe in? she had asked.

What do you believe in.

And what I wanted to say was this: I believe in you, Annie,

and I believe in your dedication to the man you want to become president, and because of that, I kept secret what happened to me and his wife and his wife's lover, so that I wouldn't destroy a campaign that was so important to you.

That's what I believe in.

I listened to the message one more time, erased it, and then spent the next few hours on the couch, watching the various campaign coverage. I didn't eat, didn't drink, just kept in view what was going on with all the pollsters, pundits, and talking heads.

I paid particular attention to the representatives from the different campaigns, for like Paula Quinn had predicted a few days earlier, each and every one of them had declared victory.

Nice to be so sure.

Oh, how I envied them that.

# TWENTY

THE DAY AFTER THE PRIMARY, freezing rain set in, and I almost slipped twice in my driveway, going up to get my newspapers, even while using my cane. The lobby of the Lafayette House was full of reporters, campaign staffers, and other various primary-related folk, all trying to get out of town to the next leg of this circus called democracy, and I ignored them all as I went into the gift shop. Stephanie Sussex was there, smiling at me, back at her old job, and for a bit I felt good. I had finally made some amends to someone.

I went to pay for my morning papers and Stephanie refused to take my bills. "Are you kidding?" she said. "Not after what you did for me so I could get my job back."

"How do you know I had anything to do with that?" I asked

Her eyes flashed at me. "Don't think I'm stupid," she said. "I got fired because Paul learned I had been through the surveillance tapes. The fact I got my job back in just over a day...I'm sure you had something to do with it. I'm positive."

I smiled as I put the papers under my arm. "Maybe so...but I have to keep a secret."

She looked about her and lowered her voice. "So. What did you do? Hurt him? Threaten him?"

I shook my head. "Nope. I just pointed out the error of his ways, and he was eager to cooperate."

That made her laugh. "Must have been a pointer made of steel, aimed at the little bit of flesh inside him called a heart. You go on home, now, and stay out of the rain. All right?"

"Sure," I said, and as I turned to make my way out of the gift shop, Stephanie murmured something and I said, "Did you say something?"

Her face looked like I had caught her at something, and she said, "Um…just a little saying, Lewis. Something I learned in catechism class, many years ago. A righteous man will get his rewards, both in heaven and on earth, and I was saying I was sure there were many rewards waiting for you. For what you did for me."

I nodded in appreciation. "Thanks, Stephanie. I appreciate that."

She waved a hand. "Go on. I'll see you tomorrow…and don't bother bringing any money, all right?"

"You've got it."

Outside in the lobby, I made my way to the doorway and then stopped. The freezing rain was coming down hard, sweeping across the parking lot, drenching those few guests coming in, holding up umbrellas or newspapers over their heads. The lobby was emptying out and even though I didn't feel any particular affection for the primary and what it had spawned, I could sense a taste of loneliness, of emptiness, as these driven people left my fair state and went somewhere else.

So I stood there, just watching the rain fall. I suppose I should have put the papers under my coat, and worked my way down to my house to watch the news of the post-primary, to see the talking heads at work, to build a fire and hunker down and be safe and alone in my home.

Like before.

That's what I should have done.

To go home, be safe, be quiet, be alone.

Like before.

But instead, I went to a nearby bank of phones, and made a phone call, and I was lucky for the very first time this day, as a familiar and friendly voice answered.

I said, "Felix?"

"Of course. Who else?"

I smiled at his teasing voice. "Just checking. I need a favor. Like, right now."

He said, "Yesterday wasn't enough, what we did with Paul Jeter and your fake Secret Service agent?"

"Oh, it was plenty, but I'd like to think you got some professional experience out of it, experience you can use down the road."

"Maybe so," he said, laughing. "Maybe so. What do you need?"

"Ride to the airport."

"Which one? Manchester or Logan?"

"Don't know yet. I'll figure it out by the time you get here."

"Where's here? Aren't you home?"

"Nope," I said. "I'm in the lobby of the Lafayette House, and that's where I want you to pick me up."

"Right now? Aren't you going to pack?"

"No, I'm not. I need to get to the airport, and I need to get to South Carolina. Today."

He laughed again. "All right, Lewis. I'll be there in just a bit. And if I can be so bold to ask, what the hell is in South Carolina?"

I looked at the cold, driving rain, and thought about a warmer place, a nicer place, and I said, "My reward. I need to get to my reward."

"Good for you," Felix said, and after hanging up the phone, I just waited, and no doubt the people coming in and out of the Lafayette House wondered about the smile on my face, but some secrets, I would always keep.

*The*

# WIFE
# WHO
# WASN'T

# The

# WIFE
# WHO
# WASN'T

## ALTA IFLAND

New Europe Books

Williamstown, Massachusetts

Published by New Europe Books, 2021
Williamstown, Massachusetts
www.NewEuropeBooks.com
Copyright © 2021 by Alta Ifland
Front cover art © 2021 by Peter Andrew Selgin
Interior design by Knowledge Publishing Services

ISBN: 9781734537918

Cataloging-in-Publication data is available from the Library of Congress.

First edition

10 9 8 7 6 5 4 3 2 1

# Part I
# Santa Barbara, California
# 1996–1997

# Samuel

For most of us it's not easy to look back and pin down the exact moment when things began to unravel and move insidiously toward a point in the future when they would boil over and explode. For Samuel Goldstein, it was easy. Date: September 22, 1996. Location: the Los Angeles International Airport. Protagonists: a woman in her mid-thirties, dressed in a burgundy business suit with a white nylon blouse and high-heeled red shoes, who, after seventeen hours of travel, is about to get off a Boeing 747, and a man in his late forties, tall, with a slight middle-age potbelly but still relatively muscular, wearing a cream linen suit, and carrying a bouquet of red roses in his right hand, and a cardboard sign bearing the inscription "Tania" in his left. Although the man is not bad looking for his age—to begin with, he still has a full head of hair—standing there with that sign, those silly roses, and, most of all, that inane smile plastered on his face, he looks like an idiot. At least that's what he thinks. He'd very much like to get rid of the flowers, or the sign, but he can't do that, so in the end he just drops his imbecilic smile. But at that exact moment, the moment when he decides to stop smiling,

he recognizes her. He recognizes the woman right away (though they haven't seen each other in over half a year), not because she is very memorable, but because there is something that makes her stand out in the crowd. It may be her hair, whose puffed-up curls remind him of the sixties, or her swinging hips, marking her territory as she advances like a lioness toward prey, or her very thick ankles straining above the high heels. When she is almost near him, he notices that her skin looks very young, white and plump like a baby's, and her lips, equally plump, have the shine and luminescence of a wet, luscious grape. She gives him a large smile and kisses him on both cheeks. As she does this, he can feel the pressure of her fleshy breasts under her restraining suit, and, when she steps back, he takes notice of the cleavage that reveals the appetizing line where said breasts begin. The woman is definitely on the plump side, but not in an unpleasant way.

In the car, before the air conditioning had time to kick in, overwhelmed by a pungent odor of female armpit sweat, he remembered how his parents used to send packages with basic hygienic items—soap, toothpaste, deodorant—to their relatives in Moldova.[1] After the death of his parents, who were born there, whatever correspondence had existed with his relatives in the old country had stopped. For him, the old country was practically fiction, a fog out of which occasional shapes emerged only to recede immediately into the same darkness. He never would have imagined that he'd end up marrying a woman from there—not in this way. In fact, he'd had no intention of ever remarrying. After the death of his wife ten years earlier, he'd surrounded himself and his (then) six-year-old daughter with an invisible ivory fence, within which he'd created a small paradise for the two of them, but which eventually proved inadequate for a teenage girl. Schooled at home, with no friends her own

age except for Bill's son, Todd, Anna had grown into a wild creature. The first time Samuel had contemplated the possibility of remarrying, Bill had come over to tell him a story he'd heard from Todd, and concluded, half-joking, half-serious, with the suggestion that Anna needed a mother, "a woman to help her with the facts of life." "It's not normal for a fourteen-year-old girl"—Anna's age at the time—"not to know where children come from," Bill added, lighting the cigar his friend offered him.

Todd had come home covered in bruises, and, when questioned, had reluctantly confessed to having received a beating from Anna. He was a few months older and strong enough to defend himself, but she'd taken him by surprise, and, after she wrestled him to the ground, had showered him with a series of quick but incredibly powerful blows. At fourteen, Anna was taller and more robust than most girls her age; part of it was, no doubt, genetics, Samuel being a tall, hefty man himself; but more than genetics, what counted were all the years she'd spent outdoors, climbing trees, swimming and running like a tomboy.

"So, you got beaten up by a girl," Bill had said, laughing. "Was it worth it, at least?"

"She's not a girl," Todd had replied, red with anger. "She's an idiot."

He'd made some allusion to "what married men and women do," and, intrigued, Anna had asked him to be more specific. Then, he'd made an obscene gesture. Indignant, she'd asked him to stop saying "dirty things." To which, he'd replied:

"These aren't dirty things! How do you think you were conceived?"

She'd grown enraged, repeating between stammers:

"What did you say about my parents? What did you say, you ugly little prick?"

In retrospect, the thing that bothered Todd most was the word "ugly." He could overlook "little prick" as an expression uttered mechanically in a moment of anger, but "ugly"? Did Anna really think he was ugly?

His body still ached from the blows and the way she'd immobilized it between her legs, as if in a vise, completely oblivious to the potential sexual implications of her position. In fact, Anna seemed to be unaware that she belonged to the female species, though there had been moments in the past when Todd had had reason to infer that she too went through the monthly ordeal all women go through.

No, it wasn't good for a girl her age to be so ignorant about this sort of thing, Samuel thought after Bill left. And this is when the idea of a "mail-order bride" began to creep in. It's not that he couldn't have found a wife on his own; what worried him was that he'd also have to marry her family and friends. He'd labored so hard to isolate himself and Anna from the rest of the world, from the vulgarity and petty noises that often passed for communal bonding! A wife from the Old World would have the immediate advantage of being an orphan, so to speak: no family, no friends. She would be like a rescued pet, entirely dependent on him. Not to mention the supplemental advantage of a woman from a world where they still believed in taking care of the head of the family! He wasn't particularly conservative, not really, but if he was going to marry at his age, he might as well try to hold onto his current privileges.

Online dating didn't exist yet, but there were plenty of agencies that had sprouted up after the fall of the Berlin Wall that tried to unite in holy matrimony the rancid poverty and hopelessness of women from one side of the wall with the taste for exotic flesh of men from the other. At the time, correspondence was still on paper (at least, for him), yet it took less than a week for

the agency to send him photographs and the contact information of the first woman. If the photographs were any indication of what the woman really looked like, she must have worked as a model, or whatever else gorgeous women did in Moldova. She was twenty-two, had long blond hair, and had photographed herself in a skimpy, lace nightgown. After he rejected the first offer, the agency put him in touch with another woman that looked like the twin sister of the first, and he spent a considerable amount of time on the phone trying to explain that he was looking for something, or rather someone, entirely different, someone "his mother would approve of." These were the words he came up with, exasperated by the standardized forms he'd had to fill out and the lack of understanding of the clerk on the other end who kept asking whether he preferred blondes or brunettes.

And so, the next batch of photos included three women in their mid-thirties, who, judging from the specifications of their height and weight, were no three graces. Two of them had little kids, so it was easy to choose. He picked the one who was free, who, as it happened, was also the prettiest. The photograph was a black-and-white close-up, in which the face, tilted to the right, was circled by the sparkling glow of a silver fur hat and a dark fur collar. The woman had an enchanting smile with cute little dimples on each side, and what appeared to be light blue (or green) eyes. Her name was Tania.

Now, next to her in his Subaru speeding along Highway 101, Samuel thought that the photo must have been at least ten years old. The youthful innocence of the girl in that picture was gone, replaced by a grimace around the mouth and a cunning expression in the eyes, which kept him on his guard. *Well, let's wait and see,* he told himself, as he always did when he was confronted with a confusing situation. *Let's just wait and see.*

# Tania

Dear Mother,

I'm still recovering from the trip, during which I thought I would starve. In fact, if it hadn't been for the apples you so wisely thought of giving me, I probably would have. When they offered us food on the plane, I was afraid to spend what little money I had, so I declined, contending myself with the aromas coming from the meals of my fat neighbors. And wouldn't you know it, it turned out that the meals were included with my ticket. Of course, by the time I realized that, it was too late.

When the car pulled up in the driveway, Sammy—that's what he said I should call him—had to help me out of the car. That's how weak I was. Now that my stomach is full again, I can tell you that *this is Paradise*. Mother dearest, *he is rich!* On our way here, after we'd left the highway, we drove up and up on a country road that snaked its way around trees and through some type of dry vegetation I'd never seen before, ever deeper into the wilderness. For a minute I thought, *What if he's some kind of psychopath and takes me God knows where?* But as soon as I finished that thought, we reached a clearing and I saw it: the house. It

was a bit of a shock: the house is black! Can you believe it? A black house. But the more I looked at it the more I liked it. It's the house of a gentleman. The car is black too. And shiny, as if he bought it yesterday. But the house . . . The way it appears, all of a sudden, from a sea of green shrubs, and beneath a clear blue sky . . . Oh, Mother, you've never seen such blue! Nothing like our gray, always-cloudy skies. Imagine a black house under the blue sky with a row of silver-leafed trees in front (olive trees, Sammy explained), and a flower garden all around . . . Nothing could be more beautiful than its sunflowers against the black of the house. And when I entered the house . . . Are you ready? The kitchen and the bathroom are black marble with golden fixtures. Everything shined as if it was brand new, but, when I asked, Sammy laughed and said that it was thanks to the maid who cleans once a week. He has a maid!

I'll tell you more about the house later. Now listen to this: when I told him I was starving, he apologized, opened the fridge and began to throw something together—something that turned out to be . . . a big salad. Yes, he welcomed me with salad! He opened a bottle of wine, too, but I kept waiting for the real food the salad was meant to accompany. Eventually, I understood that the salad *was* the meal. So, it seems that we have a problem: my Sammy is rich, but stingy. After he left the kitchen, I opened the fridge and helped myself to whatever I found there—some Swiss cheese and salami; there wasn't any bread, so I made do without. Poor man: you can tell he's been a widower for a long time. So rich and so badly fed! You better believe I'm already making a list of things to buy. I wonder if they carry vodka at the supermarket. I didn't have the courage to ask him if he had any—it wouldn't have made a good impression—but I looked everywhere and couldn't find any. I did find lots of other bottles, cognac and liqueur, and even that whiskey stuff they drink. I

tasted it, and I can tell you you're not missing anything: it tastes like a concoction made of ticks.

You're probably wondering why I haven't mentioned the daughter, Anna. Don't worry, no problems yet. It's just that we haven't been introduced. She's visiting some relatives in Los Angeles—here they call it L.A.—and will be back tomorrow. This habit of calling cities and people by their initials! I'll keep you updated on new developments. Give a big hug to Irina and a kiss to Seryozha.

Your daughter,
Tania

# Bill

For the first time in his life, Sammy locked his most valuable pieces of jewelry in the house safe. Up till then, the only times he'd done this was when he traveled and the house remained empty for days or weeks. As he did it, he felt slightly embarrassed, because he was hiding things from his wife. But she was a stranger, and the prospect of having to live, from now on, under the same roof as a stranger appeared in all its worrisome annoyance. As he always did when he had a problem, Sammy tried to reassure himself by invoking the benefits of time. *Give it a little time,* he thought, *and things will fall into place.* But in the meantime, he couldn't help worrying, and so, chose to confide in his only friend, Bill.

Sammy found him on his back porch, sipping, as was usual at that time of day, a martini; or rather, he found two Bills, one in the wicker chair, the other in the reflection of the house's mirror-glass walls, also in a wicker chair, surrounded by a profusion of grass and palm trees. Though only a few years younger than Sammy, his blasé youthfulness made it seem as if

Bill were almost from a different generation. Or maybe his dyed hair kept him forever young.

After he fixed himself his own martini and took a seat beside his host, acknowledging the twin in the mirror—a game he was happy to play when visiting his friend—Sammy wondered which complaint to begin with.

"What would you think of someone eating a ten-inch block of Swiss cheese, a pack of salami, a big bowl of salad, and then asking for something to eat?"

"I'd say they have a healthy appetite," Bill replied with a large grin.

"It's more than I've seen you eat in the entire time I've known you."

"I never claimed to have a healthy appetite. Hell, I never claimed to have a healthy anything."

This self-deprecating remark was slightly disingenuous. A steady regimen of alcohol and daily workouts had given Bill a lean, toned physique and a melancholy bluish tinge under the eyes.

The two men sat in silence, as they usually did, sipping their martinis and shooting occasional glances toward the horizon. It was beginning to cool off, and threads of cold air hung here and there all around them. Sammy got up and, as he took his leave, heard Bill inviting him once again to "bring her over." Bill had politely avoided the word "wife," but, as Sammy walked back, there was no getting around it: he was a married man and his wife was waiting for him at home.

# Tania

Dear Mother,

I never would have thought that I'd move all the way to America, live in a house with black marble in the bathrooms, a fridge as big as a closet, a cleaning woman, but no TV! Yes, I now know what, before, I only suspected: this house has no TV. When I asked my husband why there wasn't one, he answered that he hadn't owned a TV since moving out of his parents' house, that he wanted his daughter to grow up free of the influence of its "poisonous commercials." Oh, Mother, isn't life a joke? Do you remember how thrilled we were a few years ago when Moldovan TV aired its first commercials? I remember them perfectly. I'm beginning to wonder whether this husband of mine might be a communist. After all, *he is a Jew*.

Long story short, I was so upset by this incident that I began to cry. I told him that I didn't come to America to live like a stupid peasant or an African tribeswoman. He said that, if I wanted a TV, I could get one as long as I kept it in my room. And you wouldn't believe it, but a few hours later a truck stopped in front of the house and two men in overalls came

out holding a forty-two-inch color television—something that would make my former classmates green with envy!—which now rests in my bedroom. I was ecstatic at the prospect of watching *Santa Barbara*, but it turned out that the series stopped airing here over three years ago. How's that for irony? To come all the way from the other end of the world to Santa Barbara only to discover when I get to Santa Barbara that there is no *Santa Barbara*.

Speaking of "my room," when Sammy first uttered those words, I hadn't realized I'd be spending the night alone in my own room, in my own bed. Do you remember that white, gauze-thin nightgown I was so happy to get my hands on a month ago? Well, he hasn't seen it yet. At first, I was a little taken aback, but then I thought: my husband is a true gentleman. Or maybe he's waiting for me to make the first move, like those passionate women in American movies who throw their men into bed and jump in on top of them, or who appear in negligées at the bathroom door and shimmy provocatively up to the bed where the man is waiting. Well, I put on my nightgown, my skin peeking out so delightfully that no man could resist me, and entered his room. He was so surprised he literally jumped off his chair—he had been reading the paper or something.

"Can't you knock first?" he shouted.

"Knock?! I'm your wife!"

You can't imagine how humiliated I felt! Later, he came to my room and apologized, saying that "he wanted us to get to know each other first." He seemed sincerely remorseful, so I forgave him. Can you picture any of those troglodytes from back home saying, "I want us to get to know each other first"? Ha! Once again, I told myself that I was lucky. And I could tell, as he sat next to me on my bed, that he wasn't immune to my charms.

I am enclosing a photo of the TV so you can show it to those bitches, Tamara and Sofia. Tell Irina to keep studying English because I'll soon bring her here.


Your daughter,
Tania

# Anna

nna was rarely away from home, but Sammy had decided that it would be less awkward if she were absent upon Tania's arrival, so he sent her to stay with her great-aunt in L.A. When she returned, two days after the newcomer's arrival, her sensitive nose picked up an unusual smell as soon as she crossed the threshold. It may have been all those years spent outside climbing trees and chasing rabbits that led to the development of this uncanny ability: she could tell people apart by their smell. And, as far as Anna was concerned, Tania emanated the strongest, most nauseating odor ever produced by another person: the odor of a sweaty, wild creature, a sweet and sour mixture of hairy armpits that drove her insane. And so, even before Anna laid eyes on the woman, her olfactory glands already hated her with a passion. The creature walked around in a transparent nightgown, her immense breasts flapping insolently, her pink curlers framing her baby-round face.

Since Anna couldn't confide in her father about the woman he'd brought into their lives, she chose to confide in Todd. She knew the path to the Johnsons' residence by heart, every single

shrub and tree, and, whenever she walked down it, felt like a righteous guardian surveying her property. She always carried a stick when she walked, not because she needed it, but because her title and position demanded it. Privately—very privately—she thought of herself as the "Black Queen," that is, the Queen of the Black House, and of Todd as the "Glass Boy"—the boy who lived in the house of glass. The Black Queen was ruthless and unsparing, and, as she walked toward the Glass House, she savored her most recent decree: that every head wearing pink curlers be lopped off.

The path to the Johnsons' curved twice, once to the left—and then, one could see patches of bright, sparkling glass between the tall, green trees—and once to the right—and then, the house vanished from sight. Close as it was, it seemed a Fata Morgana until the end of the path, where the house emerged in all its outlandish glory. When the sun was at its zenith, like now, the house bathed in a blinding pool of light, and one had to squint until one was close enough that the reflection of the trees overpowered the shimmer of light.

Anna was hoping to find Todd outside, but there was no sign of him, so, reluctantly, she knocked on the door. She'd always had ambivalent feelings about the house, the way one had ambivalent feelings about a house in a fairytale, deep in the woods. One never knew whether the sense of mystery that enveloped such a house was a good or a bad omen and one had the foreboding suspicion that behind the colorful, tantalizing walls of sweets, an ugly witch could be hiding. Anna still remembered the day Todd had showed her the house for the first time, a house that more closely resembled an astronauts' moon-base or a high-tech laboratory than a dwelling fit for human habitation. There was a TV and a computer in every room, no rugs, and the sparse furniture, together with the

visitors' movements, were reflected in the whimsical surfaces of the glass walls. All these reflections, added to the images pouring out of the TV screens—each set to a different channel—had the momentary effect of transporting them to a magic realm, with the unfortunate side-effect of giving her a crippling headache for the rest of the day.

It was no wonder, then, that the wizard monitoring all that brittle magic from behind a glass curtain intimidated Anna. When Bill opened the door, holding the glass of whiskey that seemed to accompany him everywhere, Anna took a step back and asked if Todd was around, hoping for an answer that would allow her to leave immediately. Fortunately for her, Todd wasn't home, so, bidding Bill a quick good-bye, she turned her back to him and left, almost running.

Holding his glass, his hair in disarray, his shirt unbuttoned, Bill squinted. Following the girl with his unsteady gaze, he wondered what was different about her. There was something vaguely and imperceptibly disturbing about her, but what? Was it the fact that this girl, who used to fit in his lap, was now taller than his sixteen-year-old son? That, in some ways, she resembled a woman, although, in many others, she was the same little girl? Congratulating himself on having had the good sense to father a boy rather than a girl, he closed the door and went for a refill.

# Tania

Dear Mother,

I can finally get to what you've been waiting for: shopping for groceries. Two days ago, Sammy and I went shopping at a huge store called *Safeway*. First of all, when they go shopping, Americans always take their cars. Their stores aren't just around the corner; you have to drive a good fifteen minutes to get to them.

When we entered the store it felt as if we'd walked into an amusement park full of people who were pushing around some kind of carts on which they'd piled everything they wished to buy. And the shelves, Mother, the shelves! The best thing about American products is their sparkling, multicolored packaging. I couldn't believe how bored all the people seemed, as if the packages meant nothing to them. I wanted to stop and shake them, "Hey, look around! Look at all this beauty! Feast your eyes on it!" I never thought about it, but why did our people have to drain the color from everything? Do you realize that everything around us has always been gray or brown?

Sammy told me that I could get "anything I wanted"— anything! And I did. The more colorful a package was, the better

its chance of ending up in my cart. We spent almost two hundred dollars. I waited at the cash register, curious and impatient to see the bills, but guess what? They don't pay with cash; they use plastic cards. As Sammy returned the card to his wallet, I felt a powerful desire to hold it in my hands and pass it matter-of-factly to the clerk. I noticed that Sammy had a bunch of other cards, and I wondered if he'd even notice if one disappeared.

At home, I prepared my first meal. We were having a guest, a young man named Todd, a friend of Anna's, and I wanted to show them what a Moldovan feast looked like. I made stuffed cabbage rolls, white beans with bacon and ricotta-filled blintzes. I'd tried to find good lard in the supermarket, but the only thing that came close was some anemic-looking bacon. Even their ground meat isn't the same as ours. I don't know what it is, but the meat just doesn't taste the same. The bread too is funny: it's very soft and sweet. Now that I think of it, almost everything here tastes a little sweet, as if it were made for children.

My meal fell a little short of my expectations; still, it was the best thing I'd had since I arrived. I expected to be showered with praise by Sammy and Anna, but during dinner I noticed Sammy carefully picking out all the pieces of bacon and placing them on the rim of his plate. As for Anna, she declared, without even tasting anything, that she never eats meat, and proceeded to make herself a salad—a *salad*—instead.

"But just taste it," I said. "I promise it's the best meal you've ever had."

She refused to try it, and seemed annoyed by my insistence. I waited for Sammy to intervene and ask her to behave or at least taste the food, but he said only, "Anna is a vegetarian," as if that gave her the right to act like a spoiled brat. And I thought our Irina was the most stubborn sixteen-year-old in the world! I can see that this girl, Anna, is going to give me trouble, and

I'll have to work very hard to instill a sense of discipline in her. It's not really her fault, she grew up without a mother, poor girl! With a father weak as a lamb, what else can you expect?

The only one who seemed to appreciate my meal, and even asked for seconds, was the guest, Todd. I liked that boy. He reminds me of Ted Capwell from the early episodes of *Santa Barbara*. They even have the same name—by the way, I think the actor who played Ted was called Todd Something. It's obvious he's head over heels for Anna, and she should consider herself lucky, given that she looks more like a boy than a girl, can't eat meat and doesn't do any household chores. After he left and Anna went to her room, I shared my thoughts with Sammy. His reaction was shocking. He got very upset and said, among other things, that his daughter had plenty going for her and had no reason to consider herself "lucky" to be liked by anyone. "Besides," he said, "she's still a child."

You can imagine how that made me feel! I'd only said what I said because I was concerned about the well-being of his daughter. This is how he thanks me, by making a scene? But this taught me a lesson: Americans think very highly of their children, and, as a consequence, are incapable of acknowledging the truth. I'll try to keep my mouth shut from now on, but it won't be easy. When one has my clarity of vision, one feels obligated to speak up.

Tell Irina I know what she's up to, even from here.

Your daughter,
Tania

# Lenny

When Lenny had a party—and that happened about once a month—he invited all his neighbors and close acquaintances, so the number of guests ranged from fifty to a hundred, depending on their availability. This time, when Sammy, Tania and Anna arrived, the sun was setting on at least eighty people, who were mingling all over the property. As the new guests walked up the driveway, dozens of colorful little bulbs hidden in the bushes and the trees suddenly lit up, which prompted a series of cheerful exclamations from Tania. The only lit trees she'd ever seen were Christmas trees, and that was only one week a year—starting at Christmas and ending on New Year's. This impromptu Christmas celebration in the middle of October, with its debauchery of lights, was—like everything involving waste and excess—a sign of the triumph of lavish capitalism over pitiful, ascetic communism. With her Leica camera—one of the few things she'd brought with her from home—she was ready to capture all the signs of bourgeois decadence (as they used to call it back home) and mail them to those bitches in Moldova who would no doubt eat their hearts

out with envy. Finally, a Santa Barbara that measured up to the *Santa Barbara* she'd left behind.

After immortalizing this October Christmas, Tania took a few shots of the fairytale house whose caramel brick walls and bright blue trim stood out among the surrounding green. The house was made of three parts, the center one a two-story structure with gabled roof, and the other two on each side, one story each, roofed by crenellated terraces, like a medieval fortress. The two terraces were full of guests milling about with glasses or plates of appetizers in their hands. Inside the house there was a similar scene, people coming in and going out, laughing as if they had no worries, or otherwise lost in contemplation over one of the many paintings that decorated the walls. Tania didn't like disorder, and the environment reeked of chaos. She had attended her share of parties, either with coworkers or with her relatives or neighbors, but she'd never been to a party in someone's home where the guests moved about as if it were theirs, unattended, free to take whatever they could get their hands on. And there was plenty you could get your hands on.

The living room looked like a museum, with a large glass-topped table, under which Tania could see numerous little figurines made of bone, ivory, clay and marble. Tania moved closer to examine them and was shocked to discover that quite a few represented entanglements of naked men and women in the most bizarre (and uncomfortable) positions imaginable. Some were Chinese (or were they Japanese?) men that exposed their genitals. Others were chains of beasts—monkeys or dogs—copulating in prurient ecstasy. Breathing heavily, Tania turned her head left and right to see if anyone else shared her indignation, but apparently, either no one else had noticed the outrageous display, or no one cared. What kind of a pervert lived here, and how could Sammy bring his daughter to such a place?

As she stood there, fuming silently, she heard a voice behind her:

"Quite the amazing collection, isn't it? And not cheap, either!"

She turned and found herself facing a tall, well proportioned man with chestnut, sun-kissed hair and tanned skin, skin in which he seemed perfectly at ease. The man held a glass in one hand and a cigarette in the other—that slim, smoke-producing object Tania hadn't seen since she'd left her homeland, and which she dearly missed—and handled both with such masculine grace that Tania instinctively pushed out her breasts and flared her nostrils, as she always did when she sensed an eligible bachelor in her proximity. The man was slightly older than she was, so she couldn't be sure he was a bachelor, but his fingers were ringless, and his demeanor breathed the carefree attitude specific to unattached men, so she encouraged him with a wide smile. The man introduced himself as "Bill, Todd's father," then offered her a puff of his cigarette. Tania had often shared cigarettes with her coworkers, but didn't expect to do it in her new country. You'd think that with all their money, these people could afford to offer you a cigarette of your own.

"What brand is it?" she asked, accepting the offer. Inhaling, she suddenly realized whom Bill reminded her of: he looked like a cross between C. C. Capwell and his son, Mason.

"Oh, it's pot," Bill said, laughing.

Tania had never heard of that particular brand. In her hometown, besides the local brand, people smoked Marlboro, Kent, Pall Mall—never Pot. She took a few puffs, grimacing at the foul taste, increasingly convinced that these rich people could be very stingy when it came to basic household amenities like TV, cigarettes, or food. She wouldn't have hesitated to let Bill know what she thought of that cigarette, but she was

more preoccupied at the moment with what he'd said about the figurine collection and its potential price. Trying to appear uninterested, she asked, "Who would want to buy these silly things? And how much could they be paying for them?"

"Lots of people, I assure you. This one alone"—he pointed at the copulating beasts—"is worth thousands."

The number was much higher than anything Tania had imagined. She'd thought that some extravagant perv might pay a couple dozen bucks, but thousands? She began to examine the figurines more closely, and, when Bill left her for another guest, she attempted to lift the glass cover with her left hand, while stretching her head in the opposite direction, as if her hand was completely independent of her body. But however hard she tried, the glass wouldn't budge. She proceeded to inspect the rest of the house, room by room, amazed that no one seemed to care, and the people she occasionally ran into simply smiled at her, as if she belonged there. As naturally as she could, Tania sat down on a green couch in a room in which everything was a shade of green, and, in doing so, noticed a shelf of other small figurines immediately to her left. These were similar to the ones she had seen earlier in that they were small representations of pigs, cats and dogs, but much prettier and more colorful: pink with brownish spots, or white with black stripes, or tawny with whitish spots. She made sure no one could see her, opened her purse, and dropped the little animals inside. She closed her purse, stood up, smoothed her skirt around her hips, and left the room *allegro vivace*—a term she'd learned the day before when she and Sammy had attended the Santa Barbara Symphony.

A few minutes later Tania joined the other guests on one of the terraces. She looked around and spotted Anna ten feet away, next to a man in his mid-forties. The man, who had a certain charm, wore blue jeans, a black leather jacket and

sunglasses, and as he chatted with his head tilted in Anna's direction, a barely perceptible smile graced his lips. He was not particularly handsome, but his confidence and poise were so obvious one couldn't help but notice him. And Tania had a special gift when it came to taking notice. She compared what she noticed in this case to what she'd noticed in Bill's case, and then, compared both cases to that of her husband. Although she'd worked as a hairdresser during her last years in Moldova, she still possessed the skills she'd acquired as a clerk in a lawyer's office, skills that consisted in identifying people's best qualities and greatest weaknesses, and in filing them away in places that would later prove useful. And so, she placed both the stranger and Bill in a special file in her mind, underlining Bill's name and putting a question mark next to the stranger's. As a woman, she found Bill more attractive, but the stranger more intriguing. What was even more intriguing than the stranger was Anna's stupefied attention, the way she listened to him without moving, almost without breathing, her face raised toward his, pale and unrecognizable.

Well, that's a good one! What a silly little girl!

Stunned by her discovery, Tania congratulated herself on having arrived in the bosom of the Goldstein clan just in time to fix whatever needed to be mended before it was too late. A few seconds later, the stranger was accosted by one of the caterers and, apologizing to Anna, moved into a more private and rather animated conversation. Curious, Tania approached the two, and heard the caterer defending himself forcefully:

"I swear, all the almond-paste figurines have disappeared. We had a full platter and now it's empty."

She wasn't quite sure what the word "almond" meant, but she understood that the caterer was worried about some animal figurines, and realized that the wisest thing to do was to go back

and return them to the platter. She slipped away quickly and did what she had to. The animals had suffered some damage during their abduction: their bodies had been slightly altered and their colors were beginning to run, but they were still appealing. Unable to resist, she kept a handful for herself. She smoothed her skirt again, took out her pocket mirror, applied a thick layer of lipstick, puckered her lips in contentment, slid the mirror back in her purse, and walked out of the room.

# Tania

Dear Mother,

Two days ago, Sammy, Anna and I went to a neighbor's party. I wish you and Irina could have witnessed it! Oh, Mother! Trees with sparkling lights and Christmas decorations, some of which (and I have this from a trustworthy source) were gold. Dozens of platters with appetizers made into the shape of little animals! The owner is a strange man who has a thing for animals: he has a collection worth millions, which he keeps in the house with no protection whatsoever. Now, the bombshell: the little one, Anna, has a crush on him. Either that, or she's cleverer than she appears, and is more interested in the little animals than in the big one. Frankly, it would be unfair for such a spoiled, common girl to get her hands on such a prize. Our Irina, who is the same age, is a thousand times prettier and ten times smarter. This animal is for her. Just tell her to hang in there, and I'll find a way to bring her here.

At the same party I made another interesting acquaintance: our other neighbor, Bill, father to the boy I told you about in my last letter. I won't go into details, but there was something

in Bill's eyes that made me think we might become more than just neighbors. Oh, you'd like him! Tall, dark, and when he looks you in the eye you know you're a woman. Not like my Sammy, though as long as we're on the subject I should tell you that a few nights ago we did *it*. We did it and it was clear that there is nothing wrong with him. He's got everything it takes, and a little more, if I may say so.

Lately, he's been teaching me to drive. Yes. Yesterday we drove downtown, and, for the first time, I noticed that many cars have small signs on the back called "bumper stickers." A lot of them are about animals: "I love dogs and I vote" (so what? I thought); others are about the owner's children: "My son is an honor student at So-and-So Elementary." Ha! Can you imagine having something like that on your car in our neighborhood? I can see Sofia driving around with a sign that says, "My mother-in-law is a psychopath. May her lying tongue freeze in Hell!" One car—a truck—was even stranger. This one had a message written in large letters, not on a sticker, but on its side. The message said, "How's my driving? Call such-and-such number!" *Who cares how he's driving?* I thought. But I was curious, so I wrote the number down and, when I got home, I called it. A hoarse voice answered. It was mumbling something I couldn't understand. I said, "You wanted me to call you, so I'm calling." There was silence on the other end, then an irritated, male voice asked, "How can I help you, Ma'am?" Now, *I* was losing my patience. I said, "I don't need your help, you bumpkin! *You* asked me to call you, so I did. Frankly, I don't give a fig about your driving!" And I hung up. Of course, I said this last part in Russian. A pity he couldn't understand.

I'm telling you this so you can see how hard it is to make sense of even the most insignificant things here. But something more important happened today. The neighbor's boy, Todd—

such a handsome, smart, well-behaved young man—offered us (that is, Anna and me) a ride to a mall in a nearby town, Ventura. I know you're wondering if their malls are as big as the newspapers say. They are. Somehow, though, I was not as impressed as I thought I'd be—maybe the novelty of everything is wearing off, maybe I'm getting awe fatigue. At any rate, this giant store had trees, animals, cars, even old people jogging around inside it, as if it were a park. What surprised me more than anything were the prices: so much lower than back home! I couldn't believe my eyes. I kept grabbing dresses, piling them in my cart until the pile grew so high it threatened to spill on the floor.

I told Anna and Todd that I'd meet up them later, and they were more than happy to leave me alone. You're probably wondering, "How is this foolish woman going to pay? Did that husband of hers give her a bucketful of cash to spend on clothes?" No, he didn't. When it was time to pay, I went to the cash register with my cart brimming with dresses, shawls, blouses, pants and panties, and, very casually, opened my purse, took out my wallet and extracted the shiny credit card I had taken from Sammy's wallet that morning. The cashier examined it at length, as I played nonchalantly with my curls, then asked me for ID. That really got under my skin. Why was she asking me for ID? Just because I have a Russian accent doesn't mean I'm a thief. I told her as much, adding that next time I'd think twice before patronizing her store. (You know that here the customer is always right.) The woman apologized, saying that those were the rules—"rules" my ass. What could I do? I showed her my passport, and then she said she couldn't accept my credit card because I wasn't Samuel Goldstein. Can you believe that?! As if I was claiming I was Samuel Goldstein!

"Ma'am," I said, trying to remain calm, "I may have a foreign accent, I may even have a Russian accent, but I'm not

stupid. Of course I'm not Samuel Goldstein. Samuel Goldstein is my husband. This morning I said, 'Sammy, I'd like to do some shopping', and he said, 'Fine, honey, take my credit card and shop to your heart's content.' And so I did. Is there a law in this country that forbids a wife to use her husband's credit card?"

But the woman wouldn't give in. She went to get the manager, and when she was gone, I decided to make myself scarce. I saw a sign, "Restroom"—how nice of them to have rooms where customers can rest—and I followed it. It turned out that the restroom was a toilet, although it did have a plastic bench on which one could rest. Let me tell you, the public toilet was so clean you could lick the floors! *Now, this is a civilized country*, I thought. Until then, I'd had my doubts, but this was the moment of truth. I sat on the bench and put the credit card back in my wallet. In doing so, I found two little almond figurines from our neighbor's party. They were a little misshapen, but I was starved, so I ate them. Then, I looked at my watch and jumped: I was supposed to meet Anna and Todd five minutes earlier. By the time I arrived at our agreed-upon place, I was ten minutes late, but the youngsters didn't seem to mind. Anna had a broad smile on her face and was holding something in her hands, which she handed to me.

"A present," she said.

It was a razor and a deodorant stick. I confess, I was a little surprised. Maybe she isn't such a bad kid, after all. But I have no intention of using the funny stick, which doesn't smell like anything and leaves white flakes on your clothes. I prefer a spray like Rexona, which leaves no trace and at least smells good. I'll send you the stick. I bet Irina would happily use it. As for the razors, I have no idea what I'm supposed to do with them. Does she think I have a beard? I'll give them to Sammy.

Your daughter,

Tania


P.S. I'll add to the package a minty thread called "floss." You're supposed to place it between your teeth and slide it back and forth to remove food. Give that to Seryozha!

# Anna

Two months earlier, when Anna had accidentally spotted Lenny through the tinted glass of a pawn shop in downtown Santa Barbara, she had no idea she was starting a new phase of her life, and that that moment would later be summoned up as its fateful beginning. She was ambling along, waiting for Todd, who'd given her a ride, and who, as usual, was taking his time. Every time they went out he had to use the restroom, and each time he used the restroom he ran into an acquaintance—hence the delay.

At first, she didn't recognize him. He was wearing a black leather jacket, khakis, and black leather shoes. Hands in his pockets, head tilted to the left, he was leaning against the counter, chatting with the proprietor. It was his posture that first caught her eye, the way he leaned with such aristocratic boredom—as if he had all the time in the world—and the way his mouth moved with equal boredom—as if the man in front of him was not worth his trouble, but he was there, so, what the heck, why not exchange a few words? She couldn't hear what he was saying, but she inferred from the way his mouth moved

that he was in absolute control of the situation—whatever the situation was; the other man was totally in his power. Moreover, he didn't have to lift a finger to assert this power. It was as if his power emanated from his entire being, as if it were a function of his lungs.

Of course, Anna would never have used the word "aristocratic" to describe him; what she would have used was an image, the image of a man with whom she'd only recently become familiar: Humphrey Bogart. For her sixteenth birthday, her father had given her a camera, which, at first, she had considered with apprehension, but which, through one of those turns that our lives sometimes take, ended up becoming a kind of new appendage to her body. It took only a single click of the button for her to realize that she was in possession of a magical instrument, not because it "took pictures," but because every click brought her closer to an ideal of perfection she had not even been aware she carried within her. She framed an image and the world suddenly gathered itself into a meaningful shape, like a dancer caught leaping in mid-air. With a click, the leap was frozen in eternity. So, she clicked and clicked, to the increasing exasperation of those around her.

When Bill got wind of her new passion, he suggested that she might want to broaden her field of knowledge by watching black-and-white movies, and brought her a few tapes.

"What am I supposed to do with them?" she asked.

"Oh, I've forgotten you guys don't have a tape player."

"A tape player? Bill, we don't have a TV."

And so, Bill initiated a once-a-week movie night at his place, which immediately became a twice-a-week, or even thrice-a-week occurrence, in which Todd agreed wholeheartedly to participate. The prospect of two long, painfully delightful hours spent sitting next to Anna was an unexpected gift he wasn't

going to reject. But, as much as he enjoyed feeling her muscular leg next to his, and inhaling her apple-shampoo-scented hair, he eventually got tired of watching movies about blond women with padded shoulders and sinuous hips that extended out of incredibly thin waists. After two weeks, he let his father take his place on the couch, and disappeared into the next room to play video games.

The "movie room," as Anna and Todd called it, was different from the rest of the Johnsons' house, though Anna couldn't tell in exactly what way. Only after having established herself as a regular guest on the cream-colored sofa in front of the forty-six-inch TV screen, did she notice that the room had a warmth—tangible in the soft-edged, light wood of the furniture—that did not extend to the rest of the house. The main difference, the difference that gave the room its warmth, came from the fact that, here, instead of glass walls, there were plaster walls covered by old Hollywood posters from which bare shoulders and glistening red lips defied time. On that couch, in front of a machine that unspooled ceaseless images, occurred a transformation that was not very surprising, all things considered: Anna, who'd grown up without a TV, turned into someone hungry for images. She, who'd spent more time up in trees than on the ground, began to see the world through a lens and within a frame, and, whenever an image within that frame reminded her of one she'd seen in a movie, her heart beat wildly, as if she were about to set out on a romantic adventure.

This may explain why, standing in front of that pawn shop, her heart began to race even before she had identified the man in the frame. More than anything else, it was the image evoked by the man's Humphrey-Bogart nonchalance that electrified her. She couldn't even see half of his face, and the part she saw was marked by two days growth of beard, a sign of neglectful

masculinity that, until then, had always been a turn-off (the unmistakable mark of a species she wanted nothing to do with), but which now triggered in her a strange tingling and an emotion for which the only word at her disposal—a word repeated over and over in movies—was "love." She knew she was *in love* with the man, even though she'd have been hard pressed to tell you what he looked like. When he suddenly turned his face in her direction, she recognized him: Lenny. But, afraid he might recognize her, she averted her gaze immediately, so, on second thought, she wasn't quite sure it was him.

For the rest of the day, she remained in a haze, half-sweetness, half-nervousness, as if something monumental were about to take place, something for which she had no words, only a tingling all over her body. She kept repeating, "I'm in love," then whispering his name. But . . . had it really been him? Was she in love with her neighbor, a neighbor she'd known since she was a little girl, and to whom she'd never paid much attention? What was certain was that she was in love: maybe with her neighbor, maybe with another man, whom she might or might not recognize, should they meet again.

# Bill

Before Bill became the accidental host of Hollywood classics, he'd been languishing for days in what seemed like the dullest summer of his life, drinking cocktails and squinting at the dreary, mind-numbing sun. Seated in his wicker chair, which he placed right on the grass, he fancied himself a Gulliver who, with his enormous and outlandish piece of furniture, precipitated a crisis among the ants, locusts, crickets, and whatever other critters are to be found on the ground, and from this superior position he sipped and sipped, interrupting himself only occasionally to light a cigarette and send menacing puffs of smoke toward said creatures. He liked to imagine what went through their feeble little brains when his clouds of smoke descended upon them. Years earlier, before Michelle left him, they had taken vacations like normal people—gone camping, even went to Europe a few times. Now, the mere thought of going downtown made him so tired that all he wanted to do was lie on the grass and spend the rest of his life contemplating his navel. And the truth is, more and more, he found himself doing just that. He'd gotten used to spending the hot summer and

fall afternoons shirtless, wearing only a pair of blue jeans, and as he sat, glass in hand, his gaze wandered lazily from a semi-translucent lizard, which he admired in the sunlight, to his naked torso, which he tried to imagine from the point of view of an ant that was crawling up his abdomen. With the index finger of his unoccupied hand, he pushed the ant toward his hairy chest, and once there, the creature stopped, confused. Suddenly, it found itself surrounded by thick, dark, coarse vegetation, unlike anything it had ever seen before. Panicking, the ant tried to navigate the hairs, but got tangled, so panicked even more. Going literally into a spin, it started left, but finding only more hair, turned right, then south, then north, moving frantically like a drunk who couldn't find his way home.

"You're stuck, aren't you?" mumbled Bill, a grin on his face. He then thought of giving the struggling insect another challenge and placed it in his bellybutton. He didn't have time to assess the fruits of his experiment, however, because an unpleasant female voice rose next to him:

"I see you're resting. Good! And with no clothes. Good! I wish I could do the same!"

The voice had an unmistakable Russian accent and exhibited the paradoxical quality of being very feminine, in that its pitch moved from high to low and from low to high with a brusqueness that is typical of the female species, yet it was, at the same time, very masculine, in that it sounded like the voice of a long-time smoker. One thing was certain: the feminine and the masculine attributes of the voice combined to signal the presence of an entity Bill would have rather not dealt with. And when the entity materialized in support of the voice, he remembered: *that* woman!

"You men are lucky," the voice continued. "You can take your clothes off and it's okay. But women . . ."

"You're more than welcome to take your clothes off. Anything goes, here."

As he spoke, Bill closed his eyes and stretched out his arms, dangling his empty glass from his fingers. The woman, taking a seat beside him, giggled:

"Oh, what are you saying? What are you saying?"

She covered her mouth with a theatrical gesture that Bill caught as he briefly opened his eyes. The woman had very white, shiny skin, with two big, red patches in the middle of her cheeks.

"I'm saying," said Bill, closing his eyes again, "that you should feel at home."

"But at home I don't take my clothes off," said the woman. Even though his eyes were shut, Bill could tell that she was arching her back like a cat, opening her mouth wide, ready to swallow him whole.

"Well, you're a real lady," Bill mumbled, and, in the next instant he began to snore.

That evening, when Anna showed up for their movie, there was something new about her, something not easy to define, which gave her a radiance that shot through her dark brown eyes, lending them a soft moisture, and giving her forehead a melancholy tinge that seemed to slow her movements, imparting to them a grace hitherto absent in her boyish figure. Bill noticed the change right away, but attributed it to the two martinis he'd had on top of his regular dose of Jack Daniel's. As he was about to sit next to the girl on "their" couch, he abruptly changed his mind and, instead, sat in the armchair. They started the movie—another Humphrey Bogart—and, while the titles were running, Bill attempted, through the vapors of alcohol hanging between him and the TV screen, to determine why he had not sat next to her the way he always did. His abrupt decision

was no doubt connected to the change in her, that subtle and mysterious radiance whose cause was a mystery to him. What could bring about such a change in a girl? A man, of course. The thought of "a man," a man that could have such an impact on his . . . his student, disturbed him in unexpected ways. In fact, he was profoundly disturbed to realize how disturbed he was. When Anna asked him a question about the movie, and he had no idea how to answer because he hadn't been watching it, he began to laugh in embarrassment, at first a giggle, then more and more hysterically. She gave him a sharp look—one of those tough expressions he was familiar with, and which negated her feminine radiance ("feminine!" that's the word he had been looking for. She'd suddenly become so feminine).

"Too much bottle love?" she asked with unsparing irony.

What was this girl saying? His laughter abruptly stopped, giving way to another feeling, something from deep down inside that surged all the way up to his cheeks: shame. He opened his mouth to speak, but managed only an unintelligible murmur. He made an effort to focus on the images that were playing before his eyes. Hard as he tried, those two words—*bottle love*—materialized into a compact, unbreakable brick that struck him repeatedly over the head in a series of constant thuds. So, this is what it's come to: bottle love. He repeated the words over and over inside his head—bottlelove, bottlelovebottlelovebottl—until they stopped making any sense; he turned them on their side, exposed their hidden parts—ttlelove—licked them and spit them out—lovebot. His head hurt. He stood up to get an aspirin. Then, he went to pee and (God knows how) fell asleep on the toilet. When he woke up his groin was cold and shriveled. Through the tall window he could see the night pouring out its thick, black soul. He stumbled to his feet. Walked through the dark, groping, until he found a light switch: ten-thirty. Then

he remembered, "bottle love." Cautiously, he opened the door to the home theater. No one was there. Jesus, he must have slept for nearly two hours! Bottle love. Wait! He was struck by a bolt of inspiration. What if she said *bottled* love? Of course, it made more sense. She must have meant *bottled up love*. Groping through darkness, his hands massaging his throbbing temples, he slipped continually in and out of a maddening loop. *If she meant bottled up love, then* . . . Then what? Then, she thinks that you, that is, I . . . What a ridiculous thought! Whatever could have given her such an idea? He kept pushing the thought aside, but it stubbornly returned. Bottleduplove, bottleduplove. He stripped himself naked, the incomprehensible words dancing a witches' circle in his head, and, stepping into the shower, turned on the cold water.

# Tania

Dear Mother,

I hope you got my package. I am worried sick about Irina and that good-for-nothing boyfriend of hers. I wish I could snap my fingers and bring her here, but I need more time. Meanwhile, tell her that, if she doesn't behave, she'll see America when pigs fly. I'll send you some money for her English lessons, but first, she has to promise she'll study. I have no money to waste. Once she comes here, she doesn't even need to go to school. Did you know that some parents are allowed to keep their children at home and teach them whatever they want? It's called homeschooling. That's what Sammy does with his daughter. The education that girl is getting, let me tell you! I never imagined that an American girl could be so illiterate. I asked her how much was sixty-three times three, and she said, "let me get a calculator." A calculator! Apparently, children here can't do any math in their heads. All that Sammy teaches his daughter are his musical theories—as if anyone needed that—and all the homework she ever gets is to write in her journal. I'm not kidding: she writes in her journal, the way we used to in elementary school. I asked Sammy whether

she ever studies physics or chemistry, and he said, "Sure she does, but in a meaningful way." I asked, "What does that mean, 'in a meaningful way'?" He replied, "She has to understand the reason why she memorizes things." He said that he sees no purpose in forcing a student to memorize something without first helping her understand why—how the scientists arrived at their conclusions in the first place. Can you believe that?! Well, if you're going to teach a student all the hows and whys of this and that, you might as well forget about it. I am more and more convinced that, in this country, children rule. Even the food is made for them: everything is sweet, including the bread. Why do I need corn syrup in my bread? What am I, a fly?

This husband of mine is some kind of musician. I mean, a musician in his spare time. He sits at his piano several hours a day, but doesn't really play, just hits notes and jots stuff down on a piece of paper. When he does that, he's so focused he doesn't know what's going on around him, which is fine by me. I know how to keep myself occupied; I see our neighbor, Bill, every other day, and although he tries not to show it, I can tell he's not displeased with my visits. It seems to me that American men are a little shy, or maybe they respect women more than our Ivans do. If he was one of ours, we'd have done it already, but no, these men take their time. First, they want to "get to know you" and make conversation. It makes you feel like a lady. Now, if things begin to drag between me and Bill, I'll take the bull by the horns, that is to say by the balls, and confront him. Life is short, and I've already wasted half of mine in the shithole where you and Irina are still rotting. Don't worry, I'll get you both out! I hope she's taking birth-control pills, at least. Why did she have to break up with Matvei? The boy was good looking, was her age, and didn't touch alcohol. This new one reeks of trouble: a twenty-nine-year-old man with a sixteen-year-old girl! Find his address for me

so I can send him a piece of my mind. He should be ashamed of himself, that's what I'll tell him! Why can't he find someone his own age? I hope he doesn't use drugs. What if he's a drug addict, and he's getting our Irina involved in God knows what? I'm so worried about that girl. When she gets here, I'll break a broom over her back, I swear.

On the other hand, I should be happy with what God has given me because it could always be worse. Sammy's daughter doesn't have a boyfriend, but boy, does she have problems. Sometimes I think that maybe she's not all there in the head. When we were at the mall together I saw a black man—he was more brown than black, but he's the closest thing to a black person I've seen since coming here—and I confessed how surprised I was that there weren't as many black people around as you'd think there'd be from the movies. And do you know what she said? "Unfortunately, this city isn't very diverse." *Diverse.* That's what she said. Now, what in God's name has one to do with the other? I'm asking about black people and she's talking about diversity. I'm sure there are more of them around, but maybe they don't go to the same places we go—though the one we saw seemed very much at ease, he even went to an ATM and withdrew money. I saw him do it with my own two eyes! And they say that black people are poor!

Speaking of black people, you were right when you guessed that Goldstein was a Jewish name. How do you know these things? Since being here I've met more Jews than I had in my entire life. I wonder why there are so many of them. I asked Sammy if Bill was Jewish, and he laughed.

"Of course not," he said.

"Is Lenny Jewish?"

"Sure—though he does throw a Christmas party every year. We're always invited."

I'll give you the full report on that party, don't worry. It's already December, but most days you can still go out without a jacket. The nights, though, are getting cooler. Two days ago when Sammy reserved a table at a fancy restaurant, I wanted to wear one of the fox furs I'd brought with me from back home, the café-au-lait one: you know, the one with the beady eyes.

He was waiting for me in the entrance hall with his right hand on the doorknob—by the way, the doorknobs are round here, not L-shaped like ours—and when he saw me walking toward him in my four-inch heels, tight red dress hugging my Marilyn Monroe hips, bosom covered with a cute little black jacket, he froze as if struck by lightning. I thought he had finally realized what a catch he'd married. He stared at me for about half a minute, swallowed, and eventually, stammered:

"Is that thing around your neck real fur?"

I smiled and spun on my heels to give him a chance to see me from every angle.

"Real fur, yes," I acknowledged. A present I received from an admirer in my younger days, who bought it on a trip to Moscow."

His face fell.

"You can't wear that here. Not with me."

I expected him to be a little jealous of my previous admirer, but not *that* jealous. I smiled again, doing my best to reassure him. "Don't worry, honey. He doesn't mean anything to me anymore. But you don't expect me to throw this gorgeous thing away, do you? Just touch it. Feel how soft it is."

Suddenly, he raised his voice, and said angrily:

"I don't give a damn about your admirer! I just don't want you to wear *that!*"

Well, that was a surprise! Under that bland, grandfatherly exterior was hiding a passionate, fiercely jealous man! For the first time, I felt truly attracted to him, so I walked up to him and

pressed my body forcefully against his, whispering, "Oh, honey, if you don't want me to, I won't wear it. I'll wear another one—a different color, silver—a present from my dad. You wouldn't be jealous of my dad, would you?"

Instead of calming down, he ripped himself from my grasp, and, even angrier than before, he yelled:

"Woman, don't you understand? People don't wear fur here! They'll attack us. They'll throw eggs and paint at you. I haven't seen a real fur in fifteen years."

"Honey! Honey, don't worry! You're so agitated. Why would anyone attack me? Stop shaking and tell me what's bothering you! You can trust me, I'm your wife. If you're afraid that someone might try to rob us, then don't worry: this fur isn't that expensive!"

But no matter what I said, the poor man wouldn't calm down. In the end, I told him: "You know what? We don't need to go to a restaurant, tonight. I think you're in need of a good massage, and I might be able to help."

So, we stayed home.

Your daughter,
Tania

# Lenny

A huge pine tree decorated with sparkling red, yellow and green ornaments dominated the courtyard, twinkling to the rhythm of its colorful lights, themselves a response to the twinkling lights that outlined the house, its windows and nearby shrubs. Under the tree, big packages wrapped in shiny red paper with golden ribbons were jumbled together in the dry winter grass, and Tania wondered whom those packages might be intended for. She pressed her left breast against Sammy's right arm to let him know how thankful she was to be there. In response, he cleared his throat and looked nervously around. Anna and Todd trailed behind them, making sporadic comments and laughing. Sammy attempted to wriggle his arm free before entering the house, but Tania clung to it with even stronger determination. They entered the house as one, followed by the teenagers' lank, carefree bodies. Oh, how Tania savored those gatherings, how she wished that those stupid peasants from back home could see her now! True, she had to abandon wearing her fox fur because Sammy wouldn't let her, but still, she was like a queen in brand new, tall, leather boots, a green velvet dress, and

the pearl necklace she'd found in one of Sammy's old boxes. As she walked in with her newly acquired royal demeanor, she felt the host's intense gaze on her. She smiled to reveal her gums—which she now flossed daily—thinking that a man of such taste could not fail to notice a woman like her.

Indeed, making an effort to recall who she was and where he'd seen her before, Lenny focused his gaze on the newly arrived woman. Her face reminded him of a fresh peach—ripe, succulent, bursting with innocent, unthinking, plump flesh. In order to avoid acknowledging his lapse, he turned to Anna, and greeted her enthusiastically. The girl blushed and, to hide her embarrassment, reverted to her boyish persona, letting out a, "Hey, man, what's up?" The words had come out before she could stop them, and when they hit her ears with their screeching sound, her embarrassment spiked even higher, and her face turned the color of a California sunset all the way to her roots. Something about her behavior put Todd on guard. He wasn't sure what was going on, but he knew it was bad for him, and, from that moment on, kept his eyes on Anna. As for Lenny, uncertain of how to react, he remained silent until, fortunately for everyone, the unknown woman opened her very red mouth and broke the silence with such verve that everyone stopped in their tracks.

"Hello, Lenny! Remember me? Tania."

*Lenny*—with that unmistakable Russian accent—*glienee.* Relieved, Lenny burst out laughing. "Well, hello, Tania!"

He kissed her noisily on the cheek. At that moment, Tania let go of Sammy's arm, and immediately, he took advantage of the opening, withdrawing with the speed of a chased mouse. Anna, too, moved to safety and poured herself a Coke, all the while taking in Lenny's graceful appearance—black jeans, starched white shirt with a large collar folded over a woolen

blazer with patched elbows. She still wasn't sure whether he was the man she'd spotted in the pawn shop, but whether it was him or not, both men possessed the same masculine grace and the same detached, ironic gaze, as if they were about to take a gun from an invisible belt and, pointing it at a stunned crowd, send everyone around them into a state of ecstatic fear; then, smiling magnanimously, to put the gun back in its holster and walk out, untouched, toward other adventures.

Anna was savoring this image, when someone snatched the glass of Coke from her hand.

"You're not a little girl anymore to drink Coca-Cola," said Tania, with her usual brusqueness. "Here, have some wine, like a woman."

Anna's first impulse was to snap back at her, but, on second thought, she kept the wine. After all, a woman worthy of Lenny's attention wouldn't drink Coke, would only drink liquor or wine. She herself never drank alcohol, and the smell made her a little nauseous. Closing her eyes and holding her nose, she took a little sip; it tasted like grape juice mixed with vinegar. She forced herself to swallow it, and her mouth felt as if she'd bitten into a slightly bitter lemon. Struggling to keep the signs of displeasure from her face, she admired the muscular grace with which Lenny's body shifted from one foot to the other.

Later that night, when the party was in full swing, a group of a dozen men or so came in, making a big racket, and demanding the best Cabernet Sauvignon in the house. Lenny seemed very happy to see them and promptly brought out bottles. The men examined the labels, making knowledgeable observations and arguing whether 1989 had been a better year than 1993. Although they ranged in age from their early twenties to late fifties, they were all skinny and impeccably dressed—or so Tania thought. A few wore suits, but most of them were in khakis and v–neck

sweaters. Tania could tell that the sweaters were expensive; she could recognize cashmere from a mile away, and she moved closer to the jolly group of men. One of them, a particularly handsome man in his late forties with a white silk scarf around his neck, offered her a glass of wine. He had such exquisite manners and moved his hands with such charming delicacy that Tania couldn't take her eyes off him. When he touched her hair, exclaiming, "Oh, honey, I love your style! It's so retro!" she almost forgot about Bill. Another man heard the comment and, turning in her direction, joined in the excitement. The man had pink lipstick on—maybe a woman had kissed him earlier and he had no idea his lips were stained. Tania would have liked to tell him, but didn't want to embarrass him, so she kept her mouth shut. Soon, she was surrounded by the entire group of men who admired her hair, her attire, her accent—pretty much everything about her. God, how good that felt, all those men smelling of expensive cologne, chirping like cheerful suburban housewives. When, a few minutes later, Sammy declared that he wanted to go home, she could have wept.

"You can't go home now," Lenny intervened. "At midnight, we're all going to mass."

"To mass?" "*You* are going to mass?"

"A black mass." Lenny winked mysteriously. "I rented a bus for all of us. It'll be here in half an hour."

"I'm not going to any mass," Sammy stated categorically, "black, white or red."

Tania pouted and stamped her foot. As far as she was concerned, *he* could go home, but *she* would stay on with Anna because they deserved to go to mass at least once a year on Christmas night. Sammy sighed and replied that she could do whatever she wanted, but his daughter wasn't going anywhere. Surprised at how easily she'd won the battle, Tania dropped the

topic of Anna and was about to resume the conversation with her new admirers when she spotted Bill slipping past, light-footed as a thief. She grabbed his arm before he was able to get by, stopping him in his tracks.

"Where are you going in such a hurry, without even saying hello?"

He stammered that he was tired, but she interrupted him with that red, glossy mouth of hers that seemed to swallow the entire universe:

"I won't hear a word of it! You're coming with me."

She pulled him toward her with such force that his chest crushed her breasts, while his neck stretched away in the direction Anna had gone.

Half an hour later, a huge bus pulled into the driveway, so large that after twenty or so people had got on, it still seemed empty. It was the coldest night of the year and there was no moon and no stars; the guests shrank inside their coats and huddled close to each other on the cold seats, while Lenny urged the others to hurry. Tania dragged Bill after her and forced him to sit next to her, all the way in the back. Only when the bus moved did she notice that she was the only woman there. Even stranger was the fact that the men behaved like couples, cuddling against each other, some resting on their neighbor's shoulder, still others, well, others kissed each other on the lips. It was dark in the bus, so Tania couldn't see well, and she was nervous because the road the bus took was too narrow for its size, and its windows were being scratched by branches as they drove past. The road sloped down and down, twisting and turning, and the bus moved along, humming through the infinite darkness. She had no idea where they were headed, yet she felt strangely detached from everything. The wine, the champagne and the cocktails had mixed together in a colorful brew, and her limbs

were getting lighter and lighter, while her brain was melting into a thousand flames that were licking at one another. All she knew was that she was seated next to Bill—though, to think of it, *who* was Bill? She laughed—without really knowing why—and placed her right arm on Bill's chest. The bus—or whatever that thing was in which they sat like Jonah in the belly of the whale— kept rolling downhill. Bill sat motionless, as her hand crept toward his belt and unbuckled it. Her hand kept going, and a smile began to flutter on the lips of Bill (or whoever he was).

# Tania

Dear Mother,

The news about Irina is quite worrisome. Are you saying that she's stealing money from you?! Have you confronted her? I know *you* can't do anything about that boyfriend of hers, but have you asked Seryozha? We have to do something before it's too late. I'm sure that bastard is doing drugs, and before you know it, our Irina will be the one paying for it. Yes, I know, I have to talk to Sammy about her, but it's not easy. *He still doesn't know.* And this isn't the moment to tell him. Besides, more and more I have the feeling that something is wrong with his head. He lives inside his head, and his head lives inside his piano. But he doesn't even play; he "composes," is what he says. The other day he babbled for a whole hour about some theory he'd come up with, and how he was applying it to a new composition— something that had never been done before. *If something's never been done before,* I thought, *it's probably for a good reason.* And he forced those poor kids, Anna and Todd, to listen to him. It was obvious that they would have rather been outside, frolicking in the grass or what have you, but no, they had to sit and listen. You

know what they say: to whom God has given much wisdom, He has also given much foolishness.

I just want to see Irina here, and then I'll put myself in God's hands. Tell her I even found a man for her. His name is Lenny, he looks like an actor, and he's loaded. He's the one with the parties and the perverse little sculptures. Speaking of parties, with all this talk of Irina, I almost forgot to tell you about the last one.

Picture this: a room as large as a house, with a ten-foot pine tree in the middle, full of diamond-encrusted decorations and crisscrossed by golden tinsel. Old butlers with trays are moving around, serving hors-d'oeuvre and champagne, as music like ocean waves ebbs and flows overhead. Men in coattails and women in evening gowns are chatting in groups of three and four, sipping from tall, slim glasses. Suddenly, the music stops, and I enter in a long, black velvet dress, wearing a necklace Sammy had given me that very morning, saying tearily, "This belonged to my mother and I want you to have it." As I move into the room, the music starts again, and whispers from a dozen mouths reach my ears:

"Who's that gorgeous woman?"

"Oh, you don't know?! It's Sammy's wife, Tania."

Read this (the part about the party, I mean) to Tamara and Sofia, but not to Irina—you know she never believes anything I tell her.

I'll talk to Sammy. Soon.

Your daughter,
Tania

# Sammy

Since Tania had moved in, Sammy was no longer himself. It was the first time since the death of his mother that he had had to submit himself to another person's whims and judgments. And they were not the whims and judgments of just anyone, but the whims and judgments of a woman with a temper. His first wife, who had died when Anna was little, had been so sweet and unassuming he had never thought of her as another person, but rather, as a continuation of himself. Now, for the first time, he was sharing a roof with another self, a self that seemed to take secret pleasure in crushing his own. Or, maybe not: a self, rather, that was so averse to introspection, to any reflective activity specific to the individual, to any form of *self-regard*, that a sort of monstrous selfishness seemed to permeate her sealed-off existence. It was a conclusion he had arrived at after weeks of painful cohabitation. What was worse was that he was afraid of *that woman*. And, he was ashamed to admit, after years of living as a bachelor, *that woman* was giving him sexual pleasure. He loathed her, and shivered in disgust

when she approached him in her nylon negligée that showed her glowing white skin puffed up like a healthy baby's, her pink curlers like a strawberry shortcake, wearing soft pink slippers—everything about her soft and fluffy. Yet the loathing did nothing to hinder his physical pleasure. The greater his pleasure, the more he loathed himself. By December his self-loathing had attained such heights that he doubted his self would make it to the New Year. And this gave him a new impetus to throw himself into composing, self-less as he was. He made a discovery others had made before him: that art, in its highest form, demands the abandonment of one's pitiful self, and that to create one must reach a transparent, divinely-impersonal state. In this state, like a god drunk on its creation, he haunted his own house, wandering all through the night, the only time he felt free. The silence moved in rhythm with the grandfather clock, and, now and then, he heard his own voice—a pebble falling into a well, with damp nothingness all around.

"But of course," he heard himself saying. "Time and melody should reflect each other, since they are both rhythm."

He didn't dare turn on the lights, and so groped in the dark, occasionally tripping over some sharp object left out by Tania. The other day he'd seen her use a high-heeled red-lacquer shoe as a bookmark. Yes, unbelievable as it may sound, the woman had placed a shoe inside the book she was reading.

"What's this?" he'd asked, pointing to the perverse mélange of leather and paper.

"Oh . . ." She'd laughed and shrugged her shoulders.

And she had simply pulled the shoe from the book and thrown the book onto the bed and the shoe under it, or maybe the other way around. *That woman* had an uncanny way of making the abnormal seem like the most normal thing in the world. And

her laugh, God, her laugh! With her big, red mouth wide open, her teeth showing all the way to her gums—decent looking, but still, communist-grown teeth. How could he ever have thought that this woman would be a mother to his daughter? He must have been out of his mind.

# Bill

After the bus scene and the unfortunate weakness he'd displayed therein, Bill did everything he could to avoid Tania. One day he was lying in his Jacuzzi, holding a glass of wine in his right hand and picking crud from under his toenails with his left, when the door slid open behind him—the Jacuzzi was within an enclosed porch with a Japanese sliding door. Without turning, he yelled, "Todd, I told you not to disturb me when I'm in here."

But instead of Todd, he heard *her* voice, followed by an enthusiastic clap. "A little pool! A little pool! Oh, you mean, naughty boy, why didn't you tell me you had a little pool?"

Damn it. He'd made it clear to Todd that he wasn't home for anyone who asked.

"It's not a little pool. It's a Jacuzzi."

Before he finished, she'd already taken off her clothes, and—splash—she was beside him, giggling and wrestling him for his wine glass.

"You know something, Tania? I don't think you should be here."

"Why not?" she replied, her face taking a pouting expression Bill was now familiar with. "You want to keep this all to yourself? You can't be happy all by yourself, Bill."

Bill fought down the urge to laugh at her pronunciation of his name—*beeeel.* "Why not?" he repeated. "Sammy is *my* friend, and you're *his* wife."

"Why do you always have to mix things up? A friend is a friend, and a wife is a wife."

He waited for some continuation of her argument, which had seemed convincing enough for Tania, who now lay down next to him, cooing and moaning with pleasure. Under different circumstances, Bill might have scolded her more, told her that she was as amoral as . . . as a Frenchman's wife, which was all he could think of, even though he'd never met one. But he felt too dazed and numbed by the hot water that hugged his muscles with its "little waves," as Tania called them. Instead, he said, "You're totally amoral. You're like a wild cat."

"What does 'amoral' mean?"

"It refers to someone who . . . who . . ."

"Wait, don't tell me! Is it like 'amour' in French?"

"Yes! It refers to someone who's very amorous."

At this, she jumped on top of him and pretended to scratch his face like a cat, and then to lick it like a cat, all while making cat noises. And that was the end of his moral resistance.

# Lenny

In order for Lenny to get downtown he had to drive by Anna and Sammy's house—there was no other way. In the past, Anna had seen his black BMW and red Porsche dozens of times, without giving them a second thought. But that was before. Now, Lenny had turned from an innocuous neighbor into an enigma in a black leather jacket—negotiating shady deals with pawnshop owners, taking trips to Europe from which he returned with million-dollar paintings by old masters, throwing lavish parties that other, equally mysterious men attended. In short, he seemed like a double (a more tangible double) of that mesmerizing character, Humphrey Bogart. Truth be told, she didn't really think Humphrey was that handsome, but there was something about his disposition, the way he carried himself, the way he interacted with others, that made him irresistible. And that thing, whatever it was, Lenny had it too.

For the past two days she'd been glued to the kitchen window in order not to miss him if he drove by. The plan was to jump in her car—well, not really her car, but Sammy's second car, the one he was using to teach her and Tania to

drive—and follow him. She had to be ready at any given moment, so she slept with her clothes on, tried not to move too much to keep her hair from getting tussled. Of course, this meant she barely managed to sleep. Now she was exhausted, and her stomach was tied in knots. It wouldn't be the first time that she'd taken Sammy's car without his permission. The other times, at least, Todd was the one driving, and he had a driver's license. But there was no way she could tell Todd about Lenny! She couldn't even make something up, because the little prick was shrewd and would figure it out right away. She'd have to do this alone.

It was late afternoon when she saw the Porsche speed by and vanish in an instant. It took her by surprise, as things always do when you wait too long for them. But she put her sneakers on in a heartbeat, and soon she was pressing the gas pedal—the knots in her stomach now also in her throat. The red car was already out of sight, but there was still time to catch it further downhill. Her father's car moved easily along the slope, and her heart hummed in unison with the engine. The red car was nowhere to be found. She accelerated, turned right, then left, accelerated again, took another curve and almost lost control of the wheel. She slowed down, took another curve, and, through the eucalyptus and the pale green splashes and the purple spikes of lupine flowers, spotted a red car at the crossing of East Mountain Drive and North Coyote Road. She took a deep breath and the knots in her stomach loosened.

His first stop was at the same pawnshop where she'd seen him before. The shop was on a side street that ran perpendicular to State, and he parked right out front, so she had to make a U-turn. The knot in her stomach returned as she did, because she wasn't even sure whether the turn was legal. Then she parked on State Street, in a spot with a view of the shop. The only

foreseeable problem was that it was a loading and unloading zone with a ten-minute limit.

After fifteen minutes, and still no sign of him, she began to fidget. She worried that a police car might drive by, and sure enough, one appeared. She started the engine and began to motor slowly up the street until the car had disappeared from view. Then, she turned back in the direction of the pawn shop: the red car was gone. She cursed—she was so angry tears sprang to her eyes, but she told herself to stay calm, and stay calm she did. She found another parking spot—a good one, in a public parking lot—left the car there and went back to State Street. She decided to stroll up and down the sidewalk—One never knew!—though she doubted he was still there if his car was gone. But when she arrived at the quiet side street where the pawn shop was located, she couldn't believe her eyes: the red car was parked just a little farther down from where it had been originally. Maybe he had had to move his car because he, too, had been illegally parked. She was about to cross the street when she saw him leaving the shop, followed by its owner. They shook hands, and for a second it seemed as if he were headed for his car, but then he changed his mind and began to walk in Anna's direction. She panicked, and rushed through the first open door, her heart beating in her stomach, her throat, her temples, her mouth. She looked around and saw that she was standing in some kind of gift shop. When she raised her eyes to the window, he was right there, next to the shop, taking the long, purposeful strides of a man with a clear goal in mind. His eyes were set on the asphalt—thank God he didn't see her! As soon as he walked past the shop, she went out after him. Her heart was still racing, but this time, out of excitement. Even as a child, her favorite games had involved searching for something: a trail, the way out

of a labyrinth, an egg, a hidden object, a letter. The search was now two-fold: she was looking for something the man she loved was looking for. But what if what he was looking for turned out to be a huge disappointment? Impossible: Lenny would only be looking for something worthwhile.

Turning this and that over in her head, she almost failed to notice he'd stopped. He fumbled in his pockets, appeared to find what he was looking for, then, without hesitation, entered the store on his right. Immediately, she crossed the street and entered the coffee shop opposite, taking a seat on a stool facing it. The store was an art gallery—one of many on that street. She could see him through the window, chatting with the gallery owner, a tall woman with very long, straight blond hair, who was dressed in the impersonal, businesslike manner of women in public relations. Having always thought—a thought reinforced by reading material selected for her by her father—that women in such positions were merely puppets with the outward appearance of well-groomed dolls, she felt nothing but scorn for them. For this woman, however, it was hard to feel contempt. This was because of the way Lenny was looking at her. Anna couldn't see very well from her temporary outpost, but what she saw she didn't like. She was dying to hear what they had to say to each other, but she had to content herself with their blurred smiles and gestures. The woman showed Lenny something on the left wall, and both stared admiringly at that thing for quite some time. Then, the woman took the object off the wall—very likely, a small painting—wrapped it, set it aside, and withdrew a stack of papers from a drawer. She sat down behind the desk, and, for the next ten minutes, she and Lenny thumbed through the papers, apparently filling some out. Then the woman stood up, gave Lenny the wrapped painting, and he kissed her on both cheeks.

As soon as he was out the door, Anna left too. At first, she wanted to follow him, but realizing he was going to his car, she turned back, and headed toward the gallery. She pretended she was interested in some objects on display in the window, all the while eyeing the blond woman. From up close, she was even more doll-like than from afar.

"What a pathetic slut," Anna exclaimed, finally feeling a surge of relief.

# Theo

Sammy was in no mood to socialize, and he would have preferred to ignore the invitation from Theo, his friend and neighbor, but it would have been the second time he'd begged off such an invitation—and *that* he couldn't do. So, despite his reservations, he took the path to the strangest house in the neighborhood: a three-story, ice-cream cone-shaped dwelling, cone tip pointed up, glass panels set in orange, yellow and blue pastel walls. Theo had moved there only five years earlier, when the house, designed by the same architect as Bill's, was still under construction. At the time, Anna would frequently beg Sammy to take her to "the ice-cream house." Taking him by the hand, she would drag him all the way there, just to sit on the grass and stare at the construction site with the petlike eyes young children have.

Once, Theo happened by, and when he heard that Sammy was a musician, he confessed that he liked to collect art, "though not necessarily the kind of art most people like," and occasionally he sculpted, if he "found the right material." Sammy didn't ask what he meant by "not necessarily the kind of art most people

like," but looking at the house, he had an inkling. Later, when Theo settled in, his collection became apparent to his neighbors. Sculptures sprouted up overnight all over his property. Some found them amusing, others not so much: a "Slow Thinker" that was an homage to Rodin; two chess players hovering over a never-ending game; a row of the heads of presidents arranged in a semicircle whose unveiling was celebrated with a garden party to which all the neighbors were invited and, in consequence, had to forgive him the imposition he'd perpetrated upon them with his garish house. Less than two months after that, they woke up to the shocking spectacle of a forest of bicycles hanging from trees, wheels or whole bicycles with spokes like creeping vines balanced precariously above their heads in a way they did not find endearing. A group of concerned citizens gathered and spoke with him, but to no avail. It was his art and they'd better get used to it! Sammy and Bill had a brief fallout during this crisis, which, for a while, divided the entire neighborhood. Eventually, they got over it, and Sammy even began to feel that the sculptures had a certain charm.

The invitation he'd most recently received was for a party meant to celebrate a new series of sculptures that Sammy would "definitely find interesting." He wasn't so sure, but had no real choice. After walking a little way, he stopped: maybe Anna would like to join him? Maybe she'd be happy to visit a house that had given her so much pleasure as a child. Besides, a few hours away from *that woman* would do her good.

To his surprise, Anna agreed right away, but then took ten minutes to brush her hair and put on makeup—since when did she wear makeup? They left together, and as they walked wordlessly through the undergrowth, their silence took on the shape of uncomfortable distance—a father and a daughter walking side by side like two strangers. He'd never felt like that

next to Anna before: it was the thought of the makeup that had suddenly made her seem from the same species as *that woman*. It was her influence, no doubt about it; she used enough foundation to coat a chicken. And her mouth was always covered with such a thick layer of red lipstick it reminded him of a maraschino cherry. Now, his daughter was taking after her, and it was all his fault. He walked beside her, deep in thought, and she next to him, equally lost.

They arrived in the midst of a small but cheerful gathering of mostly men, standing near two tables set on the grass. One table was laden with a big white bowl of punch and a cooler full of beer, and the other with napkins, plastic silverware and paper plates for the buns and hamburgers that an aproned Theo was grilling, five feet away. The air was saturated with the teasing aroma of grilled meat set against a delicate olfactory background of honeysuckle, and the smoke coiled, trembling, into the unusually warm winter afternoon. All of a sudden, Anna felt happy, the way she used to when her father took her as a child to neighbors' picnics. She took the plate and the hamburger Theo offered her (with a bow), then stood in line behind two other guests at the punch table. Meanwhile, Sammy went searching for the sculptures, followed by Theo, who, abandoning his duties as host and his hamburgers to fate, began to provide a series of unasked-for explanations.

"I came up with the idea after I finished sculpting the presidents. I thought, why not some composers too? And then, of course, which ones?"

As the words tapered off, Sammy lifted his eyes and his gaze met a semicircle of five male heads, each two-feet tall, resting atop a pedestal.

"Let's see if you can guess," said Theo.

"Schoenberg," said Sammy, pointing at the one furthest to his right.

"Correct," Theo confirmed, glowing with pleasure. "Four left."

"Schumann?" Sammy tried, uncertain, pointing at the one left of the middle.

"Correct, once again."

Sammy had no idea who the other three were, but, sensing a pattern, attempted another name that started with 'S.'

"Stravinsky?"

"Yes!"

Enchanted with the result, and beginning to feel like a gambler on a hot streak, Sammy went on:

"Shostakovich?"

"Yes, but you pointed at the wrong head. The one next to it."

"Sibelius."

"Yes! You're the first one to identify them all."

"Am I going to get a prize?"

It was meant as a joke, but the host took it seriously and, regretful that he hadn't thought of it, launched into a long apology. "You *should* get a prize. Just let me think of what it could be."

As they walked back to the grill, their myopic eyes made out a male silhouette advancing in their direction, blue jeans, black leather jacket over black T-shirt—large, friendly hand gestures. A few feet closer they recognized Lenny, who carried a rectangular package in his right hand, a wide grin on his face. Further away, unseen, Anna stood drinking her punch and surveying the encounter with youthful, detectivelike eyes. She saw Lenny shake hands with her father and unwrap the package in slow, careful motions. He then held the freed object up before their eyes. They stared at it for at least five minutes, commenting animatedly. Eventually, Theo abruptly grabbed the object from

Lenny's hands, and walked away. The other two men followed him. "Hey! where do you think you're going?" shouted Lenny. When Theo arrived at the spot where Anna and the other guests stood, he held out the painting—for *it was*, as Anna had inferred, a painting, or rather, a drawing—so everyone could see.

"OK, everyone," he said. "Two things! One: our friend here, Lenny, has just purchased another masterpiece. One of Egon Schiele's most beautiful drawings."

Immediately, people clustered around him to admire the drawing, letting out exclamations of wonder, even a chuckle or two. When Anna moved closer, she understood the reason for their chuckles: the woman in the drawing had her legs spread apart, showing a generous display of pubic hair. Under different circumstances, Anna might have admired the strangeness of the drawing: the bewildering combination of surprise, defiance, and shyness on the woman's face as she covered her breasts while exposing her "hidden parts"; the line's self-assurance, as it traveled in one swift movement from the high heels to the hips, the belly and the upper body, all in ink, with the thick, short hair on the woman's head mirroring her pubic hair; two unexpected splashes of orange—the lips and the left nipple, sticking immodestly out, despite the woman's attempt to cover it. It was an uncanny drawing, everyone agreed, but all Anna could think of was that Lenny had chosen it, and he could have just as easily satisfied his thirst for art by choosing a woman who was a little more covered.

After having given a perfunctory explanation of the drawing, Theo continued:

"Second, our friend has generously offered this drawing as a gift to the person able to identify all the composers in my sculpture, and it is my pleasure to inform you that that person was Samuel Goldstein."

Before he could finish, Lenny leapt out and snatched the drawing from his hand. "Are you crazy?" he shouted. "Do you know how much this baby's worth? Almost half a million."

Theo laughed, patting Lenny on the back. "I just wanted to see your reaction." But the eyes of the others had opened wide and they were whispering in astonishment. Clutching the drawing to his chest, Lenny did not seem to enjoy the joke. A few feet away from him, her glass suspended in mid-air, Anna stared, transfixed, at the object that inspired such passion in its owner, while less than ten feet away from her, leaning against a tree, a beer in his right hand and his left hand in his pocket, stood Bill.

# Tania

Dear Mother,

You wouldn't have believed your eyes if you'd been here for the holidays. Our fridge was almost empty because Sammy had insisted on eating "as usual" and not making a big deal over "a holiday for children and people who eat the body of their so-called Savior." When I asked what he meant by that, he replied, "Don't you people eat wafers in the church pretending it's the body of Christ, and drink wine pretending it's his blood?"

I was at a loss. I really didn't know how to answer because I'd never thought about it. I guess it's true, I've heard the priest say something to that effect, but who cares? And besides, it's not supposed to be real, it's . . . What do you call it? A metaphor? An allegory? Something like that. Long story short, I didn't cook anything special for Christmas, and if we hadn't been invited over to Lenny's, I would have spent the holiest day of the year eating salad and carrots like a rabbit. I decided to compensate by preparing a sumptuous meal for New Year's Eve, so I began cooking and baking immediately after Christmas, the way we do back home. I went all the way, and prepared my favorite dishes:

chicken soup with dumplings and noodles, pigs' feet in aspic, pork roast with potatoes, roasted chicken with white sauce and mushrooms, potato dumplings with plums and cinnamon, potato salad, and Swedish pancakes, as they're called here! (Fries are "French," God knows why, and pancakes are "Swedish.") I filled them with ricotta cheese, the closest thing I found to our farmer's cheese, but it wasn't the same.

Now, you'd think that this stupid husband of mine would be happy, wouldn't you? Wrong! He kept moving around, restless, like a bottled-up fart, mumbling that there was, "No need for all this," that he was already overweight—which is true, but so what? It's not like he's a bride in search of a groom. "Who's going to eat all this?" he kept asking. Maybe we could invite some people over, I said, Bill and Todd for instance (Bill hadn't tasted my cooking yet, and I thought this might be a good opportunity). And so, we had Bill and Todd over for a few hours on New Year's Eve, and let me tell you, I made quite an impression. Bill couldn't stop eating and marveling at how good everything tasted. There was a moment of tension, though, when Sammy—thinking I couldn't hear him from the kitchen—told Bill, "Maybe you can take my place and enjoy the food, and I can take yours and enjoy some peace and quiet." I tiptoed to the living-room to get a look at Bill's face. He seemed scared. I could tell he was trying to guess from Sammy's eyes whether he knew anything, but, seeing how calm and innocent Sammy's face was, he relaxed.

Of course, that brat, Anna, hardly touched anything, what with her being a vegetarian and all. I asked her why she didn't at least eat chicken, if she didn't want any pork, and she began to explain how chickens are kept in some small cages where they can't move, and she showed me how that would feel by pinning my arms to my sides (that girl is strong! She lifts weights every day). It didn't feel good at all. I said, "Well, that's bad. I mean, keeping the birds like

that. In Moldova, they're free to roam all over the courtyard—free as a bird, as they say. Still, what does this have to do with eating them? Chickens were made for people to eat."

I don't think I finished my sentence because the brat exploded with such anger you'd have thought I killed her uncle. "Chickens are *not* made for people to eat! No creature was made for that! We should learn to treat every living thing with respect."

Treat chickens with respect! That's a good one. I'm telling you, this country is going to the dogs. If you start treating chickens with respect, where does it end? Besides, she doesn't even treat *me* with respect! I should have pointed that out. During our discussion, Bill, who hadn't been paying attention to anything except for Sammy, his plate and his glass, began to take special notice of the brat. He raised his eyes from his plate and gazed at her, a frown across his forehead. I bet he was thinking the same thing as I was, "This girl needs a good spanking." To be honest, my palm was itching for a belt or a stick. But I kept my mouth shut. Oh yes, I've learned to keep my mouth shut, and you know better than anyone how hard that is. The reason I controlled myself was because I wanted to talk to him. Sammy, I mean. I decided to start the New Year by telling him that now that God has been so generous to us, has brought me to America, has given him a wife, given his daughter a mother, it was time for him to give something in return. It was time for him to thank God. And the best way for us to thank God is by spreading his generosity, by giving to others what He has given us.

That's what I told him, trying to hide my nervousness, after Bill and Todd had left around two in the morning, and we were both ready for bed. He had slipped under the covers with the usual sigh that accompanies his bedtime ritual. As I began my well-rehearsed speech, I felt his body grow tense. He closed his

eyes wearily, pulled the covers all the way up to his chin, but he was definitely tense. Eventually, he said, "Are you trying to tell me something? If so, please make it quick, because I'm exhausted."

"Of course I'm trying to tell you something," I said. "I'm trying to tell you that I can't go on living here while my little sister is still back home, in such terrible need."

At this, his eyes shot open.

"Do you mean that . . . that . . . you're considering moving back?"

"Moving back?! Do you think I'm insane? Whatever gave you this idea?"

He then relaxed, closed his eyes, and pulled the covers back up.

"What I'm saying, honey, is that we should bring my little sister here."

This time he said nothing. Encouraged, I went on. "It just breaks my heart knowing she's there, with no future. Promise me you'll help bring her here."

When I turned to look at his face, he was already snoring, and I know he wasn't pretending.

More later.

Your daughter,
Tania

# Anna

Anna waited for the red Porsche to disappear around the curve, and when it was gone, she began to walk with determined steps in the direction of Lenny's house. An obsessive drumming had been bouncing in her head all morning, You-can-do-it-You-can-do-it, and now it had slipped down into her chest, accompanying her step and shielding her mind from anxious thoughts. What she didn't know is that she had a companion, one that moved from bush to bush at a considerable distance behind her, he too with a beat in his head.

She arrived at the house and paused to smooth out her breathing, trying to control the beat, which now went, now-or-never-now-or-never. It was a perfect Santa Barbara winter morning, crisp as a sheet of paper, of a cool brightness. Everything stood out in clearly drawn outlines: the trees, the house, even the blades of grass. She moved closer, until her hand was within reach of the wall, and stood on her toes, hoping to see through the nearest window; it was the kitchen window, that much was clear, but it was closed, and when she tried to push it

up, it didn't budge. Well, she might as well try the door. After all, most people in the neighborhood didn't lock their homes. She doubted, though, that Lenny would be so careless, what with his expensive art collections and everything. Locked. She moved to the next window but wasn't any luckier. Disappointed and relieved at once, she sat down on a rock, and took something out of one of her pockets.

*What?! She smokes?!* The young man couldn't believe his eyes. *Hypocrite! Meat is bad for you, but cigarettes aren't?* A few minutes passed, punctuated by her futile attempts to light a cigarette, but her lighter kept going out. Eventually, she must have lit it, because she began puffing. That, or she was just pretending. She looked at the sky, took another puff, her eyes staring vacantly into the distance. Her legs were in the familiar position the young man liked so much because it made her seem so girlish—knees touching, feet wide apart. She extinguished the cigarette on the rock and left the butt there. Then she stood up, and tried more windows. When she finished examining them, she paused, thinking. She looked up at the second floor. Yeah, right. She kept her head raised for a long minute, then lowered it with a sigh. She was about to circle the house one more time when she heard the distinct purr of an engine. The young man saw the panicked expression on her face, and barely refrained from yelling, "The shed!" Then, as if he had transmitted her the thought, he saw her open the wooden tool shed and disappear behind its door, moments before a red car pulled up the driveway. Lenny dismounted with his usual blasé air. What a bore, his body seemed to say, to repeat these same movements over and over, but what the hell, I'll do it again, just this once. He stretched, jangled the keys in his hand, and walked into the house.

With Lenny gone, the young man's gaze moved to the shed. Its door swung cautiously open, but, in the same instant, the door to the house reopened too, and Lenny appeared in its frame. The shed door shut itself. Lenny locked the house, then looked around, as if searching for something, a frown across his forehead. He began to walk toward the shed, and noticed— intrigued—that the latch had been tampered with. He extended his hand in its direction, but, at the last moment, changed his mind and picked up a heavy piece of metal that was lying on the ground. He carried it all the way to his car, put it down carefully next to it, opened the trunk, lifted the piece of metal and placed it inside, then shut the trunk. He opened the car door, but then changed his mind again, strode back to the shed and closed the latch.

A few seconds later the red car was gone.

# Todd

He decided to let her wait, just to teach her a lesson. In fact, she deserved to spend the night in the shed, but he didn't have the heart to put her through it. After less than ten minutes, he lifted the latch and opened the door.

She was sitting on a stool in the dark, and, when the outside light touched her face, he saw tears running down her cheeks. She looked at him with wide, scared eyes.

"You can come out now," he said. "You owe me big time."

They walked together in silence, and after they moved away from the house, Todd sat down on a boulder, inviting her to do the same, then asked for "one of those skinny white things" she kept in her pocket. At first she just looked at him, perplexed, and when she understood, she took out the pack of cigarettes, handed it to him, and asked, angry:

"Why are you following me?" She refrained from adding, *you little prick.*

"Let's not get away from the main question, here. Why are you trying to break into Lenny's house?"

Todd's tone represented an enormous shift in the power struggle between them. Usually, Anna was the one asking the questions, and he was the one dodging them—or attempting to remain in her good graces, ungraceful as he was. She wasn't used to this and she would have very much liked to punch him in the face and flatten that insolent nose of his. But she was in no position to do so. She played for time.

"What makes you think I was trying to get into Lenny's house?"

"I thought we were past this phase," he said, with a confidence he'd never before exhibited. "If this is how you want to play it, I might have to have a serious discussion with Lenny, who . . ."

"You pathetic, little prick." This time, she was unable to restrain herself. Before he had the presence of mind to protect his face, she'd left on it a long blood-red scratch. He caught her hands and, holding them, she noted with unpleasant surprise that he'd become stronger than her, overnight. She struggled, growing angrier and angrier.

"There is one way in which you could . . ."

He stopped. They were face to face, their noses almost touching. He was staring at her lips. What was wrong with him?

"Is your brain frozen?" she yelled, regaining her confidence. He continued to stare at her large, full-lipped mouth, its feminine plumpness in stark contrast with her boyish body. When she finally understood, her surprise was so overwhelming she let out a "Are you out of your mind?"—the words dropped on him with so much scorn that he let go of her hands, dismayed.

"Well, think about it," he said, trying to regain some of his lost dignity. "Just think about it."

# Bill

What Todd didn't know is that, while he was following Anna, sneaking like a thief from bush to bush, a third pair of eyes watched them both, hidden behind a clump of three man-sized succulents: a spiky Euphorbia with tiny yellow flowers, an Aloe with thorny edges, and an Agave with long, striped leaves.

As soon as the two young people had left, the man approached Anna's house and looked around to make sure both cars were gone. Then, he lit a cigarette and began to pace up and down, visibly nervous. He threw away the cigarette after extinguishing it by rubbing it against a rock, and, with a newfound spring in his step, he advanced toward the door, grasped the knob, and, without pausing, crossed the threshold. He found himself in a dark, windowless hall. In front of him: the living room; to his left: the kitchen; to his right: another dark hall. He flipped a light switch, entered the second hall and, without thinking, opened the first door on his right. It was a large bedroom of an aseptic austerity that betrayed its owner, the bed made up as if by a hotel maid. It wasn't the bedroom of

a girl that was sixteen-going-on-seventeen years old. Bill closed
the door right away. His next attempt went better. Judging from
the perfume that lingered in the air and the colorful mishmash
of scattered clothing, this could only be a woman's room. But
which woman: Anna or Tania?

His heart was now beating faster—so many years had
passed since his heart had experienced any derangement of
rhythm that he'd forgotten he had one. The room's walls were
covered in violet wallpaper, its white furniture contrasting with
the dark fixtures and black marble in the rest of the house. The
quilt on the bed was girly—squares with yellow flowers and pink
hearts—and, with a sigh of relief, he noted that there were no
dolls or teddy bears. On a nearby chair lay some brightly colored
undergarments. It was not clear exactly what they were, since
they were all crumpled up. His heart began to beat so loudly
that he could hear its pounding inside his head. As his right
hand reached for the bundle on the chair, his eyes closed, and,
very slowly, he brought it to his nose. But no sooner had he
inhaled than—with a shock that sent an electric jolt throughout
his body—he heard from behind him:

"Beeeel?! What are you doing here?"

He stood there, motionless, hoping that if he didn't move,
the gods would take pity on him and turn him to stone. But
the gods couldn't have cared less, and, a second later, the voice
materialized, taking the form of Tania's face and body. She stared
with a certain (rare, for her) analytical curiosity at the bunch of
clothes. The curiosity slowly gave way to wide, astonished eyes,
and, eventually, the beginnings of a conspiratorial smile.

"Beeel, oh, Beeel! You made a mistake. This isn't my room,
this is Anna's room."

When Bill had met Tania's eyes, all the blood had drained
from his face and traveled down into his feet. But after her

words, the blood rushed back into his head with the same urgency, and now he stood there with a mug like a sun-burnt pumpkin. Gradually, he realized that she wasn't angry, and that the evidence against him—starting with what he was holding in his hand—had an entirely different meaning for her than for him. He let his arm fall to his side, and put the clothes back on the chair.

"You devil," said Tania. "Oh, you're so devilish. Let's go to my room, and there, you can smell my clothes as long as you want."

Speechless, Bill followed her to her room, grateful that he had nothing to explain. There, he let her take his clothes off and drag him to the king-size bed, thanking the gods that this was the only price he had to pay for his transgression.

# Tania

Dear Mother,

Yesterday, Sammy dragged me from gallery to gallery until I was so exhausted I wanted to gouge his eyes out with my high heels. It was some art festival, one of those things he absolutely *had* to go to. The good that came out of it is that now I know there's a future here for my Irina. You wouldn't believe how much the people here will pay for a painting! And some paintings, they are! The first paintings we saw weren't bad, even if they were a bit weird: blue horses, women with trees in their hair and birds in their eye sockets, things like that. But starting with the third gallery, the people and the animals disappeared and were replaced by splotches of color, dots and lines—all at random, as if the painter was trying to put himself into the mind of an infant. A small painting with nothing but a mass of dark green and a tiny yellow dot in the middle was almost ten thousand dollars. Initially, I thought I got the number wrong, but Sammy confirmed that, yes, it was correct: ten thousand dollars for a patch of green. Seeing my dismay, he smiled, then, as I moved in front of another painting—this had a few more dots

than the previous one—he remarked in the constipated tone he uses when he tries to teach me a lesson, "They say that in this country the average person spends less than thirty seconds in front of a painting—but you spend less than ten. I thought Europeans were a little more attuned to art."

He often says stupid things like that, using words that make him feel good about himself because he's the only one who understands them—*attuned*—and I let him do it. Why bother, if it makes him happy? I have other things on my mind. But this time, there was something about it that really rubbed me the wrong way. Maybe I was at my wits' end after standing on four-inch heels for three hours. Whatever it was, this time I couldn't keep my mouth shut. "Really, is that what they say?" I took deep breaths, collecting my thoughts. Then, I blurted out six months of accumulated rage, "Well, you know what? They also say that every other minute someone is getting murdered, that one in four women has—or will be—raped, that if you want to know how happy you are, you should rate your happiness on a scale of one to ten, one being the lowest, and ten the highest. You people just throw numbers at each other, as if you've discovered the meaning of life. 'Just thirty seconds in front of a painting.' Bah! So what? Do you know what that means? Let me tell you what it means: nothing! Or rather, it means that the only thing you people understand is numbers. Some idiot has thought of counting the seconds people spend in front of paintings, as if that means anything! Maybe, if you people counted less, you'd have more time to spend in front of paintings. Did you ever think of *that*?"

As this scolding progressed, my voice kept rising until, in the end, I was yelling at him. It was the first time I had done that, and, when I realized it, I stopped, nervous. And you know what he did? He turned to me and, very calmly, he sized me up. It was as if he was seeing me for the first time.

"You know," he said, "you may have a point."

I waited for what would follow, but no, that's all he had to say: "you may have a point." Of course, I had a point, but that was not the point. What was the point I was trying to make? Oh, yes. Irina. Tell her that all the time she spent doodling might finally pay off. Tell her to make a pile of her finest paintings and drawings and bring them with her when she comes. It will happen soon; I'm working on it. Just be patient. Be patient!

Your daughter,
Tania

# Sammy

**H**alf an hour after Tania had dragged him to her bed, Bill was doing his best to disentangle himself from her grip without appearing too crass. He had performed, but had done so filled with anxiety, which had had the effect of making him seem more enthusiastic than he really was. Now that he'd paid the price for his stupidity, he was entitled to beat a hasty retreat. The idea of being found in bed with his best friend's wife didn't seem as funny as it usually did in movies. In reality, it was hard to imagine Sammy getting angry on account of his wife. Who knows, he might even be grateful for being handed the pretext to get rid of her!

As he considered these possibilities, Bill hurriedly put on his clothes and rushed out of the house, oblivious to Tania's caresses and cooing. But, no sooner had he taken a few steps, than Sammy's voice reached his ears, followed by a friendly handshake. Bill was already beginning to make excuses for being on his friend's turf, but, impatient, Sammy interrupted him:

"Listen, I was just thinking about you. I need your advice. Tania wants to bring her sister here, and she's constantly bugging

me about it. The girl is exactly Anna's age, so she still has a year left in high school. To tell you the truth, I'm not sure what to do. On the one hand, I'm thinking that this might be good for Anna. Especially, since she's been a little depressed lately. On the other hand, bringing another member of Tania's family here is going to bring us even closer, which is not exactly what I want. I mean, if one day I decide to . . . to extricate myself . . ." There, he said it. He, who rarely confessed anything to anyone, had made a disclosure.

Bill felt so embarrassed by his friend's trust that all he could do was mechanically repeat Sammy's words, as if he was actually considering them. "I see. I see your problem. On the one hand . . . But on the other . . . Yes, I can see the pros and cons."

They analyzed the situation while walking up the path to Bill's house, stopping occasionally for Bill to repeat a word or an idea. Eventually, Sammy breathed a sigh of relief and, patting Bill's shoulder, thanked him for his help. Bill wondered whether his friend was ironic—maybe he was being sarcastic?—but, no, Sammy's face was serious. They parted, Bill with a heavy weight on his chest, Sammy with a lightness in his step.

All this time, Tania had watched them from behind the kitchen window, feeling that something must be cooking in the curly head of that husband of hers. She greeted him with a sulky face, as was her habit—a husband should feel, daily, the chains of his circumstance: only then will he be able to truly appreciate his wife's beautiful smile, on the rare occasions of its bestowal— but when he announced, out of the blue, that her sister could come, she jumped with joy. Then she jumped into his lap and began to cover his surly face with wet kisses (*his* face was surly, not for ideological reasons, but simply out of habit), which he wiped off immediately, and then, ever more excited, she dragged him to the bed Bill had vacated less than an hour earlier. As she took his clothes off, he was already regretting his decision.

# Tania

Dear Mother,

I've been asking around about where and how to meet other women here, and everybody advised me to go to "yoga." If you want to meet women in California, they say you have to go to yoga. So, I went to yoga. Anna recommended a place downtown where she takes classes every now and then. She said, "You should start with beginners' yoga. It takes time to advance to another level, sometimes years." Nonsense! Maybe for American women, but not for me! Still, I took her advice and started with beginners' yoga. The room was full of old folks, some as old as eighty, and two women who were around my age. They all sat on plastic mats, so I helped myself to one from a pile in a corner. The funny thing was that all those old people were dressed in athletic gear, tight leggings and muscle shirts revealing their flabby, liver-spotted skin, save for the oldest one, a man in his eighties, who wore shorts and a T-shirt, and, when he sat down in a cross-legged position, I received a sudden and unobstructed view of his balls. Oh, the old devil knew what he was doing, I'm sure! I bet this was his whole reason for coming

to class: to show his balls! At first, I felt like yelling at him, "Cover your balls, you old fool," but then I thought, *Maybe this is the only pleasure he's still getting out of life. Let him have it, what do I care?*

Finally, the instructor came and the class began. Oh, she was a good one! Her body was like rubber—I expected her to start bouncing like a ball, she just didn't seem human. The other people in the room, however, were pretty bad. For my first time going to yoga, I have to say, I was top of the class. I can tell I'm going to advance quickly. But some of the poses the teacher asked us to take were quite funny. Downward-facing dog: you place yourself on the mat like a dog with your butt in the air, and you can see all the butts around you, especially the butt of the person right in front of you. These old women with their big behinds in their spandex leggings have no shame! But our teacher was amazing: she seemed like she belonged to a different species. She walked among us, talking ceaselessly while we struggled to contort ourselves into weird poses. "Breathe into your bellies!" "Bring the breath into your pelvis!" She said the strangest things, but no one else seemed to notice. I wondered if this woman had any worries in her life. All she seemed to care about was breathing. I could picture her getting up in the morning, making a cup of coffee, and, as she took her first sip, thinking to herself, "Now, let's take a deep breath." Another sip of coffee, another breath . . . this was what I was focused on when she said, "Some of you may know, we now have a class for preschoolers. Yes, for preschoolers," she repeated, as the others began to applaud, excited.

"Imagine what our lives would have been like if we had started yoga at such a young age. Imagine . . ."

I tried to follow her advice and picture it, but all I could see was my classroom with its portrait of our Dear Leader, where

we did our morning exercises under his ever-vigilant gaze, unless they forced us to do them in the cold morning air, which I hated with all my heart. Now that I think about it, those exercises were a lot like yoga, but I don't think they changed my life. With or without yoga, the portrait of our Beloved Leader would have hung above our heads. But the people around me had a different opinion. They kept nodding in agreement, seeming to say, Oh yes, our lives would have been so different, if only we could have started yoga in preschool! Our behinds would be so much smaller and we'd all be moving around with our teacher's confidence, breathing our hearts out.

At the end of the class, the teacher joined her hands in prayer, chanting in a foreign language, and I suddenly felt like I was part of a cult. Maybe the communists were right, after all. You know what they used to say about yoga and other Western occult practices.

But I forgot to mention the most important development: Bill! Well, maybe in another letter. I can hear Sammy's footsteps.

Your daughter,

Tania

# Tania and Anna

I t was their first trip as a family: Sammy, Tania, and Anna, all in his black Subaru, fighting the snail-paced traffic between Santa Barbara and L.A. Sammy was annoyed, Anna was melancholy, only Tania was in good spirits—cheerful as a toddler out for a ride. Sammy kept grumbling, complaining about the other drivers and their cars, but Tania took everything in with the ferocious thirst of an alcoholic, or as if they were having a picnic in the middle of a soaring landscape that she couldn't get enough of. Oh, look at that red car. What is it? A Corvette? That sounds nice, French. And look at that silver BMW! That's a serious, dependable car. Did you see that young man who just drove by? Wasn't he speeding? What nerve! Go after him! I see that there's no space, but he should be taught a lesson. God, look at all these lanes! Two, four, eight lanes! No, ten! Ten lanes! Can you believe it? They won't believe me when I tell them back home.

"It's because of all these lanes and cars that we have so much pollution," Anna noted dryly, wishing to put a dent in Tania's enthusiasm.

"Bullshit! What pollution? In Moldova, you can't even see the sky. Here, look at the sky: it's so blue. In Moldova, we have no cars and more pollution. Do you want to know why?"

"No."

Not only Anna didn't want to know, but each time Tania uttered the word "Moldova"— Moldova this, Moldova that— she felt like holding a pillow over her mouth to make her shut up. She didn't care a bit about Moldova, even though it was where her grandparents had come from. Before Tania had come to live with them, Moldova had been a faraway place endowed with the vague mythology of remote origins, and when asked about her family's background, Anna would name it, pleased that, like all the other kids, she too could claim that her family came from somewhere else. But ever since the name had come to be associated with *this woman,* it had taken on a certain uneasiness, even shame. *A woman whose armpits emanated an odor like a cross between a skunk and an overripe French cheese.* Anna wondered whether she had started using deodorant, given the lack of smell in the Subaru.

Their first stop was at the jewelry shop Sammy's parents had owned on Hill Street, *Goldstein's Gold,* which was now an antique store. From the outside it was as innocuous as all the other boutiques on that street, a door with a bell and a window cluttered with old, moth-eaten fabrics, peacock feathers, yellowed gloves and Chinese board games; the inside, however, was the same as it had been in the old days, Sammy told them. Even the cash register with its gilded detailing and antediluvian keys appeared to be the same. Like all antique shops, the place was dark—though it was a welcoming darkness  and exuded a slight staleness, like that of an incubator, with hidden nooks and crannies from which a jack-in-the-box might pop up, or a melody box might start playing an old tune. Numerous dolls in

lace dresses could be seen all over, and doll-size kitchen utensils and wares peppered the spaces between them. Each dark recess was lit by the discreet light of a neighboring lamp with a slender pedestal and a pastel-colored shade, and whose chiaroscuro sang an enchanted, spellbinding song.

"A Singer! A Singer!" Tania pointed at a sewing machine. "My mother had one when I was a child. Many of my clothes were made with it." Her excitement drew a smile from the store owner, but no reaction from her companions. A few seconds later: "An old iron! My mother used one just like it when I was a child." Now she pointed at a heavy, rusty iron that seemed to weigh about twenty pounds. "Why do Americans buy all these old things when they have so many other, new, better things in their stores?"

For a few seconds no one bothered to answer. Eventually, the store owner ventured, "Well, I don't think they buy them to use them; they buy them for their sentimental value. You know, just to look at them."

"Look at them? What's the point of looking at a useless sewing machine, or an old, rusty iron?"

The owner looked her up and down, as if she were a slow-witted child. He explained, in a calm, thoughtful voice, "They have charm and value *because* they're old and useless. They're part of a bygone world."

Though things were still blurry in her mind, little by little, Tania was beginning to grasp a thread of clarity that was emerging through the blur. Americans, who lived in a world of new things, occasionally took trips to islands of the past where antiquated things were stored, and they paid good money for them because they were part of a world they had killed, and now wanted to artificially resurrect. As she pondered this, wondering what old things her mother might send her, she noticed Anna

at the cash register. She was holding a big, bronze-polished Chinese pig, an obscene laugh on its piggish face, its limbs in the air, exhibiting its male genitalia.

*Christ, two hundred dollars for a toy pig,* she thought, hearing the man and seeing the credit card in the girl's hand. *This girl really is spoiled.*

What Tania didn't know was that the "toy" wasn't for Anna.

# Tania

Dear Mother,

I finally saw it: Los Angeles, the City of Angels. To tell you the truth, the most impressive part was the road there with its ten lanes and thousands of expensive, shiny cars (when I took the same road on my arrival in the States, I was so tired I didn't even notice). The reason for our trip was that Sammy was invited to the thirtieth anniversary of his high-school graduation in Beverly Hills, so we were all dressed in our Sunday best. Sammy had even given me a necklace from his mother's jewelry collection, a heavy gold chain with a little heart studded with diamonds—that woman had good taste, let me tell you! Anna refuses to wear jewelry, that is, she won't wear gold, silver or diamonds; all she wears is the silly, colorful jewelry made by Native Americans (that's what they call them here—you know, Indians!). That should tell you how unfair this world is; our Irina would know how to take advantage of everything this family has to offer. But maybe it's not the girl's fault. Anna, I mean. After all, she grew up without a mother; what does she know?

To be honest, I expected something fancier, given that these people—Sammy and his classmates—come from good, rich families. But I should have known. The restaurant was fancy enough, but the food . . . For a starter, they served us chips. I thought it was a joke—chips! Then, it got a little better. Some waiters brought around platters of finger-food: lox, cheese, ham. It was OK, but still, nothing to write home about. Drinks, we had plenty of—wine, beer, mineral water; but they gave us no real food in spite of the fact that Sammy had paid a hundred and fifty dollars for each of us. I thought it was a rip-off. I wanted to complain to someone, but didn't know to whom, so, each time Sammy introduced me to one of his former classmates, I complained to them. They all looked at me with stupid grins on their faces, as if I was speaking a foreign language. Then, they asked me where my "lovely accent" was from. They all seemed to be in love with my accent: imagine! When I said I was from Moldova, they said, "Oh," as if that reminded them of a whole world that was familiar to them. Only one of them said, "My grandmother was from there, too, but never spoke about it. But maybe I'm wrong. Maybe she was from Romania. I'm not really sure," and a few of the others exclaimed, "How interesting." It never occurred to me that there was anything interesting about being born in Moldova, but I felt proud that that's what they thought. Most of all, I was pleased that all those men with full bellies and fat wallets were so taken with me. Some of them let their eyes wander freely over my curvy body, and I can't blame them. I mean, surrounded by all those women brittle as sticks and without an ounce of flesh on them, the poor men must have been starving! Let them look, I thought. Although, on the other hand, the women were well-preserved. They must have been Sammy's age, since they had been classmates, but they barely looked older than me. Their skin was smooth, with no wrinkles.

Still, there was something strange about their noses and mouths. I couldn't quite put my finger on it. They all had the same kinds of mouths, as if someone had taken extra pieces of flesh and glued them to their faces. And their noses! They all had tiny, Michael Jackson, doll-like noses—I realize this only now since at the time I wasn't sure what they reminded me of. I spoke with a few of them, and the impression of strangeness increased. The women did not speak *with* me—they spoke *through* me. I don't know how to explain it because on the surface they seemed very nice. They looked me straight in the eye and seemed to be savoring every word I uttered—"Oh, Moldova! That's so interesting!" Everything I said was interesting. Although, come to think of it, all I said was, "I'm Sammy's wife," and, "I'm from Moldova," over and over again. And when they said, "Oh, how interesting," I started to explain that, no, it wasn't interesting, it was actually quite dull—dull and gray—that's how life was there, and I kept explaining, and the women's eyes never left mine, as if their entire world depended on what I had to say, and, at the end, they said again, "How interesting!"—although one of them said, with tears in her eyes, "You're so brave, so brave! I wouldn't have the courage to leave my own country. And you speak English so well." By the end of the night, I began to think that I really *was* an interesting woman who spoke English very well. Let me tell you, no one can boost your morale like an American.

Your daughter,
Tania

# Lenny

Lenny opened the door in sweatpants and a white T-shirt, as if he'd been working out or doing house chores. Anna had come unannounced on purpose, to see if she could spot any evidence of another woman on the premises. She was holding a square box wrapped in shiny blue paper with a red ribbon around it. At first, Lenny stared at her as if she were a solicitor, and she was afraid he would slam the door in her face, but after a few seconds, he seemed to remember who she was. "May I help you?"

The coldness of the question shrank the words in her throat. All she could think to do was extend the box wordlessly toward him. He observed the box, waiting for an explanation. Eventually, she stammered:

"I brought you something."

Only then did he invite her in, and even then, reluctantly. They were in the living room, standing, she with the box in her awkward hands, he staring at her.

"Please, sit down."

She swallowed and began to speak in a voice that sounded as if it were coming from far away. "We were in L.A. a few days ago. And, I don't know if you know, but my father, or, his parents actually, used to have a jewelry store there. We still have lots of jewelry at home, diamonds, gold and silver, but I don't like to wear it; it's for old ladies. We keep it in boxes. You could look at it some day, if you're interested."

Seeing his puzzled expression (*Why in the world would he do that?*), she swallowed hard again, and pressed on. "I mean, you don't have to. Just a thought. But that's not what I mean. What I mean is that we went to this jewelry store that's no longer a jewelry store, it's an antique shop. My father wanted us to see it, you know, for sentimental reasons, and when we walked into the shop, I saw this." She pointed to the box. "At first it seemed a little weird, but then I thought, I know someone who might like it. And I asked the owner if it was valuable. I mean, not in terms of money, but, you know, as art. Because I know you like art. And the owner said yes, it was valuable, like everything in the store, they only had things of value. And I said, OK, I'll buy it then. And here it is."

She pointed at the box again, laughing, embarrassed. Lenny took the box and began to peel away the wrapping paper. He opened the package and extracted a shiny object in the shape of a pig, its limbs up and its private parts exposed. As he examined it, he held it at arm's length, as if afraid he might get dirty. He turned the pig this way and that, observing it minutely, while Anna—cheeks aflame—tried to conjure a miracle that would turn the clock back to a time before she had knocked on Lenny's door with the damn pig. In the end, he set the pig down on a nearby coffee table, and, lifting his face toward hers—this time with a smile—said, "Thank you."

Then, changing his tone, and putting on a severe expression:

"However, I don't have to tell you that you shouldn't be spending your pocket money on—uh—presents. Please give me a moment." He disappeared for a few seconds into an adjacent room, returned, and, opening his wallet, asked:

"How much do I owe you?"

Cheeks burning, Anna jumped up, and, without a word, ran from the house.

# Tania

Dear Mother,

I decided—and Sammy agreed—that it would be good for me to get a part-time job so I could have my own pocket money, which I could spend on anything I wanted. Do you know that in this country you need references even if you apply to clean public toilets? Why would they need someone to vouch for you when all you do is clean people's shit? I couldn't understand it, but, this being the situation, I asked Bill and Lenny to put in a good word for me, as needed. I thought I should try a position as a cashier or a waitress, something that seems to be available here on every corner.

I inquired at a few places, but all the managers said no—looked at me askance, as if I might rob them or something. Finally, when I was about to lose all hope, I spotted a sign on a café with a funny name, *Café Namasté*: "Now hiring." Full of hope, I went in, but decided to change my tactic. Instead of asking for a job application, I took a seat like a regular customer, and waited for the waitress. A young woman with long, thin braids circling her head like snakes—a style they call "dreadlocks"—showed up and

ALTA IFLAND

announced, "Today's question is, 'What do you find magnificent?'"
At first, I thought she must be talking to somebody else, but when
I looked around I saw that the other customers were busily eating,
paying her no attention. She smiled. She was talking to me. *Maybe
I misunderstood,* I thought, and asked her to repeat.

"This must be your first time in our café," she said, and
when I confirmed that it was, she continued, "It's our custom
here to greet our customers with a different question every day.
You don't have to answer if you don't want to. You can just
think about it, okay?"

"That's fine with me," I said, "but what's the point of
thinking about it?"

For a second she seemed disconcerted, then she stammered,
"It . . . helps you notice the positive aspect of things. But, like I
said, you don't have to answer."

"Oh, but I do want to answer. I like this. It's like a riddle,
and I love riddles. What do I find magnificent?"

I began to think, but couldn't come up with anything.
Really, I couldn't think of anything I found magnificent. I mean,
I like good food, but is there a meal that's *truly* magnificent? For
instance, I can cook an outstanding pigs feet in aspic, but even
that can't be called magnificent.

"I can think of something outstanding," I began, "but
magnificent, I don't know." The girl seemed to be losing her
patience.

She shoved the menu under my nose and repeated:

"Really, you don't have to answer."

"I'll give you the answer before I leave," I said, and
started to study the menu. I don't know if I've told you how
complicated their menus are, but this one was strange even for
them. Each dish had a funny name, like "You are elated" or
"You are worthy" or "You are eternally youthful." Beneath the

name, there was a brief description of the dish with a list of its ingredients. And wouldn't you know it? None of the dishes had any meat. Just my luck. It was all lettuce, carrots, pine nuts, beets, cucumbers, and that funny vegetable called broccoli. I ordered a broccoli cream soup because it was the only thing that sounded at all substantial. When the girl returned with it, she placed it on the table, all smiles.

"You are worthy," she chirped.

"Thank you," I replied, realizing too late that she was referring to the soup.

Surprisingly, the soup wasn't bad. As soon as I finished it, I decided that there was no point in wasting my time and asked for the manager.

The girl frowned.

"Is there something wrong?"

"Oh, no. I just want a job application."

The girl breathed a sigh of relief, and the manager—another girl barely older than the first—appeared a minute later. She invited me to have a seat in a more secluded corner, and said that, if I felt prepared, we could hold my interview then and there. What was there to prepare? That scared me a little—I thought she might ask me some difficult questions, you know, mathematics or the like, but then I thought I had nothing to lose. I said sure I felt prepared.

"Good," she replied. "Have you ever worked in the food industry?"

"The food industry?"

"Yes, restaurants."

"Oh, no, but I'm a very good cook. In fact, I could probably teach you a thing or two. Russian cooking is very good."

"I'm sure it is. And why do you want to work at Café Namasté?"

"This was the only place that was hiring. It's not that I want to work at Café Namasté, it's that I couldn't find anything else. Frankly, I don't really want to work; I just need the money."

I was very happy that for once, I had the right answer. After all those years under communism, when we were forced to claim that we wanted to work for the good of the country, now, in freedom, I could tell the truth: I wanted to work for the money! I didn't give a shit about society, all I wanted was the money. I glanced at the manager, trying to detect some sign that she shared my feelings, but she stared straight through me:

"You know, we have some very specific rules here, and we expect our employees to obey them."

"That's fine. I'm used to rules."

"How do you feel about this: every morning, after our employees punch in, we all gather for a meeting that we call 'cleansing.' Do you understand this word?"

"I think so."

"What it means is that, before we start working, we cleanse ourselves through a process of personal reflection. To accomplish this, we hold hands . . ."

Did she say "hold hands?"

"We hold hands and cleanse ourselves of negative thoughts. For example, as a manager, I might ask, 'What do you think you don't have enough of?' and we would each take turns to answer. After that, we'd express how we feel in that particular moment. You see, we're not just a workplace. We have a philosophy that guides our work, the philosophy of sacred commerce."

"Sacred commerce?"

This time I uttered the words out loud. She watched me with moist eyes, penetrated by the loftiness of her own words.

"Yes, sacred commerce."

THE WIFE WHO WASN'T

I was more confused than ever. I had assumed that, while under communism we were forced to pretend that we enjoyed working for the good of others and not for the money, in capitalism the opposite should be true. Wasn't material reward the point of working? Now, it appeared that, while the communists were, in fact, failed capitalists, the capitalists themselves were failed ministers who felt compelled to shroud their money in the sacred veil of communal wholesomeness.

We separated, I with the words "sacred commerce," in my ears, she with the words, "We'll call you!" on her lips. And to think that all I wanted was make some money!

Your daughter,
Tania

# Sammy

Eight years after he'd begun work on his musical theory, Sammy had finally reached the point where he was ready to apply it. The day he began to compose a piece based on his theory he felt it happen; it was as if, after years of bitter separation, his heart and mind were finally coming together, joining to form an indivisible whole. He was so elated he almost wept, but stopped, troubled by a new thought: where did the body come in all this?

He recalled, with a certain embarrassment, how, on the previous night, his body had participated in a series of shameless acts initiated by his wife, a woman with whom he could not share his musical discoveries. The weight of what he had hitherto refused to acknowledge struck him: he greatly enjoyed bodily contact with a woman he otherwise despised. This brutal realization almost erased his excitement and made him eager to see Bill.

Ten minutes later, he was standing in his friend's ascetic room.

"How is this possible?" he asked, with an agitation he was rarely possessed by. "I was married for years to a woman I adored, yet I never experienced with her the physical pleasure I have with a woman I despise."

"Your situation isn't that exceptional," said Bill, trying to raise to a general condition a particular situation that made him uncomfortable.

"But if that's the case, doesn't it mean that some force in the universe is playing a cruel joke on us?"

"I think all this means is that our dicks have a logic that our minds and our hearts don't."

As he said this, Bill noticed his son in the cracked door.

"What do you want?"

"Oh, nothing. I was just looking for something."

When he returned to his room, where Anna was waiting for him, Todd whispered, smiling naughtily:

"Guess what your father and my father are talking about?"

"?"

"Sex. Your father was just saying that sex with the Moldovan woman is much better than with your mother."

Anna's fist didn't make it to Todd's face, but was caught in mid-air. Todd immobilized her arms effortlessly, and a minute later he was on top of her, demanding she "give up."

"I won't, you bastard."

He began to twist one of her arms behind her back.

"All right, you prick. Let me get up!"

His face moved closer to hers. "I'll let you get up if you let me do what I asked after I freed you from Lenny's shed."

She was in no position to negotiate, so she reluctantly agreed. Besides, she was a little curious. "Fine, but do it fast. No lingering."

She felt a rubbery tongue slide into her mouth, moving with exploratory zeal in all directions, as if attempting to uncover something. Was this—this wet suction—what everybody made such a big fuss about? If it was, she'd be happy to spend the rest of her life without it.

# Tania

Dear Mother,

Finally! Sammy has obtained the documents the American Embassy has requested for Irina's visa. He'd talked to a lawyer and was told that it would be easier to bring her here on a tourist visa, and, for that, he has to prove that he makes a certain sum of money each year. He had to show them a document from his bank, another from the IRS, and I forget what else.

But that wasn't the worst part. The worst part was when we filled out the application and got to "relationship"—that is, Irina's relationship to us. I *had* to tell him! Can you imagine? It's over now, and I'm glad I told him. But, God, he was angry!

"So, all this time, you were lying to me?"

"Lying? It's easy to not lie when you can afford it. What was I supposed to do? Would you have married me if you'd known I had a child?"

"I don't know, but . . ."

"Well, I know. You wouldn't have."

"Do you realize what you're saying is that, if you want something, you'd do whatever it takes to get it?"

"What's wrong with that?! If I hadn't acted like that, I would have died a long time ago."

"That's not the point."

"That's not the point?! It may not be the point for you, but it certainly is for me, since I'd rather be alive than dead."

He gave me a look as if he were a betrayed nobleman and I a wretched peasant, turned his back on me, and left. But later in the evening he handed me all the necessary documents, without a word. I couldn't believe my eyes. I know he's trying to prove something, but what? That he's better than me? At any rate, tell Irina that the embassy is going to get the documents very soon, and that she should prepare for her interview. God willing, she'll be here by summer.

I almost forgot: I wrote to that slacker, Vadim. Jesus, what poor judgment this girl has. A Romanian man—or half-Romanian— as if she didn't know what Romanian men are like! Has she forgotten what a good-for-nothing her father was? If I hadn't had the good sense to leave him when I did, I'd probably be rotting in prison by now, having killed him after a life of abuse and torment. And yes, I did tell this Vadim what I thought of his "ethnic background," as they call it here. I also told him that, if he doesn't leave our Irina alone, my husband—who has some very well-placed friends in the FBI and CIA—will teach him a lesson. Of course, Sammy doesn't know anything about it, he couldn't harm a fly, poor man. And I'm not speaking metaphorically! Really, he never kills flies. He says they're living beings too. No wonder America is in decline! When a world power starts to take pity on flies, it means that its empire is rotten. Pretty soon it will be a corpse covered in flies.

Honestly, sometimes these Americans seem weirder than Martians. Take the other day when we went to the movies. We left home as a family, but when we got there, Sammy just dropped

us off, then went his own way. After asking what movie I wanted to see, Anna declared that she was in the mood for another movie, so we ended up in different rooms. Imagine: they play different movies at the same time in different rooms, which they call "theaters." They have about twenty of these inside a huge, megatheater. The whole building is like a dream, or a nightmare, I don't know. The main hall has a large counter where they serve popcorn in tall paper cups, and movie titles flash across a screen overhead. The hall is full of people, noise and colors, and when you open the door to one of the theaters you find yourself groping in the dark until your eyes adjust, then you can sit in one of the numerous empty seats—there's barely anyone there—and from then on, it's only you and the screen. It's as if you've entered a magic cave or merry-go-round. You spin and spin for two hours, and at the end you're dizzy and color-full.

But that's not what I wanted to tell you. When I entered the theater, the air conditioning was turned up so high it was freezing. I went to talk to an employee and asked her to do something about it. The woman—a misshapen slob that looked like a blob with her sleeves rolled up and her shirt unbuttoned as if she was fighting July heat—looked me up and down, and said:

"If we turn the AC off, it's going to get too hot."

"How could it possibly get too hot when right now it's freezing? Besides, if we need to wear a jacket outside, why do we need the AC on inside?"

This time, she looked at me as if I was speaking Chinese. "Wait here, I'll get a manager."

A minute later another woman appeared. She was younger and in better shape—this country is run by teenagers, I'm telling you. She was carrying a bag.

"We apologize for the inconvenience," she said in a little voice like a kitten's. "Please help yourself to a sweater." As she

said this, she took a heavy blue thing out of the bag and handed it to me.

"What's this?"

"It's for our customers when they're cold."

"You'd rather have me wear *your* sweater than turn off the AC?"

"The other customers will get hot if the AC is off," meowed the pink kitten.

We were standing in the theater's open door. There was enough outside light to reveal the seats' dark outlines and the shadows of the four other guests. I looked up and, helped by the pale light, had a revelation. "Of course they're getting hot. They're all obese."

"Ma'am, I don't think that's appropriate. I'm going to have to ask you to step out of the theater."

"Not appropriate?! I'm trying to stay in shape by going to yoga twice a week and cutting out dessert, while these pigs eat to their hearts' content, and I'm the one being punished because they're too hot under ten layers of fat! Is *that* appropriate?"

As I was making my case, I was getting angrier and angrier, and my voice rose higher and higher, until a man in uniform with the word "Security" on his cap took me by the arm and dragged me—yes, dragged me—out of the theater. I was kicked out without even being reimbursed. And they say that the customer is always right! Lies, all lies.

Your daughter,
Tania

# Anna and Sammy

After the humiliation she had experienced at Lenny's, Anna decided to get him out of her mind. *I'm not really in love with him,* she kept telling herself. *I'm not in love with him, notinlovewithhim, notinlovewithhim.* But the effect was that he was on her mind more than ever, and wasn't that proof that she really *was* in love with him? She began to suffer from loss of appetite, and deep, violet circles appeared under her eyes.

One evening, all three of them—Sammy, Anna, and Tania—were in the kitchen, Sammy cooking pasta, Anna nibbling absentmindedly at this and that, and Tania, who had just returned from shopping, babbling happily about the *paté de foie gras* she'd discovered in a gourmet store. She had had it only once in her life at a party thrown by her then-boss, the lawyer, and it was the most delicious thing she'd ever tasted. Divine. As she was struggling to explain what the taste was like—the smooth, creamy, truffled, buttery taste of liver paste—Anna interrupted her.

"I can't believe you eat that stuff! Do you know how they make it? Do you know that they torture the geese—yes,

force-feed them—so that you can enjoy the 'creamy, divine taste' of their livers?"

She said that with such unusual vehemence that Tania's mouth, which had been left open in mid-sentence, stayed open, and a veil of stupefaction covered the rest of her face. When she recovered, moments later, she replied with the same vehemence. "You Americans are always so concerned with the treatment of animals, but don't give a shit about humans! If I told you that there were days in my life when I had no food to eat, you couldn't care less, but a goose that gets more food than it needs, now *that* gets your attention! Or a fly." (Here, she turned toward Sammy.)

"Maybe we Americans really do only care about animals," said Anna, "but what do *you* care about? I'll tell you what: you only care about yourself."

Tania's jaw dropped again. This time, when she recovered, she placed herself before Sammy, who, with his flowery apron and the words "Love people: Cook them tasty food!" printed on it, was trying to focus on his cooking and avoid the conflict.

"Did you hear what your daughter said to me?"

There was no way of avoiding her question, so he produced a, "Hmm," then mumbled, "Really, what's the point of fighting? Hmm, Anna, please set the table. Hmm . . ."

"Is *that* all you have to say when your daughter insults your wife? Is *that* what I came for all the way from my country?"

"No one asked you to come here," mumbled Anna under her breath. She said it loud enough that they all heard.

"That's it! I've had it! If you don't slap her right this minute . . ."

Facing his belligerent wife, Sammy, who had been hiding behind his gentle apron, changed his expression.

"I've never, ever, hit my daughter! For you to suggest that is . . . is . . ."

"She wasn't suggesting it," Anna chimed in. "She *demanded* it."

Tania sized up father and daughter. Her body stiffened.

"So it's two against one. Well, soon enough it'll be two against two."

"What do you mean?"

"I mean, when my daughter comes."

"About that. We have to talk."

Sammy turned the stove off and, with a drawn-out sigh, sat down.

"I don't think this is the right moment for you to bring your daughter here. You have to admit that things aren't working out, and we might have to . . . might have to make some adjustments."

"Wait! I don't understand a word you're saying. Speak like a normal person! What do you mean *adjustments*? And what does *working out* mean?"

"I'm talking about us. Things aren't going well between us, and I doubt bringing your daughter here will help."

"Really? You doubt that? What about your daughter? She's here and she isn't exactly helping. Besides, Irina's already submitted her application to the American Embassy. Now, we just have to wait for the process to follow its due course, and with God's help, she'll be here by the summer. And then, we'll be even: two against two."

# Part II
# Chișinău,[3] Moldova
# 1996–1997

# Tania, Olga, Irina, and Seryozha

"Building communism without alcohol is like building capitalism
without commercials."
—Vasile Ernu, *Born in the USSR*

When Sammy visited Tania's family early in the spring of 1996, he was still the naive, well-intentioned American in whom three women—Tania, Olga and Irina—had invested high hopes. Seryozha himself was rather skeptical, as any Russian male who's been around the block a few times would be when it came to the intentions (dubious, no doubt) of a middle-aged American pervert who's come here for our women, luring them with his fat wallet, which, in his mind, can buy anything. Seryozha was convinced that, like all Americans, Sammy had a fat wallet, and he was determined to keep an eye on it—an open eye and an open mind, that is.

As Sammy entered the one-bedroom Soviet-style apartment (which was neither more dilapidated nor less decrepit than millions of other similar apartments in the former empire), Seryozha looked him up and down with the discerning eye of

an expert who couldn't be fooled by a pair of Italian leather shoes that had—miraculously—managed to survive the city's pothole-filled streets without as much as a speck of dust on them. Judging from his attire, the American's wallet must have been as fat as Seryozha had imagined.

They shook hands, Sammy a little bit intimidated, and, in his confusion, handing the bouquet of roses he clumsily held in his hand to Seryozha, who considered them for a second, then, like a generous teacher to a student in need of encouragement, mumbled:

"Roses. Nice."

Next, Sammy met Olga, a rotund, jovial woman in her late fifties but who looked a decade older, with a round, soft face, dressed in a flower-print dress she kept smoothing flat, and Irina—"my sister," said Tania—a girl the same age as Anna, whose face displayed the same carnal eroticism as Tania's, the same Botticellian flesh interrupted by a flash of detached sarcasm and licentiousness that lingered at the corners of her smile. The girl wore a black leather miniskirt that revealed two muscled legs ending in high-heeled boots atop which she moved with the serpentine undulations of a less innocent version of Betty Boop. She looked Sammy over with the same inquisitive, unsparing gaze as Seryozha, but without attempting to hide the defiant spark of mockery it contained. Averting his eyes, Sammy tried to find refuge in Olga's plump warmth, and her motherly eyes answered him with a "come-to-me, son." Olga was barely a decade older than Sammy, but, like most women of her generation in that part of the world, she was a de facto mother to whomever happened to be young and helpless, and this, not so much out of generosity, but of an age-old henlike instinct, which caused her to spread her wings over everyone around her, thus giving them a semblance of protection while, in fact, transforming them into babbling children. It was no coincidence that the only

creatures who could resist her motherly appeal were Olga's own progeny, her daughter and her daughter's daughter—all three women involved in a constant power struggle, like the social classes in the Communist Party's vision, the sole distinction being that, as far as Irina was concerned, both Tania and Olga represented the dictatorship of the proletariat, while she, Irina, was the bourgeoisie, always on her guard, always on the verge of being unmasked as a disloyal element, and as a consequence, always ready to rebel and subvert their stifling dictatorship.

The three women together—Betty Boop Junior and Senior, and Mother Goose—emanated an energy that left Sammy no real choice between being sucked into its vortex and remaining in Seryozha's tight grip. Given the alternative, he chose the vortex, and complimented Olga on a "wonderful" (he hesitated before using the adjective, but it seemed less dangerous than "beautiful") daughter. At this, mother and daughter blushed with pleasure, while Irina—who displayed all the signs of an annoying, untamed teenager (thank God he didn't have to deal with her!)—produced a scornful grimace that said, "Who do you think you're fooling with this bullshit?" Sammy swallowed her scorn, which no one else seemed to notice, then washed it down with a sip of whatever-it-was Tania had poured into the shot glass in front of him. Seryozha watched his reaction, then observed in thick, mustached English:

"Traditional drink. Local."

Sammy nodded approvingly, fighting down the burning sensation in his throat.

"Good. Strong."

The verdict pleased Seryozha, who, emboldened, added, "You're supposed to drink it in one gulp. Like this . . ."

Sammy followed his future brother-in-law's example, eager to be a good sport and not disappoint, but the result was a painful

grimace on his face, which, however, the host appreciated for its homage to the drink's strength. Seryozha poured another glass, first for Sammy, then for himself, downed his glass as quickly as he had the first time, then declared:

"*Now*, we can talk."

Meanwhile, Tania had arrived with another tray, this one with bread and cold cuts, and placed it on the coffee table before Sammy. Seryozha, whose interest was aroused by the new tray, eyed the culinary assemblage with a mixture of suspicion and desire.

"Is that *my* sausage?" he asked.

His sister blushed and said something in Russian, then quickly added in English, "Seryozha sometimes does the shopping for us—you know, I come home late from work, and Mother's legs are too weak. She can't stand in line for long."

The brother picked up a piece of sausage and, bringing it near his nose, examined its veined, uneven surface with the dispassionate professionalism of a surgeon about to remove a tumor. Finally, he sniffed it, and stated categorically:

"This is *my* sausage! Who gave you the right to . . . "

Before he finished, Irina snatched the piece of meat from his hand and shoved it into her mouth.

"It's not your sausage anymore!"

A string of loud Russian words—presumably not compliments—came out of the man's mouth.

"I told you never to touch my sausage!"

"When you buy something with someone else's money it's not yours, you piece of shit."

"What?! What did you . . .?" Seryozha rose from his armchair, his sausage-red face exhibiting an array of emotions that ranged from incredulity to stupefaction, and began advancing toward the undisciplined girl, but was stopped by Tania, who interposed

herself between them. The man continued his attempt to reach the girl, who, hiding behind Tania, kept taunting him.

"Besides, if it's yours, you shouldn't keep it between someone else's *bath towels!* It's not hygienic!"

It was, alas, true that Seryozha, who, after his divorce, had bought a studio in downtown but still spent most of his time in his sister's apartment where he could get at least one free meal a day, often hid his favorite foods in the place where, with his unparalleled imagination (unparalleled except by that of a devious teenager) he thought no one would look: the wardrobe, or, more precisely, among its pile of lavender-scented bath towels.

"Stop it! All of you, stop it now!"

It was the tremulous, unmelodic voice of Mother Goose, who now took center stage, propelled by the authority of her position. Surprisingly, everyone calmed down and Seryozha went back to his seat.

"Where were we?" he asked, turning to face the guest. He then poured another glass for himself and, noticing that Sammy's glass was still full, made no effort to hide his dissatisfaction:

"This won't do! Are we brothers, or aren't we? You tell me!"

And, shooting unsteady glances at his guest, who was doing his best to empty the contents of his glass, he didn't wait for an answer. "Brother, we have to talk some serious beeezness, as you Americans say. We have to talk about my dear sister. My sister . . ."

Seryozha's tongue was heroically attempting to overcome the five or six shot glasses he'd already downed (not including the ones from before his guest's arrival).

"My sister Tania!" he exclaimed, remembering her name. "I, as her older brother, am responsible for taking care of my little sister."

By now, his tongue was having such a hard time that the words "brother" and "little sister" sounded more like "brrtr" and "llstr." The brrtr's eyes roved glassily over his guest's nervous face.

"I am *not*—you hear me?"—and here, the brrtr's finger pointed menacingly at his interlocutor—"I am not going to let some foreigner with a fat wallet take advantage of my dear little sister."

"That's enough, Seryozha," interrupted Mother and Sister simultaneously.

"Enough?! No one tells me what and when is enough."

After the interruption, Seryozha seemed to lose his train of thought, and he tried to compose himself, then, apparently having found it, he resumed. "Do you have a fat wallet?"

Coincidentally, Tania's mouth opened at the same time: "Please, have some sausage!" As a result, meat and wallet merged into a sausage-rounded wallet, and the guest replied by helping himself to a piece of said sausage, relieved from the duties of speech.

"Yes, have some sausage," added the brother, who was so touched by his own generosity that a sentimental tear moistened his right eye.

# Matvei and Vadim

A s usual on a Saturday night, this particular night too Irina could be found in the high school's dance club, which, like everywhere else in the former Eastern Bloc, was called a "disco," looking over the available males with an expert's eye. It was a pitiful crop, she thought, so when she spotted a new face among the three oldest men present—the D.J. and his technical assistants, all of whom must have graduated a decade earlier—she grew understandably excited. She couldn't see his face well in the darkness, which was rhythmically jolted by the flickering disco lights, but what she saw was good news. Very tall and lean, he wore a pair of prewashed, artfully ripped jeans, which, with their added wear and tear, looked like the indispensable garment of a cowboy that hadn't seen soap or water in years. To Irina, such an item gave its wearer a halo similar to the one that must have defined men in uniform in the eyes of nineteenth-century girls from respectable bourgeois families. Everything else, including what one would call "looks," was merely a side-effect of the above mentioned article of clothing, and was bathed in its cowboy halo. It was ironic—

and Irina would have been indignant, had someone pointed it out to her—that a cowboy was merely the American version of a Moldovan peasant, a *cow-boy*, as the name clearly indicated. And being a peasant was the most uncool, biggest turn-off Irina could think of. In fact, one of the insults she most often bestowed on her peers, especially the boys who bothered her, was "You, stupid peasant." Or simply, "Peasant!"

The Moldovan cowboy she was busy admiring that evening had nothing of a peasant about him. The rolled-up sleeves of his checkered shirt gave his attire the extra touch of a nonchalant office clerk opening, with hurried purposefulness, office doors in mythical New York City, city of blue jeans and white-collar workers who wore them. The cowboy hit buttons with knowledgeable dexterity, snaked his way among cables and speakers, and generally made a strong appeal to Irina's visual sensibility. At some point he paused and looked up, following the gaze of the other technician. He noticed the girl—the chick was visibly interested—and shot a purple-light-infused smile in her direction. Only later, on their first date, Irina spotted in the light of day his missing front tooth, which, the cowboy explained with a pride worthy of his American brethren, he'd lost in a nightclub brawl. Although, under normal circumstances, the missing tooth would have seriously diminished the young man's appeal, the explanation, or the way it was delivered, was enough to fill in the void.

His name was Vadim. Which was definitely more masculine than Matvei, the classmate—really, just a boy, a crybaby—that she'd been dating and had been trying to get rid of for some time. The problem with Matvei was that he'd do everything she asked him to. If she had asked him to lick her boots—and once, she almost did—he would have. But, really, in the end, the problem with Matvei was that he existed at all. The way he followed her

like a faithful poodle, carrying her schoolbag—only the students with well-heeled relatives abroad had backpacks—or buying her lunch with his own modest pocket money, or doing her math homework without her giving him so much as a "thank you" in return, was pathetic. The first time they had sex—which was Matvei's first time ever—he swore his eternal love. True, when he'd done that she was almost touched, but seeing his pimply little face beaming up at her in the dusk with a froglike gratitude was too much, and she had burst out laughing.

The only way to get rid of Matvei, she realized, was to crush him with the weight of a rival with whom he couldn't possibly hope to compete. She asked Vadim to wait for her after classes at the school's entrance and, when tiny Matvei saw the man— twice as tall as he was—he just stood there, paralyzed, holding her schoolbag like a rope with which to hang himself. Smiling, Irina took the bag from him, bade him good-bye, and left with his rival. It was the beginning of a stressful period during which Matvei wrote her long, tiring letters that threatened suicide. Apparently, she had miscalculated the boy's reaction: instead of retreating and leaving the field to his victorious foe, he seemed to relish the role of loser, letting himself be crushed over and over with the masochistic delight of a Proustian character. Not that Irina had read Proust (Matvei had).

Each time Irina and Vadim met, they exchanged a long, wet kiss, as Matvei watched them with clenched fists from a safe distance, then, knowing they were being watched, they burst out laughing and left holding hands. All the girls envied Irina for her Vadim. She showed them the gifts he brought her— Rexona sprays and Palmolive soaps with an overpowering smell of flowers, striped T-shirts and nylon stockings—all acquired on the black market, Vadim's main workplace, as it soon became clear, and they touched them, secretly wishing for their own

Vadims. Matvei too had brought her presents: chewing gum and roses that he stole from the city's central park, but no one envied Irina that.

In desperation, Matvei did something he'd heard others had done with various degrees of success. He went to the reference desk at the downtown library and opened a *Who's Who* with the same trepidation Saint Augustine had once opened the Bible to follow his destiny. The book opened, and his finger landed on a page next to a name Matvei had never heard of: Philippe Lacoue-Labarthe, Université des Sciences Humaines de Strasbourg, France. There was a good reason for Matvei's ignorance. He never read books on Heidegger or German romanticism, books that were very well known in certain circles where Professor Lacoue-Labarthe was highly respected. He was a who, but not to Matvei. Still, Matvei followed his initial plan and wrote to Professor Lacoue-Labarthe in his uncertain, high-school French, telling him about the pain of losing his girlfriend to a pair of blue jeans. He explained that his parents were factory workers, and a pair of jeans would cost them a whole month's income, and respectfully asked to be sent a pair of used jeans (he didn't dare ask for a new). To his surprise, two months later, when he had already forgotten about the letter, he received a package from an unknown French address. The jeans, brand new, fit perfectly. Alas, it was too late: the girl was gone.

# Seryozha

"An authentic Soviet drinker drinks by himself, starting in the early morning, and without any discernible reason."
—Vasile Ernu, *Born in the USSR*

After Tania's departure, Seryozha felt obliged, him being the only male in the family and his niece now motherless, to move in with the two women, who needed to be taken care of. True, his taking care of them was rather counter-intuitive, in that he was rarely home, and when he was, he slept on the living room couch—sending shock waves through the delicate china on the nearby glass shelves with his Pantagruelian snoring, and suffusing the atmosphere with such a strong alcoholic cloud that Olga and Irina felt dizzy each time they entered the room. This can't go on, both women said to each other and to the guilty party. Yet, it did.

Every time he came home in that state—that is, every time he came home, which sometimes happened three days after he'd

left to "visit with some friends" or "run some errands" in the
neighborhood—Olga greeted him with the same interminable
list of complaints that went back all the way to his childhood,
when he was already displaying signs—which, alas, she had
ignored!—of him being a bad seed, a bad seed that had turned
into a rotten, foul, venom-infested trunk. A drunk's trunk, that
is. The woman unearthed events Seryozha had long forgotten—
oh, she had a gift for digging things up and pulling them out—
until everything, including what had never occurred, was out in
the open—and she held them in front of his nose, asking him
to repent for his past misdeeds, repeating, once again, with the
pleasure a martyr takes in self-flagellation, that he'd send her
to an early grave. But, if there was a martyr, it was certainly
him: he who had to put up with the unstoppable blather of two
insane women (his niece too had her moments), and, during the
first hour after his return home, he behaved just like a martyr,
not saying anything, only moving slowly, careful not to throw
up on the Persian rug—thinned with years and discolored as
it was—fixing on a point in space with glassy, bloodshot eyes,
until, under the flood of words that would not stop, he'd yell,
"Shut up, you crazy, old woman! Shut up!"

And then . . . she would shut up. Startled, she'd cross
herself and take the girl as her witness to what she had to put
up with, but, after a minute of silence, she'd start again, full of
renewed zeal. Did he think she could be intimidated by a good-
for-nothing, little worm? Oh, she'd seen much worse in her life,
and if she couldn't change the way things stood, she could, at
least, tell him where *he* stood in *her* eyes, because a mother owed
it to a son to let him know that he was a miserable, good-for-
nothing, creeping worm, who'd do the world a big favor if he
put a rope around his neck and just got it over with. As for
herself, the biggest regret of her life was that, hard as she'd tried

to get rid of him while she was pregnant, he kept hanging on for dear life—he was stubborn, even then!—and, against all odds, was born with all ten fingers and, apparently, a brain, though now she doubted he had one.

With that, she would leave the room while he took a deep breath and hoped it was over—*over, for God's sake! Unbelievable, the energy of the old bitch!*—carefully lying down on the couch, his shoes still on. Half an hour later, the woman would reenter the room sporting a totally different expression, and would touch the man's forehead to see if he was asleep. If he wasn't, she'd say gently, "I made a very good chicken noodle soup, just the way you like it. You must be starving! Come and have some soup, dear."

At first, he'd push her away like an annoying fly—he couldn't give in just like that, could he?—but he always ended up following her into the kitchen, and, before he sat down at the table, she would hug him to her large bosom, beaming with love, and then kiss him on his forehead, even as he continued to squirm. If Irina happened to be present during these scenes, she would open her mouth and pretend she was about to vomit, maintaining her nauseated expression throughout the dinner. After two bowls of soup, he would begin to perk up, and his ghostly face would take on some color. Seeing that he was coming back to life, Irina would go into action. "So, when are you going to get the hell out of here and move to your place?"

She'd say it not because she expected an answer, but because the question was sure to elicit a furious reaction, which—invariably—it did. After another round of screaming, this time between uncle and niece, Olga would bring out the dessert, which they ate in knotted silence. Then, exhausted, they went to bed.

# Olga

Seryozha was Olga's little bundle of joy and pain. He could do so much more with his life, oh, so much more—"More than nothing?" (Irina)—if only he didn't waste his time with those drunks and syphilitic scoundrels. She wasn't the kind to meddle in other people's lives, but she always said what was on her mind if it meant saving someone from self-destruction. He knew, didn't he, that she'd done the same thing for his sister when she was married to that rogue, what was his name, Ilie, and even if—at the time—Tania had accused her of meddling, eventually she had understood that it was for her own good, and now she was grateful. And he too would some day be grateful, but alas, she, Olga, would no longer be on this earth to taste the sweet fruit of her labors. By then she'd be in her grave, to which he brought her one step closer each time he left the apartment.

"Woman, can't you see that I'm not a child anymore? I need to go out and find work."

"You? Work?" She spat in disgust and crossed herself, the way old peasant women did when confronted with the ways of

the Evil One. "As if I didn't know you. You go out looking for work, all the while praying, 'God help me to not find it!' And since when do they sell vodka at the unemployment office?"

"You stupid woman, you don't understand anything! Can't you see that vodka is part of doing business? You meet people over a glass, you talk business."

"You meet people over a bottle, not a glass. And don't tell me how people do business! If you had done a second of business in your life, you wouldn't be here."

The same discussion, with slight variations, had taken place fifteen years earlier between Olga and Tania's then-husband, Ilie, in a similar albeit smaller apartment, located in a town, likewise smaller, where Tania worked as a hairdresser and Ilie worked to not find a job. It was as if Olga was destined to struggle over and over with some halfwit man she had to drag along behind her, praying that, by some miracle, he would come to his senses. That's why she had been so impressed with Sammy: not only did he hardly touch alcohol, he almost never opened his mouth—no talking back. *Now, that's a man I like!* What's more, he'd saved so much money he'd been able to retire before fifty. That was a real man! And on top of it, his potbelly was the proper size— big enough to prove he was well fed, but not as big as that of some lazy lollygagger who never lifted a finger and drank beer for breakfast. All in all, he was a woman's dream. If she had been a few years younger, she would have tried to get one of those Americans for herself. Well, it was too late for her, but not for her daughter. And not for her daughter's daughter.

It wasn't until Tania's plane had become a dot in the sky that she allowed herself to believe it: her daughter had married a rich American. At the beginning, she used the word "rich" simply because it seemed to fit next to the word "American,"

but, after she received Tania's first letter, there was no longer any doubt. He *was* a rich American. Now began the struggle to reunite mother and daughter, that is, Tania and Irina, and with God's help, she might some day join them. Let Seryozha rot in this Hell, let him rot to the bone; she wouldn't lift a finger.

# Irina

Dear Mother,

You asked me to write, so: I'm writing. First of all, stop worrying! Things are exactly the way they were before you left: Seryozha spends most of his time with us, and just like before, he's barely sober enough to lift a soup spoon.

Grandma showed us the photos of you with your Japanese car and your huge TV, and then she showed them to everybody else in the building. As a result, all the beggars on our street now follow me around with their hands out, chanting apishly. You should tell her to keep her mouth shut! Who cares what Sofia thinks about your TV? Though, I admit it *was* fun to see her piggy face turn full-grown sow, as she stared, wordless, at the photos.

The other day, the senile, lame, Polish woman from across the street—you know, the one with the cane and mustache—touched me as I passed by, saying that she wanted some of my good luck to rub off on her. See what I have to put up with? And all the kids on the block are asking me for chewing gum—by the way, please send some.

You asked about Matvei. Things were over between us before you left, I just didn't tell you. And stop saying mean things about Vadim! I know Grandma has been planting ideas in your head because she thinks that all men are like Seryozha or dad. Just because Vadim is half-Romanian doesn't mean he's like dad. In fact, since you seem so concerned, he barely touches alcohol. A glass at most. Right now he's between jobs, but he freelances for some people who run an import-export business.

And what about that Anna? She sure sounds like a piece of work. I can't believe she's my age. It must be true what they say that girls in the West are less mature. She sounds like that American girl Sofia told us about who had a spider as a pet.

It's strange, though, that you haven't had a hamburger yet. When I get there, the first thing I want to do is go to McDonald's and order a Big Mac and Coca-Cola. By the way, Vadim has a source that provides him with Coca-Cola at a cheaper price than at the stalls that have been sprouting up like mushrooms lately. In our neighborhood alone, two new ones have opened since you left. Besides the things that you can find at all the other kiosks—Marlboro, Kent, juice, chewing gum, chocolate bars, candy, newspapers—at the new ones you can also get—guess what?—condoms. So, you see, you have no reason to worry.

The other day, a student—an ugly, scrawny bitch who's jealous of me because of Vadim—told me to stop speaking Russian because we were no longer in the Soviet Union, and in Moldova we speak Moldovan not Russian, and, if I don't like it, I should "go home." I called her an idiot—if you're gonna play the patriot, you should at least know that Moldovan is really just Romanian. Besides, I'm half-Romanian because my father is Romanian. I thought about telling her that, but then I thought better of it and told her she should go back between her mother's legs—and I said it in Romanian.

Last, let me remind you that my English is already pretty good, and there's no reason to keep telling me to study English, though it would help if you sent some money, so I could take more lessons.

Get me out of here! You promised.

Irina

# Seryozha and Vadim

One day, Vadim came by when Irina wasn't home, and Seryozha, who, through some miracle, had been sober for almost twenty-four hours, invited him in.

"Have a seat," he said, caressing his day's growth of beard and looking the young man up and down. Then, placing two small glasses on the coffee table between them: "Vodka or slivovitz?"

"Nothing, thanks. I never drink before sundown."

It was five o'clock in the afternoon, and Seryozha was impressed. Suddenly, the young man—who, in fact, was only a decade younger than himself—seemed endowed with the qualities of one of those ascetic figures who resist alcohol and women, and spend their afternoons at the gym—a magic realm Seryozha, groping through phantasmagoric alcohol vapors, had always dreamt of reaching. Never mind that Vadim, with his match-stick body, looked like someone who hadn't seen a gym in his life. Seryozha was impressed. Testing him further, he offered him a cigarette.

"No, thanks. I quit." (This was only half true.) "I heard that the Americans have discovered that it's bad for your health. Irina says that in America nobody smokes anymore. And for those who can't help it, they've built some special cages. So, if you smoke, they put you in a cage."

Seryozha ignored the part about the cages—his niece said a lot of crap that wasn't worth listening to—and focused on the word "America." So, the young man hoped to go to America. He had plans, plans that involved his niece, obviously.

"Yeah, they say a lot of things about America, but you shouldn't believe everything you hear. The other day a friend of mine whose brother is a student at one of those colleges, you know, Boston College or University of Miami or something like that, said that his brother said that in America they don't let you stare at women any more. They call it 'sexual harassment.' If they catch you, you have to pay the woman an amount equal to the offense. So, the women there are all rich, and the men are poor. That is, if this guy is telling the truth. But even if it's not entirely true—let's say it's only fifty percent true—I still say, 'No, thank you, I don't need your America.' No booze, no cigarettes, no women. What would be the point of living?"

"There's some truth to what you're saying—I'm not saying there isn't, but . . ."

"Of course there is!" After downing a glass of *slivovitz*, Seryozha had suddenly recovered his energy and now slammed the empty glass onto the table. "Of course there is! Look at what they did to this poor Clinton! The President of the United States of America! The President!"

"And such a handsome man," chimed in Olga, who never missed an opportunity to participate in a discussion about another country's president. And about this president in

particular, she had strong opinions. "Such a smart, handsome man to be brought down by such a silly, fat girl—that Monica!"

A fat woman herself, and one very content with her multiple layers of lipids and cholesterol, Olga had no mercy for women who transgressed their natural limitations and aspired to seduce powerful men who should have been seduced only by goddesses. True, she had no mercy for skinny women who aspired to be goddesses, either.

They chatted for a while about Clinton, women and politics, then, when they were out of things to say, Olga asked, "So, what do you do for a living? Irina wasn't very clear."

"Import-export."

This was what Vadim usually said when introduced to people he deemed worthy of respect, like grandmothers and uncles, and it wasn't far from the truth in that the items that passed through his hands—blue jeans, T-shirts, perfume, sprays, soaps—all originated in some foreign country, and, through mysterious and contorted paths, were diverted from their original destinations and directed to Moldovan addresses.

Once again, Seryozha was impressed. Import-export was the very domain he'd been trying to land a job in, and in which most of his friends were successfully un-employed. Maybe Vadim could be useful, after all.

"If you ever need a pack of Marlboros or Kent, let me know," Vadim said, as if reading his thoughts.

"I certainly will," replied Seryozha, puffing on his cheap Moldovan cigarette. "I certainly will."

# Olga

Every day at 10 AM, Olga left with the same brown canvas bag she'd used throughout the previous regime, and with the clearly defined intention of shopping. Every day she returned home an hour and a half later with a half-full bag and her head brimming with the latest news and gossip. Bags were among the first things to change after the transition, and now most people had colorful plastic bags with foreign words on them, but Olga still clung to her old bag on principle—"I don't see the point of replacing a sturdy bag with their stupid plastic ones." She had no idea that her babushka ways were prefiguring an ecological movement that twenty years later, would culminate in the banning of plastic bags in California. In 1996, in Moldova, plastic bags, which hadn't existed during Communism, were a visual sign indicating social status: that of a Western-looking hipster. Irina would never have carried a canvas bag, since being seen with one was the equivalent of wearing high heels with white socks.

And so, around eleven thirty, Olga returned with a half-full bag: a wrinkled cucumber, two or three tomatoes, three or four

potatoes, half a loaf of bread. To an outsider, this might indicate a less than successful shopping experience, but for Olga, success was measured by a different metric, one that had nothing to do with the purchase of goods; rather, it had to do with the collection of information, though the word "information" may not be quite right, either. On her way to the market, Olga stopped, first, in front of the apartment building, whose two wooden benches were usually occupied by elderly tenants who propped their bodies up on canes and greedily ogled all passersby: from where they stood—or sat, really—the world was merely a kaleidoscope of moving images. This first stop lasted at least ten minutes, as it was Olga's initial opportunity to exchange information that day. It was also the benchmark, so to speak, where one could be informed of the latest death in the neighborhood, the latest stroke or car accident. This information was invaluable, as it stood out like a shimmering red bead among all the other news of turbulent upheaval, providing the illusion that, in spite of everything, life went on, and what made it go on was death. This may be why Olga and her acquaintances loved to talk about death. Sure, they pitied the widow or widower, even shed a tear or two, but nothing in the world gave them as much pleasure as this daily exercise in decay. With every breath, giddy with excitement, they savored news of the most recent death, as if they were preparing for the arrival in town of a dear, long-awaited friend.

After these well-spent minutes, Olga would take a deep breath, as if to steady herself, and say, "Well, I'd better get going. I have things to do."

Invariably, one of the others would interject, "And what do you have to do that is so urgent? Let it wait, you've worked hard your whole life."

Olga would acknowledge, always as touched as if reminded for the first time that, indeed, she had worked hard her entire life, and for the next five minutes would repeat the same idea, after which she would suddenly take her leave ("God, how time flies!") and move slowly on, in homage to the advanced age of her interlocutors.

The next stop would occur about fifty feet or so further on, when she'd run into some acquaintance she hadn't seen in ages. The acquaintance, who was always returning from the market with her arms full of groceries, would place the bags on the ground, breathing heavily under the weight of the extra pounds she'd gained since their last encounter.

"And how is your daughter?" the woman would eventually ask—at which point Olga would launch into her daughter's unbelievable streak of good luck: her marriage to a rich American who kept her like a princess in a bed of goose down. No epithets were spared to describe Tania's phenomenal husband, as the acquaintance herself hadn't spared any when her daughter had married a Canadian. And, wouldn't you know it? She was now in the process of divorcing her Canadian, the one she had been praising a few years ago as if he were the second-coming of the Messiah.

"Well, such is life, Mrs. So-and-So, such is life," she'd say, trying to counterbalance the radiant confidence she had in her own daughter's future by donning an adequate expression of regret at the woman's misfortune. And, with this, they would part ways for another three or four years. Then Olga would accelerate her step, using the energy given her by the news of deaths and divorces, until, right at the market's entrance, another unexpected encounter would stop her in her tracks:

"Well, if it isn't Mrs. . . ."

This time, the women would size each other up, assessing the damage produced by time in the interval in which they hadn't seen each other. The point of this assessment was not to rejoice in the other's unavoidable decline; on the contrary: each had a long list of ailments that, at each encounter, they enumerated with masochistic delight, trying to outdo the other. This rivalry was predicated not on the desire to be in better shape than the other, but on the exact opposite, to prove that no one else was in worse shape. And in order to prove one's debilitating condition, a long list of adjectives and nouns was deployed, from which the words most often used were "varicose veins," "backache," "tired," "constipation," "high blood pressure," "tired," "trouble breathing," "tired."

Olga readied herself for a long battle of wits, as the other woman was ten years older, about thirty pounds fatter, and suffered from a serious case of varicose veins. By the time they were finished, she was already exhausted, and she had hardly the energy to go into the market. But such was Olga's lot and she wasn't complaining.

# Irina

Hi, it's me.

"I'm not complaining." That's what Grandma always says, but in fact, she complains all the time. She even complains about not complaining. At least Seryozha admits that he complains. He sits or lies down all day, and when he gets up he complains. What do they complain about? Me, of course; or else, each other. And who do they complain to? Who else but me?

I'm sick of their complaints!! Grandma, I forgive; but Seryozha, I swear, one of these days I'll kill him. I learned in my history class how we can poison someone without leaving evidence, and one day I'll poison the rat. Besides being a lazy, stinking rat, he tries to take advantage of me and Vadim by constantly bumming cigarettes off us. Vadim doesn't mind, but I do.

Last week I paid a visit to my elementary school art teacher, Mrs. Dvoenkin—Comrade Dvoenkin, we called her back then (once a comrade, always a comrade). I told her that I wanted to be an artist and she was overjoyed. She began to tell me again how gifted I was, and what a pity it would be to let my talents go to waste.

"But," I said, "I have no intention of being a starving artist. I want to make money with my art. Otherwise, forget it."

She laughed and said that very few artists made money with their work. But she had a friend who was an icon painter, and, lately, she had been doing pretty well, because more and more foreigners were buying Orthodox icons. If I wanted, she could put me in touch with her friend, a young Romanian woman named Maria. I said, "Why not?" Icon painting sounded good to me. Besides—but I didn't tell her this—if foreigners liked such things, maybe it would be a good way to make money in California.

Yesterday, I went to see Maria. I had to take two buses to get there, she lives at the edge of the city in a tenement building covered in graffiti. As I climbed the stairs, a fat rat scampered past my feet. If this was what it meant to be "doing pretty well" as a painter—no thanks! I almost changed my mind about the whole thing, but in the end, couldn't help knocking on her door. She wasn't expecting me because she has no phone, so I couldn't call ahead. Yet, she didn't show any surprise, as if an unannounced stranger showing up at her door was perfectly normal. I barely introduced myself and she let me in, asking me to follow her as she stepped over the clothes strewn on the floor. She wore only a pair of underwear and a dirty T-shirt full of holes, and the room she invited me into was a horrible mess. There was a twin bed on one side, covered with a dark blue bedspread on which could be seen an encroaching quagmire of paper, folders, magazines, chocolate wafers, boxes of cookies, pencils and toilet paper. In the middle of the room stood an easel with what was obviously a work in progress, a drawing (self-portrait?) of a woman lying half-naked, with a chair in front of it, and, on the parquet floor, all around, an unbelievable entanglement of shit: oil tubes, rags that had once been used for

cleaning but were now too dirty to handle, water-filled jars, jars with paint in bright or dark colors, sheets of paper on which various colors had been tested, opened chocolate bars, a bottle of something, and a dirty glass beside it. There was no other furniture in the room, and a thick curl of smoke came from a metallic saucer that served as an ashtray, it too on the floor.

Maria offered me the only chair and sat on a cushion she positioned under her butt. She lit a cigarette from the pack on the floor, offered me one, inhaled deeply, and, finally, exhaled the smoke, accompanying it by a wide smile.

"So?" she said, as if we were already well acquainted and were seeing each other after a minor separation. Only then did I notice that she had a beautiful face, olive-skinned with very large, almost black eyes, and a delicate nose. It's just that her long, unwashed hair made her look older and grungy. I explained what had brought me there, and she listened, fixing me with her deep black eyes. It was a little uncomfortable. At the end of our meeting, she asked me a question I didn't expect:

"Are you Orthodox?"

"Of course. Why?"

What a question! Isn't everybody Orthodox around here?

"Good," she said, extinguishing the butt of her cigarette. "It's important because icon painting is a spiritual art with precise rules that go back hundreds of years."

I thought, *If you can follow these rules, I'm sure I can too*, but I kept my mouth shut. The drawing on the easel wasn't much to look at, so I wasn't overly convinced of her artistic ability. As if guessing my thoughts, she began to rummage through a pile of paintings that were stacked in a corner, and she pulled out two icons, which, I had to admit, weren't bad at all. Both were tempera on wood, one a hypnotic mixture of blues—from sky blue to dark blue—the other bright red. The latter represented

the Virgin Mary, whom she called "the Mother of God," holding baby Jesus, her eyes lowered as she gazed over him, and thus giving the impression that she was sleepy. The Virgin was clothed in red, with folds outlined in black, the kind of outlines one sees in modern paintings, which created a rather surprising effect. The background was crimson, the Virgin's face very pale. The most striking thing was the quality of the color, which didn't come in brushstrokes, but rather existed in a continuum, like in photographs.

"How were you able to create this effect?" I asked. "I mean, the color doesn't look like regular paint."

And so she began to explain the difference between a regular painting and an Orthodox icon: most icons, if done properly, have four or five layers of thin paint, and the color has to be mixed with egg yolk, at least this is how they did it in the old days. Today, only a few monks still do that, and a handful of artists, who've studied with them, like her. Still, the basic technique has been handed down: one starts by applying a good priming that makes the wood ivory-smooth. Then, one divides the whole into smaller surfaces, and, using a compass, establishes the center of the whole. Everything is done with geometric precision, she explained, yet the piece's value doesn't reside in the geometric purity of its execution, but in its "inspired representation."

The other icon—in blue—showed the face of an angel (at first, I thought it was a fat baby, but Maria laughed and corrected me). It had the most striking array of blues and yellows I'd ever seen: all along the edges it was framed by a border of gold leaf, its sky-blue background beautifully offset by the yellow of the angel's curly hair. There was a thin, greenish-blue ribbon in his hair, which enhanced the glow of his golden ringlets, and, on both sides, he had snow-white wings so that he seemed ready to take flight. But what I liked most was the color of his dress: a bright

blue I'd never seen before. I kept staring at the color, unable to take my eyes off it. Maria explained that it was "Voronetz blue," that, is, the blue found on the walls of the Voronetz Monastery in Romania, where she had studied with a monk.

I told her that I wanted to learn how to reproduce that blue, and in reply she raised a skeptical eyebrow, and, puffing on her cigarette, asked:

"Don't you think you're going a little fast? It takes years to get to that blue. You don't even know the basics yet. An icon is much more than an image. Everything in it has a symbolic meaning: for instance, take this angel. Angels are messengers of the divine, and the ribbon in an angel's hair symbolizes his ability to hear God's words. Every color has its own symbolic meaning, too. There isn't a single thing in an icon that hasn't been put there for a reason. Even the position of an object—left or right—has meaning. Besides, I haven't decided yet whether I want to take you on as a student."

"Well then, that settles it. I'll let you continue drawing, and I'll be on my way." I got up and began moving toward the door. I was angry. Who did she think she was? She got up too, and when I turned to tell her good-bye, she had a wide smile on her face.

"Come on," she said, taking my right hand in her left. "Let's talk." She dragged me back to her room and ordered me to sit down. When I left two hours later, we had reached an agreement. I was going to come twice a week, and she was going to teach me.

More later.

Your daughter,
Irina

# Maria

At twenty-eight, Maria looked as if she was in her mid-thirties, with unhealthy, ashen skin and fine lines around her eyes, mouth, and on her forehead. The daily pack of cigarettes, the bottles of vodka and wine, the irregular mealtimes, the countless sleepless nights had left their mark. But behind the fine lines, the dark circles, and the tired skin, a glimmer was still visible, which could mostly be seen in her very dark, intense eyes, perfectly oval face, and high cheekbones. And, when she washed her hair—which was only every ten days or so—and its ebony glow bounced freely across her back, the tiredness slipped off her like a shed skin, and she radiated peaceful lightness.

She had lived on her own since she was fourteen, when two potbellied, gray-suited inspectors from the Education Department came to the village school, and after talking to the instructor ("Comrade Instructor," as all teachers were called back then—a title everybody shortened to "Comrade"), they had taken aside two girls: Lena and Maria. Then, in front of the rest of the students, who watched the girls with a mixture of

excitement and relief at not being in their shoes, the inspectors asked Lena to sing something. The girl's immense blue eyes rose in the direction of Comrade Instructor, who nodded her head, which was encircled by an aura of curls (the result of painstaking hours, including whole nights, spent wearing plastic curlers). "Sing," said the Comrade's eyes, and Lena sang. She chose a folksong, and, at first sang timidly, but by the end of the song her voice had found its usual strength, and the inspectors seemed very pleased. They congratulated her and asked, "How would you like to be a singer who entertains our working classes on TV?" "I'd like that," Lena said. "Perfect! You just need to work hard with the right teachers." Then, the inspectors turned to Maria. They'd heard that she was a very good painter, they said, looking her up and down. The girl said nothing and didn't shy from returning the gaze of their heavy, official eyes. She stared back at them, but her mouth didn't open. "Has the cat eaten your tongue?" One of them asked, and when the girl continued to silently stand there, while the other students began to giggle, the Comrade explained that the girl was "nervous." "I'm not nervous," Maria said with a furrowed brow. "Oh, so you do have a tongue," the inspector said, and then demanded that she show them her paintings.

Maria went to her seat, took her drawing folder, brought it to the Comrade's desk, and set it down, unopened. "Would you be so kind as to open it?" The other gray suit asked, a bit impatient. "Why can't *you* open it?" demanded Maria. The uproar that followed was a mixture of laughter, an amazed collective gasp, and a thunderous "Silence!" from the Comrade. She ordered the girl to return to her seat, then showed the paintings to the two officials herself. But the girl's misbehavior must not have affected their decision, because, the same day, they went to talk to her mother and didn't even mention the incident.

Unlike Lena's parents, who refused to send their only child to "the city," Maria's mother thought that the two big-bellied undertakers were a gift from heaven. A widow in poor health already raising another child—a young boy who was the apple of her eye—at first, she wasn't sure she understood what the two officials were proposing. Why would the government do such a thing for her: take a stubborn, ungrateful daughter off her hands and send her to school in the city? She thought there must be a catch, then, in the humble, mournful widowlike voice that Maria hated so, she said that she couldn't afford to send her daughter to the city because she couldn't pay for food and lodging. "Oh, but you don't need to," the officials replied, smiling generously. "The state will take care of that. Your daughter will receive a scholarship."

It was too good to be true. The mother, with her peasant cunning and skepticism accumulated in her genes over generations of poverty and misfortune, kept a straight face, pretending that she wasn't the kind to be impressed easily. But, as the two men were leaving, she bowed deeply and humbly before them, causing Maria's cheeks to redden in shame. That did it. She wanted to get as far away as she could from that woman, and, if going to art school in the city was her way out, so be it.

During the first year, she spent her vacations at home, but eventually, both mother and daughter realized that it would be better if they confined their relationship to the monthly package of homemade cakes the mother sent care of the dorm. They had nothing to say to each other. The mother looked at the daughter as if she were a stranger from "the city," and the daughter could no longer stand the woman who went to bed with a finger-thick layer of dirt on her callused feet—bare all day long.

By the end of her high school senior year, Maria was an adult. When the time came, she had no trouble finding a job: a

window designer for businesses, she painted window and door signs, and occasionally arranged their displays (and God only knows, with the shortages of the time, there wasn't much to arrange or display). After five years of work, Maria decided that it was time to take her first real vacation; she had spent all her others at home, but this time she would go on a tour of the famous monasteries in Bukovina and Romanian Moldova. And then . . . something unexpected happened.

# Seryozha

"Once again, we don't have a single reason not to drink."
—Soviet saying

It happened during one of his regular escapades, when he left to buy sparkling water—which usually meant that he'd be back two or three days later without the water, dead tired and so full of alcohol that you could get inebriated just from smelling his breath. But this time, he returned the very next day, to Olga's relief, which she hid by asking, "So, were your friends so tired of you they kicked you out?"

"Yeah, yeah, always full of poison, aren't you?" He said it without resentment; in fact, he seemed in very good spirits, even gave her a peck on the cheek.

"And to what do I owe this honor?"

Taking his time, Seryozha lit a cigarette, took a deep drag, exhaled, then gave her the news: he had been offered a job as an administrator of the city's camp program for high school

students. It was a dream job that came with a personal office in City Hall, where he could shuffle papers around and make phone calls for most of the year. Only during student vacations would he be truly busy. Spring vacation was just around the corner, and they wanted him to start right away.

"And how did *you* get such a job?" Olga asked, unconvinced, afraid to prematurely rejoice without some kind of official documentation.

Seryozha eyed her with pity.

"Poor woman, what do you know? Didn't I tell you that it's all about doing business over a glass of vodka? That one has to know people and cultivate one's connections?"

"And you have connections?"

"Is that all you have to say? You can't even congratulate your son?"

At this, Olga softened and gave him a passionate hug, then looked lovingly in his murky eyes, kissed his rough, manly cheek, and hugged him again.

"OK, OK, you're forgiven," he mumbled, and pushed her away.

Olga was so happy to have him home, and glad that he seemed to have found a job, that she forgot to get angry at his chutzpa. And, God help us, he did start work two days later, entering the large office that was permeated by the stale, acrid smell of unopened rooms, whose only furniture was a wooden ink-stained desk with a wobbly chair, a rotary telephone, and a tall, metallic cabinet with a lock. He entered like a king returning from exile and, opening the windows to let the air and the sun in, he filled his lungs with the breeze of freedom (freedom from his mother's chains, that is) and his long-awaited financial independence. True, his new environs left something to be desired, but with a few posters, a new chair, and especially a

wine bottle and some glasses, he could change that. The friend who'd helped him get the job brought him two chairs from his own office, and so he was able to discard the old, wobbly one. The same evening he asked Olga for a small loan.

"For the last time. I need to buy a bottle of vodka for the fellow who helped me get the job."

Olga frowned. "What kind of a man expects a bottle of vodka in return for a job? Why doesn't he want some cigarettes— Kent or Marlboro—like a normal person?"

But she capitulated immediately. Why fight now when everything was going so well? She gave him the money and, the following day, Seryozha and Vania opened the bottle in his new office, toasting with the glasses Seryozha had pilfered from Tania's numerous sets, always on display in the living room's glass cabinet. She no longer needed them, did she? She had plenty of glasses where she was now, glasses and bottles, enough to drown herself if she wanted.

"To friends," Seryozha said, and his colleague answered: "To a new life!"

They had known each other since high school, gone to the same parties, even dated some of the same women, before losing track of each other. Recently, they had met at the home of a mutual acquaintance, and Seryozha had offhandedly mentioned how his mother was driving him crazy—*get-a-job-get-a-job-get-a-job!*—and, in response, Vania had implied that he might be in a position to do something for him, though he couldn't promise anything. Yes, that's how these things happened: when you least expected them.

The two friends talked at length about their high school pals and the old days, which, in spite of everything, hadn't been as bad as all that. They had had fun, actually, and there had always been something to drink, even if it was only pump oil,

ha-ha, they had drunk life to its dregs. And saying that, they poured themselves another glass.

"Do you remember that time in the late eighties when Gorbachev decided to sober the country up, and for a while there was such a shortage of alcohol that we couldn't find anything? We were at this party, I think it was at Misha's place, and we drank all the hairspray and cologne in the guy's bathroom?"

"Do I remember it? I spent that night at the hospital. They had to pump everything out of me."

"Yeah, we were crazy."

And once again they toasted, vaguely melancholic now, congratulating themselves on having survived this and that similar adventure. Yes, they were survivors, and they should count their blessings.

For the whole first week, Seryozha spent his mornings familiarizing himself with the paperwork, and his afternoons getting to know his new colleagues. The latter activity involved considerable quantities of alcohol, some provided by him, some provided by the guests. The week passed by in a flash, an entanglement of new faces and cheerful camaraderie that was interrupted every now and then by the chief of some department or other, who, dropping by, downed a glass and, before leaving, felt obligated to add—as if admonishing a group of naughty children, "Have fun while you can, because next week we have work to do."

And then came that next week. Seryozha's first assignment was to chaperon a group of sophomore students to the train station, reassure their nervous parents—some of whom cried as if they were being separated from their progeny for life, not for merely a week—get the students to their assigned seats, stop them from fighting until the train pulled out, and, finally, wave to the departing train, together with the disconsolate parents.

This definitely called for a celebration, and, his head still full of the hustle and bustle and ruckus of the children—as if he had spent a day at the fair—he found himself, half an hour later, drinking beer with the father of one of the students. The father had been one of the parents most in need of consolation: his sixteen-year-old daughter, Gabi, an only child, had lost her mother three years earlier, may she rest in peace, and he was raising her by himself. The girl meant the world to him, and he was always nervous that something might happen to her. She was more mature than most kids her age, he said, but to him she was still a child. He often traveled on business, and the girl was used to taking care of herself, yet he never stopped worrying. Now, for instance, as they were drinking their beers, he worried that when she returned from her trip, she'd be the only student without a ride home, since, as usual, he would be traveling. Seryozha might have been a good-for-nothing, as his mother often told him, but he was not stone-hearted. Naturally, he offered to give the girl a ride home. He put his hand on the man's shoulder and urged him not to give it a second thought: the girl would be in safe hands. They separated as the best of friends, and Seryozha felt proud of himself.

A week later, he was back at the train station, surrounded by euphoric parents who kept looking at their watches, and a flow of peasants carrying heavy bundles passing by, just as they had for centuries—one wondered where these people always had to go, heavy bundle here, heavy bundle there, smelling like crap, constantly blocking the trains' corridors. The train arrived—miraculously—on time, and a gang of noisy and hyper-excited children got out, together with other passengers, yells and cries of joy from the parents and their progeny, hugs, tears, and in the midst of all this: Seryozha, running in circles, trying to convince the children not to leave because he hadn't counted them yet.

Good luck with that! Each time he counted them he came up with a different number. He took out the sheet with their names on it and put a check mark next to those accounted for. In the end, everyone was there, with one exception—wouldn't you know it?—Gabi!

He let the children go and began to look around, asking each girl if she was Gabi, but none of them were. When he had lost all hope, a young woman who appeared to be about twenty or so, with blond hair reaching down to her waist and a pair of succulent melons—there was no other way to describe them, as they really looked like overripe melons—that showed uninhibited from under a low-cut blouse, and who had spent the last ten minutes saying good-bye to a dubious young fellow, took pity on him.

"Why are you so desperate to find this Gabi?"

"I have to drive her home. Her father asked me to."

"You have a car?"

"Yes, but . . . "

"Great. I'm Gabi."

He was so surprised that he asked her for an ID. The girl laughed and produced the requested document. There was no doubting it, she was Gabi. Well, how about that? As they walked toward the car that had been lent him by the city—driver and all—he felt as if he were dreaming. He grew self-conscious and, when the girl wasn't looking, checked to make sure his breath wasn't too foul. He hadn't spent time with a woman in ages. Next to her in the car, both seated in the back, he remembered her poor father calling her "a kid," and couldn't help chuckling.

"What's so funny?"

"Oh, nothing. I was remembering a comedy starring Louis de Funès I recently watched. Do you know him?"

"No. Is he good?"

"Good? He's hilarious."

And yadda-yadda-yadda, she absolutely had to see Louis de Funès! The night was young, and he had promised her dad he'd take care of her, so why not make a slight detour to his place? He instructed the driver on how to get there, and racked his brains trying to remember if his studio, where he hadn't been in weeks, was presentable enough for company.

At the very moment the car pulled up in front of one of the newer downtown tenements, Seryozha's apartment door was being opened by a young couple who had been struggling for some time to insert the key while passionately embracing each other and kissing. Finally, they entered, and the young man rushed to the restroom. The girl, for her part, jumped onto the bed and began to take off her blouse. As she panted, blouse stretched over her head, another couple hurried in, the man heading straight to the restroom, the new girl staring at the half-naked woman.

"What the hell?" exclaimed the blond girl, taken by surprise. "Who are *you*?"

"Irina." She extended her hand, but the blond woman withheld hers angrily. At exactly that instant they heard two loud voices from the restroom, and a second later Vadim and Seryozha emerged. Seryozha went straight to Irina, hands on his hips.

"This time, you're in trouble. Give me the key."

Irina handed him the key, while Vadim tried to appease Seryozha by offering him an unopened pack of cigarettes. Seryozha pushed the pack away, but then, taking a second look, noticed that it was a foreign brand and changed his mind. He grabbed the whole pack, opened it, took out a cigarette, then, turning toward Gabi, asked her if she smoked.

"Sure," the girl said, taking a cigarette. "Aren't you going to introduce me?"

After the introductions, the blond angel who responded to the name of Gabi grew calmer, and even asked if they were going to see the comedy with what's-his-name in it.

"Forget it," Seryozha said, annoyed at how things had turned out. "Let's have a drink." And he began a frantic search, rifling through the cabinets, most of them empty, except for the cobwebs that hung in their corners. Immediately, Vadim offered to fetch a bottle from a friend who lived a block away. No sooner said than done. Fifteen minutes later, he was back with two bottles of red—"Good stuff, made for export. You can't find this in our stores."

Taking a sip from the burgundy-red wine, Seryozha thought to himself that his niece hadn't made such a bad deal, after all. He gave his full attention to the bottle, and, by the time he remembered Gabi, she was already gone.

"This Vadim has class," he told Irina the next day at dinner.

And, as uncle and niece drank Vadim's wine and smoked Vadim's cigarettes, a silent pact was born between them: I won't tell if you don't. She could have the key back, and, in return, he would enjoy the occasional bottle of wine and package of cigarettes.

# Maria

I t had happened in the summer of 1992. She knew that for sure not only because it was the summer she went on her monastery tour of Romania, but also because it was the year of the Caritas scandal. Well, it wasn't a scandal yet, it was the work of God's hand, as so many had claimed at the time, including priests and monks on Romanian national TV. Brother Simion too. It wouldn't become a scandal until a year and a half later, and, by the time of our story, it had already been forgotten.

Caritas had been one of the first private companies to appear in the city of Cluj-Napoca after the fall of communism. "You know where Cluj is, do you?" Maria asked. Irina nodded yes. "Where?" She was the teacher, after all. When Irina's ignorance became obvious, she explained that it was in Western Romania. People later found out that Caritas's business model was something called "a Ponzi scheme." They were invited to deposit their money—their monthly income, on the average—with the promise that, at the end of three months, they would make back eight times as much. If they left their money in for six months, they'd get back almost enough to buy a studio.

And they did! The local press—what was the name of that paper?—Transylvania Something, published the names of the lucky recipients by the thousands. They say that about forty percent of the families in the entire country of Romania were involved in this scheme, and up to a third of the country's liquid capital. When the pyramid scheme collapsed in the fall of 1993, about 300,000 people lost their money. About as many had made small fortunes during the two years that the miracle had held out.

"I tried to explain to Brother Simion," Maria said, "that, mathematically, some people will have to lose their money, that not everybody can make eight times more than their initial deposit."

"Who's Brother Simion?"

"I'll tell you later."

But Brother Simion didn't believe Maria. In fact, their friendship almost ended over it.

"Don't you see, dear girl, that this is God's hand helping the poor, whom no one else is willing to help? How can you say that people will lose their money when, for months, everybody has been making money? I myself know a few people who have bought cars and furniture and such."

Mathematics had no effect on Brother Simion, so Maria dropped it. In fact, she had let herself be persuaded by Grigore, Brother Simion's brother—"I'll tell you about Grigore later"— to accompany him to Cluj, and allow him to make a deposit on her behalf (not being a Romanian citizen, she couldn't do it herself). They stood in line together with another several thousand desperate poor wretches. "Have you ever seen a line of thousands of people? It's like a caravan that stretches for blocks." Family and friends took turns staying in line, and it took about two days to get to the front.

There were three of them: Maria, Grigore, and Brother Simion. It was the first time in her life, Maria said, that she'd taken a serious chance. Unlike most participants in the scheme, she was aware of the risk and what was at stake. She knew that she could lose her money, but had decided to gamble anyhow and damn the risk. She planned to leave her money in, not for three months, but for a whole year, and did it as a provocation to whatever higher power might exist up there. *I have the courage to gamble all this money away and to Hell with it.*

Grigore retrieved his share after three months, bought a suit, fixed his car, then got drunk a few times, but she, she left her money in. A year later, only a couple of months before the scheme's collapse, she withdrew enough money to buy a one-bedroom apartment.

"This?" Irina asked, looking around, as if the squalid place had suddenly turned into a palace.

"This."

She had met Grigore and Brother Simion at the end of her monastery tour, a trip organized through a travel agency, with a guide and everything. Each minute that was wasted because some idiot in the tour group had gotten lost or had to use the restroom made her feel sorry for her money—*Why didn't I go by myself?* etc.—but in the end, it was thanks to the guide that she met Grigore and his brother. She had fallen in love with the Voronctz Monastery and the adjacent village, and the guide had offered to help her find a host there, once the tour ended.

Grigore had a doll-like house in a cul-de-sac surrounded by a plot of partially cultivated land, with potted carnations lined up on the wooden rail of the covered porch, and ivy climbing on the whitewashed walls. In the summer, he often rented out his tiny bedroom and slept in the living room. She had felt safe with him

from the beginning, despite his penchant for the bottle, maybe because he didn't seem interested in women, though, she noted, he also didn't seem interested in men. It was Grigore who had introduced her to Brother Simion, a monk at another monastery a few villages away, who came every Saturday to teach the nuns at Voronetz icon painting, and stayed overnight to visit with his brother the next day. The two brothers were having lunch together—cold borscht—she remembered: Grigore invited her to eat with them. As surprising as it might seem, she was one of the few Moldovans actually from the Republic of Moldova that they had ever met. Most visitors were from Bucharest or Transylvania, or else they were foreigners from further abroad. This very likely accounted for the liking they immediately took to her, which more than once they expressed in the maxim, "We are brothers and sisters, Romanians and Moldovans, branches sprung from the same trunk."

Soon, she found in the two men two welcoming hosts, as, in the end, Brother Simion became a sort of host, too. A spiritual host, she might have said, if she hadn't come to mistrust words that were used too easily and too often. At Brother Simion's invitation, she visited his workshop at Voronetz Monastery, and he showed her the icons he'd painted and the one he was working on. He had barely begun it. The image was reduced to its outline, a Christ with nimbus, and a tremulous line that formed a quadrangle around him. Brother Simion explained that the icon was called "The Image of the Savior without Hands," that it was an icon representing Christ's face as depicted on Veronica's veil (the veil itself represented by a white square). It was this face, Brother Simion said, that was the symbolic origin of the icon as an object, which means "likeness" or "image" in Greek—a face painted, not by hands, but imprinted on the cloth by Christ's own sweat and blood. The icon with this particular

theme that he was working on now, also called a *mandylion*, was Brother Simion's personal favorite. Besides Christ's aura, which was filled with gold leaf, the rest was only an outline, naked, as it were, emanating a kind of primitive purity that seemed more powerful to Maria than the finished, colored icons she'd already seen. She noticed that the wood's surface was covered with something and asked what that was. Until then the Brother's answers had been monosyllabic, but now his face lit up and he began to discourse in complete sentences. The wood had been subjected to a treatment prior to painting. To begin with, not just any type of wood was used, but only non-resinous wood, such as lime, cypress or birch. Then, the icon and the raised frame around it were cut out, and after that, the surface was covered with a special liquid, which had to dry completely before being covered with woven linen. In the past, the linen had been glued onto the surface with glue made of animal hides, but that was no longer the case. Then, a mixture of fine alabaster and liquid called "the ground" was applied in layers to the woven linen. After each application, the surface had to be allowed to dry, and only once it had dried did he continue by applying the next layer. That was when he was ready to start the actual drawing. First, he used a pencil, then reinforced the image with a brush. Two hundred years earlier, the monks would draw the image on the ground, and, only afterward, copy the outline onto a wooden panel. Once he was able to begin the actual painting, he followed the order established by the monks of yore: first, he covered the background in gold leaf, and, only at the very end, worked on the features of the faces. He showed her how he prepared the colors in his clay pots, all lined up on a low table, like soldiers waiting to be called for inspection. He mixed in ground pigment, water, egg yolk and kvass.

"Why don't you buy the colors?" Maria asked in an unguarded moment, and was immediately sorry she had. Brother Simion went on preparing his colors, his face opaque, his lips sealed, refusing to dignify her question with so much as a grimace. Later, she got used to his loaded silences, and learned how to tiptoe around them, ignoring them just as much as they ignored her. She would look back on that time as the only time in her life when someone had bothered to share something with her out of a totally pure desire to impart it. She would remember the *quivering*—of his words; of his long, black robe; of his long, black beard and of the way it brushed against the pots of colors—and that feeling would crystallize inside her into a single block of time and space she would later call "happiness." And, when he showed her the finished Christ, she felt like a privileged witness to the veneration of a sacred mystery. She kept returning every summer, as if to a refuge after a year of meaningless labor, and the space of the monastery turned into a sort of icon too: an out-of-time, gold-framed icon.

But, talking about it with Irina, she was careful to choose her words, to leave out "grace" and "happiness." Irina, too, was careful not to burst out laughing, especially at her description of the "quivering." The girl had to bite her tongue to keep from telling a monk joke she had suddenly recalled: "What's dark, hairy, and always up at dawn?"

# Irina, Vadim, Maria, and Seryozha

"Beer without vodka is like a wedding without music."
—Russian saying (Vasile Ernu, *Born in the USSR*)

**M**aybe Irina felt guilty for having deprived Seryozha of reaping the blond harvest he'd brought home that day; or maybe she just took pity on the poor man. The fact is that one day she decided to introduce him to Maria, so she set up a double date—she and Vadim, Seryozha and Maria—at the newly renovated Ambassador Hotel.

They were a little stiff in their Sunday clothes, and Seryozha kept ogling, with a mixture of impatience and spiteful envy, the nouveaux riches languidly sipping their drinks from long-stemmed glasses as they chatted with bare-legged blondes. One second it would be, "Look at these crooks in their fake Armani suits and black market Rolex watches," and the next, "To hell with it! One day I'll be swimming in it too, mark my words."

Irina noted that Maria had taken a shower and washed her long hair, and, although she was wearing the most unassuming outfit in the bar, the simple act of washing had transformed her into the most attractive woman present. Irina, on the other hand, was not one to go for simplicity; on the contrary, her lipstick was a vermilion that rivaled the red of the Novgorod school of icon painting; her skirt barely covered her buttocks, and her boots started three inches above the ground and ended at her knees. When she'd walked with Vadim behind her, he'd whistled and slapped her behind. The third time he slapped her she unexpectedly turned and caught his nose between two of her fingers, as in a vise, and, almost touching his nose with hers, whispered to her congested prisoner, "You slap me one more time, and I'll crush your fucking nose."

Then, she wiped her fingers on his jacket, while he turned to the other couple:

"She's a passionate woman." Winking: "I like that."

They sat down, Seryozha not quite in his element but trying to appear nonchalant, a pretense he abandoned as soon as he opened the menu. "What?! Twenty lei[4] for a glass of wine? Fifteen lei for a shot of vodka?"

As Seryozha vented his frustration, Vadim placed a reassuring hand on his shoulder. "Don't worry! It's on me."

"What, me, worried? I'm not worried."

"Seryozha is never worried," Irina quipped. "You see, in order to be worried, you have to have something called a conscience."

Fortunately, or unfortunately, Irina's words were lost in Seryozha's renewed sneers and mumbles. "Crooks! A bunch of crooks putting on airs."

But he was interrupted by the waiter who, very solemnly and lacking the jovial tone of the waiters Seryozha was used to, asked for their order. Together, the girls ordered a bottle

of Moldovan red wine, and Vadim a shot of vodka. As for Seryozha, he kept turning the menu's pages, unable to decide, whistling at the prices. In the end, he picked the most expensive cocktail he could find, and, uttering its name with a defiance that seemed leveled at the "crooks" from the nearby tables—"One Atomic Bomb!"—he patted his belly as if to say, here we are, my belly and I, we've seen it all; don't think you can impress us with your fancy drinks. The "Atomic Bomb" was a holdover from Soviet times, a mixture of vodka and beer that the poorest of the poor—that is, half of the population—had favored for its extraordinary efficiency, and which had been appropriated with postmodern irony by the hip bar owner. The ironic touch consisted of an extravagant toothpick protruding from the glass, three olives impaled on its tip, which Seryozha threw spitefully under the table, then remembered how expensive they were and picked them back up. He began to reminisce about the good old times when every Soviet citizen endowed with a healthy desire to quench his thirst, manufactured his own alcoholic beverage at home or, under difficult circumstances, at work, and was thus forced to develop a complex imagination pertaining to the material resources that could be transformed, through the alchemical process of distillation, into liquor. What didn't the Soviet citizen employ in pursuit of this most noble purpose? Deodorant, perfume, nail polish, nail polish remover, bug spray, brake fluid, you name it—anything with some percentage of alcohol in it. This phenomenal period of ingenuity reached its peak when Gorbachev was in power and, together with glasnost, he happened upon an insane idea—really, the end of the Soviet empire, including of Gorbachev himself, and of our traditional way of living, Seryozha would explain to whomever happened to listen—an idea previously unheard of: namely, that there was something wrong with having a glass or two. The program of

the sobrietization of the Soviet citizen—no pun intended—touched the very core of our people; it was unnatural, and, how should one put it? Slightly obscene. When Gorbachev was seen in public drinking sparkling water while his entourage—big bellies full of beer, gray suits, astrakhan hats—drank vodka, it was like watching a naked man in a church, pardon my comparison. But don't think that the disappearance of alcohol from our stores stopped our citizens from continuing an age-long tradition, no sir. If anything, it made their imagination soar ever higher, toward realms previously unplumbed by any human mind. Sure, as with every titanic human effort, lives were lost in the process. They say that hundreds of people died at weddings, intoxicated by various concoctions of alcohol, not to mention the thousands rendered blind. But when statistics are mentioned, one never hears of the millions whose lives were given a pink glimmer of hope with each drop of alcohol ingested.

"Nor does one mention the hundreds of thousands whose brains were turned to mush by alcohol," added Irina when Seryozha had finished his soliloquy.

"Why do you always have to be so negative? You know, the Americans are gonna ship you back in a second. They don't like negative thinking."

"That's right," confirmed Vadim, who'd read his share of articles about America. "Americans only like positive thinking."

"I read that what Americans really like," chimed in Maria, "is family values. Apparently, if you are married, you have better chances of getting a visa."

"Well, you can always count on my help, sweetie," interjected Vadim, extending his arm demonstratively around Irina's shoulders. "I'm ready to sacrifice myself if you need a husband."

In reply, Irina slapped his hand and pushed his arm away. "You wish. Like I'm an idiot to end my life at sixteen."

After this exchange, Seryozha began to consider Maria in a new light, the light cast by the word "marriage:" a chick (a rather sexy chick, he had to admit) who seemed interested in marriage (even if this interest was expressed in an apparently disinterested way). This feeling must have been written all over his face, because Maria asked him in an abrupt tone, "What are you staring at?"

"Staring? Me? You must really think a lot of yourself if you think people are staring at you."

"Oh, so you're also a coward?"

At this, Seryozha's cheeks changed color, and a heated back-and-forth ensued, which was followed with utmost interest by Irina, and with some embarrassment by Vadim. The tension between the two was definitely erotic, Irina decided, and at this thought, she cuddled up to Vadim, gazing up at him with languid eyes. The next moment they were kissing, exchanging wine, vodka and tongue. She hoped that this salivary exchange might serve as an aphrodisiac for the other couple. After the kiss ended, she noticed that the bottle of wine was empty, but couldn't recall having drunk so much. She was about to accuse Seryozha, when she realized that he and Maria were engaged in a cryptic game of gazes and silences, and resolved to leave them alone. Their bellicose posturing was full of promise: as any citizen of a country that has been liberated by Soviet soldiers knows, war is the doorstep to a woman's bed, whether she wants it or not.

# Seryozha and Maria

Although Irina assumed that Seryozha ended up in Maria's bed that night, it wasn't until their third date that it happened. The next day after their drinks at the Ambassador, he dropped by to "take a look" at her paintings. He was surprised at the mess and the stale smell, which he chalked up to her chain smoking.

"Aren't you afraid you'll get cancer?" he asked, lighting first his own cigarette, then hers.

"You know what they say about smoked meat: it lasts longer."

"How about kids?"

"What about kids?"

"Well, someday you'll want to have kids. Are you going to smoke even when you're pregnant?"

"What's it to you if I'm gonna have kids or not?"

Once again, Seryozha's face turned red. Flustered, he looked around, as if searching for a helpful solution to his discomfort.

"Isn't there anything to drink around here?"

"Some vinegar."

"Ha, I get it. You want me to think you're sour. But I can sense sweetness even under the sourest appearance."

"Cut the crap! You said you wanted to see my paintings. Do you still want to, or not?"

"Sure."

"OK then."

She took him into the next room, and, after rummaging a bit in one corner, began to pull out a series of paintings and drawings. Seryozha whistled, which is what he usually did when he was at a loss for words. This woman was something. She could really draw. Or paint—he wasn't sure what the difference was. What he was sure of was that the people, the trees and the objects in the images were more gripping than reality itself. *I'll be damned!* More whistles.

"So, I guess you're are some kind of an artist or something."

"Or something." She laughed.

He felt embarrassed by his ignorance, and scratched his head, just to do something. Suddenly, he had an idea.

"Do you ever paint or draw on commission? Say, if someone wants a portrait of himself?"

"Occasionally. But I'm not cheap. It would cost you a lot."

"Money is no object," Seryozha declared emphatically. He hadn't felt so full of enthusiasm since high school. And, goddamn it, he was going to commission a portrait of himself! Not only that, but he'll have it done by this woman! Sour as she might seem, he was sure that a barrel of honey was hiding somewhere inside her. He just had to find the right way to get to it. He felt as if he were sprouting wings. Or something— something that made him feel very light and strangely proud. It was a funny, rather unusual feeling. He felt proud because he was dealing with an artist. Besides Irina (who didn't count) and Kolya's mother (Kolya was a classmate in elementary school)

who painted complicated designs on Easter eggs, Maria was the only artist he'd ever met.

"Let's start now," he said, taking off his jacket and rolling up his sleeves.

"That's not gonna do it," Maria said dryly, sizing him up with a professional eye.

"What do you mean?"

"I mean you have to take off everything. Keep on only your birthday suit."

*Jesus! What has he gotten himself into?* Normally, Seryozha had no trouble taking his clothes off in the presence of women. If anything, he had trouble keeping them on, but it wasn't the same with this woman. Later, looking back, he would finally understand the meaning of the old saying: "In the presence of a real lady, any man can be turned into a civilized human being." As he stared at her, face purple, trying to come up with the correct retort, she began to laugh.

"Ha, ha! I scared you, didn't I? Don't worry, you can keep on anything you want."

He sighed in relief, and, for the next two hours, sat there like a statue, or rather, as if he were about to be immortalized by a woman whose eyes bored into him—a most unusual, slightly unpleasant feeling—as if he were a precious object in need of restoration.

# Irina

Hi, it's me.

How many times do I have to tell you that if I'm not writing, it means that there's nothing to say, and, therefore, everything is all right? What do you want me to tell you: that Grandma fed us cabbage soup for a whole week, or that Seryozha now spends half his time in his studio downtown? There's a reason for this new arrangement, and it's not that he finally took pity on us or realized what a jerk he is for eating our food without contributing financially in any way. No. The reason is (what else?) a woman. He spends a lot of time with Maria to whom I introduced him, but don't ask me what she sees in him. In fact, it may be that she's with him because she sees nothing in him that she likes: as far as I can tell, for her, men are like passengers on a train. The problem is that our Seryozha seems to have met his match. I think he's got it bad. Yes, Seryozha—*our* Scryozha—is in love! Besides being hilarious in itself, this unexpected development appears to have nearly civilized him.

The other day, while he was having dinner with us, he told us that Maria was drawing his portrait and that he was posing for her.

I said, laughing, "'Drawing?' Is that what they call it nowadays? And 'posing'?! I'd like to see that!" To which he replied, as if he were defending a virgin whose honor was being questioned, "Watch your mouth when you talk about Maria! It may be hard for you to understand, but there are some higher beings in this world that shouldn't be sullied by your depraved mind." 'Higher Beings?' Ha! Poor Seryozha, the alcohol has finally messed up his brain, but I guess it's better that it's happened with Maria than with some 'lower being.' As for Maria, I think she likes to have him around the way she'd keep a hamster in a cage; she gives him a leaf to chew on now and then, takes him out for walks if he behaves and plays with him, if she feels like it. Still, it's been a positive development, for the most part. Seryozha has become less annoying, and has even reduced his daily intake of alcohol. In fact, he's even taken to reading, of all things! That's right. He's checking books out of the municipal library: large, heavy books about painting and painters, and even takes notes in this grease-stained notebook, which, I bet, he memorizes in order to impress his 'Higher Being'. But the 'Higher Being' is not impressed—though she is surprisingly quiet whenever Seryozha's name comes up in conversation. She's only revealed her true feelings once, when I botched an icon; it was really terrible, I'd have hidden it if I could. Examining it with profound distaste, she suggested, "You can give this to Seryozha. He might like it."

But, don't worry, things are going smoothly between the two of us. I'm making a lot of progress, at least *I* think so, I'm sure the 'Higher Being' thinks that what I'm doing is barbaric. For one thing, she wouldn't let me use any of her colors (tempera mixed with egg). I have my own store-bought tempera and oils and, frankly, I don't see much of a difference. I doubt an American buyer would either. Besides, I can tell an American buyer whatever I want. What surprises me, though, is

the interest of the 'Higher Being' in America and her eagerness to teach me everything I need to know to make icons that would earn me a profit. I can't tell whether she has some vested interest of her own, or whether she's just a good sport—but I'm keeping my eyes open.

And now, the big news: I got my plane ticket. Or, rather, Seryozha bought it for me, and I'm sure he kept a fat commission for himself. When he handed me the ticket, he had—you won't believe this—tears in his eyes. He said, choking up, "My little niece is going to America," and then, he *hugged* me! I had to push him away with all my strength just to disentangle myself from his octopuslike embrace.

Don't forget to send money for my painting lessons! As for English, I'm studying by myself; I know what I'm doing.

Your daughter,
Irina

# Irina, Tania, and Maria

**P**atience was not Maria's greatest asset. Under normal circumstances, she wouldn't have tolerated a snotty, sixteen-year-old kid (all sixteen-year-olds were snotty) for more than a few minutes. Irina, however, was different. The girl had nerve—and that, she liked. Irina wouldn't have necessarily disagreed with Maria's diagnosis about most kids her age, since she rarely sought out their company, preferring older men and women. As a child, she used to hide under the table when Olga or Tania had friends over, and listened to their women's talk, more absorbed than if they'd been telling fairytales: stories of love and betrayal, abortions, curses (with or without spitting), adultery and divorce, all enthralling, much more so than fables about silly princesses and imaginary monsters. Occasionally, her dark hair would peek out from under the table, accompanied by a mischievous smile and a comment: "Death is waiting for Mrs. So-and-So by the door with a scythe, yet she can't keep her hands off young men." Or: "The country is ablaze, yet the old hag is busy combing her hair."

For years, Olga recounted—always with the same unstoppable laughter—how once, when she and Irina stood by the window watching and chatting with a passerby, the girl, then barely six, answered a neighbor's "How are you?" with an "Oh, Mrs. —, I'm just dragging my feet along, struggling with this bloody rheumatism and pain in my joints, the same bloody business everyday: work and no rest. But what can you do? Such is life."

When Tania divorced Irina's father, who hadn't been around much anyway, the girl waved her hand in a dismissive gesture and declared philosophically, "Good riddance! One less mouth to feed!" Her philosophical attitude remained a constant, though not always in Tania's favor, even once her mother began to date other men. One had "a face like a monkey's butt;" another was "good looking enough—too bad he has a multiplication table inside his head instead of a brain" (he was an accountant); another had "looks and brains, but smokes like a Turk and drinks like a sponge." She was a hard customer to please, and didn't make concessions. But surprisingly, when Tania announced that she was "done with Moldovan men, be they Russian or Romanian," and she was going to either "get an American man or become a nun," Irina voiced her approval enthusiastically, and even helped her write her first classified ad. Since then, mother and daughter had become a team, screening the mother's potential mates together and enjoying many hours of unwholesome fun in the process.

"Check out this one, '*Former Moscovite residing in New York, dependable and without dependents, interested in long-term relationship with uninhibited, adventurous Russian woman.*" (Tania)

"The perv!" (Irina)

"Anyone who doesn't include the word 'marriage' is out." (Tania)

"And what about me? Anyone who doesn't use the word 'family' is out." (Irina)

"Listen to this one, '*Family-oriented Ukrainian-born Los Angeles businessman who enjoys birdwatching and watching in general seeks Russian-born woman with grown-up daughter.*" (Tania)

"Family-oriented my ass." (Irina)

"I'm not sure I understand this one: *American-naturalized dentist, with a passion for concavities, openings and orifices, seeks like-minded Russian female. Full dental work in exchange.* In exchange for what?" (Tania)

"Oh, mother, grow up." (Irina)

"No, really . . ." (Tania)

"Let's keep going." (Irina)

"*Folklorist and ethnographer seeks relationship with peasant female of Russian extraction who knows how to tell folktales. Sense of humor optional.*" (Tania)

"I bet you never thought one day you'd be sorry for not being a peasant." (Irina)

"Excuse me, nobody ever accused me of not having a sense of humor." (Tania)

"Nobody ever accused you of having one either." (Irina)

At moments like this, Olga would usually interject with a, "Well, it looks like the egg is smarter than the chicken." And for a while it did seem that the egg was becoming smarter than the chicken. But, after Irina started going out regularly with her classmates, her grades took a dramatic plunge, and even her sarcasm, exercised through daily duels with Seryozha and Tania, was narrowed down to a set of fixed expressions used by the same classmates, like some kind of ritualized mantra only they understood, which they repeated ad nauseam until some other fashionable phrase took its place. If, for instance, someone needed an official document, she'd say, "You need to regularize

your irregularity;" if someone stood in front of her, blocking her view, she'd ask, "Hey, do you work in a glass factory?" If some instructor or inspector visiting their school gave a lengthy speech full of bullshit propaganda about the "emancipation of women," she'd comment—loudly enough to be heard for rows around—"Down with the exploitation of women!" or "Women are men too." If her intervention provoked the hoped-for giggles from her schoolmates, she'd continue in the same spirit: "Down with the fat cats" (The inspectors were, invariably, fat). If the giggles morphed into laughter, she'd sometimes deviate from her peers' codified speech and recover the linguistic dexterity of her childhood: "Down with up, and up with down! Long live upside-down!"

It was this Irina that Maria had met, and it was to her that she agreed to impart her knowledge of icon painting. Now, you may wonder why a woman like Maria—who'd immersed herself in the mysteries of an age-old tradition and had spent summer after summer with a monk who thought of the outside world as merely noise and distracting chatter—would share this tradition and knowledge with our Irina? Our Irina who, had she met Brother Simion, would have told him to cut the crap and get real. The answer to this question is simple: 1. No one else had ever asked Maria to teach them; 2. Irina was paying her, and Maria needed the money; 3. There was nothing wrong, thought Maria, with teaching the girl something that might prove valuable (of course, she knew Brother Simion would have disapproved, could picture him saying, "Don't give lilies"—or was it pearls?—"to pigs," but she preferred not to think about it). There was, actually, a fourth reason, but it was so obscure and hard to untangle from all the other reasons that only when Irina left the country did Maria become aware of it as the two young women hugged and said goodbye in the small airport

whose rubbery smell didn't quite prefigure the otherworldly white spaces of Western airports filled with determined men and women in business suits, rolling their suitcases.

For four months, twice a week, Irina rang Maria's doorbell, and within the apartment's bare walls—strange that, although a painter, Maria didn't have a single painting on her walls— under the jaundiced light vomited from an orphan bulb, Irina witnessed the mixing of colors, the preparation of the wood and the smoothing of its surface, the application of the gold leaf, and then of the colors within pre-drawn figures: a ritual, which, like all rituals, took place within a magic circle that separated out the mundane and the extraneous.

When Irina left, Maria realized that the girl was headed toward another—very different—magic circle. Suddenly, the daily circle she inhabited seemed small and pitiful. There was another life out there, a life rich with the promise of the unknown, and those like her, watching from the ground as the plane soared higher and higher into the clouds, were pathetic pawns, forever excluded from mounting such a magic carpet. She decided, as she watched the plane turn into a dot that, no matter what it took, she would find a way onto that flying carpet.

# Irina

Hi, it's me.

Thank God, it's all over—though, in some ways, it's just the beginning. You know the saying, "Lose a son, gain a daughter," you hear at weddings. Well, I'm afraid not only didn't we lose our "son," now we have a "daughter" on our hands. Right now, Maria is sleeping on our living room couch where Seryozha used to in his bachelor days. As for Seryozha, he's probably recovering from a serious hangover with the friends that accompanied him back to his studio after the wedding.

"The bride can sleep at your place tonight. The groom has some important business to attend to," he said, and left with his pals.

"I thought the groom's business is the bride," I replied, "at least on their wedding night."

Surprisingly, Maria didn't hesitate to come with us, and didn't seem to mind at all, on the contrary, that her newly-minted husband was spending their wedding night somewhere else. She claimed she was tired, though, if you ask me, I think

she's just not that into him. She must have been the least enthusiastic bride I've ever seen. To begin with, not only didn't she wear a wedding dress, she refused to dress in white ("I'm not going to play the virgin"). She wore black linen pants with a white lace top, which, under different circumstances, would have been charming. Of course, everybody commented on her outfit, and not in a positive way. But what took the cake were her shoes: she absolutely refused to wear high heels, saying that she wasn't going to ruin her feet for the sake of anyone else, and put on some flat, everyday sandals. Seryozha, on the other hand, went to the trouble of ordering a suit for the occasion, and was dressed to the nines: white handkerchief and white carnation in his boutonnière, and so much oil in his hair that he was a fire hazard. He glowed, sparkled, radiated, and stank like a barrel of wine.

You've probably heard from Grandma that their civil union at City Hall wasn't scheduled until later, but they wanted to have the wedding before I left for the States, so we arranged everything in a hurry. We went to the Saint Paraskevi of Iconium Church at the corner of Zelinski Street and Decebal Boulevard—its *popa*[5] knows a monk that Maria knows, and agreed to conduct the ceremony on short notice. The church was brimming with people, including a few crying babies, and I wondered who'd invited everybody and how we were going to feed them, until I realized that more than half of them had hung around after a baptism that had preceded the wedding. The *popa* was as ridiculous as I expected, with a beard rivaling that of Karl Marx, short, pink, plump hands that he rested on his pregnant belly, and a nasal voice that kept announcing the end of times. "Blah-blah-blah-*acum-si-n-veacul-veciloooor*," he repeated. Grandma had given Maria a bouquet of white roses, which went well with

her outfit and her grave, unsmiling face. Next to Seryozha, she looked like a slave who'd been sold to a drunk master.

I have no idea whether the *popa*, who seemed about as smashed as Seryozha, knew what he was doing or whether he decided to shorten the ceremony because he wasn't happy with the money we gave him, but there was no "You may now kiss the bride." Instead, we bore witness to a long, convoluted ritual, in which the bride and groom placed a crown on each other's head, then, both of them, crowned like a couple of jokers, circled the *popa* while he went on and on in this nasal drone that put quite a few grandmas to sleep. We were grateful when it was over, because there was hardly any oxygen left in the church. Everybody rushed to their cars and drove to the restaurant Seryozha had rented—I don't think you know it, it's a new one, at the corner of Dante Alighieri and Cetatea Alba. That's when the problems began. We were forty people—I counted—but we had food for only thirty guests. Apparently, some people had come uninvited, so the waiters had to divide some of the portions in two, which caused muffled— sometimes not so muffled—murmurs of indignation. One of Seryozha's pals even complained, "What's going on here? I drove two hundred miles just to be served a pigeon's neck on a leaf of lettuce? C'mon, bring out the real food. Stop joking around."

Another guest, I think it was Vania, who had been given a full plate and had no reason to object, took Seryozha's side, and replied, "What's your problem, pal? Isn't your double chin enough? Are you going for triple?"

It almost got ugly. The man who'd complained rolled up his sleeves and stood, and, if the people around hadn't separated them, the meal would have started with a fist fight.

This was followed by toast after toast—I couldn't understand how we were short on food, but this shortage wasn't paralleled by an equal shortage of wine. There was more wine than we needed, judging by the fact that half of the people were already drunk before the feast began. "Why would anybody come drunk to a wedding?" I asked, and Grandma said that for some of Seryozha's friends it was their second wedding of the day, and they were probably counting on going to a third later in the evening, if they could still walk.

Needless to say, Seryozha, who was already inebriated in the church, got really smashed, and didn't even seem to notice that the bride was absent for most of the libations. I found her in the back of the restaurant, lying in a chair with an empty, very unbridely look in her eyes. I don't know if this sounds normal to you, but, as far as I'm concerned, this bride is up to something. Judging from what the groom told me a few hours later, when the guests began to thin out, I think I might know what it is. Remember how Seryozha has always said, "I don't need your America, no thanks?" Well, after he and his pals sang a couple of shameless songs about the joys of copulation—both illicit and matrimonial—he took me aside, and hugging me in that drunken octopus manner I hate so much, looked at me with bloodshot eyes and asked if I'd "do something for my only uncle." I told him to get to the point before I died of alcohol poisoning from his breath. He asked me to convince my "dear, filthy rich mother" to invite her brother and his bride to the United States so they might start a new life there because how would we—you and I, that is—live there without the rest of our family to help us in times of need? And blah-blah-blah, you get the point. The man who's never needed America, no thanks, is now dying to go. You'd have to be blind not to see that the

person behind all this is the woman who didn't even want to stay through her own wedding.

But enough of this. Exactly one week from now, I'll be on the plane, with all this behind me. I'll probably see you before this letter reaches you, but I thought I'd write everything down before I forget the details. As Seryozha says, "Ladies and gentlemen, comrades and capitalist lackeys, the die is cast!"

# Part III
# Santa Barbara
# 1997–1998

# Lenny

When Lenny received the invitation that Irina had designed by copying one of her icons, enlisting Todd's computer skills to finish the job, he had no idea who she was. Her last name was different from Tania's, so he failed to make the connection. Some visiting Russian artist, he thought. Had he known that she was the daughter of the woman with the hysterical laughter and the cherry-painted lips, he wouldn't have attended, not in a thousand years.

There he was, crossing the Goldsteins' threshold in all his stylish Saturday afternoon Lenny-ness, black slacks and white linen shirt open to the third button. As expected, Tania let out a series of high-pitched squeals at the sight of him, after which she introduced "her daughter," who Lenny now understood to be the Russian artist. The girl facing him, who looked anywhere between seventeen and twenty years old, exuded an intriguing air of self-assurance and erotic provocation that was hard to ignore. He wasn't normally attracted to girls so young, but the way this girl cocked her head with that boyish, yet sexy, close-cropped hair; her wide, dark brown eyes whose edges

were extended out with eyeliner toward her temples, and which looked straight at him; her slightly upturned nose; and her ironic, almost arrogant smile—it all made quite an impression. He shook her hand, and the girl responded instantly by shifting her weight from one foot to the other, jutting out her hips, while the mother twittered away, like an intoxicated bird.

As soon as she heard Lenny's voice, Anna retreated into her room, her heart pounding, and from there, with the door opened a crack, attempted to follow the conversation. She couldn't see the man and the young woman, nor could she have imagined the spontaneous mating dance of the two bodies that their meeting inspired, but she could hear them. She heard Irina lead him through the main hall, providing brief explanations of the paintings she'd hung on the walls.

"I painted these several years ago. They really aren't worth looking at."

"No, no, they're not bad," Lenny protested, and at this, Anna felt a wave of nausea well up in her throat.

They were looking at a series of small watercolors, mostly landscapes, that Irina had done during previous vacations when she hadn't felt like studying.

"Technically, they aren't perfect, but nevertheless, you can tell there's something there," continued Lenny, turning to face Irina.

Tiptoeing behind Lenny, as if afraid of waking someone up, and carrying a tray on which stood a glass of fresh lemonade with a few ice cubes in it, Tania offered him the glass.

"Why are you whispering?" asked Irina, annoyed.

"Am I whispering? I guess I *was* whispering," said Tania, laughing.

She had been whispering without even realizing it, because . . . well, she felt like she was in a dream and didn't want

to wake up. You'd have to be blind not to notice the honeyed gazes Irina and Lenny were sending each other, and one thing Tania was not, was blind. She would have liked to make herself as inconspicuous as possible in order not to disturb them, but she couldn't just leave them alone; she had to make sure everything was advancing in the right direction, and if there was a bump along, she'd be happy to lend a hand.

Lenny took the glass without so much as acknowledging Tania with the slightest look, and stood in the middle of the living room, fascinated. The couch was covered with four wooden icons, which were propped up like throw pillows, forming a row of colorful, two-dimensional heads with gold-leaf auras and raised hands, thumbs and ring fingers touching in the demonstrative, iconic gesture that symbolizes the Incarnation. His face alternately taking the expression of a boy in a toy store and a man in charge, Lenny moved from icon to icon, now stepping back for a better view, now getting close to scrutinize a particular detail. He placed his glass on the coffee table by the couch, and, his hands free, began to examine the icons, one by one.

"How long did it take you to do these?"

"Four months."

After inspecting each of the pieces, Lenny returned to the one representing the Virgin holding the Christ child, and kept it in his hands for a couple of minutes, as if unable to part with it.

"There is something about this one, I can't quite put my finger on it. It seems to me that there's more of you in it than in any of the others."

Saying this, Lenny's face turned to the painter, who smiled enigmatically, all the while swinging her hips. If he said so. She was ready to agree with pretty much anything he said. Though, now that she thought of it, out of everything she'd painted, this

piece was the only one that had nothing of her in it. It was the
first icon she'd done, and it was an exact reproduction of an
icon Maria had shown her on her first visit. Irina had painted it
mechanically, entirely absorbed by the technical process, eager
to master the craft as quickly as possible. What separated that
icon from the rest was the mark of a beginner. It was strange
that, of all the icons, the one Lenny preferred was the one she
had used as a tool to teach herself, and that he saw in it exactly
the opposite of what it was.

It was only after Lenny left, after he had bought the
icon, paying two hundred dollars more than the four hundred
she'd asked for it, that she tried to figure out how her most
soulless painting might appear the most soulful. No matter how
imperfect technically, most of her paintings carried a fragment
of her (let's call it) inner self, something that turned the painting
into a mirror-image of the artist. But the icon of the Virgin
had nothing of her "self" in it, yet Lenny had been fooled. She
remembered Maria stating that, unlike regular art, religious art
should transcend the artist's ego—Narcissus watching himself
in the mirror—and that the more absent the artist, the better the
icon. Was that the secret? Or was the answer much simpler, and
Lenny was just easy to con?

# Irina and Anna

As a novice artist with an unusual gift for mechanical reproduction, Irina had always believed that there must be something that distinguished even the best copy from an original. That there must be some kind of soul of the artist, which penetrated the work and imparted to it a dimension absent in a copy. She knew that her icon of the Virgin had no soul because she hadn't given it any, yet Lenny had been fooled.

As for Tania, after Lenny left, she was beside herself with joy. Her daughter had made six hundred dollars with one painting! It was more than she'd dared hope for; it was the key to their future. Brimming with excitement, she began to talk out loud about things she'd never had the courage to mention. "Do you realize what this means? It means that one day, I—*we*—can leave Sammy. And if you play your cards right, maybe Lenny will marry you, and who knows? Maybe someday Bill and I will get married too."

Irina listened to her mother with a quiet smile, neither agreeing nor disagreeing. But, when she was alone, she took out a pen and paper and began a long letter addressed to Vadim, in

which she let him know that she could send him the money he needed to pay his debts, but only if he promised he'd remain debt-free in the future. If he promised to learn English, and stay away from girls and debts, she'd save money to help pay for his plane ticket to America.

While Irina wrote and Tania daydreamed, Anna, curled into a ball on her bed, suffered in silence. She was too furious to weep, could only gasp for air, and every now and then let out a deep sigh. What a miserable turn of events! Who could have imagined that *that woman*'s daughter would accomplish in a few minutes what she hadn't been able to do in a year? She had thought that she'd succeeded in putting her "past silliness," as she now called her infatuation, behind her, but hearing his voice, and—more than anything—knowing that he was attracted to Irina, had reawakened all her past feelings. The thought of him and Irina together was maddening. She had to stop them by any means. But how? She recalled one of the first conversations she'd had with Irina after her arrival, and, although she couldn't phrase it precisely, felt that there was some connection between what Irina had said and the seduction game she'd played with Lenny.

"What would you like to be when you're done with school?" Anna had asked.

"A millionaire," Irina had answered without hesitation.

"A millionaire?! That's not a profession."

"It is for me."

"But, why? I mean, you don't need that much money to be happy."

"Maybe *you* don't, because you already have it."

"I don't have that much money! Besides, only people who are willing to exploit other people want to be millionaires."

"'Exploit other people?'! What are you, a commie?! You sound as if *you*, not I, have grown up under communists! And what will *you* do, if you don't want to exploit other people?"

"I'll work for a nonprofit that helps others."

*Well, you go ahead and help others, and I'll help myself,* Irina had thought. "Millionaire" was the answer she'd given ever since she was a little girl when asked by relatives or friends, "What would you like to be when you grow up?" Frowning in concentration over a drawing she was bringing to life as she outlined a house's drunken fence or rectified the line of a man's pants with one leg shorter than the other, she ignored the guffaws and giggles of the adults around her.

"Wouldn't you like to be an artist instead?" one of the more idealistic adults would ask.

"I *am* an artist."

# Sammy and Irina

Education had always been one of Sammy's favorite topics of discussion and reflection, and after Irina's arrival, he'd been forced to reflect on it even more than usual. Irina being the same age as Anna (well, half a year older, but in the same grade), it made sense that she would share Anna's curriculum and take the same courses. With very few exceptions, Sammy taught all the subjects. The exceptions were physical education (which Anna practiced at a yoga studio downtown) and Spanish (which she studied twice a week with an old Argentinean lady who came all the way from Ventura). Irina noticed that two important disciplines were absent from the curriculum: physics and chemistry. Accustomed as she was to a heavy dose of both subjects, she figured it must have been an oversight, but was surprised to learn that Anna (and now she) was spared any contact with the relationships between distance, speed, time, and mass, or the intricate and mysterious connections between atoms, molecules, and the configurations that, for some reason, they chose to take.

As it happens, physics and chemistry were pet peeves of Irina's, though some might go so far as to say that they were her nightmares, since more than once she had dreamed of her teachers calling on her only to find herself naked and speechless in front of an entire class. For this reason, she had never in her wildest dreams dared to imagine that one could just decide, on a whim, to nix them. Like all bad students, she thought she would suffer for eternity, and had resigned herself to her classmates laughing whenever she opened her mouth to utter another enormity. And now all that was gone! All it took was coming to America.

Irina was so awestruck by this realization, and so afraid that it might turn out not to be true, that she didn't allow herself to rejoice. The enemy—that is, Sammy—could not be allowed to guess what her true feelings were about the subjects in question. And so she adopted a devious strategy: she pretended to be disappointed.

"What kind of a curriculum is this," she said, shoving a third piece of bubblegum into her mouth, "if it doesn't include important subjects like physics and chemistry? This is a joke, this isn't school."

Sammy, to whom the criticism had been addressed, began to pace up and down the room, his hands behind his back. Very gravely and, in a measured tone (an indication he was taking her criticism seriously), he answered:

"My dear, everything we do here has been given serious consideration by me and other parents who, likewise, are teaching their children at home. Believe me, it was only after extensive reflection that I removed physics and chemistry. But, let me assure you that, if you intend to study science in college, or are considering a pre-medical track, I will find you a teacher who can teach both physics and chemistry."

It was an answer that Irina hadn't anticipated. Careful now—you're in a dangerous zone! Stretching her legs out on the desk in front of her, she blew a huge bubble and replied:

Well, I wouldn't want you to go to any trouble on my account."

"No, no, it's no trouble! I take education very seriously, and I intend to spare no expense to provide you with everything you need."

The words "spare no expense" made a deep impression on Irina, who resolved to give serious thought to the potential advantages of such a policy as soon as she had the chance.

"Tell you what: for now, I'll study the same things as Anna. We'll see how that goes, and if I change my mind later, I'll let you know."

# Todd, Anna, and Irina

Irina's arrival was a mixed blessing for Bill: on the one hand, Tania was too busy showing her daughter around to bother him as much as before; on the other hand, for some reason, Anna had decided that Irina and Todd should be friends, and she kept bringing Irina along, showcasing her with an insistence that seemed suspicious to both men. At first, Todd had been more than eager to entertain the two girls, and he had strutted around the new one with cocky enthusiasm, proudly exhibiting all his electronic gadgets, which she appreciated much more than Anna. It was clear that he was not insensitive to Irina's own, generous, display: legs showing uninhibited under her miniskirt, breasts popping from her low-cut shirt, Mascara-infused lashes fluttering above two wide, almost black eyes, and berry-colored gloss that gave the illusion that her lips were fuller than they actually were. No other girl had ever flirted with him so openly, and Todd found himself in a position no teenage boy could resist: not quite an object of desire, but an object of interest. He responded to her attention with equal solicitude, until he began to understand that they were being pushed together by Anna. Then he got mad.

One night, after Irina discovered the Jacuzzi, and, as excited as Tania had been at its discovery, asked Anna to fetch their swimsuits, Todd dared them to get in naked.

"What do you need swimsuits for?" he asked with fake indifference. He was convinced the girls would respond with indignation to the outrageous proposal, but Anna contented herself with a scornful smirk ("Keep dreaming!"), while Irina, as if struck by a revelation, gave Anna a sidelong glance and exclaimed, "He's right! We don't need swimsuits."

Anna looked her up and down, as if she had lost her mind. Todd couldn't decide whether Irina was just testing him or was seriously considering the idea.

"I'll tell you what!" Irina said. "You go first, and we'll get in after."

"Not me," declared Anna.

For a few seconds, Todd's entire body was filled with the sound of his heartbeat. He was caught in his own trap. The idea of parading naked before the two girls terrified him. At the same time, it was too good an opportunity to pass up.

"I'll do it, if both of you do it, but it has to be both of you."

"OK," Irina said, smiling.

"No," Anna yelled at almost the same instant. "If you two want to take your clothes off, that's fine. But leave me out of it."

"I won't look," Todd said, attempting to negotiate the circumstances. "I'll turn my back while you take your clothes off and get into the water, then I'll join you."

That sounded quite reasonable, but Anna still wasn't convinced. She didn't have time to argue, however, because Irina had ordered Todd to turn his back to them, which he did right away. She began to strip, and, in under five seconds, she lowered herself naked into the warm, bubbly water.

"Can I turn around now?"

But Todd received no answer because Irina was too busy splashing, giggling, laughing, moaning, and screaming. "God, this is Heaven!" She was having so much fun that Todd, burying his anxieties, hurried to take off his own clothes. Night had already fallen, and the only light came from one of the house's windows. Avoiding Anna's gaze, but feeling it on his body, Todd stepped naked into the water. Only once he was in did Irina remember his existence and began to splash him.

"Hey, stop it!"

But Irina kept frolicking, as if drunk on the bubbles. She turned to Anna, and invited her in again. Anna ignored her and instead asked Todd, "Have you got any booze around?"

Todd stared at her, surprised. "Since when do you drink?"

"That's none of your business! I just feel like having a drink."

The truth is that Anna never felt "like having a drink." It was only that she was feeling left out, was jealous of her friends' happiness, and, since she was too shy to join them, having a drink while she watched them seemed like a good compromise.

"Go to my room and look under the bed." There's a bottle of Johnny Walker there. Make sure my father doesn't see you!"

As soon as Anna left, Todd, much more relaxed now that his body was underwater, started to examine what could be seen of Irina's body in the pale yellow light. The girl's breasts were bigger than Anna's, the nipples perked up in an insolent way. He could vaguely spot her pubic hair under the dark water that seemed to unfold out of the fluid night, but the little he saw was enough to give him an erection. Although Irina couldn't know what was going on under the surface of the water, the way she was looking at him and her provocative, ironic smile made him feel as if he were completely transparent. It irritated him, but

his irritation vanished when the girl slid closer, her smile wider and wider.

When Anna returned with a half-full bottle of Johnny Walker, the bodies of the two teenagers were interlaced, and their mouths glued together, moving with a confidence that indicated previous experience. Although her plan had been all along to play matchmaker, now that she had succeeded, she couldn't help feeling a pang of jealousy. Surprised at how unhappy she was with the way things had turned out, she took a good pull straight from the bottle, and the ensuing burning sensation brought tears to her eyes. She felt betrayed by Todd and betrayed by life. "Betrayed by life" were the words that came to her mind, as she watched the dark water shimmer under the flickering starlight. The interplay of black and white made her think of a Humphrey Bogart movie. She imagined she was a heroine in a gray raincoat drowning her sorrows in a bar with a blinking neon sign. She took another swig, and this time she almost enjoyed it. Meanwhile, Todd and Irina's bodies had separated, and they now sat side by side, propped up against the Jacuzzi's wall. Smiling, they stared at each other like two idiots, completely oblivious to Anna's presence. Another swig, and an unprecedented sensation of warmth and well-being spread through Anna's body. The couple in the Jacuzzi now seemed very remote, yet, in a strange way, all three of them were tied together by an invisible thread.

"You guys wanna taste this?"

Of course they did. By the time the bottle had been returned to Anna, stars were falling from the sky, and she kept trying to catch them, her hands extended with her palms up, but the stars melted before reaching the Earth, and she kept laughing and letting out little cries of excitement. Todd and Irina laughed too, just watching her, but when Anna wanted to drink again, Todd tried to stop her.

"Are you sure you want to do this? It'll make you sick."

Defiant, Anna took another pull, then passed the bottle back. The sounds of a saxophone and a piano drifted in from one of the rooms—Bill's room, no doubt. Strange, she *felt* the sounds as if they were physical, as if they touched her skin. Even stranger, when Irina and Todd got out of the water, she could feel their dampness on her own skin, as if she were one of them. Their nakedness seemed a mere continuation of the water and of the night, part of a ceaseless, liquid state. She herself felt made of water, and to better enjoy this state of lightness, began to undress. As she advanced toward the Jacuzzi, she saw Irina and Todd walk toward her, saying something she didn't understand. Next, she felt the warmth of the water against her body, and closed her eyes, blissful.

# Anna and Bill

When she opened her eyes again, a man's face was hovering over hers, and something heavy and limp, which must have been her body, was stretched out on a chaise-longue, partially covered by a towel. She blinked a couple of times and recognized Bill, who heaved a sigh of relief.

"What happened?"

Two other towel-wrapped bodies approached.

"Nothing too terrible, except that you had too much fun with this pacifier here," said Irina, who held up the bottle of Johnny Walker as if she were submitting a piece of evidence in court.

Bill frowned. "Where'd you get this?" He turned toward Todd, who averted his gaze. "And whose idea was it to give it to her?"

As no one uttered a word, Bill let Todd know that they'd "talk later," then threw a cotton wrap around Anna and lifted her in his arms.

"I'll drive you home," he said, walking away with the bundle in his arms.

Irina looked at Todd. "Well, our friend isn't very honest, is she? She let him believe it was your idea, and now you're the one who's going to get punished."

Todd waved his hand dismissively:

"Nah, he's not going to really punish me. And who cares, anyway?"

"That's not the point. A real friend wouldn't have done that."

Bill placed Anna in the passenger seat of his car with the same care he would have if she were a porcelain doll, and as he took his hands from her body, he felt the girl's inquisitive eyes searching for his, but he avoided her gaze. He sat at the wheel and, with the girl's eyes still on him, an awkward silence settled between them. He started the engine and began to drive, thankful for its low drone. Even so, the silence was still there, between them, as if a secret had finally been revealed. He felt guilty, as if he had committed a crime, or was about to commit one, though, really, what had he done? Taken home a child who had misbehaved? Yet, somehow, the child seemed to have the upper hand, and he, the good parent, was the one being judged. Judged by whom? Well, by the girl's eyes, which hadn't left his face for a second.

After an eternity, they arrived at Sammy's. In a broken voice that sounded foreign to him, he asked if she could walk. "It would scare your father if I carried you in."

She agreed and, supported by him—as he touched her body, he felt again that the girl knew everything—she walked unsteadily to the door. Together they entered the brightly lit kitchen, Anna with her body draped in the cotton wrap that left her shoulders uncovered, and he with a look of horrible guilt on his face. He saw Sammy's jaw drop at the sight of them, and Tania's eyebrows arch dangerously.

"It's not as bad as it looks," he said, trying to joke.

# Tania, Bill, Irina, and Lenny

"What's going on here?"

"What *is* going on?"

"Don't play dumb with me! You and Anna."

Much as he hated being on Sammy's turf in his absence, Bill had agreed to see Tania when she'd called him. He'd done it only because he couldn't rid himself of his gnawing guilt, and Tania's voice on the phone had sounded menacing. Now, as he was being accused, he felt blood rush to his face and, to hide his nervousness, he hugged her, burying his face in her hair and whispering in her ear that she was being silly. But, a minute later, he stepped back, claiming he had to get home because he had an appointment with a plumber.

After he left, Irina, who believed that one should never let a good "scène de ménage" go unwitnessed, and who, for this reason, had been eavesdropping from the living room, walked into the kitchen and asked, "Trouble in paradise?"

"Men are all the same," said Tania, trying to appear less affected than she really was.

"Meaning?"

"I hope I'm wrong, but I'm afraid this idiot—Bill, I mean—has his eye on Anna."

Biting into a juicy slice of cantaloupe and keeping the same disinterested expression, Irina answered:

"I could have told you that before. I've seen how he looks at her."

This revelation made Tania lapse into her mother tongue (she and Irina were trying to use English as much as possible), since only a curse in that primal language—words dipped into the magma of visceral utterances of a long line of angry, resentful manual laborers and disaffected peasants—could truly express the rage she felt inside.

Letting her mother stew in her own juices, Irina decided to pay a visit to Lenny, from whom she hadn't heard in a few days. He greeted her with a large smile, which she returned by asking, "Hey, what's down?"

"Sorry, what was that?"

"I said, 'What's down?' This language of yours makes no sense: 'what's up?' Why should things be 'up'? Up *where*? Down makes more sense."

"I guess down makes sense if you're a Russian, but if you're an American, you always hope that things are, or will be, up."

"I see," she said, ambling along, eyeing with interest the art on the walls. "You're an optimistic people. You must be, since you have all this stuff."

She stopped in front of an Egon Schiele and stood still for a long minute.

"You like it?" he asked, moving his gaze from the girl to the woman in the painting, and back.

She nodded, silent, lost in contemplation.

"Funny, you two look very much alike. Your bone structure, your forehead, your nose, the same expression when you frown. Don't you think so?"

She laughed:

"I don't know. Maybe we look alike from the waist down."

"I see you're very down to earth," he said, emphasizing "down."

"Those who are down now, will someday be up."

He wanted to ask her if she fancied herself as some kind of a revolutionary, but changed his mind and asked if she was familiar with Egon Schiele.

"Familiar?" she repeated. "Isn't he dead?"

"Oh, he's dead all right. You're funny."

"If he's dead, then, this drawing must have been expensive. Am I right?"

"You're absolutely right. It was a very expensive drawing."

"Was it more than fifty thousand dollars?"

"Yeah."

"A hundred thousand?"

"More."

"Shit! You're a rich man."

"I guess I am. Have a problem with that?"

"That's one thing I don't have a problem with. Listen, I didn't bring my cigarettes with me. Is there anything to smoke around here?"

"I might be able to find something."

"But you don't smoke. Why don't Americans like to smoke?"

"Because Americans like to lead long, healthy lives."

"Pussies."

"Ha, ha! Where did you learn English?"

"American movies."

"It figures."

"It figures what?"

"It figures. It's just an expression."

"How come all Americans are so rich?"

"Not all Americans are rich."

"All the Americans *I* know are rich. You, Sammy, Bill."

"Sammy isn't rich."

"He is, too! He's got two cars, a big house, and jewelry that he hides in his safe."

"If he hides it, how come you know about it?"

"I know a lot of things I'm not supposed to know."

"For instance?"

"For instance, I know that there's a young woman my age who's crazy about you. No, don't look at me like that! It's not me."

"Well, I'm disappointed. I was hoping it was you. But I don't know any other girls your age."

"Yes, you do."

"No! You mean Anna?! But she's a child."

"She's my age."

"Anna? I had no idea."

"Were you really hoping it was me?"

"I sure was."

"Well, don't give up."

"You're saying I still have a chance?"

"More than a chance. You're my type."

"Oh, I'm glad to hear it. And what type is that?"

"Rich."

# Irina and Lenny

It goes without saying that Irina and Lenny were soon "an item," so, instead of describing their first kiss and first time in bed, let's focus on the day Lenny showed Irina his family photos, some of which were tacked to a large board that covered half a wall in his office. Irina immediately recognized a young Lenny in a black and white photograph among a bunch of naked children on all fours, smooshing a black, gooey mass, all with grins as large as their faces. She was curious to know the reason for their happiness and their casual attire, and Lenny explained that they were stomping grapes.

Every September, the entire neighborhood on East Mountain Drive, where his parents had built a small adobe house on the very spot where his own house now stood, gathered to stomp grapes. Actually, first, they gathered to pick the grapes in a vineyard north of Santa Barbara. One or two families in their neighborhood had an agreement with the growers, so, each fall, the entire tribe—because in those years they *were* a tribe— went there, each family in its own pickup truck or car, and, for hours, armed with baskets and clippers, picked grapes. At the

end of the day they brought the wooden crates to the house where Theo's parents lived (which was later replaced by Theo's ice cream cone–shaped house) and threw the grapes into a large wooden vat.

The stomping was preceded by a pageant in which the year's Wine Queen was chosen by all the boys and men in the community. Meanwhile, the women set the tables, and after lunch, the Wine Queen was crowned with a wreath of grape leaves. Then, wearing only her crown, the naked queen entered the vat. The queen's Dionysian union with the grapes, for which Lenny used the word "ecstatic," was merely the prelude to the real fun, which was the moment when the children, also naked, threw themselves into the vat after her. The entanglement of purple-stained arms and legs had been immortalized in several photographs, including the one with little Lenny. Other photos showed stark-naked adults, mostly young people and some ecstatic middle-aged dancers, circling the vat and unsuccessfully trying to climb in, because it was already full.

"My childhood was paradise on Earth," Lenny reminisced. "Imagine dozens of men, women, and children, all naked, taking turns to climb into the vat, stomping together, all splashed with sweet, purple juice in the slanted afternoon light, laughing for hours, laughing and stomping, drunk with happiness. And, after that, throwing themselves into an enormous tub of hot water."

Irina tried to imagine it, but, frankly, the image it conjured was more like Hell than Paradise. She couldn't understand how anyone could get so excited about picking grapes. Many of her former Moldovan classmates used to go to the countryside in the summer and help their grandparents with the chores: feed the pigs, milk the cow, pick the fruit, gather wood for the fire, and they weren't excited at all by the prospect of doing any of it. She was puzzled.

"But," she asked, "I thought your family had money. Why did they have to do this?"

"We didn't *have* to do anything. We wanted to pick grapes. It was *an event*. An event that held the community together."

"Why did the community need to be held together? I thought Americans were individualists."

"They are! That's exactly why the community needed to be held together."

That didn't make much sense, Irina thought, but she didn't press the matter.

"Don't get any ideas," Lenny continued, laughing. "This was thirty-five years ago, in the sixties, right before the hippie era."

"So, your parents were hippies?"

"Not quite. More like bohemians."

"Bohemians? You mean, Gypsies?! That's a good one: I came all the way from Moldova to get me a Gypsy."

# Theo

**E**very year in late September Theo threw a party to celebrate the grape harvest, on which occasion he invited dozens of neighbors over and opened as many bottles of wine from the previous year. It was his way of commemorating the grape-treading that used to occur at that time of the year in his parents' backyard, of which a handful of residents on Mountain Drive still had fond memories. He still had his parents' vat, which accumulated dust, cobwebs and years in a wooden shed somewhere on the edge of his property. But even if the vat were clean and functional, he would never have thought of using it! Times had changed, and today one couldn't imagine a party full of people of all ages, drinking and mingling in their birthday suits, adults and children alike throwing grape mush at each other. The resulting wine, muddy and full of sediments, wasn't even particularly good. It was a miracle they hadn't fallen sick, considering how many children must have peed in the vat while stomping. But then, if he thought back to the way they had been raised, left on their own for most of the day with no parental supervision, free to experiment

in whatever way crossed their prepubescent minds—one of these experiments, an improvised explosive, had left Theo's best friend without his right hand—Theo was amazed he was still alive. When he looked at how his friends' children and grandchildren were being brought up, though, never a minute on their own, constantly schlepped from organized activity to organized activity, like little soldiers enrolled in some kind of hypercompetitive training program, playing baseball on Mondays, Hamlet on Tuesdays, soccer on Wednesdays, piano on Thursdays, and God knows what else on Fridays—when he saw this, Theo could only shake his head. In this new world there was no place left for self-actualization, despite all the cheap talk of "self-expression." How could one express oneself when one had no self to begin with? The self could only develop when left to itself, if it was given space and time to take root and grow. No amount of knowledge or organized instruction could replace the benefits of leisure, of those moments suspended in time wherein a lone child could lose himself in a daydream or to an unproductive whim, which was the only way of building that elusive thing known as "the self." If there was a secret to becoming an artist, Theo knew that it was dreaming and knowing how to waste time. It was no accident that Freud, who appreciated a creative mind more than anything else, and was fascinated by writers and poets, searched for the secret of creativity in our dreams. It is in that inaccessible chamber of our brains that our true selves ferment night after night, giving each of us a peculiar, unique perfume. (Theo was in the habit of using metaphors derived from winemaking.)

Whether it was from his ten hours of sleep per night or some other source that Theo derived his creative juices, we don't know. What we do know is that he slept till late morning, and that noon sometimes found him in his underpants with a mug

of coffee in one hand and the *New York Times* in the other. The neighbors could all testify to this state of affairs, and he himself would brag unselfconsciously about his twice daily naps with Tom in his lap, both master and cat purring in unison, the cat under the caresses of his hand, he mollified by the cat's fluffy rotundity. Late in the evening, he'd take a long, hot bath, sweating with epicurean zest, after which he'd wrap himself in his sky-blue bathrobe, and, with Tom at his feet, listen to the nightly news on NPR. As a regular news consumer, Theo was familiar with all the woe and pain in the world, from the Clinton scandal to the Balkan wars. And, as a man of the Left, he felt guilty for enjoying his cushy lifestyle while others endured famine or violence, so he did his best to "give back to the community," as he put it (an expression Lenny too often used, Irina had remarked more than once). Among the ways Theo gave back were the parties he organized on various seasonal occasions— the Equinox, the Solstice, the grape harvest (he skipped New Year's and Christmas in order to avoid overlap with Lenny), when up to a hundred guests gathered in his backyard, eating and drinking to their hearts' content. More than anything, he liked to watch the children, including his nephews and nieces, running around and making a racket reminiscent of his own childhood.

In 1997, for many reasons including a late harvest, Theo's party fell on October first, by which time Irina had been living in America for almost a month.

# Irina

Dear Grandma,

I feel as if I left the country a thousand years ago. But don't worry, I didn't forget about you. You'll get a nice package from me, soon. What I mean is that this place is so different— not only different from our Moldova, but different from what I expected.

It was almost a month before I had my first hamburger. We never have hamburgers at home because "they're bad for you" (Sammy), so I had to wait until there was a party. It was at Theo's, a sculptor with the strangest looking home I've ever seen: it's in the shape of an upside-down ice cream cone. Stone and metal sculptures are scattered all around the property— some of them discarded objects turned into pieces of art: a clock with carrots instead of hands, a baby crib with a sculpture of a monkey inside with a (real) red ribbon around its head and a (real) pacifier in its mouth.

I thought that this Theo must be a (real) nut, but he turned out to be very cool. He spent the entire afternoon grilling hamburgers and frankfurters for us. Too bad there wasn't any

Coca-Cola! (Yes, you guessed it. Sammy doesn't allow Coca-Cola in the house either—though Mother and I sometimes buy it on the sly.) All we drank was red wine—Theo had dozens of bottles because he's a winemaker, and every fall he throws a big party after the grape harvest.

Don't tell Mother I told you, but this time she really outdid herself; she got drunk as a bicycle (this is my favorite expression in English, along with "drunk as a boiled owl"). You see, she's jealous of Anna, and whenever Anna is around Bill, Mother works herself into one of her states, and there's no way to keep her away from the bottle! At some point, while most of the guests were seated at a long table in the garden, enjoying their burgers and wine, Mother asked if we'd ever seen a Gypsy dance on a table, and if it hadn't been for Sammy and Bill, she would have gotten up there to show us. As they were struggling to calm her down and keep her seated in her chair, she almost gave herself away. She looked at Bill with tears in her eyes and said, "You don't think I'm good enough for you, do you?" Luckily, I don't think Sammy understood. He just shook his head and answered, "Sure, you are! We both know you're a great dancer, but wait until we've finished eating."

Eventually, she abandoned the idea of dancing on the table, but remained in a melancholy mood and started singing "Black Eyes" (in Russian, of course). Theo realized that something wasn't right, and kept bringing her now a burger, now a sausage link. She must have set a world record for sausage gobbling! The funny thing is that Anna, who was the reason for her bad mood, was herself in a similar state because of me and Lenny. Remember Lenny from Mother's letters? The millionaire neighbor? Well, he's my boyfriend. Mother has big plans for us; she can already picture me walking down the aisle, but, just between you and me, it's not gonna happen. Not with Lenny,

not with anyone. Mother says I shouldn't let such an opportunity slip between my fingers, and I agree, but why should it end with me in front of a priest? She really is old school, you know? I told her that there are other ways to keep a man and have some fun in life, but her infatuation with Bill seems to have blinded her. I wonder what she plans to do with Sammy if Bill . . . but Bill won't. Bill would never marry Mother.

But let's get back to Lenny. Back home you were worried about Vadim being a "bad influence" on me, but I'm sure Lenny is also involved in shady deals. How else could he have so much money? He never works. What he calls "work" is being on the phone for hours and hours, chatting with people from all over the globe. Every now and then he makes an "acquisition" or else sells a piece from his collection. Work! If that's work, then I'm the Pope.

There is, however, something I can't figure out about Lenny and Americans in general. It's hard to explain it, but I'll try. Remember the TV dramas and miniseries they used to bombard us with under communism? The protagonist was always an engineer, or a doctor, or else a factory worker, and he was always some kind of saint who was obsessed with the good of the community. We laughed, because it was such bullshit. Everyone knew that *no one* was like that. Everyone knew that no one believed in that crap. Well, no one except the Americans! It's the strangest thing, but the people who are the most anti-communist and who've never seen any of those films act as if they were raised on them! These people really believe in working for the "community"! You should hear Lenny and Theo talk about "giving back to the community"! I wanted to ask them if they *took something* from it. Now that I think of it, both Lenny and Theo are art collectors—so maybe there's something to that. Even a party, for them, is not simply an occasion to forget about

one's worries; it's a way of "keeping the community together." When they drink, they don't drink to get drunk, like us, but in order to "share" (I'm not sure what). It's as if everything has a moral tag attached to it. Really, life here is nothing like their movies—that's why it's so confusing.

Let me give you an example: Lenny showed me some photos from his childhood, and told me how back then, in the sixties, his entire neighborhood got together each September for grape stomping. He called it "an event"—a word he uses a lot, as if stomping grapes were more of an "event" than any other occasion. You should have heard him talk about those grapes! It was as if he was remembering some vacation to Paris or a week spent in a Roman villa. I told him I knew lots of peasants and even city dwellers from Chişinău, who, each September, pick grapes to make their own wine, and it's a pretty tiring "event." The only good thing about it is the wine.

When I asked him if he wasn't, by chance, a Gypsy, he laughed, and not only was he not offended, he took it as a compliment. I'm telling you this so you can see the irony of the situation. Here, people *want* to be Gypsies. Go figure! Isn't the world a crazy place? Of course, in reality, Lenny isn't a Gypsy at all, he's Jewish. I don't understand how his parents, while living like bohemians in a small adobe house—really cool, I've seen photos of it, like a house in a fairytale, with its lower part of stone, the upper part adobe, and a flight of irregular stone stairs off to one side—were able to become the biggest American collectors of one of the greatest German Expressionists. No point in asking Seryozha about the Expressionists—I'll tell you more about it later, as I myself don't know much.

Your granddaughter,
Irina

# Tania

Dear Mother,

Tell Seryozha I have the paperwork and have started working on his official invitation for the American Embassy. Meanwhile, he and Maria should get their passports ready and find money for plane tickets. If he thinks I intend to pay for them, he's wrong! As it is, Sammy is already pretty nervous about the whole thing, and keeps asking me how long they're planning to stay, and what's the rush. I assured him that they are *only* visiting, that Seryozha wants to make sure we are well taken care of, and to introduce me to his bride, but Sammy wasn't born yesterday. For once, I can't blame him for being suspicious. If Seryozha were unmarried, I might be able to find him some work, maybe as a gardener for one of our neighbors, though I doubt he can tell the difference between a tomato and a cucumber. But what's gotten into him that he's bound himself hand and foot by marrying that woman? Frankly, I don't think Santa Barbara needs another Moldovan icon painter. Our Irina, with her exceptional talent, managed to sell one of hers to a rich art collector who was so

impressed that he's now trying to convince the curator of a local art gallery to take a few others. She doesn't need the competition, as they say here.

I wonder whether there is some way to keep that woman, Maria, from coming here. Could you try to convince Seryozha? Just tell him that she can come later, that if he comes alone, Sammy would be less nervous and more likely to help him find a job. If that doesn't work, I'm afraid you'll have to resort to more extreme methods. I'm referring to Sofia. Remember when Tamara's boyfriend was cheating on her with that sleazy whore, a cashier or cleaning woman or whatever she was? Tamara came crying to Sofia, and Sofia told her not to worry, just to bring her a tuft from that woman's hair, and a week later the whore was run over by a truck?

You get my point. Besides, now that I'm thinking about it, why would Seryozha decide to marry this woman practically overnight? I smell something fishy, something downright rotten, underneath it all. I wouldn't trust this woman, not if she were made of pure gold. Does she have any money, by the way? I get a bad feeling whenever I think of her, and you know that my instincts are never wrong. Remember when my left eyelid wouldn't stop throbbing for a whole week, and afterward we got a phone call that Aunt Lena had died? (Hmm, maybe it wasn't Aunt Lena, maybe it was her sister—but still.)

You asked how things are between me and Sammy, and me and Bill. Between me and Sammy they're pretty much the same, but between me and Bill, things aren't going well at all. Why are we women always stupid and let our hearts lead us instead of our heads? I should know by now that no man is worth losing sleep over. Alas, one never learns—especially when one has a heart like mine and was born with such a passionate temperament.

As I sat down to write this letter, it dawned on me that I might want to use Sofia's skills myself. I'll see what I can do, and with a bit of luck, I'll send you a lock of Bill's hair in my next letter.

As for your breathing problems, I'm sure it's because you never stop doing things: washing the windows, cleaning the stove, mopping the floors. Stop cleaning that house! You're the only one who sees it, anyhow! Get some rest and you'll feel better.

Your daughter,
Tania

# Irina and Lenny

Irina was now spending every other afternoon with Lenny. The first two weeks they spent mostly in bed, but, after that, they began to have dinner together. Irina would pace around the kitchen and sip wine while Lenny cooked. When she had first seen him with a flowery apron around his waist, a knife in his right hand, and a bunch of raw vegetables on the cutting board before him, Irina, used to seeing only women in the kitchen, laughed. But soon she discovered that he was an excellent cook, and consequently, stopped dictating how he might do this or that, and decided that it was better to lay back and enjoy the ride.

Lenny proved to be such a charmer, not only doing well everything he did, first in bed and now in the kitchen, but telling funny stories about neighbors she'd met or would some day meet, that she began to have second thoughts about The Plan. Wasn't it too risky to go through with it, now that she could just enjoy being with Lenny? But the truth was that, although she did like Lenny, she'd never stopped thinking about Vadim, hoping that one day he'd be able to come to the States.

The Plan had begun to take shape in her mind as soon as she'd seen the Egon Schiele. At first, it was more like a vague idea, foggy and ungraspable. When Lenny had asked her if she liked the drawing, she'd almost said, "I could do something like this," but had bit her tongue and stopped herself. So, the idea must have taken root inside her mind at that moment, even if she hadn't been aware of it at the time.

Every time Lenny went out on some errand, Irina took out her sketch pad and, seated on a silk pillow in front of the drawing that graced the wall in the hall that led to Lenny's office, began to draw, her eyes fixed on the image before them. She did this for about three weeks, and, by the end of the third week, had decided that there was virtually no difference between her drawings and the one on the wall. True, the paper was of a slightly different tone, but it was the kind of thing one only noticed if one was already aware of the change. Of course, she knew that the difficult part had not yet begun. Dozens of times, she took the drawing from its hook and turned it over to examine the way it was framed: the glass, the backing, the mat, the framing points, the dust cover, the wooden frame itself. It would be hard, but not impossible.

Two weeks earlier she'd stopped by an art gallery with the intriguing name of *Totem* and asked a tall blond woman with unending legs—presumably, the owner or manager—if she knew of any framing classes in town. The arrogant blond woman had sized her up and replied, no, there weren't any such courses in Santa Barbara, as far as she knew. But, before Irina could make it back out the door, she had called her back and given her the address and phone number of a framing shop in L.A. that taught the craft to its apprentices.

It took some explaining to make the shop's owner understand that she couldn't come to L.A. but wanted to learn

the skill remotely, and wasn't there any way of doing that? At first, he was uncompromising, but Irina kept insisting until in the end, he asked her if she would please hold. When he returned, he sounded much more affable—he must have talked to someone—and said that they could sell her a video that taught one how to unframe and reframe a picture, but she could only have the video if she agreed to buy all the necessary tools and framing supplies from them. Cautious, Irina requested a catalog of their supplies, and told the shop owner that she'd get back to him once she'd seen it. She didn't have to wait long because it was in the mail two days later. According to her calculations, it would cost her exactly one hundred and thirty-eight dollars to buy the video and the equipment, which meant that she'd be left with sixty-two dollars (she still had two hundred from the sale of the icon, after sending four hundred to Vadim).

As Irina watched the video, her confidence in the success of The Plan, which had diminished lately, increased, and she was now convinced that she could do it. She got a money order from a 7-Eleven and ordered the kit. Once again, the die was cast.

# Lenny

L enny hadn't told Irina about the five Max Beckmann paintings he had placed with various art dealers, or about the Beckmann lithograph he kept in his bedroom, which she'd seen and ignored because she figured that if he hadn't mentioned it, it must not be very valuable. Nor about the gold watch he kept in a safe together with a leather-bound notebook containing a handwritten play by Beckmann and other similar items inherited from his father. Not because he didn't trust her, but because he didn't see the point. But he did tell her that there was a time when his parents had been Beckmann's foremost American collectors. His father, an aspiring writer and art connoisseur, had met him in Europe in the early 1930s, and they had become close friends in spite of the difference in their ages. At the time, Lenny's father was in his early twenties, while Beckmann was already over forty. Beckmann's paintings weren't, obviously, worth what they are worth today, so his father could afford to buy a couple of them. Then, as the political situation in Europe deteriorated, his father decided to return to the States, and Beckmann, who was afraid—and rightly so—that the Nazis

might destroy his work, sold him a dozen paintings for almost nothing. When he returned to the States in 1937, Lenny's father brought with him at least fifteen Beckmann originals.

"In 1937 Hitler gave a speech in which he included Beckmann among so-called 'degenerate' artists, and, from one day to the next, all of Beckmann's paintings were taken out of museums, so he gave many of them away to his friends, or sold them for laughably small amounts. Then he left for Amsterdam, where he stayed until the end of the war, when he moved to the States. Unfortunately, he didn't have much time left to live, and only lived in America for two or three years. He died in 1950, the same year my parents built, and moved into, the house I grew up in, here on Mountain Drive. But, while he lived in the States, my parents bought three dozen more paintings from him."

"But this means that by the time your parents moved here, they were already rich. Why did they live so modestly?"

"Well, they weren't *that* rich. Although Beckmann was a well-known painter, he wasn't yet a household name. It was only after he died that, little by little, his work grew in value, and my parents sold most of his paintings between the fifties and the eighties. The early sales amounted to little more than a pittance; it was only in the late seventies, early eighties, not long before they died, that they became, as you put it, 'rich.'"

"What do you mean, 'As I put it'? They made millions with those paintings! Doesn't that make them rich?"

"My dear, wealth is a question of perspective. What may seem like a lot to you may be nothing to other people, including some living on this very road. I know another art collector a few houses down, who has a lot more than my parents ever had. Not to mention a few Hollywood executives who live in the neighborhood."

"There are people from Hollywood around here?"

"Sure there are! Plenty of them."

"And actors?"

"Actors too."

"Oh, I want to meet Hollywood actors! Please, Lenny, please!"

"I'll see what I can do. Maybe during my Christmas party."

"Wow, I'll have to write home! They won't believe it."

# Irina and Vadim

"Stealing is a type of work too."
—Romanian saying

*Dear Vadim,*

*You'd be proud of me if you saw what I did today. I can't talk about it here—too risky—but it's big. Suffice it to say that I have—or will have soon—the money for your plane ticket. Get ready!*

*Love,*
*Irina*

This was the postcard Irina wrote on the evening of December eighth, after the most stressful afternoon of her life. Lying in bed with her eyes closed, she recapitulated to herself the incredible events of the past twenty-four hours.

It had been a week since she'd decided to move forward with The Plan, but had discovered it was impossible because, wouldn't you know it, Lenny never left the house. Finally, on

December eighth, as they cuddled in bed after a record one-hour marathon of lovemaking, the phone rang. It was the gallery owner whom Lenny had been trying to convince to take two of Irina's icons; she had finally agreed, hoping that putting them on display two weeks before Christmas might help.

"Fabulous," exclaimed Lenny, as he hung up. "She's putting them up this afternoon and wants us to come by right now to sign the contract."

"I can't go now," Irina mumbled from under the blanket. "I have a horrible headache. But we shouldn't postpone, either—she might change her mind. Why don't you go and bring me back the contract?"

As Lenny hurriedly put on his clothes, kissed her on the forehead, and left the house, Irina wondered, once again, whether going ahead with The Plan was a good idea. She compared Lenny's zeal with what she knew would have been Vadim's attitude had their roles been reversed—lighting a cigarette and telling her to go fetch the damn contract herself because he wasn't her servant—and knew, just *knew*, that The Plan was a bad idea. But something inside her kept pushing her onward, and she couldn't stop, not now that she was finally in a position to execute it, not after having spent six weeks practicing the framing, unframing, and reframing of the dozens of Egon Schiele copies she'd drawn. She knew the motions by heart, could do them with her eyes closed: 1. Unstick the felt bumpers from the back of the piece and set them aside; 2. Untwist the wire and pull it through the hole of one of the screw eyes; 3. Take the two screw eyes out of the wooden frame; 4. Remove the paper dust cover and the points; 5. Take the original drawing out and replace it with her copy; 6. Return everything to its proper place: the glass on top of the mat, the mat on top of the drawing, the

drawing on top of the backing board, and set all the above in the frame; 7. Drive new points in exactly the same spots where the old ones had been, making sure that neither the backing nor the frame had been damaged; 8. Glue down the new paper dust cover and trim it to size; 9. Put the screw eyes back in, feed the wire through one screw eye and retwist the wire; 10. Glue the felt bumpers back on and hang the drawing back on the wall.

For a whole week she'd been carrying the box of points in her backpack, the Logan frame fitting tool for driving and removing the points, and the cardboard folder with the best copy of the Schiele drawing she'd made. And now, the time had come to use them. She threw a glance at the wall clock and realized that five minutes had passed since Lenny's departure, and she was still in bed. She didn't have much time—barely enough, in fact, for everything she intended to do. She jumped out of bed, ran to her backpack, opened it, took out the Logan tool, the points and the folder, and carried it all to the wall with the drawing. She took the drawing down and began to work with a nervousness that made her hands shake. She was almost never nervous, but now her heart was beating so fast she could hear it in her ears. Once the first point came out, the rest was surprisingly easy. She was so fast, she beat all her personal records.

Thirty-five minutes later, it was over. The new drawing was hanging on the wall with a self-confidence that made her wonder whether she was still in bed, dreaming. She stared at it, puzzled how it was possible, puzzled that it had been so easy. A minute later she heard a car in the driveway, and again, she marveled at her perfect timing. She leaped up, rushed to the door, and greeted Lenny with a smile that erased everything else.

"Well, you look a lot better! Headache gone?"

"Yeah."

They kissed and he gave her the contract. As he was taking his coat off in the anteroom, she spotted her backpack in the doorway that separated the main hall from Lenny's office, where she'd left it. And, in the same moment, she remembered that everything (framing tool, points, folder) was still on the floor by the wall with the drawing. She felt Lenny's arms turning her body toward his for another kiss, and she let herself be kissed, her eyes fixed on the backpack.

# Irina and Anna

**T**hat was a close call! Irina thought, as she frantically shoved everything into her backpack, while Lenny whistled, carefree, in the bathroom.

Later, lying in her own bed, she still couldn't believe she'd done it. She'd watched Lenny as he passed by the drawing—*her* drawing!—on his way to his office, but his gaze had merely slid over it, without actually pausing.

She spent the next several days in alternating states of hyperexcitement and tension, starting each time she heard the phone ring, expecting to hear Lenny's voice on the other end after he had discovered that something was wrong with the drawing. But nothing happened. Lenny called twice and each time he sounded calm. Once, he asked why she wasn't coming over, and the other time he asked her if she wanted to go to the movies. So, it was really that easy. One could commit a crime, and life would go on just as before, with nobody any the wiser.

This is where Irina was wrong—a third observer would say. In almost every story, the person whose eyes are always watching you is someone you have wronged. For weeks, Anna

had been watching Irina, knowing that it was only a matter of time until she discovered something that would compromise her in Lenny's eyes. Lately, she'd noticed a visible restlessness in Irina's behavior, and could tell that something was amiss. But what?

One day when Irina wasn't at home, Anna entered her room and began searching. What she was looking for, exactly, she didn't quite know, but she started in her lingerie drawers—recalling that, a few years earlier, when she herself was keeping a diary, she used to hide it under her underwear. But there was nothing under Irina's underwear, and Anna grimaced at the sight of her polyester lace bikinis. Then, she opened her desk drawer and uncovered an envelope with sixty-two dollars in it, and a few letters, but they were all in Russian. Russian, of course—she'd forgotten about that! Well, she could make copies of the letters and ask someone to translate them. But, for some reason, she felt that the letters could not contain anything important.

On each side of the desk there was a wooden filing cabinet. She opened the one on the left and browsed through a few of its folders. Irina's school notes and assignments. Jesus! How could anyone have such bad handwriting? Irina's letters were huge, with *o*'s like enormous balloons about to fly away, and each letter stepping into the territory of the next, so that the words became an unintelligible hodgepodge of meandering lines and curves. Disgusted, she returned the folders and tried the cabinet on the right, but . . . The cabinet was locked!

# Anna

This year Lenny was having his Christmas party on the twenty-fourth rather than the twenty-fifth, and the invitations, printed letterpress on fine paper with gold lettering, suggested that it would be an even bigger event than usual. Maybe it was because now Tania knew more people than she had a year earlier, or because this year there was such a sense of excitement in the air—whatever the reason, Tania was filled with thrilling expectation, a feeling that something momentous was going to happen. And it wasn't just her: Irina and Anna were more fidgety than ever, even Sammy had noticed.

"What has gotten into you, girls?" he asked, exasperated, when his fourth question on atonal music met their empty gazes.

Both girls had good reasons for their absentmindedness: Irina, her recent discovery that she'd stopped missing Vadim and, in light of that, pangs of conscience over having stolen the drawing from Lenny; and Anna, her own recent discovery upon a visit to Irina's room. The discovery she had made was so shocking she knew that when she told people it would blow their

minds. *Blow their minds.* Her father would be enraged. Lenny too would be enraged, maybe also embarrassed for having gotten himself mixed up with such a person. He'd come to see the difference between her and Irina. And he'd regret not seeing it earlier and would tell her so. He'd ask her to forgive his stupidity, and she would be more than happy to.

Anna was so excited by this succession of mental images that she hadn't even heard her father's questions. Only a day earlier she'd still been far removed from the incredible piece of information she now possessed. After almost ten days of elaborate searches through Irina's room, after having shaken every item of her wardrobe and looking through all her files, she had been ready to give up. On the tenth day she opened the desk drawer again, having memorized all the little things inside, and almost mechanically she reopened the envelope with its sixty-two dollars. The money was still there, but this time, tucked between two one-dollar bills, was a tiny, golden key. Anna's heart skipped a beat. When it started again, it was faster. She took out the key and held it delicately in her palm, like a precious object. She was afraid to insert it into the keyhole of the locked cabinet, afraid of being disappointed, and it took a good ten minutes for her to gather the courage to do it.

The key turned so smoothly in the lock it seemed animated by some inner force. Anna stood in front of the still-unopened cabinet for another minute, then pulled on the knob. Darkness, a musty odor, and, inside, a gray cardboard folder. She opened the folder: her first reaction was one of frustration and resentment at having been fooled. A nude. She held in her hands the nude of a woman—a very well-drawn nude—which made her think that this must be the place Irina hid her dirty artwork. Underneath, she found a stack of similar sketches, imperfect or unfinished

copies of the first. Drawing exercises. But why would Irina keep them under lock and key?

There was something about them—the drawings; the first one in particular—that seemed very familiar. She was certain she'd seen it before, but couldn't remember when and where. Where could she have seen such a nude?

# Tania

Dear Mother,

Merry Christmas to you and Seryozha!

Today I spent all day in bed, recovering after Lenny's big party. I haven't seen so many people together since the political demonstrations in the Great National Assembly Square. Irina says there were about two hundred guests, and the cost of the food and the caterers was close to twenty thousand dollars. I met quite a few people who didn't even know who the host was, they said they knew someone who knew the host, and came. In each room there was a table with food on it, and one with drinks, and, behind each table, a waiter. You took a little plate and a napkin, and moved from room to room, getting some shrimp here, some barbecued pork there, some salmon further on—all perfectly organized, although we did have to spend some time in line, considering how many of us there were.

And the man who paid for all this, and about whom many of the guests spoke with such awe you'd think they were talking about a great dignitary or God knows what big shot is our Irina's boyfriend. Oh, Mother, you should have seen our

Irina next to Lenny in her three-hundred-dollar dress, shaking hands, throwing smiles left and right, and sucking up to the rich Americans! She was born for this, I'm telling you. At least God is on her side, because he doesn't seem to be on mine.

Now: Bill. He's been avoiding me. At the party he acted as if he barely knew me—that is, until I cornered him and gave him a piece of my mind. Do you know the expression they use in English when a man treats you like that? They say "he dropped you like a hot potato." Imagine that: being dropped like a hot potato! Well, if he thinks he can do that to me without consequences, he's got another thing coming. The man hasn't been born yet who can drop *me* like a hot potato.

I watched him closely for the duration of the party, and now I have no doubt that he's head over heels for Anna. That little princess, all innocence and righteousness, is trying to get under Lenny's skin while leading on that poor idiot—Bill, I mean! Because I think she knows what she's doing. Oh, yes, she does! But she's got her eyes on Lenny—as if he can't tell the difference between a *real* woman like our Irina, and a half-baked, meat-avoiding, animal-worshiping phony like Anna. The man knows the difference, after all, he's an art collector: he's got eyes! The only one who's truly blind to everything around him is Sammy. This man lives on a different planet, what with his music and whatever else he's got going on in his head. I'm so sick of him, and of Bill . . . Mother, I think I am, as they say here, *depressed.* I always thought that only rich Americans and Europeans suffer from depression, yet here I am. Maybe *it is* an illness of the rich—I'm living proof; I was never depressed when I was poor.

But about the party: I might have drunk a little more than I should have. I might have raised my voice to that son of a bitch when I should have just ignored him. Still, it was a fun party, and if there's anything I know how to do, it's to have fun. I made a ton

of friends and got all their phone numbers, you never know when they might come in handy. I never let my guard down, though. I kept one eye on Bill, and the other on Anna. At some point, Anna, Lenny and a couple of other guests walked up to a wall painting and stood there for quite some time, talking about it. I thought, What an idiot (Anna, that is): as if Lenny needed her to talk art when he's got an artist for a girlfriend. But after that, I noticed that he got sort of—I don't know—pensive, or maybe it was just my imagination. Anyhow, it didn't last long: by the time Irina came up to him, he'd forgotten all about Anna, but the little bitch kept spying on them, green with envy. I can tell she's up to something, and you know I'm never wrong. Yes, something's going to give, soon. I can sense it. I've been feeling like a tautly pulled slingshot the whole past month, as if I were just about to snap. Or rather, the three of us like different parts of the same slingshot: at one end, Bill—the sling—at the other, Anna—the handle—and in the middle, me—the pebble—waiting to be fired. Meanwhile, the tension is killing me. Irina keeps saying there's nothing to worry about and I should calm down, but she doesn't have my gift for divination. You know that I could always foretell things; here, people like me are called "psychic." (I was convinced the word was "psychotic," but Irina, who always has to be right, made a bet that it was "psychic." Sammy and the dictionary both backed her up.)

I tried to get a tuft from Bill's hair for you-know-what, but it was impossible. The only time I could get near him was at the party, and I couldn't do it there. I'll try at New Year's; it's my last hope. Light a candle for Irina and me when you have some time, and tell Seryozha I'm glad their visas have been approved. Tell him to let me know when he has the money for the plane tickets.

Your daughter,
Tania

# Anna and Irina

*New Year's Eve, 6PM*

The girls are each in their respective rooms, trying on dresses in a whirlwind of colors and fabrics that echoes the disorder in the other's room in spite of their significant difference in taste. Anna, who rarely wears dresses and never miniskirts, has decided to put on a recently purchased dark blue velvet skirt that stops above her knees, a black turtleneck meant to set off a lapis lazuli necklace from one of Sammy's jewelry boxes, black tights, and flat, gray boots. She observes herself in the wardrobe's mirror, changing her mind over and over about the outfit's suitability and the adequacy of her rear end in the reflection in the glass. One moment she thinks she looks sexy, the next she decides she's pathetic.

In her room, in front of her wardrobe mirror, Irina goes through a similar crisis, though not for a second does she have any misgivings about her behind. Her crisis is about the most appropriate look for a New Year's party. Should she go for a

moderately sexy look, or for a more vampish style? The choice is between a knee-length leather dress with tall, high-heeled black boots, and tight leather pants with a black satin blouse. She chooses the second option and puts on a thick silver necklace with a large pearl in the middle that she too has taken from one of Sammy's jewelry boxes.

At Tania's insistence, Sammy had opened all the jewelry boxes, including the one in his safe, and had let her and the girls choose whatever they wanted to wear at the party. As for Tania, having spent almost an entire afternoon trying to make up her mind, she picked the necklace that had seemed the most expensive, even though it hadn't been the one she liked best: a thick platinum choker with a gold flower hanging from it, a tiny diamond in the flower's chalice.

"Be careful wearing that," Sammy advised dryly. "If someone sees you, they might chop your head off to get it." For altogether different reasons, both girls had been very restless of late. After her visit to Irina's room, it took Anna some time to remember where she'd seen the woman with the spread logo. In fact, it was only after substituting the word "nude" with the words "the woman with the spread legs" in her mind that she had remembered Lenny holding it. But why would Irina be copying Lenny's drawing?

After comparing the first drawing to the rest of the stack, Anna concluded that there was definitely a difference between them: the paper of the former was yellowed, as if aged, the ink slightly faded. She also noticed a tiny scribble on the bottom right-hand corner, like someone's initials. She couldn't make out the letters, but the writing definitely wasn't Irina's. There was only one logical conclusion: the piece on top of the stack *was* Lenny's! It was possible that he had lent it to her, so she could use it as a model, but that seemed unlikely. She could have just as easily

practiced at his place, where she spent most of her time. No, it was Irina who had taken the drawing and hidden it in her drawer.

Anna had spent the week before Christmas in a state of extreme agitation, plotting scenario after scenario, and picturing the scene at Lenny's party with all the guests gathered around the Christmas tree, where, at the first gap in conversation, she'd ask him to show her the Egon Schiele nude. And they'd walk up to it together with a few other interested people and, facing the drawing, she'd examine it closely, which would force him to do the same, and then she'd say, "Funny, it looks so fresh, as if it was done yesterday." And Lenny would ask her what she meant by that, and she'd say, "Why, look at the paper and ink." And he'd begin to frown and notice that, indeed, the paper was slightly different, the ink slightly brighter, and a few other details weren't quite right. Then, she'd say something like, "Unless this isn't the *real* drawing, and the *real* drawing is in Irina's drawer." At which point, everybody would look at Irina with their mouths agape, and Irina would change colors and, eventually, Lenny would put two and two together. And then, there, in front of everybody, Irina would have to confess her misdeed. She'd cry and ask for forgiveness, but Lenny would turn his back on her, disgusted. Irina would be so disgraced that she and her idiot mother would have no choice but to return to Russia or Ukraine—or whatever country they came from.

But at Christmas, when Anna had found herself with Lenny and his guests before the drawing, she realized that she wouldn't be able to do it, not there, in front of everybody. There was Sammy to consider: she had a hunch that her father wouldn't be too pleased to have their family drawn into the center of a scandal in front of two hundred strangers. The New Year's party would be better, since it would be an intimate gathering of close friends and neighbors.

As for Irina, her week had been stressful because she'd come to the full realization that she was over Vadim, and regretted the substitution of the drawing to such a degree that she was considering returning the original. Sometimes she imagined telling Lenny, claiming she'd done it as a joke, but somehow, she doubted he'd find it very funny. There had been a few stomach-churning moments at the Christmas party, when she thought all was lost. When the leggy blond from Totem Gallery had showed up next to Lenny out of the blue, and—upon their introduction—spilled the beans about their previous meeting, Irina had panicked. At that very moment, however—and this was truly divine intervention—someone had called Lenny. The other instance that had given her pause was when Anna, that devious she-snake with a hidden agenda and the brain of a starved mouse, took Lenny aside and walked him over to the "Schiele" drawing, where they spent five endless minutes chatting and examining it. Might she suspect something?

A few times, Irina considered confessing to her mother, but lately, Tania seemed preoccupied with problems of her own—Bill, no doubt, and the possible arrival of Seryozha and Maria. December thirty-first came, and Tania, who was the hostess, was beside herself as she raced to put the finishing touches on the party.

# Tania and Sammy

It was around December first— after a discussion with Lenny about his Christmas party, during which she had offered to do some of the cooking—that Tania first knew she was going to host the New Year's party. Lenny had refused, explaining that she couldn't possibly cook for two hundred people, that he always used caterers, and preferred it that way. Seeing how hard she took this, he proposed, as a conciliatory compromise, that she host the New Year's party.

And so, almost a month in advance, Tania began to make plans, gather recipes, call friends back home about the best way to cook this or that dish, rearrange the furniture, and imagine what she was going to wear. By December thirty-first not just Sammy's fridge, but also Bill's, was crammed with pots and bowls filled to the brim. There were only a few guests—Bill, Todd, Lenny, Theo and Michelle (Bill's ex-wife and Todd's mother)— but she felt that this was a test she must pass with flying colors,

as both her future and Irina's depended on it. She'd learned the expression "to pass with flying colors" from Irina when, having asked her about her end-of-semester tests, Irina's answer was, "Passed with flying colors." Tania, who was not familiar with the expression, had imagined colors flying all over, which inspired her to hang colored paper and golden tassels throughout the house. Sammy had watched wordlessly, occasionally coughing dryly and scratching his head. Another reason for Tania's zeal was her desire to deal a blow to both her rivals, Anna and Michelle. Although Bill never talked about Michelle, his announcement that she'd spend the winter holidays with them, and that Tania would have to invite her, too, made her wonder whether Michelle was behind Bill's recent coldness.

At 7 PM Tania was in her room, putting on the gold-and-diamond necklace she'd selected, and trying to come up with a way of convincing Sammy to let her keep it after the party was over. She was wearing a dark green, beaded dress that closely followed the curvaceous shape of her body, and high-heeled patent leather shoes with black nylon stockings. Under different circumstances, she would have been extremely pleased with what she saw in the mirror, but at that moment she was too stressed out. She'd made the decision to give Bill an ultimatum: if he misbehaved tonight, that was it! She wasn't sure exactly what *it* was, but she knew that tonight was a turning point. Like most East Europeans, she attached a supernatural power to the last night of the year, endowing it with a symbolism that was supposed to be a reflection and a foretelling of the year to come.

"Dressed to kill and ready to rock," as Irina (who collected expressions she considered "awesome") put it when they crossed paths in the hall, Tania went to the kitchen to perform a last check on the dishes: stuffed peppers and cabbage rolls, potato dumplings with white sauce, pig's feet in aspic (kept in

THE WIFE WHO WASN'T

the fridge until the last minute), poppyseed cake, walnut cake, and honey cake. Covered with cloth napkins and wrapped in fragrant slumber, sleeping the sleep of the innocent before being sliced, the cakes were set next to one another on a shelf in the pantry. Even Sammy had been seduced by their insidious aroma, tiptoeing around with his nose in the air, but Tania had been unmoved. "No cake before dinner!" She had even slapped him on the wrist with a wooden spoon, causing him to retreat from the kitchen, mumbling and red-faced. The homey feeling given off by the wafting aroma of vanilla and powdered sugar made Sammy think that maybe marrying her hadn't been such a bad idea. After months of regret, self-questioning, and doubt, he was little by little coming to terms with Tania's and Irina's presence in his life. In a strange way, since Irina started dating Lenny, he'd begun to feel more fatherly toward her. Deep down he felt, of course, that there was something . . . well . . . offensive about the relationship, especially taking into account the age difference. But in the end, he wasn't displeased with its unexpected development, though he couldn't quite explain why: maybe because he'd hoped that Lenny's proximity would have a civilizing influence on the girl; this, in spite of Lenny's own uncivilized tendencies, with which he was well acquainted.

Now, peeking through the window after the bell had rung, it was with a feeling of intense domestic pleasure that he noted the arrival of their first guest, who stood before the door with two bottles of wine whose necks showed indiscreetly from a brown bag.

# Lenny

Lenny entered, bringing with him a damp, December chill that made the house's warmth even cozier. He offered Sammy the two bottles he'd brought with him, and took a seat on the couch facing the fireplace. Sammy studied the labels, seemed pleased, smiled and, manipulating one expertly, explained that the girls would be down soon. Eavesdropping from the kitchen, Tania wondered whether she was included in "the girls," and recalled how annoyed she used to be whenever Seryozha called them—Irina, Olga and herself—"geese," or some variation on the word: "chicks," "little geese," "dodos," depending on how he felt at any particular moment. "Geese, enough twittering! Less talk and more work! When's dinner?" It was impossible to imagine Sammy calling her a "dodo"—just the thought of it made her smile. In fact, had he known about Seryozha's habit, he probably would have been indignant.

She entered the living room and was greeted by Lenny, who leapt off the couch where he'd been spread out like a retired oligarch, and kissed her cheeks.

"You look smashing," he said admiringly, eyes open wide. "Now I know where Irina gets her good looks from."

Lenny, who'd never thought much of Tania's looks, was being only half-sincere, but he was in such a good mood— spending New Year's eve with his girlfriend and her family— that he wanted to spread the joy; and so it was with only his sincere half that he complimented his lover's mother, who became so excited that she forgot to act like a mother. "You, naughty boy," she gushed, waving an index finger to admonish him and swinging her hips in a way that reminded him of Irina. Had Sammy not been there, he would have laughed and played along, seeing no harm in an innocent flirtation. But he could sense that Sammy had stiffened, and was definitely not smiling. Embarrassed, Lenny took a sip of wine to avoid having to speak, while Sammy offered Tania a glass and a cold stare. Tania looked through Sammy as if through nothing, then smiled again at Lenny and toasted. "To Love!" Lenny raised his glass, and at that moment, Irina walked in.

# Bill and Michelle

The flames licked at the logs cheerfully, and the two tables that had been placed end to end by Tania were now covered with white cotton tablecloths and the Goldsteins' plates and silverware, which silently captured the fire's interplay of shadow and light. The four adults sipped at their wine with relish and abandon, feeling so comfortable and at peace that, when the bell rang again, they were a little disappointed to be disturbed. But the feeling only lasted a few seconds—after all, they were expecting more guests, and had gathered there to have some fun, not to fall asleep by the fire.

When the two new guests made their appearance, both tall, slim and graceful, he in an elegant gray suit, she in a colorful dress that swept the floor, with heavy, oblong jewelry—plastic or polished wood (it was hard to tell in the dim light)—Tania wondered who'd invited them. It took her a couple of seconds to recognize Bill, who always wore jeans and shirts with rolled-up

sleeves, in the respectable gentleman standing before her. The woman, of course, was his ex, Michelle. Tania hated her from the instant she laid eyes on her. She hated her height, her self-assurance, her ridiculous, bohemian outfit—her very existence. It's not that she had any reason to be jealous—the woman *did* look her age, after all: her dark blondish hair, which reached down to her waist, was layered with gray streaks, and her tanned, bony face had wrinkles around the eyes and the mouth. But to see her next to Bill, shoulder to shoulder (they were the same height), as if she belonged there, as if she was standing in her rightful place—*that* was unbearable. Tania forced herself to produce an American smile, but after that display of compulsory civility she disappeared into the kitchen under the pretext of domestic activity. There, she took a deep breath and assessed the situation: in spite of Bill's assurances that Michelle was visiting only to see Todd, she couldn't help but take the woman's presence as a personal insult. And, although she thought her ridiculous, dressed as if for Halloween and not a New Year's party with respectable people, she also thought she seemed dangerous. One might even say she was good-looking—that is, if one went for that kind of thing.

Tania returned to the living room with her hands full of dishes that she laid on the two tables, resolved to proceed cautiously and not let her emotions get the best of her. Better to take it slow, see what the woman was up to and not make any hasty mistakes that might cost her later.

As the three men chatted with the amiable casualness of old friends, Irina and Michelle offered to help Tania bring in the dishes. Thus, while moving back and forth between the living room and the kitchen, Tania learned that Michelle lived in Mendocino (a small town in Northern California) and was "a farmer."

"A farmer?" Tania almost dropped the platter she was carrying. "You mean, like a peasant who raises animals and works in the fields?"

"Not quite. I mostly just grow a lot of pot."

Now, if Tania had heard the above statement a year earlier, she would have been very confused—pot?! As in pots and pans? Maybe she was one of those Gypsies who specialized in aluminum cookware—but she'd learned a few things, and to show off her knowledge, she said, "I see. Do you smoke it, or you just sell it?"

"I smoke some of it, but most of it I sell."

A peasant *and* a drug dealer! Only America could invent such an . . . what was the word Irina had used the other day? Something about two opposites wrapped in one. Omni-moron?

Try as she might, Tania couldn't banish the primal scene that had marked her first encounter with pot, when Bill had offered her a cigarette at Lenny's party. She realized, with a pang of pain, that it was the first time they'd met, so pot tied them together in its poisonous, criminal embrace. How long ago that seemed, and how old she'd grown since! Her eyes filled with tears, and the tears filled her with resentment. She wasn't going to cry in front of these people! She wasn't going to cry because of some peasant dressed like a Gypsy, and a man with a name like Bill! Bill, what kind of name was that? It made her think of dollar bills and billiards.

Defiantly, Tania straightened her body and decided that her best means of revenge against Michelle was her most secret weapon: cooking. Michelle was most certainly a mediocre cook. Just look at her. All Tania had to do was show everybody what a great chef she was. She invited everybody to sit down and help themselves, but someone remarked that Theo and Todd—who had offered to pick up Theo—hadn't arrived yet, and they couldn't start without them.

"Nonsense," said Tania. "I know you're all starved. When they get here, they'll join us."

It was true that they were starved, so no one objected, and while they chewed their first bites—pigs' feet in aspic with potato dumplings—Tania scrutinized the expression on Michelle's face with a surgeon's eye. Cautiously, Michelle spooned a glob of aspic onto her plate and poked at it to test its consistency. After reluctantly placing a small bite of the translucent, gelatinous texture on her tongue, she suddenly changed color and brought her napkin to her mouth. Of all possible reactions, *this* was something Tania hadn't anticipated. The bitch was pretending to be disgusted. Or maybe she was suggesting the food was spoiled. The nerve! Before anyone had time to speak, Tania opened her mouth preemptively. "I'm sorry to say I can't give you the recipe for the aspic. It was given to me by a famous Russian chef who swore me to secrecy."

"Oh, c'mon Mother," interjected Irina, who was torn between laughing at the faces their guests were making and feeling sorry for Lenny. "Since when is Grandma a famous Russian chef?"

"I can see that four months of America have done their work. You've become a spoiled, ungrateful brat."

"Sometimes the truth needs the mouth of an ungrateful brat in order to be spoken."

The conversation would have certainly taken a dangerous turn had Todd and Theo not entered at that very moment. Todd, who had volunteered for the role of DJ, was carrying the speakers, closely followed by Theo with some auxiliary electronic equipment. A whiff of night and cold trailed in after them, but they were both in good spirits, laughing at some previously shared joke.

"Wake up, guys! The fun is about to start."

Todd put his burden down and inquired, "Where's Anna?"

# Anna and Bill

*11 PM*

Todd stepped back from Anna, with whom he'd been dancing for the past ten minutes, and retook his position in the dark nook from where he surveyed the musical equipment and directed the "special effects"—throbbing flashes of purple and yellow light that landed among, and mingled with, the dancers. The living room had been cleared of tables, and the chairs were lined up in a row against the back wall. The lights were off, but in the intimate darkness, one could make out the dancing couples moving slowly to a blues rhythm in the flickers of intermittent light: one couple young and one old. Left by herself, Anna took a seat and watched. At first, both couples, then, after a while, only the younger of the two. She watched the young woman swing her hips, laugh with her mouth open, whisper in her partner's ear and kiss him on the lips. The two had been dancing since dinner ended, oblivious to the others, enclosed in their selfish cocoon of happiness. The others had watched them for a while, envious, then Todd had invited Anna to dance, and

Sammy, Michelle. For a moment, Tania's heart had climbed into her throat, but, when she turned to face Bill, he had already disappeared. She went after him, catching up just in time to see the bathroom door close in her face.

At the end of that first dance, Sammy had walked up to Tania, while Michelle took Theo's hand and began to teach him some funny, presumably once fashionable steps. Initially, Tania couldn't understand what Sammy wanted, and, when she realized that he was asking her to dance, she answered—irritated—that she had things to do in the kitchen; but she kept standing there, waiting for Bill. Taken aback, Sammy went to the kitchen, where he was soon followed by Tania. From there, it would be easier to notice when Bill came out of the bathroom, which was at one end of the long hall, while the kitchen was at the other. Tania stuck her neck out to check every other minute, not caring if Sammy saw her; in fact, she wanted him to see—he, who never saw anything, content to live inside his own head.

By eleven, Tania had almost given up, assuming that Bill had managed to find a way to escape unnoticed. All she could think of was a pretext to go fetch him. In the living room, Michelle and Theo were dancing slowly while Irina and Lenny teased each other nearby, now moving a few steps, now pausing for another playful kiss. On a chair, brow furrowed, face dark as the room itself, sat Anna. Yet, for the man who stood in the doorway, gazing at her with an intensity spawned by years of loneliness and sexual deprivation—not to mention twenty minutes spent in a cold, black-marbled bathroom—she was light itself. Her body exuded the calm luminosity of self-sufficient things, while her head, bent in concentration, spoke of a maturity that made her all the more mysterious.

When Anna raised her forehead, she saw a hand extended toward her, and a tall male body at the end of which she recognized

Bill's face; she accepted the invitation, happy to be rescued from her state of maidenly expectation. Bill would never recall the music they danced to: the only thing that existed in those five or ten minutes was Anna's body against his, a body that was both exquisitely alive, therefore heavy, and uncannily irreal, therefore light. In the meantime, the two other couples had stopped dancing and were seated. Irina was whispering something in Lenny's ear, while Michelle and Theo carried on a lively conversation, of which the others could make out only bits and pieces:

"One must always be cautious . . ."

"even when . . ."

"two grandchildren, but . . ."

"but is life really worth living if . . ."

"not much, especially . . ."

"Pinot Noir, although . . ."

"still alone, after all these years . . ."

"and are you . . ."

The music ended and someone turned on the lights. The sudden burst of light blinded everyone, and they blinked, adjusting their eyes. This is why not all those present saw Tania advance with a stern look toward Bill and slap him, hard. But everybody heard the slap and turned their faces in its direction as if watching a tennis match. Behind Bill the wall clock showed 11:09.

# Tania, Anna, and Irina

"You call this *theft*? In this case, our worldviews are
totally opposed."
—Ostap Bender in Ilf and Petrov's *The Golden Calf*

*11:10 PM*

Sammy returned from the kitchen to find a stunned audience in
his living room.

"What happened here?" (Sammy)

"We don't need perverts in this house." (Tania)

"And no adulterers either." (Bill)

"They were just dancing." (Michelle)

"Of course, if you're a drug dealer, no perversion is going
to impress *you*!" (Tania)

"I'm sure it's your high moral standards that make you so
easily upset." (Anna)

"Anna!" (Sammy)

"No, let's all hear what she has to say! Let's hear what this innocent child with the eyes of the Madonna and the evil ways of a Delilah has to tell us about 'moral standards'! *She* should know!" (Tania)

"What are you implying?" (Sammy)

"Take that back!" (Bill)

"I will not!" (Tania)

"Take it back, or I'll . . ." (Bill)

"Or you'll what?" (Tania)

"Drop it, Mother, let Anna play with her toys!" (Irina)

"At least when I play with someone else's toys, I remember to put them back where I got them." (Anna)

"What in hell is that supposed to mean?" (Irina)

"Oh, nothing. Just that you've borrowed a very expensive toy from someone, and if you had your mother's high moral standards, you'd return it." (Anna)

"Don't push your luck, you . . . *alternative* Mother Teresa! Mother Teresa with a libido!" (Irina)

"Aren't you curious to know what toy I'm talking about? Or is it just that you don't want the others to find out?" (Anna)

"I said, don't push your luck! I'm the daughter of a Russian slut and a Romanian drunk, and you have no idea what I'm capable of." (Irina)

"Anna, what are you talking about? If you have something to say, then say it." (Lenny)

"Very well, then. I'll tell you, but first I have to show you, otherwise you won't believe me." (Anna)

Anna started toward the door, but Irina blocked her passage and held her arm.

"You aren't going anywhere!"

"Let her go!" (Lenny, menacing frown)

Anna left, and returned in less than a minute, a gray folder in her hand.

"It's in here. I'm sure you'll recognize it."

She opened the folder and passed it to Lenny. The audience's gaze moved from Irina to Anna to Lenny, who was holding a piece of paper with something drawn on it. Increasingly incredulous, Lenny stared at the paper, and finally, asked both girls:

"How'd my Egon Schiele get in here?"

"I think you should ask *her*."

Lenny turned to face Irina, but before their eyes met, Irina let out a shriek and lunged forward, cursing in Russian and throwing punches in the air, which, thanks to Bill and Sammy, failed to reach Anna. Only Lenny stood still, staring at Irina.

"I never want to see you again," he said, tucking the folder under his arm, and walked out the door.

# Irina and Tania

*Midnight*

Outside, firecrackers popped in wreaths of light that crisscrossed the sky. Inside, the unexpected sound of a champagne cork startled everybody. Seeing Theo with an open bottle in his hand and an apologetic smile on his face—"I'm sorry to interrupt the drama, but still, it's the New Year"—everybody relaxed and reached for a glass. Everybody save for Irina, who had rushed into the darkness after Lenny's car, and Tania, who had slipped away in the confusion caused by Irina's attack. They clinked their glasses and kissed each other on the cheeks, breathing a collective sigh of relief, as if they had escaped some mortal danger.

"The cakes," Sammy suddenly remembered. "We still haven't had dessert, and she's made these fabulous cakes." He dashed to the pantry and returned with two platters full of walnut cake, poppyseed cake, and honey cake. The atmosphere warmed up, tongues loosened, and Todd even attempted a few jokes.

As our six cake eaters abandoned themselves with such primal delight to gastronomic pleasures, Irina was nearing Lenny's house. She had walked briskly in the cool night air, and was breathing heavily—a mist balloon suspended from her parted lips. She paused to catch her breath, then started again, taking longer and longer steps, until, at last, she found herself on Lenny's doorstep. She had not given herself time to think, because she knew that, if she did, she would turn back. She knocked, and, when no one answered, she pleaded, "Lenny, open the door! Please open the door!" She heard her own voice as if coming from someone else's mouth, and, with a jab of annoyance, realized that she sounded like her mother. The lights in the house were on, though, and she wouldn't give up. "Lenny, please. We need to talk!"

The door opened a crack, and Lenny appeared just long enough to say, "You should be glad I didn't call the police. If you don't leave right now, I will." Then, the door slammed in her face, and she stood there, trying to connect the sound of the closed door to her life. After a few seconds of perplexed silence, she moved away from the door and sat down on a rock, her mind like a buzzing beehive, thoughts escaping in all directions, as she struggled to pull them into a single thread of unified sound. She sat there for a long time, fifteen, twenty minutes— maybe more—and when she got up, her mind had quieted down, reduced to a single persistent thought: he was going to pay! If he could get rid of her just like that, without giving her a chance to explain herself—if the words of that . . . that pathetic little bitch counted for more than hers—then so be it! She felt a rush of energy pushing her body onward, and, clinging to the invisible thread in her mind, advanced in the direction of the shed. There, she undid the latch, opened the door, and fumbled through the

thick darkness until her fingers grabbed the gasoline can. She emptied its contents with slow deliberation, first, circling the shed, then, walking up to the house, its path lined by rows of cacti and shrubs. The liquid, soaked up by the earth in places, and gleaming in the moonlight on the stone slabs, infused the night with an acrid smell that made her dizzier than she already was. The can was small, so, by the time she got to the house it was already empty. She dropped the can and returned to the shed where she knew she would find matches, struck one and threw it onto the wet trail.

She did not look back.

She ran, suddenly afraid. For some reason, she thought that there would be an explosion, but the night remained as impenetrably quiet as before. Halfway between Lenny's and Sammy's houses she stopped to catch her breath. It seemed strange to go back now, so she changed direction, and set course for Bill's house. She walked with determined steps, eyes fixed on the ground, and, when she raised them, she spotted a figure sitting by the road, bathed in pulsing rays of moonlight. For a second, she thought she'd walked too far—had arrived at Theo's, and the black shadow with a golden glaze was one of his sculptures, but when she got closer, she saw that its head moved. Neither afraid nor curious, she continued to walk, following the same inner thread that had led her to empty the can. In the viscous darkness that was intermittently interrupted by pale moonbeams, it was only when she was a few feet away from the shadow that she recognized her mother.

"What are *you* doing here?"

Tania shrugged and offered her a cigarette.

Irina sat down on the boulder next to her mother, and lit her cigarette with the tip of her mother's. They sat in silence for some time—time had turned into a foreign substance, and

it was hard to tell how long it lasted and how it stretched—then Tania began to talk.

She had left the house during the altercation between Anna and Irina, and had walked, full of vengeful rage, to Bill's place. She had no plan in mind, all she had was her anger, but when she saw the ax resting by the woodpile some twenty feet from the house, she grabbed it without even thinking. *She* wasn't thinking, but her hands must have been, because her hands put that ax against every single window with all the venom they had accumulated over the past several months. But the material the windows were made of must have been some fancy American shit, not Russian crap, because it took her a lot of effort to break it, and even when she managed to, she was only able to break it in two places, and to make a few cracks here and there. She hit the glass and yelled, until she got tired, and then she began to weep.

They sat together on that rock, mother and daughter, in the cold American night, and when they got up, they knew what they had to do.

# Everybody minus Tania and Irina

*1:00 AM–4:30 AM*

It was Todd who first saw the fire: an orange dot suspended in the dark that rapidly morphed into a fireball. They called Lenny, who didn't answer, then they got in Sammy and Bill's cars and drove there, bringing buckets with them. By the time they arrived, the shed was unapproachable—a reddish conflagration writhing in painful anger, from which a second fire moved in a straight line toward the house. A hose in each hand, Lenny struggled to stop the red invasion, and the others hurried to join him. For a while, the flames seemed to be retreating or diminishing, but then the shed collapsed with a long, drawn-out sigh, and red splinters sprang in all directions, starting new fires and feeding the old, tired ones. It wasn't until after two o'clock that the fire truck arrived, having found its way with difficulty on the narrow, meandering road into the hills. A few minutes later and it would have been too late, as the flames were lifting their hissing mouths to the sideboards of the house. Luckily, the surrounding vegetation wasn't tall,

and the only tree was some distance away, fire still sniffing at its roots. By three, disaster had been averted, though the fire still smoldered here and there, and what remained of the shed shuddered in the torment of its last, crackling gasps. Only the firefighters continued to work, everyone else rested, exhausted, either sitting on rocks or standing, drinking water or beers Lenny had brought out. They left a little after three-thirty, agreeing to reconvene at Sammy's.

They entered the house like miners after a day's work, and hurried to the bathroom and kitchen to wash the soot from their hands and darkened faces. At Sammy's request, Anna made coffee, a little nervous since it was the first time she was making it for anyone other than herself, and while she busied herself in the kitchen, she heard her father's anxious voice, "Has anyone seen Tania?"

Two minutes later he emerged from his bedroom:

"She took all the jewelry from the safe."

"Have you checked her bedroom?" asked Bill. "Are her clothes still there?"

"Some are, but most are gone. Same for Irina's."

Bill, Anna, and Todd exchanged tired, predawn looks, as Sammy grabbed his coffee mug, spooned some sugar into it, and kissed Anna on the cheeks. "Good coffee. Thanks." Suddenly calm, he took a sip, and said, "They must have taken a taxi."

"Aren't you gonna call the police?" asked Theo.

"What for? So I have to go down to the station and bail them out?"

"What about Lenny? Did he call the police?"

Sammy shook his head: no.

"Why not?"

"Because. He got his drawing back."

"But the fire . . ."

"Let's just enjoy this cup of coffee in peace," said Sammy. "It's getting cold and there's nothing worse than cold coffee."

"I can think of a lot worse things than cold coffee," Theo pressed on. "Like having your house burn down."

"Theo," chimed in Bill, "drink your coffee and shut up."

They fell silent, and for a while only the liquid darkness of sipped coffee could be heard. Then, a muffled sound came from Sammy, and when they looked at him, he was chuckling like a schoolboy.

"Are you OK?" Bill put one arm tenderly around him.

More chuckles, followed by a sonorous burst of laughter. "It's so funny," managed Sammy, when, finally, he could speak. "I lost all my family's jewelry, and I could be sued by my neighbor for property damage, but I think it might be worth it. I'm a free man!"

Bill and Anna attempted a smile, but Theo and Michelle looked at him reprovingly.

"I don't think it's funny," Michelle said.

"That's because you didn't know Tania," Bill replied.

Calming down, Sammy noticed that Todd had fallen asleep on the living room rug, and proposed that they all get some sleep for a couple of hours. Michelle could sleep on the couch, Theo and Bill would take the armchairs, and Anna could go to her room.

"I'll lie next to Todd," she said.

As for himself, he wasn't sleepy, and was planning to do some chores around the house. Indeed, his body felt strangely energized and, as soon as the others went to sleep, he entered Tania's room and began to pull her clothes from the hangers. He then folded them and placed them inside a suitcase, which he took down to the basement. Next came the drawers. With every little thing he disposed of, his chest felt lighter, and as he walked around the house, his feet grew wings that carried him along, singing to him, "I'm-a-free-man, I'm-a-free-man."

# S & M

Dawn caught Sammy asleep with his head on the kitchen table. A cold sun—what in Moldova they call "a sun with teeth"—strove to pierce through the bluish morning fog, claiming victory here and there when a ray managed to clear the fog for a few brief minutes. In the living room, Theo stretched his limbs, mumbling to himself, "Jesus, what a night! What a night." Bill, who had just woken up, looked around with a stupefied expression until his gaze fell on Todd and Anna lying on the floor, she with her head on his shoulder, he with an arm around her waist. After the night they'd been through, he thought that there was something touchingly pure about that scene, and he sat there for some time, watching them. But, when Theo got up, he decided to follow him into the kitchen.

"Coffee?" asked Sammy, and, without waiting for an answer, began to prepare a pot.

"I should go," said Theo.

"I'll give you a ride," offered Bill, "but let's have coffee first."

Soon, the aroma of the coffee spread throughout the house, and Todd and Anna could be heard talking softly in the living room, the sun having dispersed the fog at last. The New Year had brought with it a touching domesticity and, as everybody listened to that quiet breath of normality, the engine of a car purred down the road and into the driveway. They looked at each other with raised eyebrows: who could it be at this hour, on the first day of the year?

"I'll go see," said Sammy.

He left, praying (to No One, for such is the lot of the atheist), *Anyone, let it be anyone but them, please!* Outside, squinting in the already bright sun, he spotted a candy-pink limo that filled the whole driveway, from which emerged, a few seconds later, a man in a white linen suit wearing a white fedora and white shoes, followed by a dark-haired woman in a red dress and red patent-leather shoes. He was sure he'd never seen the woman before, but the man looked vaguely familiar. He'd seen that mustache somewhere. The limo driver extracted two large pieces of luggage from the trunk, and the **man in white searched** for something in his pockets. He took out some bills and put them in the man's hand, but in the end it wasn't enough, and the man in white looked around until his gaze landed on Sammy. His face lit up, and he waved to him energetically.

"Hey, I need ten dollars," he screeched in a thick Russian accent.

Maybe God—or his evil twin, the Devil—did exist, after all. What else could explain such a joke of cosmic proportions? Sammy advanced slowly, as if in a trance. When they were close enough, the man kissed him on the cheeks, patted him vigorously on the back, then turned toward the woman.

"May I introduce you to my wife, Maria?"

# Part IV
## Santa Barbara and Chișinău
### 1998–1999

# Seryozha

**B**ill, Theo, Michelle, Todd, and Anna sat at the dining table that faced the French doors to the back of the house, sipping coffee and throwing empty morning looks around the room when the front door opened and Sammy entered followed by a man in a white suit and a woman in red. The friends put their cups down and stared at Sammy.

"I have the pleasure of introducing my brother-in-law, Seryozha, and his wife, Maria," declared Sammy with uncharacteristic jovialness.

There was a long silence, after which Bill burst out laughing. He pointed at the two newcomers, shaking with laughter. "Brother-in-law," he repeated. "Wife," as if he'd never heard anything funnier. After Bill calmed down, Seryozha interjected in his Russian-inflected English:

"Say, is there something wrong with the weather? Or are you Americans using propaganda even when it comes to the temperature? I had this suit custom-made for California, and here I am, freezing my balls off—pardon my English."

"It's January," they replied.

"So what? It's California."

"But it's January."

"I told you," Maria said reproachfully in barely comprehensible English, then added something in Russian.

"Women always know," Bill said, winking in Seryozha's direction and getting up. Todd, Theo, and Michelle followed suit, and they all left—Bill alone, the rest in Todd's car.

After the guests' departure, Seryozha rubbed his palms together with an air of contentment.

"And where are my dear sister and niece hiding? Still in bed? Too much vodka at the party last night?"

Anna who, until then, hadn't uttered a word but had watched the couple with a long, unsmiling face, replied:

"Tania and Irina aren't here. They left like a couple of . . ."

"Not now, dear," interrupted Sammy. Then, turning to Seryozha and Maria, he said:

"It's a long story. You should probably rest first."

He gave them Tania's room, as if to make sure there would be no place for her to come back to, and rushed to answer the phone. It was Bill.

"You have to see this," said Bill, his voice betraying an unusual degree of agitation. When did he have time to get drunk again? Sammy wondered, but he agreed to come over.

When his car pulled up the driveway and he saw the broken windows, he grew frightened. Were there other surprises left in store for him by the two women? Guided by Bill, he took a tour of the wounded house, and immediately offered to compensate him for the damage. Bill refused flat out. He kept searching Sammy's face for accusatory signs, convinced that Tania's behavior must have aroused suspicion, even in an unsuspicious man like him. Yet Sammy acted as friendly as ever, even friendlier, given that he considered himself partly responsible for the damage, as

husband to the guilty party. Did he think that Tania had acted the way she had because she was flat-out crazy, or did he simply not care that she'd had an affair with his best friend? And if he didn't care about her having the affair, what did he think about him, Bill? Bill would have very much liked to have an answer to these questions, but lacked the courage to ask them.

"Don't worry, I was planning on changing the windows anyhow," he lied. "I'm sick of the mirror effect. I'm getting smoked glass." And then: "Let's have a drink."

"I can't. I have to figure out what I'm going to do with my new Russians."

"The new Russians, right. Well, when it rains it pours."

"What do you mean?"

"I'm sure your mother-in-law will show up any day now. I mean, what's she going to do there, all by herself?"

"Hey, that's not funny! Anyway, Seryozha and Maria are just visiting."

"Are you sure?"

"Sure I'm sure."

Sammy was right, it wasn't funny, and it became even less so when Sammy explained to the new Russians (actually—it turned out—only one Russian, since Maria was Romanian) the reason for Tania and Irina's sudden departure. Seryozha eyed him suspiciously, as if Sammy were responsible for the disappearance of the two women, and launched into an accusatory tirade.

"Are you telling me that my sister and my niece, two women who've never hurt anyone, have attempted to destroy two people's houses? Women who . . . who . . ."

Seeing that he needed help, Maria, who never missed an opportunity to use a Romanian expression, added sarcastically, "Were as good as God's bread."

"Two women as good as God's bread," Seryozha repeated. "I find your story hard to believe, but if it's indeed true, something must have happened to push them over the edge. *Someone* must have pushed them over the edge." With these words, Seryozha eyed Sammy with the diffidence he'd seen on Inspector Clouseau's face when, mustache trembling, Clouseau unveiled the last piece of the puzzle and all the pieces came together.

Later, when Seryozha and Maria were alone, she convinced him that not only was it unwise to make an enemy of Sammy, who was their only means of survival, but that he (Seryozha) should drop any silliness about "calling the police," a threat he kept repeating, puffing up his chest and pacing back and forth, "like a bozo drunk on his own (questionable) self-importance" (Maria's words). If they wanted to stay in the States, it was definitely not in their interest to alert the police, was it? Well, he had to admit that she was right about that, he knew he'd married "a smart chick," he noted proudly, and kissed her behind the ear. Maria wiped off her ear with an impatient brush of her fingertips.

"If I were you, I'd try to find out more about both men—Bill and Lenny—and figure out what really happened with Tania and Irina. You can be sure that Sammy hasn't told us the whole story."

Congratulating himself once again on having married such a smart little woman, Seryozha asked Sammy to take him to Bill's so he could see the damage with his own eyes. But, once there, he seemed to forget the purpose of his visit, and got lost in intense esthetic contemplation—whistling, producing interjections, and winking at Bill to signal his admiration for such a magnificent abode (his reaction upon his arrival at Sammy's had been seriously compromised by his exhaustion).

"Nice hut you got yourself here," he told Bill, though what he said sounded more like *"nicehootyewgut."*

Judging from the wink that it must have been some kind of joke, and having no idea what it meant, Bill laughed loudly and winked back. Sammy had left him alone with the mustachioed Russian, and he wasn't sure what was expected of him. As always in such circumstances—or in any circumstance, really—he thought that Scotch or whiskey might help, so he invited the man into the living room, where the whistling reached a climactic pitch. *Why would Tania want to destroy this?* Seryozha wondered. The poor woman must have lost her mind after being blessed with so much, and turned into one of those people who win the lottery and whose lives, after having been focused on this one goal like an arrow aimed at a target, fall into disarray once the target has been hit.

As if to prove him right, at that very moment Bill opened a cabinet at that very moment, and the image that unfolded before Seryozha's eyes would become the Eden he would return to time and time again in the years to come: staring at Seryozha with the calm radiance of the inhabitants of a Promised Land were about two dozen bottles of the most varied shapes and sizes—round, oval, elongated, square, striated or smooth, with inviting labels whose restrained colors (white, red, and black) suggested that they were guardians of highly refined contents, ranging from pale amber, to reddish and dark brown.

As he sank into a deep leather armchair with his Scotch on the rocks in his right hand—*These American bastards, the more they have, the stingier they are! Imagine diluting such a divine drink with ice!*—Seryozha knew that he'd finally found his life's purpose. To be the owner of such a cabinet and such a chair—what more could one want? Hell, he wouldn't mind spending his entire life in that chair, drinking that Scotch.

When Bill refilled his glass, Seryozha relaxed a little and asked, with a coy smile:

"So, you and my sister . . ."

Pretending he didn't understand, Bill stared at his glass.

Seryozha finished his drink, asked for another refill, and said:

"Hey, you can trust me. I'm her brother."

Bill refilled both Seryozha's and his own glass and attempted to change the subject:

"You and your wife . . ." He left the sentence suspended in midair, in a sort of syntactical brotherhood with his guest.

"Me and my wife, you and my sister . . ." Seryozha laughed, and Bill laughed, too, without knowing why.

Two hours later they were still laughing and had decided they had to do this again. And again. Every time they got together, they couldn't stop laughing and patting each other on the back, as if they couldn't get over the miracle of having found each other. An involuntary observer would have been stunned to see how well the two men got along despite the language barrier. But some friendships are like love: logic and reason have nothing to do with them.

"Your sister was a good woman." (Bill)

"Yes, she was . . ." (Seryozha, with a deep sigh)

"Well, I hope she still is . . . wherever she is." (Bill)

"You mean she might be . . . I've been told this country of yours is a dangerous place." (Seryozha, sinking even deeper in his armchair)

"Have you and your wife given any thought to the future?"

"Thought?! Thinking is all that woman does! Let me tell you, if there was ever a chick who could think, it's my wife! She is the chick of chicks, the queen of chickens."

Seeing his host's puzzled look, Seryozha began to flap his arms in imitation of a bird's vocal output:.

"Cluck-cluck!"

"Oh, you're thinking of raising chickens?"

"Raisinchickens? No, no! Woman-chicken!"

"You mean your wife plans to? Well, I don't blame you; I wouldn't want to raise chickens, either. And what are *your* plans?"

"*My* plans?" Seryozha pointed a finger at his own chest, surprised that anyone would be interested in his projects. "I'll tell you a secret!" Drawing closer to Bill, he whispered into his ear, "I've never been happier in my life." Then, withdrawing, he raised his voice: "My plan is: This!" And he pounded the arm of the chair, as if to establish the kind of jocular male bond a father might intend with a friendly punch to his son's arm.

Bill raised his eyebrows, while, on the same hushed tone of secrecy, as if sealing a pact between the two of them and the chair, Seryozha continued:

"I'm your friend, Bill. Forever."

The word—"forever"—rang in the room with a foreignness that awoke Bill from his reverie and convinced him to speak to Sammy. Forever? Bill had never done anything "forever," and, much as he liked his new friend, he felt he had to pull the word up by the root.

Sammy, who'd been watching their budding friendship with a jaundiced eye and was getting more restless with the passing of each day, was relieved to hear Bill's complaint. He agreed that the weed that had taken root in his friend's living room had to be pulled out. He was, however, more ambivalent about the man's wife, Maria, who seemed cut from a completely different fabric than her sister-in-law. Unsure of how to treat her, Sammy mostly avoided her and told Seryozha that they needed to have a talk, "man to man." Seryozha, who reeked of alcohol, as usual, let out a jovial "sure," and, taking a seat, looked around the room as if he'd lost something.

"What's wrong?" asked Sammy.

"Couldn't we discuss this over a glass of something?"

"You just put your finger on the crux of the problem. You see, since you arrived here you've had a lot of glasses of something, and, as much as Bill enjoys your company, he's a busy man."

"Busy with what?" interrupted Seryozha.

"He's a busy man," Sammy continued, "and you keep him from doing anything. But"— he added quickly, when Seryozha wondered aloud whether Bill had complained about him— "this is not the issue. The problem is that you . . . How should I put it? The motive of your visit is unclear. You don't really seem to care that Tania and Irina are gone, and are content to just sit around, with no concern for the future. I'm beginning to wonder what your plans are."

While Sammy delivered his speech, Seryozha kept fidgeting, and at the last word, he excused himself, walked out of the room, and returned a minute later with a half-full bottle and two glasses. He poured two fingers of the amber-colored liquid into each glass, offered one to Sammy, and, taking the other, took a good swig and smacked his lips in contentment. Sammy put his glass aside, dryly swallowed his rebuke, and waited.

"I understand your problem," Seryozha began.

"*My* problem?"

"Oh, yes! Yes, I understand. *You*" (Seryozha pointed at Sammy, squinting his eyes) "are afraid."

"Afraid?"

"Yes." Seryozha nodded.

And then, something strange happened to Seryozha's language, something that often happens to the language of adults when speaking to babies: while, until then, he'd made an effort to use English in all its problematic complexity (albeit a version of his own, with the verbs mostly in the present tense, the nouns a combination of Russian root and English suffix), now

he began to drop most articles and even some verbs, keeping his language in its essential infant purity: noun and adjective.

"You," Seryozha continued, "afraid of Russian man. But that OK. No problem. American propaganda make Russian man bad. You afraid of Russian man, no problem. But I tell you secret: not to be afraid! Russian man hard worker. For centuries Russian peasant more hard worker than American worker, although American worker too hard worker. We brothers." He placed his hand on Sammy's arm.

After several unsuccessful attempts, Sammy finally managed to get a word in edgewise: no, *this* was not his problem. He was not afraid of the Russian man, and he had no doubt that the Russian man could be a hard worker. (Well, he had his doubts, but kept those to himself.) His problem was not with the Russian man, his problem was with Seryozha.

"Well, then," Seryozha said, getting up, and miraculously recovering his linguistic abilities. "I'm sorry you can't let go of your grudge against my sister. I liked you, actually. But—no problem—I won't bother you any longer. I'll go stay with my friend, Bill."

Before Sammy could think of an answer, Seryozha walked out of the room. Half an hour later, Seryozha-fedora-and-suitcase were already outside of Bill's front door.

It wasn't Bill who answered, it was Todd.

"Hi kid," Seryozha said casually, the way he'd seen in American movies, and, without waiting to be invited in, crossed the threshold with his suitcase, walking past him into the living room.

# Sammy, Maria, Seryozha, and Bill

S eryozha and Tania differed in many ways, but they had one thing in common: whatever space they inhabited became theirs. When Bill returned home later that night, he found Seryozha asleep in the guestroom, his suitcase opened and half unpacked, a bottle of Scotch and an empty glass on the nightstand by the bed. The room was dark, but the windows had no shades, and, unhindered, a moonbeam revealed the face of a peaceful sleeper.

Meanwhile, Sammy had been unable to decide whether Seryozha's sudden departure should make him happy or worried. He opted for "cautiously happy," but then he remembered that there was also Maria to consider. Strange, he kept forgetting about her, maybe because she was rarely home, and when she was, she rendered herself almost as invisible as Tania had been obtrusive. During the first days of the new year, Michelle had taken her sightseeing and shopping, and, after Michelle left, Maria began to take long walks on her own. On the rare occasions Sammy saw her, she avoided him, and she almost never opened her mouth.

The night Seryozha left, Sammy waited for Maria to come home, then invited her into the kitchen for a talk. They sat down next to each other at the kitchen table, and under the harsh, violent light, Sammy was able to take a good look at her for the first time. She had walked for a long time in the chilly winter air, and her cheeks had taken on a rosy color; her eyes were bright and inquisitive, and Sammy was surprised to discover that she was quite attractive. This was so unexpected that, for a minute, he forgot what he'd wanted to talk about. She wasn't sexy (or at least not in the way Tania was, thank God) and there was a severe expression in her eyes, but there was something impressive, almost intimidating, about her.

It was she who asked where Seryozha was. As he tried to reproduce the conversation he'd had with Seryozha, he became aware of her unfocused gaze, and realized, suddenly, that she didn't understand a word of English. He paused and stared at her, helpless, then made a gesture with his right hand in the direction of Bill's home, which he accompanied with the words, "Seryozha . . . Bill."

"Oh," she said.

He liked the way silence settled in around her, as if it were an emanation of her long, dark hair—no, not an emanation, he corrected himself; rather, an exaltation. He took another sip of the red wine he'd been drinking, and offered her a glass, which she accepted quietly, and he himself began to feel exalted, as if a door that had long been closed, had finally opened. He started to talk, reticently at first, about Tania and Irina—about "what happened"—but the more he talked, the more encouraged he felt. The fact that she apparently understood no English had no bearing upon her ability to *understand*—he was talking to her silence and to her eyes and felt perfectly understood. You see, he told her, it was Tania's incapacity to understand that had driven

him crazy. For a year and a half, he had lived with a wall; when he spoke to Tania his words ricocheted back at him, hitting him in the head, and he had been beginning to wonder if *he* was the crazy one. And now, talking to her—to Maria—was like recovering his sanity, *Do you understand what I'm saying,* and Maria nodded her head, smiling, and he went on, clinging to the light in her eyes.

It was long past midnight when Maria excused herself and went to bed, but the scene repeated itself the following night: same actors, different bottle. He talked and asked her questions to which he gave the answers, too, and she followed his words with the same quiet smile, the same glimmer in her eyes. When he seemed anxious or in doubt, her face too borrowed his anxiety or doubt; without a word, she was there. He'd never met anyone so intensely present, had never felt so understood. Night after night, he opened up to her and night after night, she sat there like a silent mirror. At the end of the week, when he had finally run out of things to say, they went to his bedroom and took off their clothes, and he felt more understood than ever.

The very next morning Seryozha-fedora-and-suitcase were back.

He too had enjoyed a magical week, him talking, Bill mostly listening and pouring Scotch into their large crystal glasses. Seryozha explained how different life was "back there," and how much he preferred to live in America. Because words often failed him, he used hand gestures to convey to Bill the chronic lack of the most basic daily necessities under communism, such as toilet paper.

Listening, Bill had nodded along in supportive acknowledgment:

"I see," he said. "Things weren't very clean there."

"Clean?! Everybody smelled like shit. Shit was everywhere. Sometimes the water didn't run, and, for days, shit piled up in the toilet: no paper, no water, just shit."

Bill, who took two hot showers a day, sighed to show his sympathy, and they both toasted—"To water!"—downing their Scotch.

Seryozha hadn't been so happy since the days he'd spent working as a summer camp administrator, when he'd entertained his colleagues with vodka. But what a difference between the wobbling chair, like a single tooth implanted in the gaping maw of his former office with its bare, echoing walls, and Bill's enormous leather armchairs, from where their voices lazily emerged! No, this was better than anything Seryozha had ever experienced. As he spoke, his eyes grew moist with affectionate gratitude, and, when he was too worn out to speak any more English, he switched to Russian, while Bill listened, his head drooping lower and lower until, finally, he began to snore. Bill's snoring was a pleasant murmur, not the loud, disruptive wheezing of some men, but more like the rustling of a carpet of leaves over pebbles, and Seryozha let the snoring accompany his Russian-spoken monologue until he too dropped off to sleep and began to snore.

A week went by without incident, so when Bill told him out of the blue that he had to leave, Seryozha was shocked. He insisted on being given a reason, but Bill kept repeating that things couldn't go on this way and that it was probably better for him to return to Russia.

"Moldova," corrected Seryozha.

"Sorry, Moldova."

Seryozha packed his few things and, with tears in his eyes, hugged Bill. If he was ever in Chişinău, he should look him up, because *there* people were happy to receive guests, and he, for

one, would be thrilled to host him. His mother, who cooked like a goddess, would give him the royal treatment. Although they were poor folks—their entire apartment could fit inside Bill's living room—he wouldn't starve, oh no! And it wouldn't be anything fancy, potatoes, cabbage, bacon, you know, poor folks' food, but the taste, the aroma . . . Nothing like the plastic tasting dishes he'd had since being there—no offense.

"None taken," Bill replied, and, with a pat on the back, he led Seryozha out and closed the door behind him.

This is how Seryozha-fedora-and-suitcase found themselves left out in the cold in the middle of January, and, without wasting any time, they walked straight back to Sammy's.

# Seryozha and Maria

S ammy and Maria stared at the man who stood in the doorway holding a suitcase, as if they were having trouble remembering who he was. Seryozha walked in, gave Sammy a strong handshake, kissed his wife on both cheeks, and, putting his suitcase down, announced, "Pack your things. We're going back."

"You're free to go wherever you want," the wife replied. "I'm not going anywhere."

As they exchanged words in a language he didn't understand, Sammy watched them apprehensively, realizing how different the woman was from the mysterious creature he'd spent a week with. The woman's tone was harsh, and the sounds coming from her mouth had a roughness that contrasted with the reassuring tranquility he'd felt around her. It was as if an invisible hand had suddenly drawn the precise contour of a body of mist, and its mystery was being expelled by reality's lack of appetite for shapelessness. The two were now arguing, buried under an avalanche of words, and Sammy left them there to hide in his room. The truth is, Seryozha, too, was taken aback by a side

of his wife he hadn't seen before, a cruel determination verging on cynicism. Did he think she'd sold her apartment and spent a fortune on their plane tickets only to go back? To go back to what? When Seryozha reminded her that they still had his studio, she laughed mockingly. Neither of them had a job anymore, and if he thought she'd go back to live on his mother's meager pension, he was out of his mind. But what was she going to live on, here? Did she think she had a chance of surviving among foreigners? That was none of his business, he should just go home to mommy and enjoy her noodle soup. What did she mean it was none of his business? She was his wife! Not anymore, not if she stayed and he left. Oh, so that was her plan all along! Yes, it was, and now get out of my life!

Luckily, Seryozha's return ticket was already paid for—they'd had to buy return tickets in order to get the visas. He just had to call the airline and make a reservation. He left on a Saturday morning in the same white suit he'd worn upon his arrival, accompanied, from behind the blinds in Anna's room, by her spiteful gaze. Maria, whom he'd tried again to persuade to come with him, was notably absent. Only when he opened the door of his empty studio in Chișinău did he fully understand that he'd lost her, and he burst into uncontrollable sobs.

His return to Chișinău, which was welcomed with such an outpouring of joy by Olga—crosses, tears, hugs, more crosses, spitting to chase away the evil eye, more tears, thanks to the Almighty—that he was afraid she might have a heart attack was the beginning of a long chapter in Seryozha's life that he would later refer to as "the heartbreak." At first, he contented himself with drinking alone in his studio, writing laborious letters to Maria, which he peppered with love poems—yes, *his own* love poems—in which he compared her to a rose, a nightingale, or a witch, depending on his mood. Then, when his grief was too

much to bear alone, he moved in with Olga, and, between stormy arguments and stupor-inducing episodes of drunkenness, continued to write letters and poems, which grew ever more bitter and reproachful. The poem he was most proud of was called "The Evil Woman," which he learned by heart and took to reciting in pubs after he had exhausted all his anecdotes about America:

### The Evil Woman

Once I was handsome and smart,
Now I nurse a broken heart.
In the heatless, forlorn room
I drink my vodka full of gloom.
I am toothless, sad, and lonely,
You are cruel, mean, and horny.
You have practiced your deceit
As if I were but a piece of meat.
For a dress to show your ass
You turned into an evil lass.

It isn't certain whether or not Maria read Seryozha's poem, but all his drinking buddies did, or rather, heard it from the author's mouth, and clapped and cheered enthusiastically, encouraging him to send it to *Molodezh Moldovy* (*Moldova's Youth*). Seryozha, who was in grade school the last time he'd read a poem, and had never dared imagine that anyone would be interested in the inner workings of his head, much less publish them, suddenly envisioned the possibility of a public declaration that would show Maria "who he was" and possibly melt away her resistance. Heart thumping with anticipation, he enclosed his handwritten poem in a stamped envelope on which he wrote the

newspaper's address and prepared himself for an anxious period of waiting. He gave them five days, after which, every time the mail arrived without the much-expected answer, he drowned his disappointment in another bottle of vodka. He knew that if Maria saw his name printed in such a respectable publication, she'd realize whom she had been dealing with, and would come crawling back to him. Well, come to think of it, maybe she wouldn't come crawling, but at least she'd be wobbling back. Maybe she wouldn't come back at all, but at least she'd answer his letters.

He waited. And waited. Two weeks passed and there was no word from the paper. At the beginning of the third week, he "grabbed his heart with his teeth"—as Maria used to say when she translated literally from Romanian into English—that is, screwed up his courage, and called the newspaper office. They transferred him from one person to another, and he kept repeating his request, which for some reason caused a prolonged silence on the other end of the line, until finally, someone said, "Hold on," then he heard someone say, "Hey, this is the guy who's been dumped by his woman," and a chorus of giggles and laughter ensued. After waiting another five minutes, he heard the dial tone, and hung up.

The disillusionment caused by this episode was the last drop in a glass so full that, upon reaching its bottom, Seryozha drank himself into an alcoholic coma. When Olga discovered him in the middle of the night, lying motionless in a pool of his own vomit, her screams woke up the entire neighborhood, and, as a consequence, the white van of the Municipal Hospital's Emergency Department arrived in record time. (Truth be told, most of the city's residents had never seen this van, which for reasons having to do with endemic lack of fuel and the need for

repairs that the hospital couldn't afford, only made occasional appearances on TV.)

When he woke up in a strange room with a tube in his veins, Seryozha thought that he was back in Santa Barbara after what must have been an accident, but the sight of Olga sleeping with her mouth open in a chair at his bedside brought him back to reality. It was a reality he wanted no part of, so he closed his eyes, pretending to be asleep. All he wanted was to die in that hospital, "like a dog among strangers," and for Maria to find out and then be tortured by remorse for the rest of her life. He might have gotten his wish, had it not been for the doctor, a no-nonsense woman who had him released on the grounds that they needed his bed for patients with "real problems."

Back home, an ugly surprise awaited him: everything that belonged to Maria—clothes, a few paintings, even a Romanian-English dictionary—had disappeared. Faced with Seryozha's breakdown, Olga confessed that she had burned everything, hoping to cleanse the apartment of Maria's evil spirit, and to free Seryozha from her diabolical spell. But instead of being freed, Seryozha broke all the porcelain his sister had left in the glass cabinet in the living room—Cleanse the place, you say? There, how about this? Is this clean enough for you?—and cups and plates flew everywhere, shattering into a thousand pieces on the cement floor.

Two hours later, when the storm had passed, Olga swept the floors clean, and, after tossing all the shards into a large plastic bag, put on a flowery apron with the words "Kiss the Cook!" that Tania had sent from Santa Barbara, and turned on the stove to make chicken noodle soup.

# Sammy, Lenny, Bill, and Maria

Seryozha's departure ushered a period of unexpected happiness into Sammy's life. Maria was there whenever he needed her, yet she seemed barely present, as she never asked for anything and never voiced an opinion. She was Tania's opposite in every way. Sammy wondered whether he could be *that* lucky, and it was this fear that stopped him from fully enjoying his newfound happiness. It was the same fear that was at the root of his occasional nightmares about Tania, dreams in which he'd hear her obscene laughter and realize, with a jolt of panic, that she'd returned. Jesus, what would he do if she *did* come back?

As for Maria, all she seemed to need were her daily walks, her brushes, a canvas, and a box of colors. She took the daily game she played with her brush very seriously, though, whenever he asked her a question about it, she just shrugged. It wasn't just her English that was the problem—on several occasions he'd had evidence that her English was better than she let on; she just wasn't much of a talker.

At the beginning, he loved that about her. But after a few weeks, he began to wonder whether they were really "communicating," as he put it.

"My dear, don't get me wrong, I love a woman who knows how to be quiet, and you have the loveliest way of keeping quiet. But communication is important, and I don't want to discover, someday, that we have nothing to say to each other. We have to communicate more."

She met his eye with that disarming look of hers, and asked:

"What do you want to communicate about?"

"Anything. Ask me anything you want to know about me."

"Do I have to?"

"No, you don't have to; I thought you'd like to."

"Not really. I think if there's something you want me to know you'll tell me yourself; if not, what's the point in asking?"

"The point is that people have to communicate."

"People don't *have* to do anything. You're just saying this because everybody around you says it."

"No! I'm saying it because I want us to communicate!"

"Aren't we communicating now?"

"No! Your questions are stopping us from really communicating."

"You said I could ask you anything."

"Anything that might lead to real communication."

"So, some communications are real, and others are not."

"Precisely."

"Well, you should have told me at the beginning."

"What?"

"That our communications aren't real."

At the end of one of these conversations he'd wonder, stupefied, whether there was something about himself that invited such inscrutable women into his life, or whether there was nothing wrong with him, and the constant misunderstandings were simply the result of cultural differences.

"What do you mean, 'cultural differences'?" Maria asked him the first time he used the expression.

"Well, for instance, the fact that you Moldovans don't care about communication."

"We care about it if there is something we need to communicate."

"There's always something to communicate."

"No, there isn't! Let me tell you an anecdote about the greatest modern Romanian poet: his name was Lucian and he didn't say a word until he was six years old. His parents were, naturally, very sad and worried. Then, one day—when he was about six—he came running to his parents and said, 'The cat ate the parrot!' His parents were in tears, they couldn't believe that little Lucian was speaking, and asked him why he'd been mute for all that time—'mute as a swan,' as he'd say many years later in a poem titled 'Self-Portrait.' 'There was nothing to say until now,'" the boy answered.

Sammy laughed: "*Now* we're communicating."

"Are we?"

These conversations aside, things between Maria and Sammy ran smoothly, and life was peaceful. Even Anna seemed to accept her, though every now and then her sensitive nose caught a whiff of something that reminded her of Tania's body odor.

About three months after Maria's arrival, Sammy introduced her to Lenny, who had finally gotten over his disenchantment with Irina. Sammy hoped that Lenny would do for Maria what he had done for Irina, that is, help her to exhibit her work in

one of the local galleries. It was a delicate topic, since Lenny was understandably not in the mood to help another Moldovan artist, but, after a few visits, he and Maria seemed to hit it off, and soon, one of Maria's icons was on display in Totem Gallery.

As everything was seemingly moving in the right direction, the phone call Sammy received one late afternoon toward the end of April was the last thing he expected.

"I'm not coming home tonight," Maria said, after mentioning that she was at Lenny's.

The statement was so matter-of-fact and, at the same time, so strange, that Sammy didn't know what to make of it. Eventually, he decided to take it at face value: for whatever reason, she had decided to sleep over at Lenny's. The next morning, however, when he woke up, and she wasn't home, something definitely seemed off. Little by little, the suspicion that she wasn't just sleeping at Lenny's, but *with* Lenny, became harder and harder to brush off.

Two days later, the couple arrived holding hands, and Lenny explained, slightly embarrassed, that it was something they hadn't planned. It just happened, and he was truly hoping that Sammy wouldn't be hurt, and all three of them could continue to be friends. Indeed, Maria stopped by regularly, as if nothing had happened, and after a brief period of confusion, Sammy too began to act as if nothing out of the ordinary had occurred. In a couple of months, Maria became Totem Gallery's artist in residence, and her paintings sold so well that, reluctantly, she had to make some changes to her wardrobe in order to appear somewhat presentable at the numerous receptions held in her honor. Her bank account would have made Tania and Irina green with envy. What could go wrong?

In August, Anna and Todd went away to college, he to Stanford, and she to a small liberal arts college on the East Coast.

They were sent off with a big party on Bill's front lawn, on which occasion he got so intoxicated he began to cry, holding his "sweet boy, who's going away" in his arms—reminiscing about Seryozha and wondering whatever had become of "that poor lad with a heart of gold." It was during this party that Maria got to know Bill a little, since, until then, they had barely spoken. Maybe he was so drunk he did something he couldn't undo later, or maybe they saw in each other something they hadn't had the opportunity to see until then. Who knows? Whatever the case was, two weeks later Lenny got the same phone call Sammy had received four months before.

At first, Lenny thought she was pulling his leg. But when midnight came, then dawn, and she hadn't returned, he began to reevaluate his situation. He climbed into his Porsche and drove to Sammy's, who listened to him with sympathy, and opened a bottle of Johnnie Walker. They drank and spoke little, and when, two hours later, Bill and Maria showed up, Sammy brought out two more glasses. A couple of hours later, the three men had agreed to share the expense of a lawyer in order to deal with Maria's application for permanent residency.

# Seryozha

Nine months after his return from the States, and a month into Maria's third new beginning (of which he was, of course, unaware) a new opportunity arouse for Seryozha: the apartment building's caretaker, a woman in her early sixties, died suddenly of a heart attack and the tenants needed someone to replace her. Using her connections, Olga secured the position for him, announcing as she opened the apartment door, "I found you a great job! You start work tomorrow!"

The job consisted mainly of mopping the stairs of the four-story building, and of doing occasional chores, such as replacing burnt-out light bulbs or fixing the plumbing. For these expenses, Seryozha was to be given a monthly allowance by the super, an amount so insignificant that it was barely sufficient to buy a screwdriver, but the words "monthly allowance" were nonetheless enough to trigger certain images in Seryozha's brain, and with these images before his eyes, he accepted the offer. From then on, every morning he could be found holding

a mop with which he traced wet lines on the stairwell, as the tenants hurried past him on their way to work on the recently washed stairs. Sure, some people complained that the stairs were even dirtier than before he'd cleaned them, but he wasn't about to start listening to every idiot with an opinion, was he?

After he finished mopping, he used his plumbing allowance for a quick drink at the corner pub, where some fans of his "Evil Woman" still met. Well, maybe it wasn't always quick—maybe sometimes it took him three or four hours to get back—but how could he go on living otherwise? He needed their company and a sympathetic ear. In fact, it was one of them who, seeing how Seryozha racked his brains to come up with a trick that would bring back Maria, suggested breaking into a doctor's office.

"Cancer. It always works."

He just had to convince Maria that he had cancer, and, unless she was a stone-hearted bitch, she'd come back. Unfortunately, the plan required a doctor's cooperation, or, at least, a doctor's letterhead and rubber stamp.

He left the bar that day with a spring in his step and cancer on his mind. He remembered that the cleaning women at the Municipal Clinic unlocked all the rooms, including the doctors' offices, at seven AM, but that the doctors never came in earlier than nine, so their offices were unsupervised for two whole hours.

The next day, he left home at seven in the morning, carrying a duffel bag with the blue dungarees he'd inherited from the building's previous caretaker, and which were identical to those the cleaning staff wore in all the city's institutions. He arrived at the hospital at seven-twenty, and promptly removed the dungarees from his bag, then put them on over his clothes.

It was a quiet morning, and, with the exception of a few cars parked in the front lot, there was no sign of another human being. He began to pace nervously up and down, and, when his watch showed seven-thirty, entered the building.

No one in the main lobby. No one in the hall. According to the directory, the doctors' offices were on the second floor. He wasn't sure what was safer, the elevator or the stairs. If he took the elevator, someone would surely notice. If he took the stairs, he ran the risk of coming across one of the cleaning women. He decided to take the stairs. No one there. The entire building seemed empty. When he arrived on the second floor he noticed, with a sigh of relief, that the doors had all been left open, as if expecting a visitor. He entered the first—"Dr. Mara Ursu," read the inscription on the door—and began to yank on drawer handles. None of them budged—all were locked. He looked around to see if he could find a letterhead, but the only piece of paper he came across was a laundry list under a stack of women's magazines. Finally, when he was about to leave, he spotted a rubber stamp near the sink. He grabbed it, but before he could read what was inscribed on it, an angry female voice asked, "Have you people no shame?"

Startled, he looked up to find himself facing a plump nurse with a red nose and puffy cheeks.

"Give me that," she ordered, and mechanically, he handed it to her.

"Really, have you no shame? You're the third person in the past two days I've found trying to steal this. Look at you, young and strong, no limbs missing. Is it that hard to work, the way normal people do? No, you all need some excuse! Doctor's excuses. That's why this country is going to hell: everyone wants a piece of it, but no one wants to work for it."

While the nurse was busy talking, Seryozha tried to steal away, but she grabbed him by the arm, stopping him in his tracks: "Wait! Where's your mop and bucket?"

He mumbled something, but before he finished his sentence, he was presented with a mop, and sighing, he began to clean the floors.

# Seryozha and Maria

Seryozha's unsuccessful trip to the doctor's office was his last attempt to reclaim his wife. After he had mopped a whole floor at the Municipal Clinic, he returned home in a state of increased depression: if the nurse saw in him no more than a mop handler, maybe that's what he was, and, if that's what he was, what right did he have to ask Maria to come back to him? She deserved more, he mused, holding his mop. People went up and down the stairs, stepping with their shoes on the wet stairs he'd just mopped, and the odd rascal would point at a spot and say, "You forgot to clean here." Then, adding, "See, it's dirty," he'd step on the spot where he'd pointed. The first time this happened, he chased the little devil down the stairs, trying to hit him with his mop, but, as luck would have it, an old hag who lived on the first floor was just exiting her apartment and saw him.

"Aren't you ashamed of yourself," the old woman lashed at him, "a grown man beating a helpless child?"

Of course, the woman spoke as loudly as she could, and in less than a minute two other doors opened, each with its own

hag in the doorframe, shaking her head and adding her own commentary: "This is what's wrong with this country. Give him a mop and he acts like he owns us!"

By then, the child had already disappeared, and all Seryozha wanted was to disappear, too—which is not that easy when one is holding a mop—so he beat a shameful retreat up the stairs, while the women kept on. Eventually, though, they grew quiet and returned to their uneventful lives, leaving Seryozha alone on the stairs. Exhausted, he sat down, set the mop beside him, took his head in his hands, and began to weep.

When, a few weeks later, he received the divorce papers in the mail he was so drained from weeping that he just stared at them in numbed prostration. And, when he got tired of staring, he went to the neighborhood bar, ordered drinks for all his buddies, and, once again, told them stories about a magical house in the California hills, a house made entirely of unbreakable glass, with a TV and a computer in every room, and an enormous bar in the living room whose drinks, like the fountain of youth, were ceaselessly replenished. The owner of this house, a gentleman called Bill, was the kindest man you could imagine, and if, by a miracle, any of them happened to find themselves in the hills of Santa Barbara, they just had to knock at his door and they would receive a royal welcome.

"If this guy was so generous," one of Seryozha's friends inquired, "why'd you come back?"

"Better to be a king among apes than an ape among kings," Seryozha replied, embracing his audience with a large gesture.

Of course, Seryozha had no idea that, at that very moment, his own wife was enjoying a royal welcome from his former friend. As a matter of fact, she, too, had spent that day drinking with friends. They were celebrating her first interview with the Immigration and Naturalization Services, which, it seemed, had

gone very well. Of the three friends that surrounded Maria at that moment, the one who was least enthusiastic about the prospect of her receiving permanent residency was the one who shared her bed. The memory of Tania's possessiveness and of Seryozha's declarations of eternal friendship were still so vivid in Bill's mind that he shivered at the mere mention of the word "permanent." On the other hand, the man whose bed Maria had most recently abandoned was probably the one who shared her happiness the most: he truly appreciated her as an artist and felt that, in retrospect, their brief relationship had been unnecessary. "Why keep a cow when milk is so cheap?" had always been Lenny's motto when it came to women—a motto he'd regretfully forgotten while in the polished claws of that little Russian thief. As for Sammy, his thoughts were shadowed by his lingering feelings for Maria and by the secret hope that someday she'd come back to him.

And come she did. The friends celebrated New Year's at Sammy's, with Anna and Todd, who were home for the winter holidays, and Michelle and Theo, who had been dating casually for the past year. At the end of the night, when Bill asked Maria if she was ready to go home, she looked him straight in the eye and replied, "I'm not going. I'm staying."

# Epilogue

**M**aria stayed with Sammy, and they all remained close friends until the tragedy of November 2008, which put an end to the entire neighborhood's way of life. I was lucky to get a glimpse into this world when chance brought me there only a few months before it ended.

It was summer, and all three houses still stood: Sammy's coal-black house, gleaming, like a huge piece of glazed pottery against the light blue sky and the sage-green foliage, shrubs and tangled undergrowth; Lenny's villa, like a medieval fortress at the end of a long driveway where, once a month ascended shiny BMWs, Porsches and Jaguars, spitting out loquacious guests; and Bill's house, built in the late eighties with money from various secret projects, on which he'd worked with some of the young tech guys who in a few years would be known as the Silicon Valley moguls. Had he been more ambitious, Bill too would have been one of them, but he enjoyed doing nothing too much, and, as soon as he had a decent amount in savings, he'd retired. His house had been his only ambition, and he'd breathed into it the very spirit of Silicon Valley, the spirit of a world of reflections, screens, and images.

The house had enormous, slanted panes of glass, made of two-way mirrors, so that the trees and all the vegetation around were captured in them, as if floating in a sea of shimmering silver. Every now and then a small-brained, suicidal blue jay would land beak-first on that frozen sea, but luckily, the deer and other creatures were oblivious to the otherworldly construction.

When I was there, some of the mirrors—presumably, the ones that had been damaged by Tania's belligerent attack—had been replaced with smoked plates, so that the house had a rather unbalanced look, as if the owner couldn't make up his mind about the house's guiding aesthetic. I remember the sense of abandoned Paradise exuding from the area, the hummingbirds drunk on the scarlet bugler flowers and the pink malva rosa, and the red-tiled roofs of the white Spanish houses one could spot further down the hill.

On the afternoon of November 13, 2008, a fire, which apparently started at the Santa Barbara Tea Gardens, and which, for this reason, is now known as the Tea Fire, blazed through the dry vegetation along Mountain Drive and Coyote Road, engulfing everything in its path. In just hours, dozens of houses were destroyed, among them Bill's, Lenny's, and Theo's. They say that Theo's cone-shaped house could be seen melting from miles away, dripping to the ground like ice cream. They also say that, at daybreak, an eerie beauty suffused the entire area, a ghostland from which rose gray columns that had once been part of a chimney or support beam—a land layered with uncanny rows of ash, once books, that now formed neatly arrayed, immaterial pages. Days later, the former owners returned to haunt the smoldering ruins, dazed, scraping for mementos amidst the ghost-things. Theo's sculptures had been reshaped by the fire but were still standing, twisted, defiant in their disfigurement. He was one of the few owners who decided

to rebuild. Lenny left without giving a forwarding address, and his only correspondence has been with the mysterious foreign woman who, a year after the fire, bought his land. Bill left for San Francisco, where he now works for a tech company led by one of his former coworkers. Around the same time Lenny's land was bought, Bill's property was acquired by his former wife.

Through some miracle, Sammy's house made it through untouched. He still lives there, and as far as anybody knows, Maria is still his partner. She and Michelle are busy decorating the houses they've rebuilt on the scorched earth. The four of them—Sammy, Maria, Theo, and Michelle—still celebrate New Year's together, but Anna is never there. She has her own life.

As for our Moldovan heroes: Seryozha still mops the floors of the building in which he shares an apartment with his mother, and only goes to his studio on the rare occasions he entertains a female acquaintance. No one complains about his mopping anymore, and even the children have learned to ignore the downtrodden, middle-aged man who, now and then, sets his mop aside, and, lighting a cigarette, plummets into prolonged bouts of daydreaming. If a neighbor happens to stop by to chat, Seryozha will open his wallet and proudly exhibit a photo of his niece, rather scantily clad and gripping a pole, and a photo of his sister, who, somewhat more covered, can be seen presiding over a poker table at which are seated a bunch of don't-mess-with-me types. Both women work in a casino in Reno, the former as an exotic dancer, the latter as a hostess.

No one in Santa Barbara has heard from Irina or Tania.

*Santa Cruz, California, 2013–2014*

# Acknowledgments

My deepest thanks go to Lucas Lackner, one of the victims of the 2008 Tea Fire, for reading the manuscript and letting me appropriate his history as an art collector, and specifically, a collector of Max Beckmann. His knowledge about the history of East Mountain Drive was invaluable.

Two books have helped me reconstitute the atmosphere of Santa Barbara in the 60s and of Moldova during communism: *Mountain Drive. Santa Barbara's Pioneer Bohemian Community*, compiled and edited by Elias Chiacos (Santa Barbara: Shoreline Press, 1994); and *Nascut în URSS/Born in the USSR* (Iasi: Polirom, 2006—the translation of the quotes from Romanian into English is mine) by Vasile Ernu. I am grateful to both authors. I tried to recreate the atmosphere of the Santa Barbara hills by replicating, as much as possible, the real houses that were once there. The "ice cream cone" house and the sculptures on its grounds were inspired by the descriptions in *Mountain Drive*, but the owner of the house, Theo, is entirely fictional.

I am also indebted to Mikhail Iossel for his insightful comments on the impact of the American soap *Santa Barbara*

on post-Soviet Russia, to Andrew Lenz for sharing his expertise on picture framing, to Moni Stanila and Tatiana Tibuleac for imparting their knowledge on life in the Republic of Moldova in the nineties, and to Stephen Kessler and Eireene Nealand for editorial suggestions.

I am grateful to the Ragdale Foundation for the time and space provided me in 2014 when I was revising this novel.

Excerpts from this novel have been published, in slightly different forms, in the following publications:

"Seryozha, Maria and the Mop" in *Trafika Europe*, Spring 2020.

"Matvei and Vadim" in *The Ink Pods*. Literary Podcast for *The Blue Nib*, Dec. 2019.

# Notes

1 The Republic of Moldova gained its independence from the Soviet Union in 1991 and is a separate entity from the region of Moldova, which is situated in eastern Romania. Both Moldovas had been part of "Greater Romania" until the Soviet takeover during World War II. Ethnic Romanians comprise the majority of the Moldovan population. Moldova is the poorest European country, has the highest alcoholism rate in the world, and a quarter of its population works abroad.

2 *Santa Barbara* was an American TV soap opera that aired from 1984 until 1993, focusing on the complicated adventures and drama of the wealthy Capwell family. It was the first American soap to air in Russia, where it became the longest-running television series (1992– 2002), and it was hugely popular in much of Eastern Europe.

3 Chișinău (or "Kishinev") is the capital of Moldova.

4 The *leu* (pl. *lei*) is the Moldovan and Romanian currency. At the time in which this novel is set, the average income in Moldova was 200 lei a month (about 50 dollars).

5 A *popa* is a Romanian Christian Orthodox priest.

# COMING IN 2021–22
# FROM NEW EUROPE BOOKS

978-1-7345379-1-8

**A journalist's personal account of why one small European nation's path away from liberal democracy carries vital lessons for us all**

"Skytt's great service to the reader is that he shows why so many Hungarians love Viktor Orbán so much. And through that gateway, he strides out onto the bigger political battlefield, to help us understand: why do so many people round the world love other leaders like Viktor Orban so much?"
**—from the foreword by Nick Thorpe, BBC Central Europe Correspondent**

# COMING IN 2021–22
# FROM NEW EUROPE BOOKS

978-0-9973169-2-6
copublished with Academic Studies Press

**A long-overdue second edition of the acclaimed, first-ever
comprehensive popular history of Eastern Europe in English**

## PRAISE FOR THE FIRST EDITION

"Jankowski displays an ease and familiarity with cultural minutiae
while briskly covering intense topics of genocide, religion, and
Communist implosion. . . . His history of the region serves as a
welcome introduction or refresher course." —*Publishers Weekly*

# COMING IN 2021–22
# FROM NEW EUROPE BOOKS

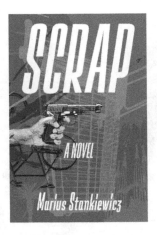

978-0-9995416-6-1

A riveting debut noir novel that takes us from Brazil to Barcelona, with a millennial, political edge

978-1-7345379-3-2

A scintillating, comic novel about one young American and his fellow expats caught up in a student loan scheme in an imaginary Eastern European capital

# COMING IN 2021–22
# FROM NEW EUROPE BOOKS

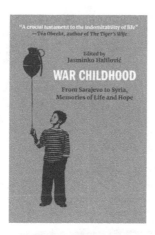

978-0-9995416-1-6

In this informative & inspiring book of quotations and
color photos, adults reflect on their childhoods in a siege
that came to define one of the late twentieth-century's
most brutal wars

"Not only a compendium of the most intimate details of
one of the 20th century's greatest tragedies, but also a crucial
testament to the indomitability of life." —**Téa Obreht,
author of *The Tiger's Wife***

# Also Available
# from New Europe Books

New Europe Books

**Williamstown, Massachusetts**

Find our titles wherever books are sold,
or visit www.NewEuropeBooks.com for order information.

# ABOUT THE AUTHOR

**Alta Ifland** was born in Romania, took part in the overthrow of
its communist dictatorship, and emigrated to the United States
in 1991. After earning a PhD in French language and literature,
and several years of university teaching, she now works as a full-
time writer, book reviewer, and translator (from/into French and
Romanian). She is the author of two books of short stories—
*Elegy for a Fabulous World* (2010 finalist for the Northern California
Book Award in Fiction) and *Death-in-a-Box* (2010 Subito Press
Fiction Prize)—and two collections of prose poems, including
*Voix de Glace/Voice of Ice* (bilingual, self-translated, 2008 Louis
Guillaume Prize). She lives in Northern California.

CPSIA information can be obtained
at www.ICGtesting.com
Printed in the USA
JSHW040513110421
13460JS00004B/6